Elle J[illegible] [illegible]ted writin[illegible] [illegible]e a romance novel. S[illegible] [illegible] raised three wonderf[illegible] [illegible]d even tried ranchi[illegible] [illegible]otic birds (ostriches, emus and rheas). Ask her, and she'll tell you what it's like to go toe-to-toe with an angry 350-pound bird! Elle loves to hear from fans at ellejames@earthlink.net or ellejames.com

Amanda Stevens is an award-winning author of over fifty novels, including the modern gothic series *The Graveyard Queen*. Her books have been described as eerie and atmospheric and 'a new take on the classic ghost story.' Born and raised in the rural South, she now resides in Houston, Texas, where she enjoys binge-watching, bike riding and the occasional margarita.

Also by Elle James

Homicide at Whiskey Gulch
Hideout at Whiskey Gulch
Held Hostage at Whiskey Gulch
Setup at Whiskey Gulch
Marine Force Recon
Show of Force
Full Force
Driving Force
Tactical Force
Disruptive Force

Also by Amanda Stevens

Little Girl Gone
John Doe Cold Case
Without a Trace
A Desperate Search
Someone Is Watching
Criminal Behaviour
Incriminating Evidence
Killer Investigation
Pine Lake
Whispering Springs

MISSING WITNESS AT WHISKEY GULCH

ELLE JAMES

LOOKS THAT KILL

AMANDA STEVENS

MILLS & BOON

First Published in Great Britain 2022
by Mills & Boon, an imprint of HarperCollins*Publishers* Ltd
1 London Bridge Street, London, SE1 9GF

www.harpercollins.co.uk

HarperCollins*Publishers*
1st Floor, Watermarque Building,
Ringsend Road, Dublin 4, Ireland

ISBN: 978-0-263-30353-7

0822

MISSING WITNESS AT WHISKEY GULCH

ELLE JAMES

For my mother, who loved to read and showed what fun it was to get lost in a story. Wish I could pick up the phone and call you.

I love and miss you, Mom.

Chapter One

Olivia Swann wrapped her fingers around the spinning clay, molding and shaping it into the custom vase she'd promised a wealthy client in Peoria, Pennsylvania.

In the back of her little shop, in Whiskey Gulch, Texas, she smiled at the thought of her work finding homes in places all over the US and other countries around the world.

It helped that she was a gifted artist, though she seldom thought of herself as such. Sure, she made beautiful pottery. What helped even more was having a sister who worked in a high-end art gallery in Dallas that displayed unique works of art that lured art enthusiasts from around the world.

It'd been a miracle that her sister, Jasmine, had gotten Olivia's work included.

Now she had more work than she knew what to do with—so much that in order to deliver any on time, she had to be selective in what projects she commissioned. Because of the popularity of her decorative vases, bowls and platters, she had been able to remodel her shop and her parents' home, bringing it up to the current century in style and habitability.

Jasmine loved the updates. Their mother would have

loved it. Her father…not so much. He'd resisted change, insisting on keeping outdated furniture and his favorite easy chair, much to their mother's frustration. She couldn't argue too much. They'd loved each other until parted by death…a day that had come all too soon.

Olivia dipped her hands in the murky water beside her. She placed them on the damp clay and continued shaping, pulling and forming the large vase on the potter's wheel. The hum of the motor and her focus on the clay calmed her in a way nothing else could match. She was in her element, living the life she was meant to live, free of worry and the complications of relationships.

Since a failed engagement to her high school sweetheart, she'd sworn off men. Her parents' deaths had pushed dating and love to the bottom of her priority list. Olivia honestly thought she couldn't possibly find a love like her parents had enjoyed.

They'd been perfectly matched: both artistic, both free-spirited—and so into each other, no one else existed.

Not Mike. He'd said he loved her and wanted to marry her, but he hadn't stopped looking around. Especially when on one of the many conferences he attended in Vegas as part of his job.

Olivia had happened to be in his apartment when he was in the shower, getting ready for their date, and a text came through from a woman by the name of Kiki Cox.

Curious about the name, she'd looked her up online, only to find she was a hooker in Vegas.

When she'd confronted him—purely out of curiosity, never suspecting he'd strayed—she'd been stunned when he admitted to having a pre-wedding fling with the woman. Mike had assured her he was just sowing wild oats, and it wouldn't happen again after they were married.

Olivia had calmly removed the engagement ring, handed it to him and left. She hadn't talked to him since. That had been three years ago.

Other than the biological clock ticking in her ear, reminding her she had wasted some of the best years of her reproductive life, she had no regrets.

If she ever married, it would be to someone who didn't feel the need to look elsewhere for love or sex.

The bell over the shop door rang as a man entered and stood still, waiting for his vision to adjust from the harsh Texas sunlight to the cooler, dimmer interior.

Olivia glanced up from her project, her breath catching in her throat at the sight of a tall, muscular man with broad shoulders, striking ice-blue eyes, a military haircut and a scruffy five-o'clock shadow. Wow.

The vase on the wheel wobbled against her fingertips, reminding her to focus on the task. She glanced down, recovered the project—just barely—and asked, "Can I help you?"

"I'm looking for a present for my mother."

Not only was he an outstanding physical form but he also loved his mother. How much more perfect could the man be? Sigh… He was still a man. Men had faults, as she well knew.

"I'm in the middle of a project. Have a look around. If you see something you think she might like, I should be at a stopping point in a few minutes."

She risked another glance, her pulse quickening.

The man's eyes narrowed. "I hear a voice, but I don't see who it belongs to."

Olivia chuckled, returning her attention to the vase. "I'm at the back of the shop, working."

She could hear footsteps nearing her work area. The man came to a halt in front of her. "Ah, there you are."

When she glanced up, her breath caught…and she couldn't help staring.

He smiled, a twinkle in his blue eyes. "Hey."

Her heart thumped against her ribs. "Hey." Her hands shifted, and the vase she'd been working on wobbled once more and flopped over as it whirled on the wheel.

"Damn!" Olivia switched off the motor and stood up, looking down at the mess.

"Wow," he said in his deep voice. "I'm sorry. I should have done like you asked and waited until you were finished."

She sighed. "It's okay. I'll just start over." *When I'm not distracted by a drop-dead gorgeous guy taking up all the air in the shop.* She didn't say it out loud, but she was sure thinking it. "A gift for your mother, you said?"

He nodded. "Yes, ma'am. She appreciates handmade items, being that she makes things as well."

Olivia's heart warmed. "What kinds of things does she make?"

"Nothing as difficult as these," he said, sweeping his hand out to encompass the contents of her shop. "She knits blankets for foster children and beanies for newborns. But she's been collecting unique pottery, displaying it around her house in San Antonio. I think the items in your shop would be right up her alley."

"Let me wash my hands, and I'll help you." Olivia hurried to the sink at the back of the shop and washed away the residual mud from her elbows to her fingertips. Once she'd dried her hands, she checked her reflection in the mirror, her eyes widening. She had a spot of clay on her nose, which she quickly wiped away before turning back to smile at the man, who was waiting patiently.

His lip quirked upward on one side. "You missed a spot." He reached out and brushed his thumb over a smudge on her chin.

Heat rose up her neck. She raised her hand to where his was, bumping into his fingers. "Here?"

He shook his head. "No." Wrapping his fingers around hers, he guided her hand.

Warmth spread throughout her body at his touch. With her cheeks on fire, she scrubbed at her chin and dragged her gaze from his striking blue eyes. "Did you see something you liked?" she asked, anxious to draw attention away from her dirty face to the contents of her shop.

"Actually, yes."

His deep voice sent shivers up and down Olivia's spine. She shot a glance back at him to discover he was looking at her, not her pottery.

Her heart thumped hard in her chest. Her reaction to this man was getting more and more ridiculous by the minute. If he didn't leave soon, she'd be begging to have his baby.

What was wrong with her? Olivia shook her head. He was just a man—and therefore, like most men she'd run across, probably not trustworthy, most likely overbearing and possibly narcissistic. She didn't need to fall all over herself because one man was extremely ruggedly attractive and had a voice that could melt chocolate on a frosty day.

No, Olivia had renounced men after Mike. She considered herself better off without the complications of relationships. Trust wasn't easy for her.

He paused in front of one of her slender three-foot-tall vases in stunning shades of cobalt blue and black. The piece was displayed in a glass cabinet to keep people from handling it. She'd sold one like it to a wealthy client in Dallas during an art show Jasmine had curated. The vase she'd been shaping on the wheel would be similar.

"This one is beautiful," he said in that tone that made Olivia's knees weaken. He glanced her way. "You made this? You're Olivia?" Before she could answer, he shook his head. "Of course you're Olivia. You were making another creation when I interrupted. I might as well be a bull in a china shop." He clasped his hands behind his back. "I'll leave all the touching to you."

His words inspired a shiver of awareness to ripple across her skin. An image of her hands running across his broad chest made heat build at her core.

Maybe swearing off men was a bit drastic. She didn't have to commit to any one man.

"What kind of pottery does your mother like?"

He shrugged those broad shoulders. "She has a couple of large bowls. One she uses for fruit. The other is front and center on her coffee table. She has a colorful array of platters hung on her wall. What she doesn't have is a vase like this." He nodded toward the cobalt blue vase in the glass cabinet. "This vase would make her happy."

Her mouth twisted into a wry grin. "Perhaps we should start with how much you want to spend on this gift?"

His brow wrinkled. "That much, huh?"

She nodded. "The techniques and materials used to create that particular color combination are expensive and time-intensive."

"I can only imagine," he said. "It's an impressive piece. My mother visited an art gallery in Dallas. When I told her I was coming to work in Whiskey Gulch, she insisted I look for the artist she discovered at that gallery." He grinned. "Olivia Swann was the name she gave me." The man held out his hand. "My mother will be thrilled I actually met you. I'm Becker Jackson. My mother is Linda Jackson."

Olivia took his hand. "Nice to meet you, Mr. Jackson."

"Becker." He smiled. "Mr. Jackson was my father." He held her hand a little longer than necessary, his eyes narrowing as he stared down into her face. "I didn't expect Mom's artist to have such pretty green eyes."

Her cheeks burned. She wanted to tell him that he had the prettiest blue eyes, but thankfully, her tongue was too tied to make coherent conversation.

"Look..." he said, still holding her hand, "I just got to town. I don't know anyone. You wouldn't happen to want to have dinner with me, would you?"

Her brows shot up.

He chuckled. "You can tell me to get lost if I'm asking too soon, but I like your grip and your eyes. And I don't like to eat by myself." He paused. "That is, if you're alone... I mean, not married or you don't have a significant other." He scrubbed his spare hand through his hair. "Wow, talk about a lousy first impression." He pressed a kiss to her knuckles and let go. "Let me start over."

Becker performed an about-face and marched out of the shop, the bell reverberating throughout the space.

Olivia shook her head, her hand still tingling where he'd touched her. "What the hell just happened?"

Before she could form another thought, Becker entered her shop again.

"Hi," he said. "I'm looking for Olivia Swann." He winked.

Olivia frowned. "I'm Olivia. But then, you already know that."

"Humor me. I feel like a putz." He crossed the room and held out his hand. "I'm on a mission to find a gift for my mother. She won't settle for anything less than an Olivia Swann creation."

She tentatively took his hand. "I'm not sure I can help you." Her lips twitched at the corners.

"If you're Olivia, I know you can." He nodded toward the black-and-blue vase. "That vase will do. Is it for sale?"

Olivia nodded.

He let go of her hand and pulled his wallet from his back pocket. "How much do I owe you?"

"Three thousand, five hundred dollars."

Becker dropped his wallet on the ground.

Olivia laughed. "I have other vases not quite as expensive."

He scooped his wallet off the floor. "I need to have a talk with my mother about her spending all of my inheritance." Becker winked. "Seriously, I still want it. It'll have to be her birthday and Christmas present for the next five years."

Olivia shook her head. "Don't feel obligated to purchase the vase. I'd feel awful if I broke your bank."

He pulled out a credit card. "Take plastic?"

"I do."

"Can you ship it?"

She took the card from him, nodding. "Yes, I can."

"Insured?"

"Absolutely." Her frown deepened. "Are you sure?"

"Absolutely." He pulled out a card and scribbled a name and address on the back. "Here. You can have my very first business card, with my mother's address."

She stared down at the front of the card. "Outrider

Security?" Olivia glanced up. "Isn't that Trace Travis's security company?"

Becker nodded. "It is. Tomorrow is my first day with them. He sent my business cards ahead to lure me in."

"Is that all it took? A few business cards with your name on them?" she asked.

He spread his arms wide. "I'm here, aren't I? You're my first stop before I head out to the Whiskey Gulch Ranch to meet up with my new boss."

"Won't he want to take you to dinner?" she asked.

"I secured a room in town for the night. I won't meet up with him until tomorrow morning." He lifted his chin. "Don't feel obligated to go out with me just because I bought a vase. I'll be fine on my own." He looked out her front window. "Though I *would* like a recommendation for a place to grab a bite."

"The diner is always good," Olivia said. "And if you still want me to join you, I'd like that. My refrigerator is all out of leftovers."

"In that case, I'm delighted to be your second choice over leftovers." He grinned. "Want me to pick you up at six? Or, if it makes you feel better, we could meet at the diner at six."

"I'll meet you at the diner at six. I need to clean up before I eat." She stepped behind the counter, ran his card through her credit card processor and handed it back to him with the receipt for him to sign. "And I'll ship your mother's vase to her on my way home."

Becker grinned once more. "Thank you. Then I'll see you at six. And if you don't show up, I'll know I made a helluva first impression on you, and you had the good sense to stay home and eat popcorn."

She laughed. "Are you always this…?"

"Charming? Adorable? Sexy?"

"Maddening? Exasperating? Incorrigible?"

Becker winced. "Ouch. And I was leaning toward *sexy*."

Olivia waved toward the door. "Go on. I still have to close up shop, shower and change if I want to get to the diner by six."

His face brightened, a twinkle shining in his blue eyes. "So you're not discouraged."

She fought hard to keep from smiling and failed miserably. "If I say I'll be there… I'll be there."

He took her hand again, raised it to his lips and brushed the backs of her knuckles once more. "I'll be counting the minutes. Until then…" He left the shop, the bell ringing over the door.

As soon as the man was gone, Olivia let go of the breath she'd been holding and giggled like a schoolgirl.

Had she just said yes to having dinner with him?

Yes. She had.

After years of refusing to have anything to do with men, a stranger had walked through her shop door, and she'd reneged.

But now that she'd said she'd be there, she would make good on that promise.

A glance at the clock made her yelp. Five after five? If she was going to make it to the diner by six, she had to get moving.

Olivia locked the front door, flipped the Open sign over to Closed and hurried to package the beautiful vase for Becker's mother. She had until five thirty to get it to the FedEx drop point.

Using copious amounts of Bubble Wrap and foam

packaging, she wrapped the beautiful vase and placed it in a box.

After moving the clay on her wheel into a bucket to keep it moist, she washed her hands and carried the box out to her slate gray Jeep Wrangler.

The drive across town didn't take long. Whiskey Gulch wasn't that big. Olivia arrived at the shipping store in time to send the box out to the address Becker had given her. After insuring the vase and paying to ship the gift, she hurried back to her Jeep and drove to the opposite end of town and parked in the driveway of the house she'd inherited from her parents.

Once inside, she shed her clothes as she ran through the house to the en suite in the master bedroom. She was in and out of the shower in under ten minutes, with fifteen minutes to spare. She'd have just enough time to dress, dry her hair and dab on a bit of makeup before she had to race to the diner to be there by six.

Why had she agreed to have dinner with Becker at six?

Because the twinkle in his blue eyes had utterly captivated her, and she couldn't wait to see him again.

Was she insane? Hadn't she learned men couldn't be trusted?

"It's only dinner," she said as she stepped out of the shower. She dried off and wrapped the towel around her body.

A sudden creaking sound came from another part of the house.

Olivia froze, straining to hear it again. The house had been built in the early 1940s. No manner of updates would change the fact that it still made noises when the wind blew and when it didn't.

She heard a soft thump that sounded like someone running into a wall.

She raced across the bedroom to the nightstand and grabbed the baseball bat she kept by the bed. Her heart racing, she crept over to her open bedroom door and leaned out.

Now wasn't the time to remember she'd disconnected her landline phone. Nor was it a good time to remember her cell phone was in the kitchen on the counter, where she'd dropped her purse and keys.

Olivia peered down the hall.

Nothing seemed out of the ordinary.

Click.

Did someone just close my back door?

Olivia had two choices: She could go into the kitchen, possibly confront an intruder, and risk being attacked, subdued, raped and killed. Or she could branch off the hallway before reaching the kitchen, run out the front door into the yard and yell for help. She'd have to run a block; her closest neighbor was deaf.

With the bat gripped tightly in her hands, Olivia inched out into the hallway, afraid to breathe, lest she miss hearing something.

Chapter Two

Olivia's pulse pounded so hard through her veins, it thundered in her ears. She tensed her muscles, ready to make a dash for the front door and out into the open.

Before she took the first step, a strangled sob sounded from the kitchen.

"Olivia?" a faint, feminine and familiar voice called out.

She knew that voice. It was the voice she'd grown up with—her sister's.

Still carrying the bat, Olivia ran for the kitchen. "Jasmine?" As she entered the room, a hand reached out, snagged her arm and dragged her to the floor.

Her first instinct was to shake free of the grip, but fingers dug into her skin and refused to release her.

Olivia dropped to her knees beside her sister and stared into her tear-streaked face.

"Jasmine, sweetie." She cupped her sister's cheek, which was smeared with dirt and scratches. "What happened?" She hadn't heard from her in three weeks. Guilt tugged at her gut. She'd been so busy with her work, she hadn't picked up her cell phone to call Jasmine.

"I'm in trouble," she whispered.

"Do we need to get you to a doctor?" Olivia tried to stand.

Jasmine stopped her. "No. I can't," she said, choking on her words. Tears welled in her eyes. "I'm scared."

Olivia sat back on the floor with her younger sister and pulled her into her arms. "Why? What's wrong?"

"I witnessed a m-murder." Jasmine used her balled fist to cover her mouth. "I witnessed a murder, Olivia."

Olivia's stomach roiled at the horror reflected in her sister's face. "Oh, baby."

"I had returned to the gallery because I'd left my phone on my desk there. The back door was open. I knew I'd locked it and set the alarm, but it was open. The alarms were disengaged. When I went inside, I saw… I saw them. They were arguing. I recognized Nico Salvatore. He'd been in the gallery earlier that day. I didn't know the other guy. I've since learned it was Eduardo Romano. Romano had something in his hand that looked like a painting. It was wrapped in brown paper, but it was the shape of a picture frame. I wanted to tell him to put it back, but I couldn't. They didn't see me. If they had…"

"You were right not to say anything," Olivia said, thankful her sister had kept quiet.

"Maybe if I had spoken up, Eduardo would still be alive."

"Or both of you would be dead."

Her sister drew in a shaky breath. "I was scared. They were both bigger than me. I didn't have any way to protect myself, so I hid behind a cabinet and waited for them to leave. I was going to call the police then."

"You did the right thing."

Her blue eyes widened, and her bottom lip trembled. "But I saw everything."

"Oh, Jaz." Olivia held her sister's hands.

"The man with the painting turned to leave. Nico

grabbed him from behind and…and…slit his throat." The tears spilled down her cheeks.

"Oh, my God, Jasmine." Olivia hugged her sister tighter. "Did you call the police?"

Her sister nodded. "I did. When I told them what I'd seen, they checked for video footage. The cameras had been turned off. I was the only witness to the murder. Once they realized that, they put me in witness protection and stashed me at a safe house."

Olivia leaned back, her heart hammering. "When did this happen?"

"Two weeks ago."

And she hadn't bothered to call her sister during those two weeks to even know something was wrong. "Oh, Jasmine. I'm so sorry. I should have called you sooner."

"You wouldn't have been able to get me. I had to give up my cell phone, my job, my apartment. Everything. The marshals didn't even give me a chance to go back and collect my own clothes. I've been in witness protection since. Until yesterday."

"I don't understand." Olivia shook her head. "Why didn't they arrest Nico?"

"They did."

"Then why did they put you in witness protection?"

Her sister's mouth twisted. "You don't know who Nico Salvatore is, do you?"

Olivia's brow furrowed. "Should I know that name?"

"I only know it because he and his father have been patrons at the gallery where I work…*worked*." She swallowed hard, more tears slipping down her face. "Vincenzo Salvatore. He's a very rich Italian American with links to the Sicilian mafia. If being the son of a mafia kingpin wasn't bad enough, Nico killed the nephew of

Giovanni Romano. He's just as rich and powerful as Nico. Either man could pay anyone enough to silence a witness to any crime."

"Holy smokes, Jaz." Olivia stared into her sister's face. "But the US Marshals had you at a safe house. It should have been…safe."

Jasmine shook her head. "Compromised. Apparently, the Salvatores have connections. Thankfully, the place had an underground tunnel leading into the basement of a neighboring store. While the marshals held off the attack, I escaped through the tunnel and ran. I didn't stop running until I got here."

"You didn't run all the way from Dallas. How did you get here?" Olivia asked.

"I made my way to a truck stop and hitched a ride."

"Jeez." Olivia pressed a hand to her chest. "Hitching a ride could have gotten you killed."

Jasmine snorted. "*Either way*, I could have gotten killed. I hated leaving the marshals to their fate. The cartel hit the safe house with automatic weapons. I can't imagine anyone coming out of that alive."

"Oh, no," Olivia whispered.

"I came to the only place I knew. Home." Her fingers gripped Olivia's arms. "I need money and some clothes. And hair dye, if you have any."

Olivia frowned. "I can give you money and clothes, but you can't run forever."

Jasmine buried her face in her hands, her shoulders shaking with her sobs. "I need to hide… At least until they convict the killer. Maybe even…longer."

Olivia stroked her sister's back. "Sweetie, that's insane."

"I know." She raised her head. "I can't go back to

work. I can't have a career. The US Marshals weren't able to keep me safe." She flung her hands in the air. "I don't know what to do." Jasmine stared into her sister's eyes. "But I have to leave as soon as possible. My being here places *you* in danger."

A chill slithered across Olivia's skin. "This will be the first place they look."

Jasmine pushed to her feet, crouching low. "I have to get out of here."

Olivia rose. "Not without me."

"No, Olivia, this is my problem. I can't let you get dragged into it."

"I'm already in it," Olivia said. "You're my only sister. My only family. I can't let you leave without me."

Jasmine hurried down the hallway toward her bedroom. "Do you still have my old clothes?"

"They're right where you left them three years ago."

"I'll need a suitcase." Jasmine quickly closed the blinds and drew the curtains. Then she rummaged through the closet, throwing jeans, shirts and shoes into a pile on the quilt-covered iron bed she'd slept in as a child.

Olivia pulled a suitcase out of the back of her closet and laid it on the bed. "*We'll* need suitcases," she said. "You are *not* leaving without me. We'll figure this out together." She didn't wait for her sister to respond. Instead, she ran to her bedroom, dressed, grabbed her own suitcase from her closet and started packing, her mind racing.

If the US Marshals couldn't keep her sister safe, the mafia would know where to look next. It was only a matter of time before they came looking for her in her hometown of Whiskey Gulch.

Olivia's hands froze. They didn't need to pack. They needed to leave.

Now.

"Jasmine. You're right." Olivia spun and ran toward her bedroom door. "We need to leave. Forget packing. We can buy what we need wherever we land." All she needed was her purse and her car keys. "Hurry."

"Coming." Jasmine wheeled the suitcase down the hallway, stopping before she reached the living room to button the shirt she'd changed into.

"I'm going to grab my purse, and then we're out of here."

Jasmine's brow wrinkled. "You didn't pack a bag?"

"No. If this mafia group knew where to find you at the safe house, they will know to look here. We need to leave immediately."

On her way through the living room to the kitchen, Olivia grabbed the photograph of herself, Jasmine and their parents. She had just stuffed the picture into her purse, grabbed her keys and was heading for the front door when something crashed through the front of the house. Glass, wood and debris exploded into the room, filling it with dust, making it impossible to see clearly.

Olivia stumbled backward in time to avoid being hit and fell, landing hard on her back, the wind knocked out of her lungs. She rolled over and managed to get up onto her hands and knees, coughing as dust filled her nostrils and lungs. She blinked to clear her eyes and gasped.

A large black SUV stood in the middle of the living room, and the doors swung open. Two men wearing dark ski masks hopped out, their silhouettes shadowy in the fog of dust.

Olivia crawled behind the couch, working her way toward the other side of the room, where Jasmine had been standing in the hallway.

Shards of glass cut into her palms and through the denim of her jeans, piercing her knees. Biting hard on her tongue to keep from crying out, she continued crawling along behind the couch. She had to get to Jasmine and get her out of there before—

A scream ripped through the air.

The men carried a wiggling, kicking, yelling Jasmine toward the SUV.

Olivia jumped to her feet. "Let go of her!" she yelled. She rolled over the back of the couch and ran after them, leaping onto one man's back.

He released his hold on Jasmine and backhanded Olivia, his knuckles catching her temple. The blow sent her flying backward. She hit the wall and sank, her head swimming, her vision going black.

When she came to, the doors to the SUV had closed and the vehicle was backing out of her living room.

"No!" she screamed. She pushed to her feet and raced out of the house through the hole in the wall. The SUV whipped around and sped away into the dusk.

Olivia ran a few steps after them and stopped. She couldn't catch them on foot. She spun around toward her vehicle. Even if she'd had the keys, it wasn't going anywhere—the tires had been slashed.

She hurried into what was left of the house that had been her home all her life and picked her way through the rubble, searching for her purse in the dust and debris.

When she found the bag, she dug out her cell phone. The screen was cracked, but it still worked. She dialed 911 and waited.

When the dispatcher answered, she had to swallow hard past the lump blocking her vocal cords. "You have to stop them. They kidnapped my sister. Please." Her voice cracked. "Help her."

BECKER WAITED UNTIL six thirty at the diner Olivia had suggested. He'd already had two glasses of water, shredded three napkins and apologized to the waitress for taking his time with the menu. He waited another five minutes before concluding he'd been stood up.

Disappointment had robbed him of his appetite. He tossed a twenty on the table and left without ordering. As he exited the diner, a sheriff's vehicle raced past him, strobes flashing and sirens wailing, followed by a fire truck and an ambulance.

He sighed. Someone else was having it worse than he was. Being ditched was lousy; needing first responders was worse. Becker hoped whoever was in trouble would be all right. Though Olivia had chosen not to show for their dinner date, Becker wasn't going to give up. He just had to try harder.

Olivia was the first person he'd met in Whiskey Gulch. Being new in town, he could use all the friends he could get. It wasn't like he was going to marry her. He'd given up on that institution a long time ago. But he liked company, and he liked her green eyes and shiny black hair—and that she didn't mind getting her hands dirty.

A grin tugged at the corners of his mouth. Since he wasn't going to have dinner with her, he might see if his new boss was up to meeting with him that night instead of in the morning.

He pulled out his cell phone and dialed Trace's number.

Trace answered on the first ring. "Becker! You made it to Whiskey Gulch?"

"I did," he answered.

"Get on out to the ranch. I'm grilling steaks, and Mom and Lily are putting all the fixins on the table. Everything should be ready by the time you get here."

"I don't want to intrude on your family meal," Becker said.

"You're not intruding. As it is, you can meet the other members of the Outriders. They're all here. When I mentioned steaks and beer, they came running."

Becker laughed. "Can't blame them, can you?"

"They know Whiskey Gulch Ranch beef is the best. Should only take you fifteen minutes to get here from town. We'll be looking for you."

"I'll be there." Becker ended the call and climbed into his truck.

A sheriff's SUV raced by—this time, in the opposite direction—lights flashing, siren wailing.

"Wonder what's going on," he muttered, checking all directions before he pulled out onto the main street running through Whiskey Gulch.

He slowed as he neared Olivia's pottery shop. Had she gotten caught up in her work and forgotten what time it was?

The lights were out, and the Closed sign hung in the window.

As he passed the shop, his cell phone rang. He fished it out of the cupholder and glanced down at a number he didn't recognize. Usually, he would ignore unknown callers, as most were call centers trying to sell him extended warranties on his vehicle or siding on the house he didn't own. But on the off chance it could be Olivia, he answered.

"Hello?"

"Becker?" Olivia's voice sounded in his ear.

Becker pulled into the parking lot of her shop. "Olivia?"

For a moment, she didn't respond.

He could swear he heard a sob, and then her voice came on again, shaky and not at all normal. "I need your help."

He clutched the phone tighter in his hand. "Sweetheart, are you okay?"

"No. I'm not okay." There was no mistaking the sob this time; she was crying.

"Are you safe?"

She let out a bark of laughter that didn't ring true. "I guess."

"Where are you?"

She gave him an address, followed by, "I'm sorry I missed our dinner, but it couldn't be helped."

"I'm on my way. Stay on the phone with me." He entered the address on his map application, turned the truck around and headed away from Whiskey Gulch Ranch and toward the other end of town. "Do I need to call an ambulance?"

"No. They're here."

His heart plummeted to the pit of his belly. "Are they taking care of you?" he asked.

"They tried. But they can't help me. That's why I called you."

As he turned at the last road before leaving town, he could see the sheriff's vehicle, fire truck and ambulance even before he reached her house.

His foot hit the accelerator hard, sending him shooting toward the scene of whatever disaster had befallen Olivia. When he neared the emergency vehicles, he slowed to a stop, shifted into Park and dropped down out of the truck. The GPS map had brought him to a house that appeared as if an armored tank had rammed through the middle, making a huge hole ringed in splintered wood and siding. The roof dipped low in the middle, the support beams destroyed.

Sheriff's deputies stood around with firefighters and EMTs, staring at the damage. In the middle of them was Olivia, her dark hair gray with dust, her hands covered in bandages and the knees of her jeans stained a dark red, almost black, from blood.

Becker's pulse raced, and he broke out in a sweat. The last time he'd seen blood… He shook his head. This wasn't a helicopter crash in Afghanistan—though the house appeared to have been the victim of a crash of some sort.

He breathed in and out several times, a technique he'd learned from the psych doctor he'd been forced to visit for six weeks upon his return from deployment. When his heart slowed enough and he felt more in control, he stepped forward.

His movement caught Olivia's attention, and she looked up.

As soon as she saw him, her tearful eyes grew large and her face crumpled.

Becker opened his arms, and Olivia fell into them, pressing her cheek against his chest.

"What happened?" he asked, his tone calm despite the full-on panic attack that had threatened to overwhelm him only moments before. He wrapped his arms around her and stroked the back of her head in a slow, calming motion.

For a long moment, she didn't speak.

The sheriff's deputy filled him in. "From what Ms. Swann reported, a large black SUV plowed into her home. Men jumped out, grabbed her sister and left."

"Your sister?" Becker tipped her chin up and stared into her watery, red-rimmed green eyes.

Olivia nodded, more tears streaming down her face. "They took her. Oh, dear God. They have my sister."

"Do you know who they were?" Becker cupped her cheek in one hand, brushing away the tears. "Can you describe them?"

Olivia shook her head. "I think they wore ski masks, and they were covered in dust. When I tried to stop one of them, he slammed me against the wall. I must have blacked out for a second, because when I came to, the SUV was already backing out."

Becker frowned down at her, studying her face through the coating of dust. A bruise was forming on her right temple. "Did you have the EMT check you for potential concussion?"

One of the EMTs leaned into the conversation. "I did. She appears to be okay, but it wouldn't hurt to keep an eye on her. She refused to go to the hospital for a night of observation."

He brushed his thumb gently across the bruise. "If you blacked out—"

Olivia grabbed his hand and captured his gaze with her green-eyed one. "They took my sister. I'm not going anywhere unless it's to find her."

Becker's glance shifted to the deputy.

"We have an all-points bulletin out for a dark SUV with a damaged front end. Dispatch was going to pass that information on to the state police to be on the lookout for it as well."

"It might already be too late," Olivia said. "The people who are after her are only after one thing."

"And what's that?" Becker asked.

"She witnessed a murder." She stared up at him, her voice shaking as she added, "A dead witness can't testify."

"We passed information about your sister witnessing a murder on to the state police and the feds," the deputy said. "They'll start an investigation to find the people responsible."

"In the meantime, they're getting farther and farther away." She took Becker's hands in hers. "Please, help me find my sister."

"The authorities are doing their best."

She shook her head. "You're going to work for Trace Travis. He has a security firm. I'll hire you. I'll hire all of his team. I'll do anything to get my sister back. Alive." Her fingers squeezed his. "Please. She's the only family I have left."

Becker nodded. "I can't speak for Trace, but I can for myself. I'll do whatever I can to help you. And I'll bet Trace will too." He gathered her to his side and turned to the deputy. "Are you done with Ms. Swann?"

"Yes, sir." He handed Olivia his business card. "If you think of anything else, let us know. Even the smallest detail can be helpful."

"You can't stay here," Becker said.

"I have nowhere else to go," she said. "This was my home."

"You're coming with me." Becker herded Olivia to his truck, helped her into the passenger seat and secured her seat belt. He quickly rounded the front of the vehicle to climb into the driver's seat.

"Where are we going?" she asked.

"To get the help we need." He turned the truck around. "We're going to talk to the leader of the Outriders—my friend and former brother in arms Trace Travis."

Chapter Three

"You knew Trace Travis before he hired you?" Olivia asked as the truck passed through town.

Darkness had settled over Whiskey Gulch, and the stars illuminated the Texas landscape, casting the trees, bushes and hills in a deep indigo blue.

"Trace Travis and I served together as Delta Force operators." Becker's focus remained on the road in front of him. "He's saved my life a number of times, and I've had his back as well."

"He's brought a few of his old army buddies to Whiskey Gulch, hasn't he?"

Becker nodded. "Irish and Levi were members of our team. I'm sure as others leave active duty, they'll come as well."

"Are you all that close?"

"We're closer than blood brothers," he said. "And working for Trace's Outriders, we can use some of the skills we learned as Deltas."

"What exactly does his security firm do?" Olivia studied the man beside her, desperate for anything to keep her mind off what could be happening to Jasmine.

"Provide protection and investigative extraction services when the authorities are short-handed or their hands are tied. Or the mission is out of their jurisdiction."

Olivia frowned. "Are you some kind of vigilante group?"

Becker shrugged. "We don't break laws, if that's what you're asking. At least, not if we can help it."

Her jaw hardened as she stared out into the darkness. "Frankly, I don't care if you do break a few laws, as long as we get my sister back alive."

"I believe Trace's father had connections here in Texas and with the feds. Hopefully, Trace can encourage those connections to get the ball rolling."

"I hope so." She couldn't imagine what Jasmine was dealing with and didn't want to. She had to be optimistic and do everything in her power to find her.

Becker turned off the highway and pulled up to a gate with the words *Whiskey Gulch Ranch* across a wrought iron arch.

He leaned out his open window and pressed the call button on the keypad.

"That you, Beck?" Trace's voice called out.

"Yes, sir," Becker answered.

"Get up here, man. Steaks are getting cold."

A loud click sounded, and the gate swung open.

Becker drove on and followed the winding road through a stand of oak trees. As they emerged, the lights from the ranch house came into view.

He parked at the side of the house, got out and helped Olivia down from her seat.

They climbed the steps to the long wraparound porch, and a petite woman with blond hair and blue eyes walked out and greeted them on the front porch. "You must be

Beck." She held out her hand. "Everyone is gathered in the dining room. I'm Lily, Trace's fiancée."

Becker took her hand. "Lily, pleased to finally meet you. Trace has nothing but good things to say about you."

She smiled. "He's had nothing but good things to say about you as well." When she turned to Olivia, her brows dipped. "Good Lord, Olivia, what happened to you?"

Olivia grimaced. "It's a long story." She knew Lily and Trace from way back when they were kids, growing up in Whiskey Gulch.

"One I'm anxious to hear." Lily hugged her. "Come in. I'm sure Trace will want to hear it as well. No need to tell it more than once to this group."

She hooked her arm around Olivia's elbow and led her through the living area and into the dining room, where there was a long table with seating for up to fourteen people.

The men and women standing around the table turned toward them as they entered.

Trace's mother, Rosalyn Travis, had just set a basket full of bread rolls on the table when she looked up and gasped. "Olivia! What happened?" She hurried forward and touched her bandaged hands. "Come in and sit."

"I'm okay," Olivia said. "Really. I'm sure I can remove these bandages now that the bleeding has stopped."

"*Bleeding?* Good Lord, look at your jeans." Rosalyn's gaze swept over her. "Honey, let's get you cleaned up. You can tell us all about it when we get back to the table."

Olivia let the older woman lead her out of the dining room, thankful for the reprieve. "I'm sorry to show up to your house when I'm such a mess."

"Don't you worry. We'll have you fixed up in no time."

Over her shoulder, she called out, "Don't wait on us. Eat while it's hot."

Rosalyn led her up the stairs and straight to the master bedroom, where she rummaged through her closet and pulled out a pair of jeans and a lightweight calf-length sundress in a soft blue floral print. "Which would you prefer?"

"If it's all the same to you, my knees are scraped up from the glass. The dress won't rub against them."

"The dress it is." She put the jeans back and dug in a drawer in her dresser. "My husband gave me this bra-and-panty set before he died, and I haven't had the heart to wear them. I think they will fit you. We're almost the same size."

Olivia shook her head. "I couldn't. He gave them to you. I was so sorry about his death. Your husband was loved by so many in Whiskey Gulch. He helped so many people. Myself included."

Rosalyn smiled and held out the offering of undergarments. "Please. He would have wanted you to have these. He'd understand. That was who he was."

Olivia accepted. "Thank you."

Rosalyn led the way into the spacious bathroom, switched on the shower faucet and adjusted the temperature. "The towels are fresh. There's shampoo, conditioner and bodywash. There's a brush in the top drawer. Help yourself to anything you might need. I'll be downstairs with the others. Take your time. I can warm your supper when you're done."

Olivia's eyes filled at the woman's touching welcome. "Thank you, Mrs. Travis."

"Please, call me Rosalyn. And don't you worry. Everything will work out."

"I hope so," Olivia whispered as the matriarch left the bathroom, closing the door behind her.

For the first time since the SUV had come crashing through her house, Olivia looked at her reflection in the mirror and gasped.

A thin coat of dust covered every inch of her body and made her black hair appear gray. She stripped out of the torn and bloody clothes, the contaminants dirtying the shiny white tiles. She spread a towel on the floor, wrapped her dirty clothes in it and set it aside to take to the laundry room when she was done.

She stepped into the walk-in shower and let the water wash the dust and debris from her hair and scalp. Using a generous amount of shampoo, she quickly washed and rinsed. Afterward, she lathered a washcloth with liquid soap and scrubbed all her nooks and crannies until the water ran clear.

Though she felt better, she couldn't help thinking about Jasmine, frustrated that she was getting clean when she had no idea what was happening to her sister.

A hard knot of guilt formed in her belly as she dried, dressed and found the brush in the top drawer.

Moments later, she was clean, her hair straightened and pulled back from her forehead. Anxious to get downstairs and see what Trace Travis and the Outriders could do to find her sister, she didn't take the additional time to dry her hair.

The undergarments and the dress fit a little loose but were close enough. Olivia could only feel grateful for the clothing Rosalyn had provided.

Feeling a little more in control of her emotions, Olivia gathered the dirty clothes wrapped in the towel and carried them down the stairs.

Lily met her at the bottom. "I'll take those," she said with a smile. "Please, join the others. They're waiting to hear about what happened. We need to know, in order to help you."

"Thank you." Olivia lifted her chin and marched into the dining room, determined not to shed another tear. Crying accomplished nothing. To find her sister, she needed action.

WHEN OLIVIA WALKED into the dining room wearing the blue dress—her hair slicked back from her forehead, her head held high—Becker had to catch his breath.

The woman had just experienced a traumatic event, yet she stood before him like a Valkyrie ready to charge into battle.

Still, she was magnificent, strong and beautiful.

He rose from his seat and held out the chair beside him.

When she sank into the chair, he leaned close. "I told them they would have to wait for you to come down until we went into what happened. They're champing at the bit. Do you want to tell them, or should I?"

She gave him a smile. "Please, I'd like you to tell them." Marching in with her head held high was one thing. Retelling the story of her sister's abduction would destroy any confidence she might have built up in the shower.

Becker passed a platter of steak toward her.

"No, thank you," she said. "I'm not hungry."

"Take your time, Olivia," Trace said. "At least drink something. I'm sure this is all difficult for you. We can start by introducing you to the team." He nodded toward Lily. "You've met my better half, Lily."

Lily winked. "We've met."

Lily was petite and spunky. Becker liked that Trace had a woman who could stand on her own. "Trace speaks highly of you, Lily. He said you could face down cowboys twice your size without batting an eyelash."

She lifted her chin. "The key is to never show fear."

Trace chuckled. "I don't think there's anything Lily is afraid of."

Lily leaned against Trace's shoulder. "There is one thing..." Her gaze met his. "Losing you again."

"Baby, I'm not going anywhere," Trace said. "You're stuck with me."

"I can live with that." She smiled up into his eyes.

Becker's heart contracted in his chest. When he was younger, he'd always imagined himself married to someone who would look at him the way Lily looked at Trace. For a brief time, he thought he'd found that person in Brittany. Until Brittany stood him up at the altar and ran off with an accountant. She'd claimed she couldn't handle that he would be gone all the time, doing dangerous things that could get him killed.

He'd been up-front about his work in the army. Apparently, she'd expected him to give it up for her and settle into a low-risk admin job.

The thought of spending his day behind a desk gave him hives.

Trace nodded toward the man to his right. "Beck and Olivia, this is my brother, Matt Hennessey."

"*Half* brother," Matt corrected.

Olivia's brow puckered. "I sense a story behind that."

Trace nodded. "A story for another time. Anyway, Matt's my brother and part of the Outrider team. He had prior service… Marine Force Recon. But we won't hold that against him."

Matt glared at him. "Jealous because you were a lowly Delta?"

Trace grinned once more. "Matt's woman, Aubrey, isn't here tonight."

"She's a home health-care nurse," Matt said. "One of her patients needed some help this evening."

"Moving right along—" Trace nodded toward the familiar face of a man with black hair and blue eyes "—Joseph Monahan, one of my former teammates from the army."

"They call me Irish," he said. "Nice to meet you, Olivia. And it's good to have Beck around again."

Becker nodded. "Good to be with people I know."

"On Irish's other side is his significant other, Tessa Bolton," Trace continued. "An angel of mercy amongst us."

Tessa grimaced. "I'm no angel. But I am a nurse at the local hospital."

Trace smiled at the older woman seated at the table. "You've met my mother, Rosalyn Travis. She's the glue that holds us all together."

His mother's cheeks filled with a soft shade of pink. "He'd be just fine without me. Lily could handle everything without me around."

Irish leaned toward Tessa and muttered, "Note she didn't say Trace could handle everything."

Trace held up his hands. "I've been gone fighting wars in foreign countries. Before that, my father had a tight fist on how he wanted this ranch run. Since his death, my mother and Lily have been picking up the pieces. They are fully capable of running the ranch operations without my help, giving me the time to pursue my vision for the Outriders."

Trace turned to the last two people at the table. "Levi Warren, also a former Delta from our team."

Levi held up a hand in a short wave. "Nice to meet you. Glad you're with us, Beck. We missed your ugly mug." He winked and cracked half a smile.

"Back atcha, Levi." Becker tipped his head toward the woman seated beside his former teammate. "Who have you got with you?"

Levi grinned and stared down at the woman with sandy-blond hair and gray eyes. "She's only the smartest, prettiest badass in the county sheriff's department. Deputy Dallas Jones, my fiancée."

"Now that all the introductions are out of the way..." Trace looked around the room. "I trust everyone is up to speed on the abduction of Olivia's sister?"

As one, each person at the table nodded.

Dallas leaned toward Olivia. "I got a call about the BOLO they put out on the black SUV. I'm sorry about your sister."

Even as Olivia's eyes welled, she squared her shoulders. "We'll get her back."

Becker only hoped they would get Jasmine back *alive*. He launched into an explanation of what had happened.

"Excuse me," Trace said after Becker had finished. He left the table and returned with a laptop. He opened it and waited for the system to boot.

"Says here, Nico Salvatore's initial court date is a week from today. They will arraign him then. According to the press releases, he's pleading not guilty. They have no evidence. The murder weapon is still missing, and his girlfriend claims he was with her at the time of the murder."

"He was if she was also at the scene of the crime." Olivia shook her head. "My sister *was* there. If she said it was Nico, it was Nico. She has no reason to lie. Jasmine also said Eduardo was carrying what appeared to be a painting. She didn't have time or access to determine which painting he was carrying. Nico took it from Eduardo and left."

In between bites of his steak, Trace's fingers flew across the keyboard. "I found a report on a missing painting from the Cavendish Art Gallery in downtown Dallas."

Olivia's eyes widened. "That's the gallery my sister curated."

"The report says the police have no suspects at this time, citing faulty or disarmed security cameras. They do mention the curator, a Miss Jasmine Swann, is missing. By stating the curator has gone missing, the reporter is leaving it to the readers to infer Ms. Swann might be the one who stole the painting."

"But she didn't," Olivia cried. "Nico did."

Trace toggled back and forth between articles. "Nico was arrested the following morning. That gave him time to hide or dispose of the painting."

Irish speared a piece of his steak. "With Nico's life hanging in the balance, Salvatore would have every reason to want your sister dead. I'm sure his father does not want his son rotting in jail." He popped the steak in his mouth and chewed.

Becker's eyes narrowed. "If all Salvatore wanted was to keep his son out of jail, why didn't he have his people kill Jasmine instead of taking her hostage?"

Olivia stiffened next to him. "Unless it wasn't Salvatore who kidnapped my sister."

Becker turned to her. "Who else?"

"Eduardo Romano's family," Levi said. "They have reason to want Jasmine to testify. That way, Nico would pay for his crime. Texas has the death penalty."

Trace glanced up. "The other question is, what happened to the painting?"

"If Eduardo had it initially, do you think the Romanos want it back?" Lily asked. "Could they be the ones who actually kidnapped Jasmine? I mean, they didn't kill her. They obviously wanted her alive, or why not just burn the house down with her in it? Or shoot her?"

Becker reached under the table to grip Olivia's hand. Her fingers curled between his.

"Do you think they might want to bargain with the Salvatores?" Tessa said. "The witness for the painting?"

"What was so special about the painting that Nico would kill to get it?" Levi asked.

Trace tapped his fingers against the keyboard a few times and turned the laptop around so that everyone could see the image on the screen.

A woman stood with her back to the artist in a field of wheat, her long dark hair whipped by the wind, her body naked, blending naturally in the late-afternoon light of a fading sun.

"She's beautiful," Rosalyn whispered. "It's like something Andrew Wyeth would have done."

Trace nodded. "That's because it is. It was commissioned by one of Wyeth's patrons. The man had Wyeth paint this portrait of his wife. The patron has since passed. The wife and her family wanted the work displayed for all to see before they sold it to the highest bidder."

"Wow. No wonder both mafia families want it," Olivia said. "It's an original Wyeth."

"But why display it at the Cavendish Art Gallery?" Becker asked.

"Good point," Tessa said. "Wouldn't it have been better to place it with other paintings from Wyeth's collection?"

Olivia shook her head. "Wyeth's paintings could be on tour from one gallery to another around the world. The family might not want the painting that far away. Art enthusiasts who love Wyeth would come to see this newly discovered treasure."

"Some would pay big bucks to own it," Trace said. "An Andrew Wyeth painting could sell for millions."

"All the more reason to steal it," Dallas said. "They're going to sell it on the black market."

"They might already have a buyer lined up," Becker said.

Trace's lips twisted. "I bet both families had the same idea. They might both have a buyer—maybe even the money already in their hands."

"Then that's all the incentive they need to snag the painting," Olivia said. "Even if they have to kill someone to get it." She squeezed Becker's hand beneath the table. "Jasmine has to be okay. They kidnapped her for a reason, and it wasn't to kill her. They're going to use her as a bargaining chip."

"I've read there are auctions set up specifically for black market items," Dallas said. "Seems they could get a bigger payoff if more than one person is bidding on the painting."

Olivia's brow furrowed. "Hopefully, they haven't delivered the painting to a buyer yet. It's been a couple of weeks since it went missing."

"If Nico was smart," Becker said, "he hid it and didn't tell anyone where it is. All the more reason for his entire family to want to get the murder charges dropped and Nico out of jail in a hurry."

Trace closed the laptop and set it on a buffet table behind him. "We have a lot to think about. It makes sense to keep Jasmine alive if she's to be used as leverage for the painting."

"We need to locate the painting," Olivia said. "We could use it in trade for my sister's life."

"Not if you turn it over to the police," Dallas said.

Becker stared at the sheriff's deputy. "Are you saying we should withhold evidence?"

She held up her hands. "I wouldn't exactly put it in those terms. But once that painting is back where it belongs, you won't have anything to bargain with."

"She's right," Olivia said. "We might have to be just as crooked as the mafia long enough to get my sister out of trouble."

Dallas covered her ears. "This is where I have to step out of the discussion. I made an oath to uphold the law. But what I don't know, I can't report."

"Let's table this discussion until after dinner," Rosalyn said. "Please, eat. And when we're done here, I have pecan pie for dessert."

Becker finished his steak, all the while his thoughts churning, a plan forming. His idea might be way off base, but it was just crazy enough that it might work. He glanced over at Olivia, knowing she would want to be in on the plan. The hard part was that this plan, if they chose to go with it, would place both of them in danger and right in the middle of rival mafia families.

But if it worked, they stood a chance of snagging the painting and getting Jasmine back alive.

He was up for the challenge. His training as a Delta had given him the fighting skills he would need if he was backed into a corner.

Olivia, on the other hand, wasn't a fighter. She was an artist. She'd be in way over her head.

But if he didn't take her with him, she'd find a way to follow and get herself into all kinds of trouble anyway. If she insisted, he'd be better off knowing she was by his side rather than off by herself, a loose cannon on a rocking ship.

Becker polished off the last bite of his food and waited impatiently for the others to finish. When Rosalyn rose from the table, he rose too, helped clear the dishes and carried them into the kitchen.

"Rosalyn, Trace—" Dallas set her plate in the sink "—thank you for dinner. I'll just see myself to the door so your team can make plans I might not want to know about." She leaned forward and brushed a kiss across Rosalyn's cheek. "Keep them somewhat in line, will you? I don't want to put any of my people in jail if I can help it."

Rosalyn patted Dallas's cheek. "You haven't always played by the rules, my dear."

"Good point. But I did that out of self-preservation." She turned to Trace. "I might be stepping out of this conversation, but I'm around if you need me. I'll always have your back. After all, you had mine when I needed the help." She reached for Levi's hand. "And you have my back."

"Always, darlin'. Always." He walked her out.

Once they were out of the house, Becker met Trace's gaze. "I have an idea."

Trace nodded. "Let's help with the cleanup. Then we can take it to my office."

"Normally, I'd make you stay and help," Lily said. "But Olivia needs you more." She pushed up on her toes and pressed a kiss to Trace's lips. "We've got this. Go."

"Thank you." Trace led the way through the door. "I believe we have your first assignment as an Outrider agent."

Becker nodded. He hadn't been sure what to expect. Playing the bodyguard or providing security at events, yeah. But going undercover with the mafia hadn't even been a passing thought.

Chapter Four

Olivia followed Becker as they walked down a hallway to a set of wood-paneled doors.

Trace opened them to reveal a large office with a massive desk at one end and a conference table at the other. He waved toward the table. "Have a seat."

Becker pulled out a chair for Olivia.

She didn't really feel like sitting. Her natural inclination was to pace. But she didn't want to argue, so she took the proffered seat and waited to hear what Becker had to say, praying his idea was sound and would lead to them getting Jasmine back safe and sound.

Matt, Irish and Levi took seats around the table. Trace closed the doors and sank into the chair at the end of the long table. "What have you got?"

"I understand you have connections," Becker said. "Do you happen to have any in the dark web?"

Trace frowned. "Maybe. Why?"

Becker's jaw hardened. "We need to gather all the information we can get about the Salvatores and the Romanos. We also need to find out who else has enough money and interest in art to purchase a stolen Andrew Wyeth—someone I can impersonate."

"That's a lot to ask." Trace leaned back in his chair.

"I might be able to help you with the dark web," Matt said. "My mother helped a young hacker once when he was cornered by some mean rednecks. Saved his life. I'm sure he'd want to return the favor."

Becker nodded. "Tap into that resource. Look for an auction that might be selling stolen art. I'll need as much of that information as I can get. In the meantime, I'll need to craft my new identity with a driver's license, credit cards, clothes and an expensive sports car."

Trace laughed. "This kind of thing takes time."

"We don't have a lot of time," Olivia said.

Trace sobered. "Of course," he assured her. "We'll make it happen."

"And while your hacker is at it," Olivia said, "make sure he gets information on what your rich art-loving sleazebag likes in the way of women." She shot a glance at Becker. "If you're going undercover, I'm going with you."

He took her hands. "You realize we'll be dancing with dangerous people?"

She nodded. "Been there. You saw my house. Besides, we're talking about saving my sister. I refuse to stand by and do nothing."

"They might recognize you," he said. "You have pretty distinctive features."

She lifted her chin. "I can change my appearance. We both have to do something to impersonate whomever the hacker can find."

Matt shifted in his seat. "How soon do you need this information?"

"The sooner, the better," Olivia answered. "My sister might not have much time."

"We'll also need you to have the hacker spread the

word that we are in the market for an Andrew Wyeth painting and will pay top dollar." Becker tapped his fingertips on the tabletop.

Matt grabbed a pad of paper and a pen from the middle of the table and jotted down notes. "Should we spread other rumors about more potential buyers?"

"Yes," Becker said. "Hopefully, they'll be greedy enough to want a bidding war. Maybe they'll arrange for an in-person auction." He glanced at Olivia. "We'll want an invite to that."

"It all sounds too fantastic." Her brow knit. "Can we pull off something this complicated?"

Becker nodded. "We have to lure the two factions out in the open."

"In the meantime, Matt, Irish and I will be searching for Jasmine," Trace said. "If we find her first, we can save you the trouble of all the pretense."

Becker nodded.

If only it was that easy. Olivia feared it wouldn't end that quickly. "As long as the Romanos think Jasmine is of value, and they don't have the painting, they'll come after her again."

Becker drew in a deep breath and released it slowly. "Then we return the painting to the rightful owners."

"That will help with the Romanos but not the Salvatores," Olivia said. "Until Nico is locked up for good, Jasmine will remain a target."

"Then once we find her, we'll get her to a safe location."

"Can you guarantee her safety?" Olivia asked. "The US Marshals couldn't."

Trace's brow dipped. "You have my word. I can assign one of my men to protect her."

"For how long? Weeks? Months? Years?" Olivia shook her head. "You can't commit to that kind of long-term protection."

"Wanna bet?" He leaned toward her. "Let's get her back and take it from there."

Olivia forced herself to breathe normally. She couldn't freak out now; Jasmine needed her to keep a calm, cool head. Especially if she was going incognito in order to rescue her.

Trace glanced at Matt, who was scribbling notes on the pad. His eyes narrowed. "This hacker you know… Do you trust him?"

Matt looked up. "With my life."

Trace's lips quirked. "I wouldn't happen to know him, would I?"

Matt's mouth twitched. He held Trace's gaze for a long moment in silence.

Olivia studied the two men as they communicated without saying anything.

Trace nodded. "Enough said."

She almost laughed. If she'd read their looks right, Matt Hennessey not only trusted the hacker—he *was* the hacker.

The knowledge made her feel a little better. At least they were keeping this operation within the team. A random hacker might be up for sale.

Olivia glanced around the room at the men who'd worked, fought and would lay down their lives for each other. She was in good hands. If anyone could find and rescue her sister, it was these stalwart men.

Her heart warmed as she sat beside Becker, glad he'd walked into her shop that afternoon.

He was different from other men she'd known. Becker

was nothing like her former fiancé. Mike would never have put himself in danger for anyone. He would have walked the other way. Not Becker. The man was planning to put himself in harm's way for her, a veritable stranger.

Like he had done earlier, she reached beneath the table for his hand and gave it a gentle squeeze.

His lips turned upward, and he responded in kind.

"Are you sure you want to do this?" he asked. "You don't have to. I can handle this operation on my own. I'd feel better if I did."

She shook her head. "And who would have your back?"

"Trace or Irish."

Both men nodded.

Olivia shook her head. "It would look more natural for the rich guy to bring his girlfriend. He'd want to impress her with the money."

"She has a point," Irish said. "They might be more open to you if you have a woman with you rather than a couple of bodyguards."

Trace tipped his head. "Although, we could be your bodyguards even if you take Olivia in with you. A rich man would travel with them. He'd be a target for kidnapping and ransom."

"We'll play it by ear," Becker said. "Let's get our stories down, hijack the identity of a man who's most likely to purchase a stolen painting and see what happens then."

"On it." Matt pushed to his feet. "I'll have my contact get to work. Hopefully, we'll have something by morning."

Olivia met Matt's gaze. "Thank you." She turned to the others in the room. "I appreciate what you're doing for my sister." For the first time since she'd found her sister cowering in her kitchen, Olivia was optimistic.

Trace nodded. "We'll do our best. In the meantime, I'll send my foreman over to your place tomorrow and see what he can do to mitigate the damage and weatherproof it until we can get a carpenter to repair the structure."

Her heart swelled and tears sprang to her eyes. "I don't know what I would have done if Becker hadn't shown up in my shop today."

Trace's brow wrinkled. "I don't know what that has to do with us helping."

She smiled through the liquid swimming in her eyes. "It brought me to all of you."

"My mother will probably have a room ready for you. You're welcome to stay with us as long as you like. It will take time to repair your home. You can go with the foreman tomorrow and gather some of your belongings and bring them here."

Olivia swallowed the lump in her throat. "Thank you."

They left the room and returned to the kitchen, where Rosalyn, Lily and Tessa sat around the kitchen table, drinking coffee.

Rosalyn popped out of her seat. "There you are. Did you find a way to save the world? Or at the very least, Olivia's sister?"

"We're working on it," Trace said.

"Well, while you're working on it, let me show our guest to her room. I'm sure all the trauma of the day has taken its toll." She hooked her arm through Olivia's. "Let me show you where you'll sleep for the next few weeks."

"I could sleep over my shop in town," Olivia insisted. "There's a storage room I could convert into sleeping quarters."

"Is there a bed?"

"No. But I could bring one from the house."

"Is there a bathroom with a shower?"

Olivia shook her head, the events of the day hitting her like a ton of bricks. "No. I should just quit arguing and say thank you, shouldn't I?"

Lily laughed. "Yes, ma'am. When Rosalyn Travis gets in mama mode, she won't take no for an answer."

"She's right. And you, my dear, could use a little mothering." She led her out of the kitchen. "I knew your mother. She was a lovely woman and a talented artist. I have one of her paintings. Did you know that?"

Olivia couldn't resist the comfort Mrs. Travis provided. It was almost as good as having her own mother there to tell her everything would be all right.

Rosalyn spoke softly of her friendship with Olivia's mother and the time she took painting lessons from her. "Alas, I didn't have the talent—or was it the patience?—to learn." She shrugged with a smile. "That's when I bought one of her paintings. It's hanging in the room you'll be sleeping in. I figured if I couldn't paint, I should at least help someone be successful at what she did best by purchasing one of her works."

At the top of the stairs, she turned right and led her to a room two doors down. "This is the blue room. It has its own bathroom. You won't have to traipse down the hallway." She pushed the door open.

Olivia's heart swelled when she saw the painting hanging over the white iron bed. Her mother had painted a picture of a white wooden porch overlooking a sandy beach, the blue green of the ocean waves shimmering beyond.

The bed was covered with a seafoam-green comforter and matching pillows.

Rosalyn crossed the room to the French doors on the other side. "I like to open the window or door at night to let the cool night breeze flow through." She pulled open the doors and walked out onto the porch. "It's a beautiful night. The breeze is so peaceful." She lifted her face to the sky, a slight smile softening her features.

Olivia joined her on the porch and stared up at the night sky, where a blanket of stars stretched in all directions. "It is a beautiful night," she said. "When we were little, my sister and I used to lie outside under the stars with our parents and point out the constellations and make wishes on shooting stars." Olivia chose to remember the good in those memories, not the loss of her parents and the danger her sister faced.

"I used to do that with Trace. He loved learning about the stars and planets. For a while, I thought he'd be an astronaut. But he chose to join the army." She sighed. "I didn't want him to. I was afraid every time he deployed. I didn't want to be one of those parents visited by a man in a fancy uniform, there to tell me my son was coming home in a body bag." Rosalyn turned to her with a crooked smile that faded away. "As it was, my son came home when my husband was murdered. He was safer at war than his father was at home."

Olivia touched the older woman's arm. "I'm so sorry."

Rosalyn covered her hand with her own. "I am too. But life goes on. I'm glad Trace is home, but I hope he didn't stay because of me. I never wanted him to be trapped by this big ol' ranch. Lily and I could have managed." She snorted. "Or we would have gone down fighting."

"I've seen Trace around town. He seems to love what he's doing. He's always got a kind word and a smile."

"Thank you, dear." Rosalyn smiled. "He and his boys will find your sister. Don't you worry. They're good at what they do. Now, I've laid out a nightgown, a robe and slippers. There's a new toothbrush in the bathroom and all the toiletries you might need. If you need anything, please let me know."

"You've done more than enough for me. Thank you." Olivia hugged Rosalyn.

When she left, she closed the door behind her.

Olivia was finally alone in a pretty room with her mother's painting. Her sister was out there somewhere, being held captive by the animals who'd carried her away screaming.

How could she go on?

By putting one foot in front of the other and taking care of herself. She would be of no use to her sister if she didn't get enough rest.

She changed into the pretty, semi-sheer nightgown and lay on the bed.

She was exhausted and weary.

As soon as she closed her eyes, images of the SUV crashing through the wall of her home flashed over and over in her mind like a video on a loop.

She opened her eyes to dispel the images and stared up at the ceiling, following the shadows created by the starlight shining through the windows.

After thirty minutes, she sat up and swung her legs over the side of the bed. Maybe a drink of water would help. She was anxious. After wrapping the robe around the nightgown, she slipped her feet into the soft terry-cloth slippers and padded to the door.

After a quick peek into the hallway, she stepped out and descended the staircase to the first floor.

The lights were off, but several night-lights provided enough illumination. She made it to the kitchen, where someone had left a light on over the sink.

She searched until she found the cabinet with the glasses and filled one with tap water and several cubes of ice.

The thought of going back up the stairs to lie alone didn't appeal to her, so she walked out the back door and onto the porch.

Rosalyn was right: the cool night breeze was peaceful.

Olivia crept across the porch to the end, where a swing swayed slightly in the gentle breeze. She set the glass on a table and sank onto the cushioned seat with a sigh. Maybe she'd rock herself to sleep.

"That was a deep sigh," a warm, resonant voice said in the darkness. Becker pushed away from the wall of the house, emerging from the shadows.

A tremor of awareness rippled through Olivia. "I thought you had a room in town?"

"I do, but Trace insisted I stay. Saves time if I'm here instead of all the way in town. He and Matt are working in the office. I imagine they'll be there all night."

"And you're not with them?"

"I was for a while, but there were only the two computers. I didn't like crowding them by hanging over their shoulders."

"Matt's the hacker, isn't he?" Olivia grinned. "Why doesn't he just confess?"

"Hacking can get you thrown in jail, and worse, if you break into the wrong systems," Becker said.

"I guess you're right." She drew her fingers across her lips. "I know nothing about any hacking going on."

"Neither do I."

Olivia scooted to one side of the porch swing. "You can sit. I promise not to bite."

He settled on the cushioned seat beside her and leaned back. "What if I want you to?"

"I'm sure we could work something out," she shot back.

"Why aren't you sleeping?" he asked. "I would think you're pretty tired after what you went through today."

"I am. But I can't get my mind to relax."

He slipped his arm around her shoulders and pulled her close. "If you want me to stay with you until you go to sleep, I can."

"You've already done so much for me," she said and yawned. "But okay. I accept." She leaned her body into his, her cheek resting against his chest.

"That can't be all that comfortable," he said and shifted his body. Turning to the side, he scooped her into his arms and deposited her in his lap, guiding her head onto his shoulder. "Better?"

She melted against him, loving how hard his body was compared to her softer curves and how warm he was in the cool breeze.

His arms wrapped around her, holding her close.

Olivia rested her cheek against his chest, the steady beat of his heart calming the storm of memories rushing through her mind. She inhaled deeply, and on a slow exhalation, she released some of the day's stress.

She'd just met him earlier that day; yet here she was, draped across his lap, dressed in a nightgown and a robe, feeling cherished in his strong arms.

She couldn't help thinking it would be nice to be loved by someone like Becker. The woman he married would be one lucky lady. He would stand by her, protect her, and never destroy the sanctity of their love and trust for one another by hiring a prostitute.

That thought led to another. "Have you ever been married?"

He shook his head. "No."

"How is it that you're still single?" she whispered.

"I came close once," he said, his voice as warm as melted chocolate.

"'Close'? What happened?"

"I showed up. She didn't."

Olivia leaned back and stared into his face. Her heart fluttered. "She stood you up at the altar?"

He grimaced. "I know. My life is a cliché. I haven't had the desire to repeat the humiliation since."

"She must have been blind and stupid." Olivia shook her head. "I can't believe she didn't show up for her own wedding."

He chuckled. "She realized at the last minute that she couldn't be married to a military man who wouldn't be home for her birthday, Valentine's Day, Christmas. She married an accountant."

Olivia rested her cheek back on his chest. "They deserved each other. She settled for boring when she could have had you."

His laughter rumbled against her ear. "I'll take that as a compliment."

"You should. She wasn't the right woman for you. You dodged a bullet."

He nodded, his hand coming up to stroke her hair. "I know that now, but I can't lie… It hurt when I was standing there, waiting for a bride who never showed up."

"Hurt your pride, most likely." Olivia bit her tongue. "Sorry. I shouldn't have said that. Did you love her?"

He didn't answer at first.

Olivia regretted asking the question. She hadn't intended to put him on the spot or make him uncomfortable.

Finally, he said, "I was young and stupid. I think I was more in love with the idea of being married. Of having someone to come home to more than having the right someone to spend my life with."

She glanced up at him. "That's pretty profound. Did you realize that at the time?"

He snorted. "I realized it just now." Becker pressed a kiss to her forehead. "It took meeting you for my thoughts to become clear enough to understand why I was so hurt at the time."

"And why was that?" she asked.

"I wanted all of it. Marriage, kids…the love of a good woman." His chest rose and fell beneath her cheek. "I just didn't take the time to find the right person to do all that with. Then I told myself I shouldn't marry. The job makes any relationship too hard. I gave up."

"When you could have found a woman who would have accepted you for who you are and understood that your military service meant so much to you." Her hand rested over his heart. "And now?"

His arms tightened around her. "I think there's hope for the future." Again, he kissed her forehead.

"I'm glad I could help," she said. "Not that I did anything."

"You did everything," he said. "You asked the questions that made me think past my pride. Thank you." With a grin, he cupped her cheek and kissed her on the lips.

With her hand resting on his chest, it wasn't hard to move it up to circle the back of his neck and deepen the kiss. Olivia made that bold move so naturally, she didn't realize she'd done it until her fingers pushed through his hair.

His tongue swept across the seam of her lips, urging her to open to him.

She did, meeting him thrust for thrust, their tongues entwining in a sensual caress.

Heat surged through her veins, dispelling the coolness of the breeze and sending fire to her core, where it coiled and intensified.

His hand slid down her arm to her waist and lower to smooth over her hip…and lower still, finding the hem of her robe halfway down her thigh.

Yes.

She wanted to feel his hand on her bare skin, riding up beneath the robe and the gown to cup her bottom, pressing her body closer to his.

Beneath her, she could feel the hardness of his erection digging into her other hip. All she had to do was shift her weight, straddle his hips and lower herself over him to consummate the burgeoning desire flooding her system.

It wouldn't be impossible. Tricky, considering the swing. But not impossible.

When she started to move, he broke the kiss and leaned back, dragging in a shaky breath. "I'm sorry. I got a little carried away." He lifted her and sat her on the seat beside him. "If you like, I'll walk you to your room and wait with you while you go to sleep." He raised his hands. "I promise not to take advantage of you. Just be there so you can sleep without bad guys driving into your home."

Inside, Olivia was screaming, *No, no, no!*

They couldn't stop there.

She wanted so much more.

Chapter Five

Still shaking from the intensity of her desire, all Olivia could do was nod.

Becker stood up and held out his hand.

She laid hers in his and rose to her feet. Her slipper slid off her foot, and she fell forward.

Becker caught her and held her longer than was necessary to regain her balance.

Olivia didn't complain. She was back in his arms, loving the feeling of strength and security he imparted.

When he pushed her out to arm's length, the cool air between them felt too empty. She considered propositioning him.

All the way up the stairs, she mentally rehearsed asking him to stay with her, to make love to her and hold her through the night.

When they reached her room, he swept her up into his arms once more and carried her over the threshold, laying her across the bed.

Then he bent to press another kiss to her forehead.

Olivia lifted her face to him, circled her hands behind his head and brought his lips to hers. Forehead kisses were for friends and children. She didn't want to be just his friend. And she wasn't a child. Her heart slamming against her ribs, Olivia kissed him long and hard. All the words she'd rehearsed in her head flew from her mind.

"Stay with me," she whispered against his mouth.

"I shouldn't."

"Why?"

"We just met."

"Bad reason. Try again." She resumed the kiss and pulled him down onto the bed beside her.

He sank down on the mattress, lay on his side and brushed her hair back from her forehead. "I don't want to rush you," he said. "Whatever we're feeling is special. I can't blow it. I want it too badly."

"And so do I," she said softly. "We're not kids."

"No, we're not," he said, sliding his thumb across her jawbone.

Olivia ran her hand over his shoulder and down to the small of his back, applying pressure, reminding him of the hardness digging into her hip. "We're consenting adults."

He brushed a featherlight kiss across first one eyelid and then the other. "Mmm. Yes, we are."

"I'm not asking for forever," she said. "I don't want to be alone tonight. Please." There it was—she was so desperate to be with this man, she had been reduced to begging. She knew no shame, but she didn't care, as long as he stayed.

He paused his onslaught of kisses on her face and lifted his head to stare into her eyes. "If I stay, it won't be just kisses."

"I want more." She took his hand in hers and guided it to the hem of her robe, sliding his fingers beneath the soft silk and then beneath the thin chiffon of the gown beneath.

Her breath caught at the feel of his skin against hers

as she moved his hand up over her hip and across her torso to cup one of her breasts. She held him there, her breath ragged as if she couldn't quite get enough air into her lungs.

For a fraction of a second, he hesitated. Then his fingers curled around her, finding the tip and teasing the nipple into a tight little pearl.

Her back arched off the mattress.

More. She wanted so much more.

Becker reached for the belt of her robe, untied it and opened the lapels wide.

The nightgown did little to hide Olivia's attributes. Not that she wanted it to. She wanted to be completely naked with the man. Impatient, she sat up, ripped off the nightgown and flung it against the wall. It slipped softly and soundlessly to the floor.

Olivia lay back against the mattress and slid her hands beneath the hem of his T-shirt, bringing it up and over his head. She tossed it aside, and it landed on top of her gown. He was all muscle and sinew, and she reveled in running her hands over his smooth skin and impressive chest.

The man was magnificent.

When she reached for the button on his jeans, he brushed her hands aside, ripped open the rivet, unzipped and stepped out of the jeans to stand before her in all his glorious masculinity.

She held her breath as he came to her, parted her legs and dropped to his knees.

"I want you inside me," she said. "Now."

He shook his head. "Not yet. I want you to want me as much as I want you right now."

Olivia collapsed back against the mattress with a moan. "I already do."

"I'm here to prove you wrong."

As soon as he parted her folds and touched his tongue to her most sensitive spot, she knew he was right.

Shocks of electricity rippled through her at the first touch. The second flick of his tongue had her sensations pulsing, lighting her nerve endings, making her body sizzle with anticipation.

Olivia dug her hands into his hair, the ecstasy so profound, she didn't know whether to push him away or bring him closer.

She chose closer.

He swirled and flicked and licked her there until her body writhed to the pace he set.

Her hips rocked, rising and falling as she let go of her worry and embraced the moment.

Beautiful tension rose within her, her muscles tightening, her heels digging into the mattress as she savored everything he was doing to her.

Tingling started at her core and spread outward until she was consumed by her release.

She rode the wave for as long as it lasted and then finally collapsed back against the pillow—her breathing coming in shallow gasps, her heartbeat raging.

For a long moment, she lay still, reveling in the afterglow. But only for a moment. They weren't done. Not yet. She wanted to feel him inside her, filling that space that had been empty for too long. Had it ever been filled? Mike hadn't touched her quite as *completely* as Becker had. This was…different…more intense…so much better. Olivia didn't want it to end.

She sank her fingers into his hair again and pulled.

“Hey,” he chuckled. “The hair is attached.”

“Now,” she managed to say. “I need you now.”

“Well, then. Okay.” He climbed up her body, settled between her legs, pressed his staff against her channel… and stopped.

Olivia groaned, grabbed his buttocks and tried to bring him home.

He shook his head. “Wait.”

“No.”

“Trust me, you’ll want to wait.” He leaned over the side of the bed, grabbed his jeans and dug into the back pocket for his wallet.

It was then that Olivia realized Becker was thinking more clearly than she was. He was right. She was glad he’d waited as he rolled the protection down over his engorged staff.

Then he was back between her legs, nudging her entrance. He leaned up on his arms, staring down into her eyes. “You are a beautiful, amazing and talented woman, Olivia Swann.”

She looked up at the gorgeous man—even more beautiful naked than any man had a right to be. “You’re pretty talented yourself.” Her hands wrapped around his hips, her fingers pressing into the taut skin of his buttocks. “Make love to me, Becker. Before we forget where we left off.”

He laughed. “I have a memory like a—”

Before he could utter another word, she lifted her hips and came down on him, hard and deep.

BECKER HELD ON TO his control by a thread. The woman was so hot, sexy and willing, he wasn’t sure how much longer he could hold back. But he did, wanting to make the moment last even longer.

What they were doing—how he was feeling—was pure magic, and he never wanted it to end.

Taking his time, he moved in and out of her. Slowly at first.

Her fingers dug into him again, urging him to pick up the pace.

He complied, the tension mounting inside, his body tensing even more with every thrust and parry.

Her muscles tightened, and she gripped him like a fitted glove, providing slick friction that ignited every part of his soul.

Soon, he was pumping hard and fast, past the point of no return, ready to take her all the way. As he neared the peak, he let go of his restraint, and with one final thrust, he spasmed. He pulsed inside her as wave after wave of ecstasy washed over him, reminding him of how good it felt to make love to someone incredibly special.

Olivia was that someone. He'd known it the moment he'd found her at the back of her shop, her hands gray with wet clay, smudges of it drying on her face. She'd looked up at him with those incredible green eyes, and it was as if he'd been sucker punched in the gut.

He knew he had to see her again. All the years of telling himself he wasn't marriage material, that no woman would or should marry a Delta Force operator, had been his way of pushing women away. He hadn't wanted to risk rejection again.

Until a talented artist, covered in clay and charm, had smiled up at him.

He held his body stiffly, absorbing every bit of his

release, relishing the moment in her arms. Olivia was the real deal.

Maybe it was too soon to think about forever, but he was determined not to fail this time. If she really was the one, he'd do everything to win her heart.

As he returned to Earth, he lowered himself onto her and rolled them both to the side, maintaining their intimate connection as long as possible.

He held her close in his arms and pressed his lips to hers in a gentle kiss he hoped conveyed even a fraction of his joy.

When his heart slowed enough to where he could breathe normally, he asked, "Are you all right?"

Olivia raised her hand to his cheek and smiled. "More than all right." She breathed deeply, her breasts pressing against him.

"You should rest," he said.

She yawned and nodded, closing her eyes. "So should you."

"I will as soon as I know you're sleeping peacefully."

"You'll stay?" she whispered, her hand dropping to rest on his chest.

"I'll stay," he promised. "Now, sleep."

She nestled close, her body pressing against his. Her breathing slowed, and finally, she slept. From what Becker could tell, she wasn't fighting bad guys in her dreams—probably not dreaming at all.

He held her tight. He was almost afraid to sleep. Afraid that when he woke, what had just happened would have all been a dream. He'd be alone in his bed, and Olivia would have been a product of his imagination.

To keep the dream alive, he stayed awake, his gaze on the woman he held, hoping this was the real deal.

For a few short minutes, while making love with Olivia, Becker had pushed aside the mission he'd proposed, focusing instead on this woman and the chemistry between them that neither could deny.

He couldn't do that again. Not until they'd successfully located Jasmine, retrieved the painting and put Nico behind bars permanently. Until then, Jasmine and Olivia were in danger.

His resolve firm, he drifted into half sleep, his awareness not far from the surface. When they woke the next day, they would have work to do. He needed all his faculties operating at 100 percent.

His sleep was plagued by images of Olivia covered in dust, her arms and legs bleeding. He wouldn't let that happen again. Not on his watch. He'd protect her with his life, if that was what it took.

He hoped he wouldn't have to make that decision, because he only had one life to give. Then who would take care of Olivia and make sure she was safe for the rest of her life?

His last thought as he faded into sleep was that he wouldn't let this mission get to the point of sacrificing his life to save another. He had to stay alive to be there for her.

Chapter Six

Becker slept for a few hours and woke as the gray light of dawn edged through the windows.

He lay on his back for a few minutes, enjoying waking beside Olivia, wondering if they'd ever have the opportunity to do it again.

If he had anything to say about it, they would. But first, they had to find Jasmine and the painting. Once they were secure, he could pursue Olivia. How far *she* wanted to go with *him*, he still wasn't sure. For Becker, forever seemed to be floating around in his mind.

Frankly, that scared him. He'd just met her, and he was already thinking about the long term. Was he so in love with the dream of finding a family that he was jumping ahead when he should be taking it slowly?

To keep from waking Olivia, Becker eased out of bed. Once he'd dressed, he slipped from the room and paused when he turned to close the door behind him.

Olivia slept with abandon, her arms splayed out, her cheeks a rosy pink, her dark hair fanned out around her head on the seafoam-green pillows.

His heart tugged at him, urging him to go back to her, lie down in the bed and hold her once more. With the plan he had in mind, he might not get that chance again anytime soon.

Just as he was about to take that step, he heard another door open at the end of the hallway.

To avoid awkwardness for himself and Olivia, he pulled the door closed and hurried to the head of the stairs. As he glanced back, he caught Rosalyn's gaze.

She smiled and nodded, indicating he should continue down the stairs.

He didn't, preferring to wait for his host instead.

She carried a basket full of laundry, which he removed from her hands.

"I can carry it," she insisted.

"I know," he said with a smile of his own. "But my mother taught me to help with all household chores."

"As she should. There is no such thing as women's work or men's work. We all pitch in to get things done." She grinned. "I think I would like your mother."

"She would like you."

"Does she live close enough to visit?" Rosalyn asked as she followed him down the stairs.

"She's in the Dallas area. I visit as often as I can. Now that I'm out of the military, I hope to make that more often."

"And your father?"

Becker's chest tightened. "He passed away several years ago."

"I'm sorry," she said, her smile slipping. "It's hard to lose someone you love."

He nodded. "Yes, it is. We were all sorry to hear of your loss. We were there when Trace got the news." Becker paused at the bottom of the stairs.

"This way." Rosalyn led him down a hallway, passing

the entrance to the kitchen and turning through a doorway into a spacious laundry room with cabinets, countertops and a utility sink. "You can put the basket on the floor. I'll sort the items after breakfast. If you need anything washed, you can leave your things in the laundry room. We'll get around to it today."

"Thank you. I'm all caught up."

They walked into the kitchen in companionable silence.

Trace was pouring water into the repository of the coffee maker. "I hope you like your coffee strong," he called out over his shoulder. "We need it after last night."

Matt entered the kitchen, his hair damp, wearing a T-shirt and faded blue jeans. His feet were bare, and dark shadows lingered beneath his eyes. He stopped in the middle of the kitchen and stretched his arms above his head, working the kinks out of his body.

"Long night?" Rosalyn asked. "Did you sleep at all?"

Matt dropped his arms to his sides. "No, ma'am," he said. His gaze met Becker's. "But we have most of the information you'll need to infiltrate the black market–art circles. Apparently, there's an entire group of dirty-rich patrons of the arts who are willing to spend big bucks on hot commodities."

"Great."

Trace pulled coffee mugs out of the cabinet and lined them up on the counter in front of the coffee maker. "We found your guy."

"Really?" Becker crossed his arms over his chest, his interest piqued. "Who will I be impersonating?"

"Gunter Kraus," Trace said.

Matt stepped in. "He's a little older than you, at forty-two, but approximately the same height and coloring, with blond hair and blue eyes." He pulled out his cell phone and brought up an image of the man in question wearing a black tuxedo with a red rose pinned to the lapel. On his arm was a beautiful woman with raven-black hair and dark eyes. She wore a striking red dress, the front of which plunged all the way down to her belly button.

Becker tipped his head toward the cell phone. "Who's the woman?"

"Monique Jameson," Matt answered. "We found her in a number of the photographs. She appears to be one of his regulars."

"Good. Her coloring is similar to Olivia's."

"We thought so too," Trace said.

Becker took the phone and studied the man. "Do we have any videos on this guy?"

Matt nodded. "After breakfast, I'll show you what we found. This guy is internationally known as a playboy. He gets what he likes because he has a massive trust fund and investments he inherited from his father and grandfather. From what we learned from the dark web, he likes to collect artwork to display in his château in the Swiss Alps."

Trace added, "He isn't too concerned about following laws. He thinks his wealth makes him exempt from rules others have to follow. He was a suspect in the disappearance of a young college girl on vacation at a resort in Mexico. The case was swept under the rug before it could make it to the Mexican court."

"Did they ever find the girl?"

"No." Trace's lips pressed together in a tight line.

Matt crossed the kitchen to stand beside Trace at the coffee maker. "Gunter arrived on a Greek island two days ago. His reservation at a resort there indicates he'll be there a week."

Becker nodded. "So we can be relatively assured he isn't coming to America anytime soon."

Matt shook his head. "You'll have to be flexible. The man has a fleet of jets at his disposal and he's been known to change his mind. He could be back in the States as we speak or within a few hours. The only reason we don't think he's here now is because he likes to be the center of attention."

Trace nodded. "Where he goes, the paparazzi follow. We'd know if he was stateside." He picked up the carafe of coffee, poured a mug full and held it out to Matt. "Coffee?"

"Yes." Matt took the mug and sipped the steaming brew. He closed his eyes and sighed. "Man, I needed that."

Trace poured another cup and offered it to Becker. "Think you can pull off impersonating this guy?"

Becker took the mug, breathing in the fragrant aroma mixed with the steam. He dared to sip the liquid before answering, "My German is rusty."

"No worries. He was raised in the US in a posh penthouse apartment in New York City." Trace poured another cup of coffee and handed it to his mother. "I doubt he learned to speak much German, despite his heritage."

Still holding Matt's phone with the picture of Gunter, Becker nodded. "In that case, I can do it."

"Then we'll need to make sure you're equipped with everything you'll need to be convincing."

"Like…?" Becker cocked an eyebrow. He had an idea of what he'd need, but he wanted to hear what Trace and Matt considered important.

"Clothes," Rosalyn piped in. "If Gunter is a playboy,

he probably dresses to the nines in the latest men's fashions, showing off his wealth."

"He likes Ferraris," Matt said.

Trace leaned against the counter and sipped his own coffee. "I have a friend who owns a black Ferrari Enzo."

Matt straightened, his eyes widening. "An Enzo?"

Trace nodded. "A 2003."

Matt let loose a long, low whistle. "Did you know they have 650 ponies and can go 0 to 60 in 3.1 flat?"

Trace nodded.

"Does he owe you a favor?" Becker asked.

Trace's lips quirked at the corners. "He does."

"Must be a big one, if you think he'll loan you his Enzo," Matt said. "I wouldn't let that car out of my sight, much less loan it to a stranger."

"He will. He has a whole collection of expensive sports cars and planes."

"Who did you kill for him?" Matt asked.

Trace's brow wrinkled. "*Kill?* No. It's nothing like that."

"He'll do it for me," Rosalyn interjected. "Ross has always had a...thing for me. When James was murdered, he offered to help. He said if there was anything I needed—anything—he was there for us."

"Does rescuing a kidnapped stranger qualify as anything?" Olivia asked from the entrance to the kitchen.

Becker turned toward the woman who was quickly capturing his heart. She was wearing the clothes Rosalyn had provided the night before. She'd brushed her hair back from her forehead and secured it in a ponytail at the base of her neck, making her look younger and more vulnerable.

The older woman nodded. "If it's important to me,

he'll live up to his promise." She crossed the room to take Olivia's hands in hers. "It's important to me for us to find your sister."

Olivia's eyes filled. "Thank you."

Rosalyn gave her a quick hug and then marched to the refrigerator. "I'll have breakfast ready in less than fifteen minutes. Trace, pop some bread in the toaster. Matt, slap some bacon on the griddle."

"I'll set the table." Lily entered the kitchen and went straight for the cabinet with the plates.

"I'll help." Olivia took the stack of plates while Lily grabbed glasses from another cabinet.

A pretty woman with red hair and green eyes staggered into the melee, yawning. "What can I do?"

"Sit and drink some coffee," Rosalyn said. "Matt?"

"On it." Matt paused in his effort to stretch strips of bacon on the griddle. He hurried over to the coffee maker, poured a cup and carried it to the table.

Becker took over at the griddle, finishing what Matt had started. He manned the bacon, careful to let the slices cook to a perfect crispness without burning.

Working together, they had breakfast on the table in the fifteen minutes Rosalyn had promised.

Irish arrived at the back door as Rosalyn was setting the platter of scrambled eggs in the middle of the large kitchen table. He grinned and clapped his hands together. "Did I time that right or what?"

"Perfect," Rosalyn said. "Where's Tessa?" She turned to add another plate and silverware to the table.

"She had to work at the hospital today," Irish said. He claimed a seat at the table. "I stopped by the sheriff's office. Levi and Dallas are following up on a report out of

Fort Worth about an abandoned black SUV with damage to the front of the vehicle."

Olivia sank into a seat on the opposite side of the table. "Do they know who it belonged to?"

Irish nodded, took a slice of toast off the top of the stack and laid it on his plate. "It had been reported as stolen yesterday morning from a limousine service in Dallas."

Becker took a seat beside Olivia, noting how her shoulders sagged at the news. "At least we know she's probably somewhere in the Dallas/Fort Worth area."

She shot a glance in his direction. "There are over seven million people in that area. How will we find just one? And they aren't going to make it easy."

"We'll find her," Becker promised. He wasn't sure how, but he'd do everything in his power to make it happen.

"So what's the latest?" Irish asked as he scooped eggs onto his plate and piled several slices of bacon on top.

Matt filled him in on what they'd learned about Gunter Kraus.

Irish grinned. "Gunter, huh?" His eyes narrowed. "I can see it. The blond hair and blue eyes..."

"The real Gunter Kraus is blond-haired and blue-eyed," Trace said. "And he's in Europe."

"Even better. If you're impersonating someone, it's good if he doesn't show up where you're pretending to be him." Irish laughed. "That would be awkward."

"And potentially deadly," Becker added, his gaze going to Olivia.

She lifted her chin. "I don't care how dangerous. I'm going with you. I've seen some of the news articles on

Kraus. He's a player, and he always has a woman on his arm. You show up without one, and they might get suspicious."

"Good point," Trace said. "But maybe we should recruit Dallas, instead of sending you. She's a trained law enforcement officer and was in the army. She might be better suited for the undercover work."

Olivia's gaze went from Trace to Becker. "She's my sister. If you don't take me, I'll find a way in by myself. I won't be left behind."

And Becker wouldn't be able to pull off his part knowing Olivia was somewhere else, possibly getting into trouble. "You're going with me," he said. "But I expect you to do what I say. Both of our lives could depend on it."

She nodded, her jaw set. "I might not be combat trained, but I will have your back. And I was a pretty good actor in my theater class in high school." Olivia gave him a crooked smile. "I promise not to do anything stupid."

Becker wasn't so concerned about her doing something stupid as he was about the mafia getting wind of their deception and taking matters into their own hands. Whether the Romanos or the Salvatores were responsible for the attack on Olivia's home, one thing was certain: they weren't averse to playing rough.

OLIVIA PUSHED THE FOOD around on her plate. She couldn't focus on eating when she was faced with the prospect of walking into the belly of a mafia family, pretending to be someone she wasn't. If she slipped up and exposed them, they could both end up at the bottom of a lake, wearing concrete shoes. Then Jasmine would be on her own.

She squared her shoulders and forced the dark thoughts

from her mind. Their undercover operation would work. It had to.

"Excuse me." Trace laid down his fork and pushed back from the table. "I need to make a few phone calls." He left the room, and the conversation turned to everyday life on the ranch. Lily and Rosalyn discussed the chores that needed to be completed since the ranch foreman had left before sunup to secure Olivia's house.

Irish and Matt offered to take care of feeding the livestock. When the meal concluded, they all pitched in to clean up.

After the last dish was dried and stored in the cabinet, Lily glanced at Olivia. "Let's get you ready to go shopping."

"'Shopping'?" Olivia frowned. "I don't need to go shopping, but I would like to go back to my house to get some of my belongings."

"You won't have time." Trace entered the room. "You and Beck need to be at the airport in fifteen minutes."

Olivia's heart skipped several beats. "What? Why?"

Trace grinned. "Like Lily said, you're going shopping."

"Why do we need to go to the airport to do that?" Olivia asked.

"Because Whiskey Gulch doesn't have what you and Beck will need to pull off this charade." He tipped his head toward Becker. "I've arranged for you two to fly to San Antonio, where you will be met with a car and taken to the upscale La Cantera shops. There, you'll be outfitted with clothes befitting a wealthy jet-setter."

"Shouldn't we do that in Dallas?" Olivia protested. "We'd be closer to where we need to be."

Trace shook his head. "With Kraus, it's all about being

the center of attention. I'm working on your entrance. You need to be in full Kraus form when you land in Dallas."

"In the meantime, you need something nice to wear when you arrive in San Antonio," Lily said, ushering her out of the kitchen. "I have a dress that might do, even if you're a few inches taller than me." She glanced down at her feet. "And I think we might be close to the same shoe size."

"Just so you know," Olivia said, "I can pay for my own clothes. I might be homeless, but I'm not broke."

"Sure, honey," Lily said. "But I'm betting you don't have an outfit that Gunter Kraus would appreciate."

"And you do?"

"Sweetie, I have some connections of my own." Lily led her up the stairs to the room she shared with Trace.

Olivia had lived in Whiskey Gulch all her life, so she knew what Lily's mother had done to provide for her daughter. The woman had used the only skills she possessed to put food on the table and clothes on Lily's back.

Lily had paid the price for her mother's profession. Many of the boys in school had thought she was as loose as her mother and had hit on her every chance they got. Her father—a liar, thief and swindler—had been a piece of work as well.

Olivia admired Lily for emerging from her crummy childhood a strong, independent woman who could stand up for herself.

Lily flung open her closet door and dug into the back behind hangers holding jeans, chambray shirts and sundresses. After a few swear words, she pulled out a sleeveless off-white dress with simple lines and a narrow black belt.

She held it up. "It was my mother's, a gift from a gentleman…friend. I tossed most of her clothes, but this one was too nice to burn."

Olivia held up her hands. "I can't wear that. It would fit you perfectly, but you're a lot shorter. That dress would be a miniskirt on me."

Lily grinned. "I know, right? It will be perfect for a woman Gunter Kraus would be with. I saw the photos of the women he surrounds himself with. All I can say is that they show a lot of skin."

Olivia stared at the pretty dress with the plunging neckline and short skirt. "I don't know. It's not me."

"And you won't be you when you're with Gunter Kraus. It's all part of the act." She shoved the dress into Olivia's arms, turned her toward the adjoining bathroom and gave her a gentle shove. "Try it on. It will at least get you to the stores, where you can buy designer outfits. Just remember—when you do purchase clothes, they have to fit the lifestyle you want to portray."

Lily was right. Olivia had never been a risk-taker where her own clothing was concerned. Since she worked with wet clay, she preferred to wear jeans and a heavy apron. Anything else would be ruined. Whenever she dressed up, it was usually in light cotton sundresses or tailored trousers and modest tops.

She entered the bathroom and jumped when the door clicked shut behind her.

"I can do this," she whispered to herself.

"Yes, you can," Lily said through the wood panel.

Olivia grinned. "You weren't supposed to hear that."

"You're going to be fine. Just remember who you're supposed to be."

Olivia shed the clothes she had on. The neckline of the dress was so low, she couldn't wear a bra with it. She slipped out of the undergarment as well and pulled the dress over her head.

It slid over her curves, the material lying soft against her skin. The hem stopped just below the slope of her buttocks.

Olivia faced herself in the mirror and gasped.

"Does it fit?" Lily asked. "Can I come in?"

"Yes, sort of. And yes," Olivia responded, staring at the alluring woman in the mirror. Never in her life had she considered herself sexy. But in that dress…

The door burst open, and Lily swept in, coming to an abrupt halt as her gaze landed on Olivia. Her eyes grew wide, and her mouth dropped open. "Wow." She shook her head and repeated, "Wow."

Heat rose up Olivia's neck and covered her cheeks. She chewed on her lip as she continued to stare at her reflection. "It's too much, isn't it?"

"Not at all," Lily said. "It's perfect for a little shopping spree in the Alamo City. Come on—you don't want to waste time. Trace has a tight schedule he's working with."

"Right." Olivia followed Lily into the bedroom. "I really feel like shopping will waste even more time."

"I know. You want to get to your sister. But you won't fool anyone if you don't dress the part." Lily dived back into the closet, coming up with a pair of black stiletto slides to match the belt. "These might be a little small, but they should work."

Olivia slid her feet into the shoes and tried walking in them. "I'm likely to kill myself in these."

"Practice. You need to be convincing." Lily turned toward the door. "Come on. Trace is waiting in the truck."

Olivia held on to the rail as she descended the stairs and walked out onto the porch.

Irish was standing beside a black pickup while Trace sat behind the steering wheel. "Wow," Irish said under his breath when he caught sight of Olivia.

Becker rounded the front of the truck and held out his hand to her.

She laid her palm in his.

"You look amazing," he whispered, his gaze seeming to drink her in.

Warmth rushed through her body, reminding her of the night they'd spent together. How she wished they could turn back the clock and crawl into bed and forget about impersonating playboys and deceiving the mafia. "Thank you."

"Ready?"

No.

But she nodded and let him help her up into the front passenger seat.

All the while, she tugged at the hem, certain she was exposing more of herself than she intended as she climbed up on the running board and settled on the leather seat.

Becker and Irish settled into the back seat as Trace hightailed it off the ranch.

THE LITTLE AIRPORT outside of Whiskey Gulch wasn't much more than a landing strip for private planes and crop dusters.

Olivia had driven past it all her life, every time she headed to Austin or San Antonio, and never gave it much thought.

Trace drove right up to the runway, where a plane was taxiing to a stop.

The pilot cut the engine, and the propeller slowed to a stop.

A hatch opened on the side of the aircraft before a set of stairs was lowered to the ground. A man poked his head out. "Trace, I got here as soon as I could."

Trace hopped out of his truck and crossed the tarmac to shake the pilot's hand. "Good to see you, Pete. Thanks for coming on short notice."

"Glad to do it," Pete said. "I needed to get some flight time in to keep current on my license. This gives me a good excuse to get the plane out of the hangar."

Pete ducked back into the plane to allow the others to climb aboard and settle in the leather seats.

Trace made quick introductions.

Pete gave them a brief description of the safety features on the aircraft as he secured the door and slipped into the pilot's seat, settled his headset over his ears and started the engine.

Trace sat in as copilot. Pete handed him a headset and went through his checklist before he turned the plane around and took off down the runway.

Olivia had never flown in a plane this small. She wasn't sure she was going to like it.

As the aircraft left the ground, she gripped Becker's hand.

Once they reached their cruising altitude high above the rugged terrain of the Texas Hill Country, Olivia willed herself to relax and take in the scenery below.

Without a headset, she couldn't hear what Trace and the pilot were saying, nor could she carry on much of a conversation with Becker or Irish.

She sat back and thought about what was ahead when they reached Dallas. Shopping in San Antonio would give her a chance to practice her role in front of people. She and Becker had to be convincing if they hoped to fit in and find her sister.

Oh, Jasmine.

Olivia's stomach knotted whenever she thought about her. She'd been so scared. She prayed she was okay and that the men who'd stolen her away hadn't hurt her. If Trace and Becker had theorized correctly and the Romanos had been the ones to kidnap Jasmine, they would want to keep her alive until the Salvatores handed over the painting.

She clung to their assumption, unwilling to imagine the alternative.

Chapter Seven

The trip to San Antonio usually took a couple of hours by car. Flying cut that time in half. They landed at a small airport to the northwest of the city, where a black Suburban waited for them in the parking lot.

They thanked Pete and crossed the tarmac to climb into the SUV. The driver took them along Interstate 10 to La Cantera, a posh shopping center located on the outskirts of the city.

"We have exactly one hour to get what we need and meet back here," Trace informed them as the driver pulled into the parking lot.

"One hour?" Olivia shook her head. "I don't even know where to start."

Trace climbed out of the vehicle and held the door open for Olivia. "My mother called ahead. She has a fashion consultant standing by to help. All we have to do is deliver you to the shop, and the consultant will take over."

Seeming relieved, Olivia sighed. "Thank goodness. I'm clueless when it comes to style."

"You'd look good in anything," Becker assured her. "I think that dress you're wearing now is amazing."

Trace nodded, leading the way. "It is, but you'll need more than one outfit—and the bigger the designer name, the better. The shop also has a makeup artist. They'll do it today and, if need be, show you how to apply it yourself."

"This is insane," Olivia said. "All that can't be done in an hour."

"It can," Trace said. "Let the professionals handle it."

The shopping center was an outdoor mall, tastefully designed and landscaped to encourage shoppers to take their time and spend their entire day visiting the array of stores.

Trace led her straight to one of the high-end women's shops and paused outside the door. "This is your stop. We'll be back to get you when we're done."

Becker didn't like leaving Olivia alone. He would be with his team; she had no one.

A well-dressed woman stepped through the entrance, her gaze sweeping Olivia from top to bottom. "Are you Miss Swann?"

Olivia nodded. "I am."

"Please, come right in so we can get started. We understand you only have a limited amount of time. Mrs. Travis called ahead with your size requirements and style preferences. We have items ready for your approval, and our makeup artist standing by."

Becker grinned as the woman took charge and whisked Olivia through the door.

If he'd been skeptical about adhering to the hour, he wasn't anymore.

"Come on, Beck," Trace said. "She's in good hands."

Becker had always known that Trace came from money. But it was never more apparent than at that moment. The man was as comfortable in jeans and riding a horse as he was in an expensive men's store, selecting button-down shirts and tailored trousers suitable for someone like Gunter Kraus, who had more money than sense.

Becker had never owned an outfit that cost more than what he could afford with his army paycheck. The fabric quality was amazing and felt good against his skin, but the cost left him feeling uncomfortable.

"Don't think about it," Trace said, as if reading his mind. "Consider it your uniform for the job. The company will cover the expense. Besides, you're now Gunter Kraus. He wouldn't give it a second thought."

With his role in mind, Becker lifted his chin and practiced the entitled sneer he'd noticed on Gunter Kraus's face in all his photographs.

For a man with as much money as Gunter had, he didn't appear terribly happy in any of his pictures.

"There! That's what I'm talking about." Trace grinned. "You have his look."

Becker didn't need the fancy clothes, expensive sport cars or castles in Switzerland to be happy. All he needed was a modest roof over his head, good friends, and a woman who appreciated him and the simpler things in a life.

As he selected a suit, a couple of shirts, casual trousers and a leather jacket, he wondered how Olivia was getting along with her team.

Based on how overwhelmed she'd appeared, she was probably a lot like him. Then again, she'd rocked that dress Lily had loaned her. He couldn't wait to get back to Olivia.

Forty-five minutes into their shopping trip, Becker had what he needed, including underwear, socks and matching shoes. Trace and Irish bought black trousers, black shirts, ties and black suit jackets to look the part of Gunter's usual bodyguard entourage. They dressed in their new clothes and bagged their jeans and T-shirts.

Trace had purchased suitcases and a garment bag from another store while Becker had worked with the salesman. As Becker and the sales team selected items, Trace had a clerk ring them up, remove the tags, steam any wrinkles out and add them to the garment bag or suitcase.

Becker tried to draw the line when Trace insisted on purchasing a Rolex watch. Trace won the argument, and the watch was added to the stack.

By the time they left the store, they'd racked up thousands of dollars in purchases.

"Wow," Becker said, still in sticker shock. "That was a lot of money."

"Look, I don't expect you to pay for all of this," Trace said. "I just don't want you walking into a hostile environment without the tools you need to convince them not to kill you." He gave Becker a brief grin. "You're part of the team. My friend and brother. I want this plan to work."

"It *will* work," Becker said. It had to. Not only did he have to find Jasmine, but he also had to prove to Trace he hadn't made a mistake in hiring him.

Leaving the army had been one of the hardest things Becker had ever done. It had meant leaving the family of brothers he'd been with through some of the hardest times he'd ever endured.

Having a job to go to with some of his brothers in arms had been his saving grace—a job working with the men he'd fought alongside and trusted with his life. It had been a godsend. He owed Trace more than money could ever buy. The man had thrown him a lifeline into the civilian world when he'd left everything he'd known.

Two minutes after they left the men's shop, they arrived in front of the store where they'd left Olivia.

Before Becker could reach for the handle, the door opened, and a woman stepped out.

For a split second, he didn't recognize her—but only for a split second. She wore a bloodred dress in a silky, flowing material that hugged every inch of her delectable body, from the fullness of her breasts to the narrowing curve of her waist and the gentle swell of her hips. The hem stopped a few inches short of midthigh, exposing her incredibly long and beautiful legs, trim ankles and sparkling rhinestone-encrusted high heels.

Her black hair had been swept back from her forehead and hung straight down, with a delicate loose curl caressing her cheek.

The subtle colors of the makeup enhanced the natural beauty of her skin, while bold eye shadow illuminated her eyes.

She was drop-dead gorgeous—nothing like the woman with mud up to her elbows and smudges on her face who'd captured his heart.

She walked toward him.

No...she *stalked* him like a cat on the prowl.

When she stopped in front of him, his pulse kicked into high gear.

"Hey, good-looking," she said in a low, sultry tone that set his blood on fire. She leaned into him and trailed her finger along the hard line of his jaw. "Let's say you and I blow this joint and head for Big D."

His hands automatically rose to encircle her waist. He had to swallow, hard, to get his tongue to move. "If by Big D, you mean Dallas, I'm game, sweetcakes. Lead the way."

Irish laughed out loud. "Dude, you should see your face. Priceless."

Olivia frowned. "Did I get it right? I was channeling my inner vamp. I practiced that line in my head a hundred times. Was it not at all convincing?"

Irish snorted. "Not convincing? Beck's tongue practically hit the floor. He knows you, and he was completely convinced."

Trace shook his head. "You need to work on your inner sleaze, man. Kraus would have been all over her in a heartbeat. He's not known for being subtle or a gentleman."

"I'll get it right. I just wasn't expecting…this." His gaze swept Olivia from head to toe. Everything about her was perfect: the clothes, the hair and the makeup.

Becker was attracted to her in a big way. But he more so wanted the woman who'd lain naked with him last night. Her hair had been mussed, and she hadn't worn fancy clothes or expensive shoes, but she'd made love with him without holding back. She was passionate and sexy without even trying.

He tightened his hold around her waist. "Hey, doll," he said. "Want to have dinner with me tonight in Paris?"

She shook her head and walked her fingers across his chest. "That would take too long."

"How about I fly you to the moon and back?"

Her lips curled. "Now you're talking."

"Give me a little time, and I'll do just that." He turned her toward the parking lot. "In the meantime, life's one big adventure if you stick with me."

"I'm counting on it," she said and crossed one leg in front of the other, walking with a pronounced swing to her hips.

Becker liked how Olivia had thrown herself into the role of Monique Jameson. Now, if he could quit drooling over her and get himself together, they might just pull it off.

OLIVIA WALKED BESIDE BECKER, loving the feeling of his arm around her, holding her close against him. She'd even liked coming on to him as if she were the real Monique Jameson and he was Gunter Kraus. The surprise in his eyes had quickly changed to heat.

The dress had done its job. If Becker had been that distracted, surely the mafia members—being mostly virile males—would find it difficult to focus on hurting her or Becker. And while she held their attention, Becker, Trace and Irish could look for clues that would lead them to Jasmine.

The SUV hadn't moved from where the driver had parked. As soon as they were all on board, the driver shifted into gear and pulled out of the parking lot and out onto the highway leading into San Antonio.

"Aren't we flying out of the same airport we flew into?" Olivia asked.

Trace shook his head. "The runway is a little short for the jet to land on."

Olivia sat back against the leather upholstery and cocked an eyebrow at Trace's back. "We didn't fly in a jet. I distinctly recall a prop on that plane."

Trace shot a glance over his shoulder. "We're not flying out in the plane we flew in on."

Olivia's brows rose. "No?"

"No," Trace said. "We're flying to Dallas in a jet."

"A jet." Olivia's brow dipped. "Wouldn't it just be

faster to drive? It takes almost as much time to clear security checkpoints."

Trace shook his head. "Not at all. We aren't flying commercial. We can be there in minutes versus hours. Let's do this."

The frown on Olivia's face must have tickled Becker's funny bone because he laughed. "What's wrong?" he asked.

Her lips twisted in a wry grin. "My usual day consists of sitting for long hours, shaping pottery in a quiet room all by myself. I'm not sure I'm cut out for the business of espionage."

"Me neither." Becker's brow knit. "But if it's the only choice we have, we'll make it work."

"And we'll be there as backup," Trace said.

During the drive to the airport, Trace was on the phone with Matt, his conversation hushed. Matt must have been doing most of the talking.

Olivia wished she could hear what Trace's brother had to say. Hopefully, he had more information that would help them pull this off.

They didn't go to the main terminal where commercial travelers waded through TSA security. Instead, the driver dropped them off at the door to the general aviation entrance.

With his back to the building, Trace addressed the others. "From here on out, you're in character."

Olivia fought the urge to nod. Instead, she flipped her hair back over her shoulder and hooked her arm through Becker's.

Becker raised an eyebrow and stared down his nose at Trace, his friend and boss. "You're in the way."

Trace's lips quirked, but by the time he turned to enter the building, he was all business.

The woman at the counter asked if she could help.

"I'm with Gunter Kraus," Trace said. "Our transport should have arrived by now."

Becker stepped up behind Trace and lifted his nose in the air. "Can we get a move on? I don't want to be late for my massage." He settled a pair of sunglasses on his face and looked toward the sliding glass door leading out onto the tarmac.

The woman behind the counter straightened. "Yes, sir. Your jet arrived five minutes ago. Could I get you a bottle of water to take with you?"

He curled his lip in his best sneer. "A martini would be better."

Her cheeks flushed. "I'm sorry, sir. We don't serve mixed drinks in the FBO."

"That's a pity," Becker said. "If you can't get me a martini, could you at least let us board? I'm sure my staff will be able to accommodate me."

"Of course." The clerk's cheeks reddened, and she quickly punched a button behind the counter. The glass door slid open. "Have a nice day," she said as Becker strode through with Olivia draped on his arm, followed by Trace and Irish, who looked like bulked-up bodyguards in their solid black ensembles.

A plane about four times larger than the one they'd flown in from Whiskey Gulch stood at the ready. The stairs came down, and a man in black trousers and a white shirt with decorative epaulets stood at attention at the bottom. "Good morning, Mr. Kraus."

Becker sailed past him. "I'll need a dry martini, two

olives, before we leave the ground. Monique, be a gem—make sure it's shaken, not stirred."

"Sure, Gunter, baby," Olivia said.

Olivia's low, sexy voice brought images to Becker's mind of her lying naked in bed, writhing beneath him. Now was not the time to get excited. Then again, the element of danger and the secrecy of their undercover operation spiked his adrenaline and desire.

Becker stepped inside the plane and inwardly marveled at the opulence. "Not one of mine," he said, "but it'll have to do."

Trace, Irish and Olivia all sat and pulled their seat belts across their laps.

The male flight attendant who'd greeted them outside the plane leaned close to Becker. "Sir, you'll need to sit and secure your seat belt."

"That martini? Pronto?" He stopped himself short of snapping his fingers, unsure of just how far he should take Gunter's privileged attitude.

The attendant scurried to the other end of the cabin and opened a cabinet, revealing a fully equipped bar.

Becker dropped into the seat beside Olivia and secured his seat belt.

The attendant returned with his drink and hurried to close the door and inform the pilot they were ready to take off.

Minutes later, they were in the air, climbing to altitude above San Antonio, swinging north toward Dallas.

Beside him, Olivia was stiff, her gaze fixed on the window.

Becker reached for her hand and lifted it to brush a kiss across the backs of her knuckles. He too felt the strain of the charade. He sipped on the martini to take the edge off but didn't get too far before he realized he didn't like martinis. In fact, he didn't like gin, preferring beer and whiskey over the fancy drink any day.

He glanced at his watch. Jasmine had been missing less than twenty-four hours. The sooner they got to Dallas, the sooner they could begin their search for the missing painting, which might be the motive for a murder and the key to finding Olivia's sister.

Becker had been on many dangerous missions during his time as a Delta Force operator. Never had he thought he'd be on one just as dangerous in his own country.

And he was going into the operation unarmed and with an untrained woman at his side. Red flags waved all around him, but it was too late to turn around and come up with a new plan. He and Olivia had to make their way into the inner circles of the black market for illegally acquired works of art. The stakes were high. The people involved wouldn't bat an eye at shooting someone if they thought they would expose them to the authorities.

Becker studied Olivia's profile, regretting his decision to bring her along on this operation. He wasn't sure he could protect himself, but he sure as hell would do his best to protect her.

Chapter Eight

Olivia gripped Becker's hand as the plane landed at one of the small executive airports near Dallas. She never felt comfortable flying.

"Looks like the paparazzi got wind of your arrival, Gunter," Trace commented and winked at Becker. The head of the Outriders had probably let it "leak" that jet-setting playboy Gunter Kraus would be landing in Dallas at that exact airport and approximate time, on a different airplane than one of his own.

A crowd of reporters had gathered on the other side of the fence surrounding the airport.

Trace was on the phone the moment the plane landed and didn't hang up until they'd taxied to the small terminal and come to a full stop.

Becker immediately popped open his seat belt buckle.

Trace pocketed his cell phone and met Becker's gaze. "You have been invited to an exclusive showing at the Madison Gallery in downtown Dallas at six o'clock this evening. In the meantime, we'll get you and Miss Jameson checked in to your suite at the Ritz-Carlton."

The flight attendant hurried through the cabin to check with the pilot before he hit the switch to lower the stairs. Then he stepped back. "Enjoy your stay in Dallas."

Becker pushed to his feet, held out his hand for Olivia and pulled her up to stand beside him. "You ready?"

"Always, when I'm with you." She ran her hand across his chest and smiled. Pretending to be his girlfriend had its perks. She could touch him as much as she wanted. Monique would be all over Gunter.

Trace was first off the plane, followed by Becker, Olivia and Irish.

Olivia glanced toward the swarm of reporters pressed against the chain-link fence, snapping pictures of Gunter Kraus…or so they thought. Olivia hoped Gunter wasn't one to follow the news on the internet. Their cover would be blown pretty quickly, if he saw someone impersonating him in Dallas, while he was vacationing in Greece.

Becker turned and held out his hand for Olivia as she descended the last step. Then he swung her into his arms and kissed her soundly as cameras clicked and reporters shouted questions about his relationship with Monique. Was she the one? Were wedding bells in the future?

When he set her back on her feet, her heart was pounding, and she felt a little light-headed. Man, he was a good kisser. She could get used to playing Monique to his Gunter.

They passed through the terminal and ran the gauntlet of reporters, with Trace and Irish playing their part as the bodyguards protecting the rich man and his girl.

Several times, a reporter got close enough to shove a microphone in Becker's face.

Becker gave his best sneer for the cameras and moved on without comment, tucking Olivia against his side, shielding her the best he could from the rudest of the paparazzi.

She loved that he was so protective, but she hoped he wouldn't sacrifice his own safety for hers.

A chauffeur in a black suit stood beside a shiny white limousine. As Becker and Olivia approached, he opened the door. Olivia got in first and slid across the seat. Becker dropped in beside her.

The chauffeur closed the door, loaded their luggage and got into the driver's seat. He raised the barrier between the front and back with the push of a button. The window tinting effectively blocked them from the view of the media mongers, giving them a relative sense of privacy.

A black SUV was parked in front of the limousine. The driver got out, handed the keys to Trace and walked away. Trace slipped behind the wheel, Irish took shotgun, and they pulled away from the terminal and out into traffic.

With moderate to heavy traffic flowing through the Dallas metro area, it took thirty minutes to reach the Ritz-Carlton hotel.

Becker spent the time holding Olivia. She assumed he was still playing his part. Having little experience with plush limousines, she didn't know if the driver had access to sound or video of what was going on in the back. Becker and Olivia had to pull off their ruse. They had to get Jasmine back, safe and sound.

The fewer people who knew the truth about Gunter Kraus's visit to Dallas, the better.

Olivia sat beside him, holding his hand like a lifeline. Though she absolutely looked the part of Monique Jameson, she felt as if others would see right through her act. She didn't want to be the one who blew their cover.

When they arrived at the hotel, a bellman was there

to collect their luggage from the trunk. The chauffeur got out and opened the door to let them out.

Trace and Irish escorted them into the lobby, where they were met by the manager, who personally escorted them to the penthouse suite.

Once the manager left and the bellman delivered their suitcases, the room fell silent.

Using a bug detector, Trace and Irish scoured the room, checking beneath table edges, inside lampshades and behind paintings on the wall.

Olivia was amazed at how thorough they were.

Then Trace entered the huge bathroom, turned on the shower faucet and let the water stream down, making enough noise to drown out their words. He waved Becker and Olivia into the bathroom, where they huddled close to hear each other talk.

"You can't be too careful," Trace said. "If people are considering Gunter Kraus as a potential buyer for the stolen painting, they will be watching him closely. That includes bugging your room."

Olivia shivered and wrapped her arms around her middle. The thought of someone spying on them gave her the willies.

"Watch anyone who comes into your room for any reason at all. And perform a bug check every time you leave and come back." Trace looked into their faces, his own tight, concerned. "Keep in mind at all times that whether you're in this room or wandering around Dallas, you will be watched."

Olivia nodded. Dealing with stolen goods would make the buyers and sellers paranoid. And rightly so.

Trace continued. "Once the media releases footage of Gunter arriving in Dallas, word will spread to the two families. That's why we staged that arrival in front of the media. For now, hang tight, relax for a while and then change into evening clothes for the art exhibit. It's by special invitation only. The people who will be there will be wearing their finest."

"What do we hope to achieve at the show?" Becker asked.

"Vincenzo Salvatore is supposed to be there. It's safe to assume he'll be looking for a buyer."

"Like Gunter Kraus," Olivia said.

Trace nodded. "Rumor has it that collectors from all over the world are coming to Dallas or sending representatives in hopes of acquiring the Wyeth painting."

Olivia shivered again. "And all I want is my sister back."

"I read in the news earlier today that Nico will be released tomorrow if they can't produce any substantial evidence that he killed Eduardo. His alibi insists he was with her the entire night. The witness who accused him has gone missing, and they only had her word that she saw him at the gallery that night."

"Won't the Romanos be after him to avenge Eduardo's death?" Olivia asked.

Trace met and held Olivia's gaze. "Not if Nico is the only one who knows where the painting is."

"Thus, the reason for keeping Jasmine alive," Olivia said.

"If Nico is smart, he won't have told anyone where the stolen art is," Becker said. "It's even more reason for his family to want to get him out of jail."

Travis's eyes narrowed. "That painting is going to be worth a lot more on the black market. The Romanos could have lined up a buyer, who might have put down a deposit or actually paid the full price and is waiting for delivery of the product."

"Great motivation to get Nico to reveal the location of the painting," Becker said.

"In exchange for the girl, the Romanos get the Wyeth. Nico gets the witness, and he can do whatever he wants with her to stay out of jail."

Olivia flinched. "There are a lot of moving parts to this story," she noted. "The Romanos can't make their demands until Nico is released and can lead them to the painting."

"They can't kill Jasmine and offer up the body, because dead people can't testify in court," Becker said. He touched Olivia's arm. "Sorry to be so blunt about your sister—but in this case, it's a good thing that it's more beneficial to them to keep her alive until they have the painting in hand. She's their only leverage."

Olivia's hands curled into fists. "We have to be there if and when an exchange is made."

"Or get to the painting first and make the trade ourselves," Irish said.

"If they release Nico tomorrow—" Trace tipped his head toward Irish "—we'll tail him."

Irish laughed. "You mean *I'll* tail him. Gunter doesn't go anywhere without a bodyguard. And I wouldn't feel right leaving these two without backup."

Trace's mouth twisted. "You're right. Irish would tail Nico." He tapped his chin with the tip of his finger. "I think we could use Matt and Levi up here. I'll step out of the hotel long enough to place a few calls. We can have them in Dallas by morning."

"Matt needs to stay on his hacker and plugged into the internet," Irish said.

"He can do that from here." Trace drew in a deep breath and let it out slowly. "Things might start moving faster if they turn Nico loose. We'll need all the help we can get."

Olivia stood among the men, feeling a little more hopeful than she had when standing in the middle of her shattered living room, watching the taillights of the stolen SUV disappear along with her sister.

If anyone could pull this operation off, it was the Outriders.

WITH A FEW HOURS to kill before they had to leave for the art exhibit, Becker shrugged out of the casual blazer he wore and stretched out on the bed. He'd learned to rest when he could to conserve energy he might need for later.

Trace and Irish had left the room. Trace would be outside the hotel by now, making arrangements to get Matt and Levi up to Dallas. Irish would be standing outside their door, as the first line of defense for Gunter Kraus.

While Becker lay on the bed, Olivia paced.

"You'll be worn out before we even begin the evening." Becker patted the bed beside him. "Relax."

Olivia snorted. "I can't. I keep thinking of…" She bit her lip to keep from saying the name of her sister. Her heart hurt at the thought of how scared and alone she must be feeling. She was frustrated about doing nothing while her sister suffered.

"You need to have a store of energy in reserve for the night to come." He patted the bed again. "You won't enjoy the exhibit if you're so tired that you can barely stand."

She slowed to a stop beside the bed. "I know you're right. But it's hard."

"Then fake it until you feel it." He grinned. "That

sounded suggestive, didn't it?" He gave her a gentle look. "Do this…" He inhaled and let the air out slowly. "Breathe."

She laughed, but she wasn't smiling. "I can't. I feel like my chest is constricted. I've felt that way since we left this morning."

"Try it with me." He drew in another deep breath.

Olivia pressed a hand to her chest and gave it a shot, pulling in a long breath.

"Now hold it in for a second," he said.

She held it.

"Let it go slowly." His voice was low, rich and resonant.

His words alone slowed her heartbeat. She released the air from her lungs, and her body relaxed a little.

When Becker patted the bed beside him once more, she complied and lay down on the mattress.

The last time she'd been in bed with Becker, they'd been naked—making mad, passionate love.

Now they lay side by side, fully clothed, without touching.

The fact that someone could bug their room at any time made her paranoid. One small mistake had the potential to reveal them as the fakes they were.

Olivia had never been very good at lying. Acting was easier when she memorized the lines; she wasn't as good at ad-libbing. But she'd insisted on being part of the mission to save her sister. She'd better get her act together. Her sister's life and the lives of Becker and his teammates depended on her getting it right.

Becker reached over and took her hand in his, squeezing it gently. "Breathe."

She did, repeating the long, slow inhale-and-release

process until it came more naturally. Her muscles relaxed, relieving some of the pressure constricting her chest.

The silence stretched on.

A number of times, she opened her mouth to say something but closed it without uttering a word. She wanted to learn more about this man—who he was, what he wanted out of life, his favorite color, what he liked to eat...everything. All of that discovery would have to wait until they were back in Whiskey Gulch, with her sister safely away from the mafia families using her as a pawn in their tug-of-war over a painting.

Olivia closed her eyes and continued to practice the slow, steady breathing Becker had prescribed.

When she woke, the room was darker; she must have fallen asleep. She reached for Becker, but the bed beside her was empty.

Her pulse quickened, and she sat up straight.

"I'm here," he called out in the huge room.

She turned to find Becker silhouetted against the floor-to-ceiling windows overlooking the Dallas skyline.

"How long was I asleep?" she asked, pushing her hair back away from her face.

"An hour and a half."

"Did I miss anything?"

He chuckled. "Nothing. It's almost time to get ready for the exhibit. I thought we might want to get something to eat along the way."

Her stomach rumbled at the mention of food. "That would be nice." Olivia swung her legs over the side of the bed and stood, smoothing the wrinkles out of her red dress. "Did I hear right? Trace said the patrons of the arts like to dress up for exhibits?"

"That's what he said. What you have on should be fine."

Olivia glanced down at the dress. "I like it, but I have another outfit in mind. The lady at the designer store said a woman can't go wrong with a little black dress. Since the people who attend these events like to dress up, I'll do the same." She gave him a quick smile. "If you want in the bathroom, go now. Once I'm in there, I might not come out until I'm completely ready."

"I'd like to shave before you barricade yourself inside."

She laughed. "Go ahead. I'll gather my clothes and makeup while you're doing your thing."

Becker unearthed a shaving kit from his suitcase and carried it into the bathroom, leaving the door wide open.

Every time Olivia walked past, she couldn't help but look inside.

Becker had removed his shirt and was standing in front of the mirror, rubbing shaving cream across his jaw.

The man was far too attractive for Olivia's own good. It only took her one trip to gather everything she needed; the other trips past the open bathroom door had been out of pure curiosity—and the burning heat that had begun in the pit of her belly and was spreading throughout her body.

She glanced at the clock, wondering if they had enough time to…

With a firm shake of her head, she reminded herself to stick to the plan until they got her sister back. Hopefully, there'd be plenty of time for lovemaking later.

On Olivia's next pass in front of the little bathroom, Becker emerged, his shirt flung over one shoulder, his broad chest naked and sun-kissed.

Olivia's feet slowed as she looked up into his clear blue eyes.

"I'm finished in there," he said. "It's all yours."

She was tempted to run her fingers over his fine chest. They tingled with the memory of doing that the night before. She hoped she'd have another opportunity soon.

For now, she squeezed past him, careful not to touch any of his magnificent flesh. She was already too confused by the desire raging through her to keep her head on straight. One touch might set off a firestorm of desire she wouldn't be able to defuse.

If she gave in, and the man was willing, they'd fall into bed and make love. With Olivia's luck, Trace and Irish would pick that moment to enter the room and catch them in the act.

They could say they were just getting into character, but it would be a lie—and it wouldn't help them free Jasmine either.

She entered the bathroom, closed the door and leaned against the cool wooden panels. Staying in the same room with Becker could be a joy or a challenge. Olivia struggled to keep her hands off the muscular Delta Force soldier.

Focus.

Olivia changed out of the red dress and into the black one. Her hands shook a little as she reached behind to pull up the zipper.

The art exhibit would be the next big test of their acting skills. Hopefully, they wouldn't run into anyone who knew Gunter or Monique personally. In a world full of people, the rich and famous tended to run in the same circles. That scared Olivia.

Once she had the dress on, she slid her feet into the shiny rhinestone-encrusted shoes she'd purchased at the store and straightened in front of the full-length mirror.

Wow. She looked like a different person from the artist who spent her days with mud up to her elbows. She looked every bit as good as any celebrity in Hollywood or the high rollers in Dallas. Seeing it for herself helped boost her confidence.

They would be in a public place with lots of other people. Hopefully, the Salvatores and the Romanos wouldn't do anything crazy.

Olivia wished she had a weapon she could hide underneath her dress. Not that the dress would hide anything—it fit her body like a second skin, and the slit up the side ran from the floor up to her midthigh. No. Even if she had a knife or small gun, the dress wouldn't hide anything.

If things got crazy, she would have to rely on her charm, wit and her former Delta Force protector.

Chapter Nine

Becker sat in the back seat of the stretch limousine beside Olivia. He'd thought nothing could top that red dress she'd worn earlier. He'd been wrong. The black sheath gracing her lithe body invoked such a rush of desire, he could barely think.

The limousine delivered Becker and Olivia to Madison Gallery, which was not too far from the Ritz-Carlton. A uniformed attendant hurried forward and opened the door.

Reporters stood on either side of the velvet ropes cordoning off the entrance.

As soon as Becker got out, cameras flashed and reporters shouted.

"Mr. Kraus, could you answer a few questions for us?"

"Mr. Kraus, are you and Ms. Jameson engaged? Is there a wedding date set?"

"Gunter, is it true that you fired your former assistant after you got her pregnant?"

Becker ignored the questions and turned to extend his hand to Olivia.

She laid her palm in his and swiveled on the seat. One slender leg emerged through the door, the slit of her dress rising up to the middle of her thigh.

Becker's groin tightened.

Olivia was a beautiful woman. She looked fabulous in that black dress, in the red dress, in jeans and a T-shirt, and in nothing at all. He pulled her to her feet and into his arms. "Do you know just how gorgeous you are?"

She gave him a sultry smile. "You're not so bad yourself."

Then he kissed her in front of the attendants, valets and the army of reporters. He told himself it was what Gunter would do. The truth was, he wanted to kiss her, and he was happy to play the Gunter card to get what he wanted.

She leaned into him, her fingers curling into his shirt, dragging him closer.

For a moment, he forgot where he was, who he was supposed to be and why it was important. It was just him and Olivia.

A honk sounded on the street in front of the gallery, bringing him back to Earth. A black limousine pulled in as their white one drove off.

An attendant opened the door, and a blonde in a long white dress stepped out, her hair swept up and back in a sophisticated style. She smiled and approached them. "Oh, good. I don't have to go in by myself." Her brows rose. "You are going to the exhibit, aren't you?"

Olivia nodded. "We are." She held out her hand. "I'm Monique. This is—"

"Gunter Kraus," the woman said. "I saw the news of your arrival in Dallas on television." She flipped her hair toward the crowd of media personnel snapping photographs. "The paparazzi never leave you alone. How do you put up with it?"

Becker shrugged. "You get used to it." He held out his hand. "And you are?"

"Tacey Rogers, fellow art enthusiast. Do you mind if I go in with you? My date was unavoidably detained. Which is short for, I was stood up."

"Please, join us," Becker said. "The more, the merrier." He held out his elbow to Tacey, as he suspected Gunter would do. Though the man was most often seen with Monique, he was seen with other women as well. Based on the tabloids, he was never one to turn down a pretty woman he might get into his bed later.

Tacey hooked her hand through the crook of his arm and smiled up at him.

Then Becker held out his other elbow to Olivia and winked down at her.

She took his arm, cocking an eyebrow as if questioning his proclivity to collect women.

Gunter wouldn't give it a second thought. He was a ladies' man. The more women who surrounded him, the happier he was.

Becker, on the other hand, was a one-woman man. The kiss he and Olivia shared hadn't been pretense. His only regret was that they weren't alone to enjoy it longer. He hoped to remedy it later when they were back at the Ritz.

"I almost didn't come tonight," Tacey was saying.

"No?" Becker glanced down at the blonde. "Why?"

She grimaced. "Well, after the murder at Cavendish Gallery, I wasn't sure how safe we would be. Frankly, I'm surprised this event wasn't canceled."

"If you were that concerned, why did you come?" Olivia asked.

"Morbid curiosity as to who would show up. I'm betting most of the people coming are more interested in the stolen painting than those on display at this exhibit." She smiled up at Becker. "What about you? Surely you didn't fly all the way into Dallas for this show."

Becker gave a secretive smile. "Let's just say I'm intrigued by the events. Especially considering the Cavendish curator is missing."

Tacey's eyes widened. "She was the one who reported the murder, the only witness who saw Nico Salvatore do it."

Olivia stiffened on Becker's other side.

"Makes you wonder," Becker said, "doesn't it?"

Tacey glanced away. "The Salvatore family want the public to believe the curator did it and got away with the Wyeth painting."

"What do you think?" Becker asked.

"I think Nico did it, and he's the only one who knows where that painting is." Her lips twisted. "If they let him out of jail, you know he'll be followed and he'll be in the market to sell that painting before he gets caught with it. Everything seems to be hinging on a painting no one knew existed until a couple of weeks ago."

"Which makes the event tonight even more interesting," Becker said.

Tacey nodded. "I had to come."

"Why do you think the curator disappeared?" Olivia asked.

The other woman's mouth thinned. "Who knows? If I were her, I'd have kept my mouth shut. Squealing on a Salvatore is like signing your own death certificate."

"Why is that?"

The blonde leaned around Becker, her eyebrows cocked. "Do you really not know?"

Olivia blinked. "Know what?"

Becker almost laughed at her innocent act.

"Nico's father is Vincenzo Salvatore, one of the richest men in the country."

"So?" Olivia quipped.

"*So* he could buy any verdict he wants from any court in the land. He's that rich. And if that didn't work, he could pay to have the accuser silenced."

"Sounds like she put herself in danger," Becker said.

"Yes, she did," Tacey said softly. "I don't think she understood the ramifications. I'll bet she does now."

"You appear to be pretty informed about the art community here in Dallas," Becker said. "Why would Salvatore's son kill a man for a painting if his father could afford to purchase it outright?"

"Eduardo was stupid. He wanted the money the painting would bring on the black market."

"Did he need the money that badly?" Olivia asked.

Tacey snorted. "That's just it—his uncle Giovanni has almost as much money as the Salvatores. Or at least, he did. Who knows, with the world economy the way it is these days? Maybe he lost it in the stock market, or his ships ran aground, or his money manager absconded with it. The Wyeth was estimated to be worth at least three million if sold legitimately."

"Interesting," Becker said.

"Enough to kill for," Tacey said.

By then, they had entered the lobby of the gallery, where other patrons had gathered.

"If the Wyeth is worth so much, it could make sense that the curator might have been in on the whole thing," Becker suggested.

Tacey shook her head. "I think she was in the wrong place at the wrong time and witnessed something she shouldn't have seen. Her biggest mistake was opening her mouth and doing the right thing by reporting a murder. I kind of feel sorry for her, with both families after her."

"*Both* families?" Olivia asked. "I would think the Salvatores would be the only ones wanting her to disappear. Why would the Romanos want her out of the picture?"

Becker was enjoying Olivia's wide-eyed, innocent act.

"Good question," Tacey said. "Why don't you ask them?" She tipped her head toward a man with a shock of white hair, bushy brows and dark eyes. He stood in the middle of a group of bulky-looking men who had to be bodyguards. "That's Giovanni Romano."

The man wasn't paying attention to the people around him. He was glaring at another man across the room.

The other guy was taller, with silvery-gray hair and his head held high, bearing a distinguished presence.

"Who's the silver fox?" Olivia asked.

Tacey laughed. "Giovanni's rival, Vincenzo Salvatore. Both men are from fine Italian stock, with quick Italian tempers. I'm surprised they let them in the gallery at the same time. It's a good thing they have metal detectors at the door."

She looked up at Becker. "Gunter, Monique, thank you so much for accompanying me to the door and helping me save face for having been stood up."

"It was your date's loss and our pleasure."

"Monique." Tacey turned her smile to Olivia. "Thank you for sharing Gunter with me."

"You're welcome."

With those parting words, Tacey left them and walked across the room to join Giovanni Romano.

"If you'll excuse me," Olivia said with a smile, "I'll take a moment in the ladies' room and give Trace a call to have Matt conduct a background check on Ms. Tacey Rogers. She seems to know a lot about the Salvatores and the Romanos."

Becker nodded. "I was about to suggest I do the same."

Olivia shook her head. "You need to stay with the others. You're the potential client in the market for hot paintings. Nobody cares about Monique Jameson or will miss her if she disappears for a few minutes."

"I'll miss you," Becker said, his eyes narrowing. "I don't like you being out of my sight for a moment."

She smiled again and batted her eyelashes at him. "I'll be fine."

Becker's gaze followed Olivia until she disappeared down a corridor. His inclination was to follow her. With both mafia bosses in the room, anything could happen—and he didn't want *anything* to happen to Olivia. He and Trace had discussed wearing listening devices, but they hadn't wanted to risk being caught with them. Cell phones were expected. Being caught with a listening device would send up red flags with the mafia.

Once Olivia was out of sight, he turned his attention to Tacey, who was now talking with Giovanni—and not like casual strangers either. The blonde's brow was creased in a frown, and she appeared to be having harsh words with the man. After a few more moments arguing with him, she left his side.

Giovanni started across the floor, heading for Vincenzo Salvatore.

Becker moved closer, hoping to eavesdrop on any conversation the two rivals might have.

Before the two mafia kingpins could collide, a man with a microphone invited the guests to enter the gallery.

A crowd of people surged forward, blocking Giovanni's path to Salvatore.

Salvatore joined the others moving through the double doors into the art gallery. Giovanni altered his trajectory and fell in step with the others, his entourage of bodyguards bringing up the rear.

Becker hung back. He didn't want to enter until he had Olivia in his sights. About the time he was ready to go in search of her, she emerged from the hallway. When she caught sight of him, she nodded, indicating she had completed her mission.

He met her halfway across the floor, slipped an arm around her waist and walked with her into the gallery. He felt better knowing where Olivia was, but he didn't feel good at all about being in the same building as two very powerful men with ties to warring mafia families.

He'd liked it better when he was fighting the Taliban in Afghanistan. At least then he had been armed and could defend himself and his team. Here, in what most people considered a more civilized environment, he didn't know who might be the enemy or what he would do if someone decided to raid the party and shoot everyone in the room.

ALTHOUGH OLIVIA GLANCED briefly at the works displayed, she spent more time studying the people around them. If this was truly where they intended to make the exchange, the folks milling around were willing to take risks and break the rules to get what they wanted.

The patrons wandered from room to room, admiring the artwork of a number of artists, local and nationwide. Different rooms had different themes: one was impressionist; another, realist; and yet another contained art employing odd textures and different mediums.

When Olivia stepped into the farthest room, she immediately understood why the exhibit within was so much more special than the others. Each painting on the wall was on loan from the estate of Andrew Wyeth. Several of the patrons were gathered in this room, admiring some of Wyeth's most famous works.

Security guards stood inside the room to ensure no one got close enough to damage or steal anything.

Everyone, including Becker and Olivia, stared at the displays, enchanted by the realism of each of his works. The man truly had been talented.

"Now can you see why someone would want one of his paintings?" a feminine voice whispered into Olivia's ear.

Tacey stood to her right, her gaze on a portrait of a woman in a field. "This one, like so many others, makes you feel. If it doesn't, it makes you wonder what the woman in the field is feeling. You can practically smell the grass." Tacey inhaled and let the air out slowly. "I know who you are."

Olivia froze, her eyes still on the woman in the painting, not the one who could rat her out to anyone who might take issue with her stolen identity. She was only slightly relieved by the unarmed security officers in the room.

"I don't know what you mean," Olivia said.

"You're not Monique Jameson."

"Yes, I am," Olivia argued in as calm a voice as she could while her heart pounded in her chest. She was terrified their op had been compromised before they had located the painting or Jasmine.

Tacey shot a quick glance her way. "I wish I could say I don't care who you are—but, as it happens, I do care. And that's what will end up getting us both in trouble."

Olivia shook her head. "I don't understand."

"You will. Now, shut up and listen. We don't have much time before others get suspicious. And don't look at me." Tacey tipped her head as if trying to get a different perspective of the painting on the wall. "Monique and Gunter are still island-hopping in Greece."

Olivia drew in a deep breath, ready to refute Tacey's claim.

Tacey continued before Olivia could say anything. "I spoke with Monique this morning and asked her how Gunter was doing. You see, Monique and I met the last time she and Gunter were in Dallas for an art show. We bonded over the fact that neither one of us cared much for expensive art. She'd never tell Gunter that. He's obsessed with owning something that other people could never have. When you're that wealthy, and can have anything you want, finding something unique becomes a challenge. They were on a yacht in Mykonos, about to head for Santorini. Don't worry. I think I'm the only one here who knows this. But that's not the point. When I told you I felt sorry that the curator disappeared, I meant it."

Olivia's heart beat faster. She pressed a hand to her chest, sure everyone near her could hear it.

"Just so you know," Tacey whispered, "she's still alive."

Relief washed through Olivia.

"I've seen her," Tacey said. "Spoken to her. Sat in the same room with her."

Olivia fought the urge to look toward Tacey.

"I wasn't sure at first, but now I know—" Tacey paused and pointed at the painting on the wall as if commenting on some aspect of the work "—you're her sister, Olivia."

"How—"

"She described you as having beautiful black hair and green eyes." Tacey's lips turned up at the corners. "Monique has black hair and gray eyes. She's a little taller than you and maybe a little thinner. She was a model before she hooked up with Gunter. Most people wouldn't pick up on the differences between you and her."

Olivia didn't care at all about Monique, how tall she was, or if she slept on the right side of the bed or the left. All she wanted to know was how to find Jasmine. "Where is she?" she said in a low whisper.

"In one of Romano's warehouses, the last time I saw her," Tacey said.

"Why are they keeping her?"

Tacey gave her another wry smile. "I would think it's obvious. They want the painting, like every other collector in this room. The curator is in a warehouse near the south Dallas train yard. I saw her last night, but there's no guarantee she's still there."

"Why are you telling me this if you're on *their* side?"

"I don't believe in trading a life for a painting." She shrugged. "I told you, I'm not a big fan of art. Not like some who would kill to own that Wyeth original."

"The address?"

"I want to go there first and let you know if she's still there."

"Let me go with you," Olivia begged.

"Can't. Not only would that reveal the fact I told you, but it would also be a waste of time if they've already moved her."

"I'm willing to take the risk."

"I'm not. I'll text you the location once I've made sure she's there."

"You'll need my number."

"Tell me what it is," Tacey said. "I have a good memory."

Olivia told her the number.

Tacey repeated it verbatim.

"How is she?" Olivia asked.

"Shh," Tacey said. "Someone's headed our way."

A stately older man in a black tuxedo with a balding head stopped behind them and studied the painting of the woman.

As one, Olivia and Tacey moved to another work—a watercolor of a seascape in various tones of blues and greens. Keeping her tone low, Tacey leaned slightly toward Olivia. "Hang tough until I send you the location."

Olivia nodded. "Thank you."

"Don't thank me until you get her away from Giovanni and his family."

"Why are you doing this?" Olivia asked. "Won't you be in trouble with the Romanos?"

"I already am. I'm tired of all the drama and corruption. I don't agree with using an innocent as leverage. And they don't really care about their own. They sent Eduardo—the only good man of the lot—to steal the painting as a test of his loyalty to the family." Her chin lifted, and the lines around her mouth deepened. "They were more upset about losing the painting than losing a family member."

Olivia's heart constricted. This woman was putting her life on the line to save a stranger. "Will you be okay?"

"One way or another." She turned away from the painting and smiled at a woman across the room. "Mrs. Mortenson," she called out, "I haven't seen you in forever.

How is your son, the doctor?" Tacey left Olivia standing in front of the seascape.

For a long moment, Olivia continued to face the painting on the wall without seeing it. Her head spun and her heart raced. They'd come to the exhibit to learn where the missing Wyeth was. But now…

An arm slipped around her and pulled her against a solid wall of muscle.

Becker.

Olivia leaned into him, absorbing his strength.

"She knows," she whispered softly.

Chapter Ten

Becker had been across the room, pretending to admire a landscape while doing his best to eavesdrop on a heated conversation between Salvatore and Romano. The two men spoke in hushed tones, and Becker hadn't been able to hear enough to make sense of their words. When he moved closer, they moved away to continue their discussion.

He'd seen Tacey approach Olivia. At first, he thought they were just discussing the artwork in front of them. But when Olivia stiffened, Becker knew it was more important than opinions on style and color. He'd given them the space to finish their conversation. When Tacey moved off to speak with another guest, Becker went to Olivia.

She was holding it together like a champ, but he could tell by the tightness around her mouth and the way she curled her fingers into fists that her control was slipping.

"She knows about us?" Becker asked.

Olivia nodded and looked up at him. "And where they're keeping her."

He forced a smile as he looked down into her eyes. They had to appear to be the carefree playboy and his girlfriend, even when they were on the verge of getting the information they were after. "Where?"

"She said she would text the location when she was certain they hadn't moved her. She did say she was being held in a warehouse on the south side of Dallas, near the train yard."

Becker's brow furrowed. He wasn't sure he trusted the woman. "Why would she tell you that?"

Olivia shook her head. "I think she was in love with Eduardo."

"The victim?"

"If not in love, she cared about him, and his death made her realize the Romano family isn't where she wants to be." Olivia glanced toward the door. "Look."

The woman in question was leaving the Wyeth room.

"Does that mean you're ready to go?"

"Have you accomplished what you came here to do?" She looked around at the other men and women in the room. "Have you sufficiently networked to ensure an invite to any potential sale?"

Becker shook his head. "I have yet to gain an audience with either Salvatore or Romano."

She gave him a tight smile. "Then we need to make that happen before we leave." Her gaze swept the room again, and she paused.

Following her glance, Becker saw that Salvatore was finally alone, studying the painting Tacey and Olivia had been standing in front of.

"There's a painting you need to see." Olivia hooked his elbow and marched him over to where Salvatore stood.

"I think this is my favorite so far," Olivia said as they approached the silver-haired man. "What do you think?"

Salvatore nodded. "It has merit. I appreciate the realism in the artist's work."

"It makes me wonder about the painting that disappeared from Cavendish Gallery. I would like to have observed it in person to see if it elicits the same emotion. What do you think? Did it make you feel the same?"

"I would like to say it does, but I have not had the pleasure of viewing it, other than the image presented in the media. I was unable to make it to Cavendish before its untimely disappearance." His lip curled into a snarl. "Did you come over to accuse my son of murder and stealing the Wyeth too?"

Olivia's eyes widened. "Of course not, Mr. Salvatore. It's just that Gunter and I are big fans of Andrew Wyeth's creations. We wish we'd been able to see that painting before it disappeared."

"You and many others," Salvatore said, his tone abrupt. His glance moved to Becker. "I understand you have quite the collection of artwork in your château in Switzerland."

"I do," Becker said. "It's an expansive château, with room for more."

Salvatore's eyes narrowed and shifted from Olivia to Becker. His gaze held Becker's for a few seconds longer than necessary. Then he gave an almost imperceptible nod. "If you'll excuse me now." The older man turned and left the room.

Olivia smiled at Becker. "One down, one to go—and here he comes."

Romano was heading their way from across the room.

Her smile broadened as Giovanni Romano approached.

His two bodyguards hung back. The older man nodded as he stepped up to the painting, pretending to study it while glancing sideways at Becker.

Olivia tilted her head to one side. "I like it," she said loud enough for Romano to hear.

Romano nodded toward her and turned to Becker. "And you?" he asked.

Becker nodded. "One of my favorites. But then, I love beautiful women. I find the woman in the painting quite exquisite."

Romano's gaze returned to Olivia. "As I see. I'd read that you were touring the Greek islands recently."

Becker's mouth twisted into a wry grin. "I was, until I heard of the opportunity to add a Wyeth to my collection. It was worth an abrupt pause in my vacation."

Romano looked back at Olivia. "And did you feel the same? Was it worth disrupting your tour of the islands?"

Olivia gave the man a cute pout. "I admit, I was a little disappointed. However, the Greek islands will always be there. We can always return. The chance to own an Andrew Wyeth is once in a lifetime. So, yes, I was all for flying back to see what it was all about." She sighed. "I was quite saddened when I found out the painting had been stolen. I do hope it reappears soon." She touched Becker's arm. "I know how disappointed Gunter would be if he couldn't have it. He has the most perfect spot to hang it in his Swiss château."

Romano nodded toward the others in the room. "There are quite a few interested in the whereabouts of the missing painting. I hope it will be recovered soon."

"Me too." Becker's eyes narrowed, and his chin lifted a fraction. "I want it. Money is not an object."

"Money always becomes the issue," Romano said, then pressed his lips together.

"I really don't care who has the painting. I just want

whoever has it to know—I'm willing to pay whatever it takes."

Romano nodded.

Becker cupped Olivia's elbow. "Have you seen enough?" he asked.

"I haven't seen the painting of the old man in the window," she said with a hint of a whine.

"Monique, darling, we need to leave now if we're to make our dinner reservation."

Olivia nodded and gave him a smile, albeit a tight one. "I'm ready when you are."

Becker glanced at Romano. "If you'll excuse us, I promised to feed my date."

Romano gave a slight dip of his head. "Enjoy your dinner."

Becker held on to Olivia's arm as he guided her toward the exit of the Wyeth room. In the next viewing area, he noted Salvatore was speaking with a barrel-chested man in a black tuxedo.

As Becker and Olivia passed them, the two men turned, watching them as they walked through the room.

Olivia looked back over her shoulder and gave them a perky smile and a wave.

Becker almost laughed, amazed the woman could still play the part when she had to be tied in knots, waiting for Tacey to text her sister's location.

Once outside the gallery, Trace and Irish appeared out of the shadows. Moments later, the white limousine and the black SUV rolled to a stop in front of them.

The ride back to the Ritz was accomplished in silence. Olivia held her cell phone in one hand, staring at the blank screen.

Becker could feel the tension in her body. He reached

out to take her other hand and held it all the way back to the hotel.

Once the limousine slid to a stop in front of the Ritz-Carlton, Olivia and Becker got out.

The limousine pulled away, and the SUV rolled up to the curb.

"Get in," Trace said.

Becker held the back door for Olivia. She got in and tucked her skirt around her.

Becker rounded to the other side and slipped in beside her.

"How was the exhibit?" Trace asked.

"Interesting," Becker responded.

"You can tell us all about it in a few minutes." Trace gave Becker a pointed look in the mirror.

Becker nodded. They wouldn't talk about the event until they were out of the vehicle.

"Are you hungry?" Trace asked.

"Starving," Irish responded, rubbing his belly with a grin. "Standing around for hours has a way of making you think about food."

Trace chuckled. "You're always thinking of food. I don't know how you stay so fit."

"High metabolism," Irish said.

Trace glanced again in the rearview mirror. "Steak sound good?"

"Sounds good to me." Becker turned to Olivia. "Are you okay with it?"

She nodded, her attention on the cell phone as if it were a lifeline to her sister. In a way, it was.

They didn't have to go too far to find a steak house. Once Trace parked the SUV and they all piled out, Trace said, "Give it to us. I didn't want to say anything in the vehicle. It could have been bugged while it was parked in the garage."

Becker nodded toward Olivia. "We had an interesting conversation with Tacey Rogers."

"I assumed you had when Olivia texted her name to us. I had Matt do some digging on the lady. He got back to us pretty quickly."

Olivia glanced up from her phone. "What did he find?"

"She used to date Eduardo Romano. They broke up a couple of months ago but remained friends."

"Apparently, she's still in good with the Romano family even after her breakup," Olivia said. "After a brief conversation with the two of us, she came to me while I was alone and said she knew who we were."

Trace shot a glance at Olivia. "Did she blow your cover?"

Olivia shook her head. "No. She cornered me to say she knows where my sister is, that she's seen her and she's alive."

"Did she tell you where she is?" Trace asked.

Olivia shook her head. "No. I gave her my phone number. She said she'd let me know when she made sure they hadn't moved her from her last known location."

"You realize that by telling you where your sister is, Tacey is putting herself in a lot of danger." Irish frowned. "The Romanos have a way of eliminating people who betray the family."

Olivia nodded. "Tacey has to know that, but she was more than willing to let me know about her. She doesn't like that they're using her as a pawn in a showdown with the Salvatores."

"Is your cell phone fully charged?" Trace asked.

"Yes." Olivia checked the screen again. "It's killing me to wait."

Trace waved a hand toward the restaurant. "We can blow some time eating. It will help take your mind off the passing time. Besides, you need to keep up your energy."

"That's right," Irish said. "When that call comes through, we'll need to be on our way immediately."

"And while we're waiting for our order, you two can tell us about the others you ran into at the exhibit," Trace said.

Throughout dinner, Olivia stared at her cell phone as if willing it to ring. She barely touched the fillet Becker had ordered for her.

Becker gave a detailed account of the people they encountered at the event.

"Any more news on the dark web about any black market auctions scheduled soon?" Becker asked.

Trace shook his head. "Matt's monitoring the web. He said social media sites for rabid art collectors have been passing veiled messages about the missing painting. A lot of people speculate that the piece is already in the hands of the new owner." Trace took a bite of his steak.

Irish picked up where Trace left off. "Nico wasn't arrested until the following day. That would have given him time to pass the painting to whoever he had in mind to sell it to."

"Or to stash it somewhere until the authorities had time to process the murder scene and the body Nico hadn't had the time or inclination to dispose of," Becker suggested.

"He didn't know when he left the scene that my sister had been there and witnessed the murder," Olivia said.

"He might have been more concerned about establishing his alibi in case the police came looking for him."

"No matter who has the painting or where it is, we've confirmed the Romanos have Olivia's sister," Becker said.

"And the last time Tacey saw her, she was being held in a warehouse in south Dallas near the rail yard," Olivia said. "And she was alive."

"They are keeping her alive for a reason," Irish said.

"The Romanos know the Salvatores have the painting." Becker nodded toward Olivia. "They will leverage Olivia's sister to trade for it."

"The question is," Trace said, "are the Salvatores as mercenary as the Romanos? Will they be willing to give up the prize to keep Nico out of jail?"

"The Salvatores might not have a choice," Becker said. "If Nico is the only one who knows where the painting is, everyone has to wait until the authorities release him to find it."

"The Romanos can't negotiate a trade with anyone but Nico. They have to keep Olivia's sister under wraps until Nico is free. They can't risk the Salvatores killing Jasmine before they know for sure Nico has the Wyeth painting. Nico has the most to lose if Jasmine resurfaces to testify in court that he was at the gallery that night and killed Eduardo."

Trace nodded. "Nico won't want to go back to jail. If he knows where the painting is and his family doesn't, he might be willing to trade the painting for the witness. His family might not be as willing, even if it means Nico goes to jail for life."

By the time they'd finished dinner, Becker could tell the stress was getting to Olivia. "Let's go back to the Ritz."

"Just remember," Trace said, "you can't talk in your room, even if you check for bugs. The Italian mafia didn't get so wealthy playing by any rules or moral standards."

"We'll bear that in mind," Becker said.

"If you need to talk to us, text us. We can meet in the lobby." Trace paid the bill and then pushed back from the table and stood.

Becker rose and extended a hand to Olivia. She was still holding her cell phone in her hand. Dark shadows were beginning to form beneath her eyes.

He hated seeing her so worried and stressed, and he hated even more that he could do nothing to help take away her pain. All he could do was be there for her and take action when the call came through.

Once again, Becker and Olivia claimed the back seat of the SUV, with Trace driving and Irish riding shotgun.

At the Ritz, Trace hesitated handing the keys to the SUV over to the valet. "Could you park it as close as possible?" he asked. "There's a possibility we may have to leave in a hurry."

The valet arranged to have the SUV parked in the drop-off area throughout the night instead of driving it around to the garage.

Olivia stared at the SUV sitting at the end of the loading-and-unloading zone. "I feel like we should be driving toward the rail yard. We could wait close by for the call."

"What if they've moved her?" Becker said. "To the north end of Dallas?"

"We will have wasted time, and it would take longer to get there from the south side of Dallas." Olivia sighed. "I know. I need to be patient. It's hard."

Becker slipped an arm around her waist.

"We'll move quickly when you get that call," Trace

promised. "In the meantime, Irish will see you two up to your room. You okay with that, Irish?"

Irish popped a salute and a grin. "Yes, sir." He turned to Becker and Olivia. "Are you going straight up to your room, or do you want to make a pit stop at the bar for a drink?"

Olivia shook her head. "I want to go to our room. At least there I can stare at my phone and people won't look at me funny." She gave him a weak smile. "I'd like a drink, but I need to keep a clear head for when I get that call with the location of where they're keeping my sister."

"I get that," Irish said. "And as much as I'd like a beer, I'll pass."

Trace lifted his chin at Becker. "I'm going to touch base with Matt one more time. I sent a plane to pick them up. I have a strong suspicion we're going to need them soon. Especially if we get caught in a war between the Romanos and the Salvatores."

With Irish as their bodyguard, Becker and Olivia rode up the elevator to their floor and entered their room. Irish went in with them and helped conduct a search for listening or video devices. Once they were fairly certain the room was clear, Irish stepped out to stand guard in the hallway.

"Thanks, man," Becker said before his teammate left.

"No worries," he said with a wink. "I've got your six." He pulled the door shut between them.

Becker turned to find Olivia. When he didn't see her in the sitting room, he went to the bedroom. It was empty too, but the bathroom door was closed.

Moments later, Olivia came out, wearing black slacks and a black blouse. She'd pulled her hair back in a ponytail and wore matching flat shoes. "I'd rather be in my jeans and a T-shirt, but at least I have these." She nodded toward his suitcase. "You might want to change into something less fancy. When we get the call, we won't have time to change."

He crossed the room to her and gathered her in his arms. "I love that when you're crazy worried, you hold it together." He kissed her forehead. "I'll be out in a minute."

Becker gathered slacks, a dark polo shirt and a leather jacket before disappearing into the bathroom. Less than five minutes later, he was ready to go.

As he emerged from the bathroom, he heard the ping of a text message coming across on Olivia's cell phone.

He hurried out to the sitting area, where he found Olivia staring down at the screen, her eyes wide, her face pale.

"Is it her?" he asked.

She nodded. "She sent a GPS pin." Without waiting for his response, Olivia spun and ran for the door.

Becker hurried to keep up.

When they burst out into the hallway, Irish asked, "You get the call?"

"Yes." Olivia didn't slow down until she reached the elevator. She paced as she waited for the door to open.

On the way down, Irish sent a text to Trace.

By the time they emerged into the lobby, the SUV was waiting for them out front.

Olivia handed her cell phone to Irish, who brought up the directions. Within minutes, they were on the major highway, speeding through the city, heading south toward the rail yard.

Becker prayed they'd get there in time to find Olivia's sister safe and sound—and that they weren't being led into a trap.

Chapter Eleven

Olivia sat in the back seat, perched on the edge, looking over Irish's shoulder at the map on her cell phone. Ten minutes had passed, and according to the app, they were halfway to their destination.

Becker laid a hand on her back. He didn't say anything, but he was there. And that made Olivia feel a little better. She wouldn't be all right until her sister was safe and away from the Romanos.

Trace glanced in the rearview mirror. "There's a 9 mm Glock under your seat. Irish and I have weapons as well."

Becker reached for the case beneath his seat and removed the gun from inside. He checked the magazine and slid the gun into the pocket of his jacket.

The gun should have made Olivia even more nervous. Instead, it gave her a little sense of relief. Knowing where her sister was didn't guarantee they'd free her without a fight. The Romanos would be armed and dangerous.

A shiver rippled over Olivia's skin.

"When we get there, Olivia, you should stay in the vehicle," Trace said.

She was already shaking her head before he could finish. "She's my sister."

"If you go in, we'll be worried about you and not focusing on getting to your sister," Becker said. "It puts every one of this team in danger. We need someone on the outside, watching to make sure no one comes in behind us. We need someone to have our six."

Olivia chewed on her bottom lip. "The last thing I want is for one of you to get hurt. But hanging back—"

"Will be difficult but necessary," Trace said. "With only three of us, we need a fourth to warn us if this turns out to be a trap."

"We have another gun in the back," Irish said. "Have you ever fired a pistol of any kind?"

She nodded. "I have an HK 40 handgun. I got it after my parents died and I was living alone. I practiced with it until I became proficient, and I go every other month to the range for a refresher."

Becker grinned. "I learn something new about you every time I turn around."

"You'll find the other gun in the bag," Irish said. "It's a little bigger than you're used to, but it's smooth and easy to figure out."

Becker leaned over the back of the seat and snagged the bag from the floor, bringing it up to place on the seat between them. Inside was another case, several boxes of ammo and a bulletproof vest. He handed the vest to her. "Put this on."

She frowned. "Shouldn't you three be wearing one of these?"

"We only brought the one," Trace said. "We'd all prefer for you to wear it."

She frowned but slipped into it and buckled the front clasps.

Once she was in it, Becker handed her the gun. "Familiarize yourself with it." Then he handed her the magazine full of bullets. "When you feel confident about its functionality, you can load it."

She held the weapon in her hand, testing the weight and checking the safety features. She pulled the slide back to check that there wasn't a bullet already chambered. Satisfied that it was very much like hers, she slid the magazine into the handle without chambering a round. She would only do that if the situation called for it.

"We're two miles from the destination," Irish said. Trace pulled off the main highway onto an access road and turned right, heading into a seedier part of town.

"We'll park the SUV close, but not close enough so that their sentries will see it," Trace said.

He slowed a few blocks away and pulled into an alley between two businesses. "We'll park here."

Olivia shook her head. "I'm not staying in the vehicle. Not if it's this far away from you guys. I can't see what's happening to the building where you're headed if I stay here."

"You'll be safer," Becker argued.

Anger surged inside Olivia. "And you three won't." She frowned, her jaw set in a hard line. "I'm going to get close enough to have your back, even if I don't go inside the warehouse with you."

Trace shot Becker a look. "She'll be out in the open. What if someone sneaks up on her?"

"I'll find a position in the shadows with my back against a wall," she said, getting angrier that the men were talking as if she weren't there or didn't have a say in what happened to her.

"Look, I'm here—let me help," she said. "I get it that I'm not trained for clearing a building and you guys must have done it a few times on active duty. But I can handle a gun, and I will watch from a reasonable distance for anyone else showing up on the outside when you're already inside."

"Makes me nervous," Becker said. "But she makes sense." He met her gaze. "Only if you promise not to follow us inside. We could end up shooting you, thinking you're the enemy."

She nodded. "I promise."

"Okay, we're wasting time," Trace said. "Let's move out."

As soon as they opened the doors to the SUV, Olivia smelled smoke. At first, it was only a little bit, but as they emerged from the end of the alley and onto the street, she looked up to see a glow a couple of blocks away. Smoke billowed into the night sky, the lights from the city reflecting off the clouds it formed.

Irish glanced down at the GPS location on the cell phone and looked up again. "Folks, that's where we're headed."

Olivia's heart skipped several beats. Then she was running, her eyes filling with tears, making it difficult to see where she was going. She had to get to the warehouse. Her sister was inside, probably tied to a post and surely scared out of her mind.

As Olivia rounded the corner of a brick structure, she ground to a halt and stared at a warehouse completely engulfed in flames.

Sirens started to wail nearby, and soon a fire engine was rolling up to the front of the building, followed by an ambulance.

Firefighters leaped out, pulled a hose from the side of the truck and connected it to a hydrant.

With a firm grip on the hose, a fireman gave a quick

turn of the valve, releasing a gush of water from the other end.

Other firefighters suited up in tanks and masks and headed into the burning building.

Her heart thundering in her chest, Olivia staggered forward and then ran toward the crew working the fire.

Becker caught her before she could reach them. His hands held her in an iron grip.

"Let me go," she said, fighting to free herself from his grasp. "Jasmine's in there. We have to get her out." When he refused to release her, she cried, "Please. Oh, please. She's all the family I have left."

"Sweetheart, I know. And I want her out of there too," he said, his voice shaking. He swallowed hard and continued. "You have to let the firefighters do their job. They're trained and equipped to handle this. If there's anyone inside, they'll get them out."

Olivia knew he was right. Her heart in her throat, Olivia stood back, out of the way, wanting with all her being to rush into the building and bring Jasmine out.

Becker's hand remained on her arm, holding so tightly, his fingers would likely leave a bruise.

Trace approached the captain.

Olivia couldn't hear what he was saying. As soon as they finished talking, the chief turned and spoke into a handheld radio.

Near the front of the building, a man wearing a full mask and oxygen tank kicked open a locked door at the entrance and stood back as smoke billowed out. Once the smoke had cleared a little, he ducked inside.

For the longest few minutes of Olivia's life, she held her breath and prayed.

Becker folded her into his arms as she watched the

door. He whispered over and over, "It'll be okay. It'll be okay."

Trace and Irish stood on either side of Becker and Olivia. It felt like a show of solidarity. They were there for her no matter the outcome.

Olivia didn't feel alone. She was thankful for the Outriders. Mostly, she was thankful for Becker holding her so close. With him close, she could handle almost anything.

The longer the firefighter was inside, the more her stomach churned and the more labored her breathing became. Her chest hurt so much, she thought she might be having a heart attack.

"Breathe, sweetheart," Becker whispered against her ear. "Breathe." He said the words almost as if he needed to hear them himself.

She drew in a breath, let it out and did it again. On the third breath, she gasped.

A firefighter was backing out through the door.

As he cleared the threshold, Olivia could see that he was dragging someone by the arms.

A female with blond hair.

Olivia pressed her palms to her cheeks, her heart dropping into the pit of her belly. "Oh, dear God, please."

She lunged toward the firefighter, only to be restrained by Becker. "Let go of me."

"You'll only be in the way. Let them save her."

The paramedics surrounded the woman and went to work on her.

Tears slipped down Olivia's cheeks. "No, no, no," she cried. "Jasmine!"

The woman was loaded onto a stretcher and rolled

toward the ambulance. They started an IV and covered her mouth and nose with an oxygen mask.

The firefighter in charge checked with the medical crew before walking over to where Olivia and the Outriders were standing. "Can you identify her?"

Olivia nodded, a lump lodged in her throat, making it hard to breathe and speak. She managed to say, "Let me see her. Please. I know her."

"Come with me. They're loading her for transport to the hospital. If you're a family member, they'll want you to follow."

Olivia and Becker hurried after the firefighter, approaching the ambulance as the techs prepared to load the victim.

With her fingers pressed to her lips, Olivia asked, "Is she…?"

"Alive?" an EMT said with a tight smile. "Yes. But she's a long way from being in the clear. She's suffering from smoke inhalation, and it appears as if she took a blow to the head."

Olivia reached out to brush back the blond hair from her face. The mask covered most of her facial features, and her eyes were closed…but something wasn't right.

Then Olivia noticed that the woman was wearing a white dress. Granted, the dress was covered in soot and damaged beyond repair, but there was no denying it had been white at one time.

"Jasmine wasn't wearing a white dress," she said. Her eyes widened, and she looked back at Becker. "This isn't Jasmine."

Becker frowned. "If it isn't Jasmine, who is it?"

"Oh, dear Lord," Olivia said as recognition dawned on her. "It's Tacey Rogers."

The first responders loaded the victim into the ambulance, closed the door and drove away.

Becker stood by Olivia as she turned toward the smoking building. His heart hurt for her.

"That can't be it." Olivia shook her head, her eyes widening. "Sweet heaven… She's still inside that building." Before he could stop her, she ran to the man who'd brought the woman out of the warehouse.

The firefighter had shed his mask and was shrugging out of the breathing apparatus when she reached him. "You can't stop now," she cried. "My sister was in that building."

He shook his head and set the tank on the ground. "My buddy went in after me." He nodded toward another man who was stepping out of similar gear. "I only found one person."

Olivia ran to the other guy. "Please," she begged. "Was there anyone else inside that warehouse?"

He shook his head. "I checked all the rooms. The warehouse was fairly empty but for a few busted wood pallets. No one else was inside."

He moved past her to stow his gear on the truck.

Becker was there for Olivia as her knees buckled. He caught her on the way down, pulled her into his embrace and held her until she stopped shaking. "They tried to kill her."

"It wasn't Jasmine," he said.

"But it was Tacey. She told us about Jasmine, and they must have found out. She did it for Jasmine, and it cost her."

Trace and Irish had caught up with them and stood beside Becker.

"I'll meet with the police," Trace said, "and let them

know that she'll need protection in the hospital." He crossed to where a police officer was standing, talking to the fire chief. Already the flames had been reduced; the fire appeared to be under control.

Moments later, Trace returned. "So far, they're treating this incident as an attempted homicide and arson. They will provide Ms. Rogers with protection while she is recuperating in the hospital."

"Jasmine was here," Olivia said, choking on a sob.

"Yes, but she's not here now," Becker said.

"Which means they still need her alive for a trade to get that painting," Trace said. "Matt reminded me in a text that Nico Salvatore is being released tomorrow if no evidence is presented by then."

"He'll find that painting."

"And if he doesn't negotiate the trade...they'll kill Jasmine." Olivia pressed her fist to her mouth.

"We won't let that happen," Trace said.

"How will you stop it?" Olivia demanded. "We don't know where they have her. We need to get to that painting before Nico does. It's the only thing they want—the only thing they'll take in exchange for my sister's life."

"Matt and Levi will be here within the hour. I have a plane flying them up as we speak," Trace said. "Let's get back to the Ritz. They'll meet us there."

Olivia glanced once more at the smoldering warehouse.

Becker's arm tightened around her waist. "She wasn't in there," he reminded her.

She looked up at him with haunted eyes. "But she's with people who would do what they did to Tacey."

"Don't." He pressed a kiss to her forehead. "You have to stay positive. For Jasmine."

She nodded, her brow dipping, her jaw hardening. "We have to *do* something. No more standing around waiting for the Salvatores or the Romanos to make the next move."

Becker turned her around and they started back to where they'd left the SUV parked in the alley. Irish and Trace led the way.

"Hopefully, Matt will have more information when he gets here," Trace said.

"Like where they've moved Jasmine," Olivia said.

"Or where the painting might be hidden," Irish said. "We have to search for both. One might be key to getting the other."

"I'm to the point where I want to burn that damned thing," Olivia said through gritted teeth. "Jasmine wouldn't be in the situation she is now if that painting never existed."

Becker agreed. But wishing rarely achieved results. Intelligence and hard work were more likely to produce a positive outcome.

Once Matt and Levi arrived, they'd put their heads together. He'd worked with Levi, Irish and Trace on difficult missions in the past. With Matt's internet savvy and his former team's tactical planning and combat skills, they should be able to initiate a plan to resolve this issue quickly.

And hopefully, without anyone else being hurt or injured.

By the time they reached the Ritz-Carlton, Matt and Levi's plane had landed, and they were on their way to the hotel.

"We'll meet in the bar since it's still open," Trace said.

They found a table large enough to hold six people in

the far corner of the room and waited for the other two men to join them.

Each person ordered a nonalcoholic drink, then discussed the fire and Tacey Rogers in between sips. The only one not talking was Olivia.

Becker leaned close and asked, “Do you want to go up to our room?”

She shook her head. “No. I want to be here when Matt and Levi arrive. Matt has to have something else that will help us.”

The two men chose that moment to enter the bar. Matt carried a backpack on one shoulder.

Olivia started to rise. Becker touched her arm, and she sank back into her seat.

“Traffic was heavier than I expected this time of night.” Matt swung the backpack off his shoulder and set it on the floor. “Makes me glad I live in Whiskey Gulch.”

They all made room at the table for the two men and waited while they ordered drinks and a couple of hamburgers.

Once the waiter left, Trace filled Matt and Levi in on what had happened at the exhibit and the warehouse.

Matt let out a long, low whistle. “At least we are fairly certain they’re holding your sister as leverage. It’s too bad they took it out on Ms. Rogers.”

Olivia leaned forward. “Do any of your folks on the dark web keep up with the Romano mafia? Could they have any idea where they’re keeping my sister?”

Matt shook his head. “You’d have an easier time finding the painting than your sister. My sources say the Salvatores are scrambling, searching for the painting as much or more so than the Romanos.”

Olivia sat back, a frown denting her brow.

Becker could almost see the wheels turning in her head as she processed Matt's words. Her hands clenched into fists, and her pretty lips pressed together in a hard line. Finally, she looked up and met Matt's gaze. "If the Salvatores are looking for the painting, that means Nico is the only one who knows where it is. What do we know about Nico?"

Matt's eyes narrowed. "He's married, no children. His wife lives at the family estate in Dallas. He has a mistress who isn't a secret from anyone. Rumor has it his wife condones it because the other woman keeps him away from her. Wife gets to spend his money. He gets to fool around. Win-win for both of them."

"Could he have stashed the painting at his home or his mistress's place?" Olivia asked.

"The police are still working on a search warrant. With no witness and no evidence that he was even at the Cavendish Gallery that night, the judge isn't issuing one."

"I'm not a judge and I'm not in law enforcement," Olivia said. "I'd be willing to search the woman's home for that painting."

"That's breaking and entering," Trace said. "It's illegal."

"And so is kidnapping my sister and using her as a bargaining tool for a stolen painting." Olivia leaned across the table, her face intense. "I'll break any rule or law around, short of killing someone, if it leads me to my sister. I *might* even kill someone if he or she gets in between me and Jasmine. The point is, we don't have much time."

Becker understood her frustration. "She's right. If Nico's out tomorrow, he could get to that painting, sell it and put a hit out on Jasmine before noon. For that matter, his own family might want to get their hands on the witness to use as leverage against Nico to get him to hand over the Wyeth."

"What do you propose?" Trace asked.

Olivia lifted her chin. "We need to search the mistress's apartment, Nico's office—any property Nico might have access to where he could have hidden that painting."

"His mistress, Lana Etheridge, was his alibi," Matt confirmed.

"The authorities had to have questioned her," Irish said.

Matt nodded. "They did, and they searched her apartment, where Nico claimed to have been all that night. He even produced video from the security system showing him arriving early that evening and leaving the next morning."

"Were there any gaps between the time he came and the time he allegedly left?" Becker asked.

Matt shook his head. "No gaps or erasures. But the video only captures the door entrances, not the windows, which was noted in the investigation. Still, they don't have any evidence he was at the gallery, because the security system was deactivated before Eduardo entered the building."

"Someone had access to the computer system from a remote location?" Irish asked.

Matt nodded. "The preliminary findings indicate a hacker got in and disabled the alarms. Eduardo was able to walk right in and take the painting, and he would have made it out if Nico hadn't arrived first. It would have been a clean heist."

"For either man, except my sister forgot something in her office and returned in time to witness the murder."

Olivia placed both hands on the table. "Where does this Lana Etheridge live? The police might have missed something. Or Nico might have hidden the painting in a shed, attic or a secret panel in the floor."

"It would make more sense for him to hide it in a storage unit or an office-supply closet."

"It could be anywhere," Levi said.

"Then the sooner we start looking, the sooner we find it," Olivia said. "I'll check out Lana's place." She met Matt's gaze. "I'll need the address."

Matt glanced from Trace to Becker and back to Trace. "Are we doing this?"

Trace shrugged. "We don't have anything else to go on."

Matt nodded. "Nico is involved in a building project in the downtown area not far from the Cavendish Gallery. It is possible he could have swung by there, dropped the painting at the mobile office unit. No one is there at night, and he could have had a key to it since he's reported to have been working closely with the engineer."

Levi raised his hand. "I can check it out."

"Any chance he would have taken it by the Salvatore estate?" Becker asked.

"The detective on the case reviewed the videos of vehicles coming in and out, as well as people entering the house that night. That place has cameras everywhere." Matt shook his head. "No sign of Nico and no gaps in time on any of the videos."

"He had to be scared after killing Eduardo," Trace said. "Stealing is one thing. Murder is another, with greater consequences if caught. I doubt he went anywhere with cameras, and even then, since he ended up at his mistress's place, he knew where the cameras were and avoided them altogether."

"So we need to look for places he could have hidden the painting that don't have video cameras."

"We might be shooting in the dark," Olivia said, "but it's better than sitting around doing nothing."

A pinging sound came from her pocket. Olivia frowned and pulled out her cell phone. She glanced at the screen, and her face paled.

Becker rose to stand next to her, peering over her shoulder to read the message. "Who's it from?"

Olivia frowned. "Tacey's cell phone." She stared at the words and then handed him the phone. "We have to do something. Now."

Becker read the words aloud.

"'I don't know who you are, and I don't care what happens to the girl. But maybe you do. Whoever gets the painting to me, gets her.'"

Becker's gut clenched. "We all know Tacey didn't send that text. Romano has it and is using you to get what he wants. That settles it for me." Becker looked up, his eyes meeting Trace's. "I'll go with Olivia."

"I'm with Levi," Irish said.

"Matt and I will continue to monitor the internet and look for other sites close to the Cavendish Gallery where Nico could have hidden that painting. If we find something interesting, we'll head there. Keep in touch." Trace paused, his brow furrowing. "And whatever you do… don't get caught."

Chapter Twelve

"Phone on silent," Becker said as they climbed out of the SUV a block away from Lana's home on a quiet street in a decent neighborhood.

Olivia verified she had turned off the sound on her cell phone. No need for a calling card. Lana could be home alone, with a gun tucked beneath her pillow.

Thankfully, it wasn't a gated community. Nico might be paying her rent, but he hadn't gone overboard with security. Perhaps he thought the security system was enough to keep his ladylove safe.

And from what Matt had indicated, the cameras only focused on the main entrances to the home.

Becker and Olivia approached the residence, clinging to the shadows of the other buildings along the street.

When they were within a few yards, Becker stopped and held out a hand, blocking Olivia from going farther until he could recon the area.

"There it is." He pointed to a modest brick home that had probably been built in the nineties. The front entrance had a small covered porch.

Nothing about the house screamed *murderer*—or *hiding place for a priceless work of art*—but then again, Olivia hadn't expected it to.

"Let's move around the back," he whispered. "There has to be a window Nico could get in and out of that's out of view of the cameras."

"Did Matt mention dogs?" Olivia asked.

"I'm betting since he didn't mention them, there aren't any. The authorities reviewed the videos. If there had been barking dogs, that would have been an indication of someone entering the house."

Olivia hoped he was right. Guns and dogs were deal breakers. She almost snorted. Like she knew the best methods of safely breaking and entering the home of a murderer.

A tremor rippled down her spine.

She'd never committed a crime in her life. Her parents had raised her to respect the law and the authorities. Yet here she was, ready to commit one and drag a good man into it with her. "Look," she said. "You don't have to go in with me. If I get caught, it'll just be on me. I don't want you to pay for my crime."

He frowned at her. "Sweetheart, I'm not letting you go in there without me. We don't know if Lana is home or if she's armed. What would you do if she pointed a gun at you?"

Olivia shrugged. "Try to talk her out of shooting me?"

"Before or after she pulls the trigger? A lone woman with a mafia boyfriend might shoot first. And she'd have every right to, since you'd be trespassing in her house."

"Still, it was my idea to search her house. You don't have to go down with me. I don't expect you to."

"Are we going in or not? Either I go in with you or neither one of us goes in." He waited for her response.

Olivia was determined to find the missing painting. "I'm going in. If you come along…well, then, that's on you." She lifted her head in challenge, hoping he'd back down and opt to stay outside.

He tipped his head toward Lana's place. "Then we're going in."

Becker swung wide of the house, looking at it from all angles, judging which side would be best to enter from. Starlight gave them enough light to see where they were going.

Olivia did her best to remain in the shadows. When Becker came to a sudden halt, she nearly bumped into him. "What?"

He nodded toward the garage, where a light suddenly blinked on. The garage door opened, and a small red Mazda Miata convertible pulled out into the driveway and paused until the garage door closed. Then the car raced down the street, disappearing around the next corner.

"That was the only vehicle in the garage," Becker said.

"Wonder why she left at this time," Olivia said.

"Whatever the reason, she might be back soon. If we're going to do this, it's now or never."

Olivia nodded. "Through the window on the west side?"

He nodded. "We want to stay out of view of the cameras and the neighbors." Becker led the way, staying in the shadows of the bushes until they were directly across from the window they would enter.

As quickly as they could, they crossed the open ground and made it to the side of the house.

"What are the chances the window is unlocked?" Becker whispered. He placed his fingers on the window and pushed upward.

Olivia held her breath.

At first, the window didn't budge. Then it moved and rose slowly up the tracks. Before Olivia could protest, Becker pulled himself up and through the window into the house.

He leaned out the window and whispered, "Stay here."

"But—"

Becker disappeared into the house. Time crawled for the minute or two it took for him to get back to where she stood beneath the window.

Then he reached down, grabbed her arms and pulled her through. She landed gracelessly on the floor and struggled to her feet.

The window was to a bedroom that had a wood-framed bed pushed up against one wall, its mattress without sheets or pillows. Piles of clothing obscured the bed, and the rest of the room was filled with moving boxes that had been opened but not unpacked.

"Is the house empty?" Olivia asked softly.

"Yes. We need to make it quick." He looked around the room. "This would be a good place to start. I'll get started on the rest of the house."

Olivia didn't like letting him out of her sight any more than he liked letting her out of his, but they had a lot of ground to cover in a short amount of time. Using a tiny flashlight she'd brought with her in her pocket, she dug through the stack of clothing on the bed, checked under the mattress and looked beneath the bed.

Then she worked her way through the larger open boxes, digging down to the bottoms, finding nothing but knickknacks, photographs, sheets and blankets.

The closet in the room was filled with clothes on plastic hangers and shoes stacked on the floor and on the shelves above. The woman liked her stilettos. She had some in every color and style, including a pair of ankle boots completely covered in rhinestones.

Olivia checked the back wall of the closet for hidden doors but found none.

When she emerged from the bedroom, she almost ran into Becker in the hallway. "I checked the master bedroom. Nothing but a lot of shoes."

Olivia snorted. "Her shoe collection overflowed into this room as well."

"I'm headed for the living room," Becker said. "There's another guest bedroom, if you want to take that."

She nodded and crossed the hallway into the other guest room, which had a white iron bed, this one covered in a floral-print comforter with matching pillows.

Olivia started there, feeling under the pillows and sliding her hands beneath the blankets and sheets. She checked between the mattress and box spring—nothing. She dropped to the floor and slid beneath the bed, checking the underside of the box spring. Other than a few dust bunnies, she didn't find anything.

The closet contained empty suitcases. She checked each one, only to be disappointed when she found that they were all empty. Again, she checked the back wall of the closet for any hidden doors.

The only other items in the room were a dresser, two small nightstands and a print of a spring garden that hung over the headboard.

She checked all the drawers in the dresser and nightstands, even pulling them out to look behind and beneath them. Getting desperate, she lifted the print off the wall and checked the back, but it didn't appear to have been tampered with.

Out of options, she headed for the living room. As

she emerged from the hallway, headlights shone through the picture window as a vehicle passed on the street and slowed to a stop.

"Becker!" she called out.

A door creaked from somewhere beyond the dining room.

The vehicle pulled up in front of the little house and parked next to the curb.

Her heart beating like a snare drum solo, Olivia ran through the dining room and into the kitchen. "Becker!" she called out again in an urgent whisper.

He stepped out of the walk-in pantry. "What?"

"A car," she said. At that moment, the rumble of a motor sounded: the garage door was opening. Which meant Lana was back.

Olivia pushed Becker back into the pantry and stepped in with him, closing the door to just a crack as the door between the kitchen and the garage swung open.

A woman carrying a paper bag entered and flipped the light switch, bathing the kitchen in soft yellow light. She left the garage door open as she set the bag on the counter and pulled out four full bottles—two of red wine, one of whiskey and the other of gin.

"Whiskey on the rocks?" she called out and headed for the refrigerator, snagging a glass from a cabinet on the way.

"Sounds good," a male voice responded. A moment later, a man with graying hair, wearing black trousers and a black long-sleeved shirt, entered, pulling a necktie loose from around his throat. He tossed it on the counter and unbuttoned the top button of his shirt.

The woman Olivia assumed was Lana handed him a

glass filled with whiskey and a couple of cubes of ice. "Better?" she asked with a smile.

He took a long swallow, downing half the liquid in the glass before responding. "Yes."

Olivia held her breath, praying Lana didn't decide to stow the other bottles in the pantry.

"He gets out tomorrow?" the man asked.

Lana nodded. "Yes, he does."

"Are you sure he'll be back here?"

"Absolutely. He hates his wife. She only stays married to him so she can live on the family estate. She made it clear that she doesn't much care for him, and she actually gets along better with his dad. Nico and Briana haven't lived together for over a year." Lana chuckled. "Since he moved in with me."

"If he comes back here, we'll see less of each other," the man said.

"That means we need to make the most of tonight." She took the glass from his fingers and set it on the counter; then she wrapped her hand around the back of his neck and pulled him down for a kiss.

He dragged her body up against his and deepened the kiss.

She hooked one of her calves around the back of his thigh, her short dress rising up.

"Ummm," he growled. "Let's take this and the whiskey to the bedroom."

She laughed, grabbed the bottle of whiskey and his glass, and led the way through the kitchen and out of view of the pantry. The light blinked off, leaving Olivia and Becker in the dark.

"So," the man said, "Nico didn't tell you where he hid the painting?"

Lana snorted. "Do you think I'd still be in this stinking house or this stinking town if he had?"

"No. I guess not. If I had it, I'd have been long gone."

"I looked all over this house. It's not here. I have no idea where it is. I just hope when he's out and sells it, I get some of the proceeds for being his alibi. Still can't believe he killed Eduardo. He'll be lucky to make his next birthday if the Romanos have their way. Sadly, that would mean I'll lose this house."

Her voice faded the farther away she moved.

A moment later, music sounded from the living room, and Olivia could hear Lana's laugh.

When she started to open the pantry door wider, Becker touched her arm. "Wait," he whispered.

She let her hand drop and did as he'd suggested.

After what felt like an hour—but was probably only ten minutes—Becker pushed the pantry door open and stepped around Olivia and into the kitchen.

He tiptoed across the tile floor.

Olivia followed, careful not to bump into anything in the darkness. Fortunately, starlight filtered through the windows, giving them just enough light to find their way through the dining room and living room.

In the hallway, the only light came from the half-open door to the master bedroom.

Muffled voices rumbled from within. A giggle, an answering deep laugh and silence. Footsteps sounded.

Becker ducked through the door to the guest room they'd come in through. He pulled Olivia in after him and pulled the door to.

The creaky sound of another door broke the silence.

"I'll be right back with my wine," Lana called out. "Do you want anything?"

"Just you, darlin'," the man responded.

Becker and Olivia made their way through the maze of boxes to the window and waited for the sound of Lana returning to her bedroom and closing the squeaking door before making their exit.

"You first," Becker said.

Olivia swung one leg over the windowsill, then the other, and dropped softly to the ground.

She turned and waited for Becker, who soon landed beside her.

He gripped the bottom of the window and pulled it down as far as it would go before he had to place his fingers on the glass and ease it down the rest of the way. Then he took off his shirt and used it to wipe away any fingerprints he'd left behind.

Throughout the process, Olivia watched the room for movement.

A light blinked on in the hallway, shining a sliver of light through the crack in the door.

A moment later, the door swung open.

Olivia grabbed Becker's shoulder and pushed him down below the windowsill.

The light in the bedroom flashed on.

"I thought I heard a sound," they could hear the man say.

"Oh, you're being paranoid. They aren't letting Nico go until tomorrow morning. That is, if that woman who claimed she witnessed him murdering Eduardo doesn't show up out of the blue to keep that from happening. I bet Nico's family got to her. They won't want her blabbing and keeping Nico from getting out to show them where he left that stupid painting."

The window above Olivia and Becker slid open. "Don't you ever lock your windows?" the man asked.

"If I did, how would Nico use me as an alibi?" She huffed. "If it makes you feel better…" The window slammed shut, and the locks clicked in place. "Happy?" Lana asked, her muffled voice moving farther away from the window. "Now, can we have a little fun before Nico shows up?"

Becker touched Olivia's arm, and he tipped his head toward the bushes.

They ran for the shadows, working their way around the yards and back to the SUV. They jumped in.

As Becker turned the SUV around in the street, he glanced at Olivia. "Let Trace know what we found."

"Basically, nothing we didn't know," Olivia said. "And no painting." She pulled out her phone and sent Trace a text.

No painting at Lana's. Lana showed up. Overheard her with another man. As suspected, she's lying about Nico's alibi.

He responded within seconds.

No painting in the office at the construction site. Levi and Irish heading back.

Same. Any other locations we should look?

It will be morning soon. We'll tail Nico when he's released.

Roger.

"We're back to square one." Olivia sighed, her heart aching. "And my sister is still a hostage."

The only thing holding her together was the fact that she was with Becker. He was her rock in this sea of uncertainty.

She glanced at the time on the dash. It was nearly three o'clock. Like Trace had said, it would soon be morning.

Nico would be freed. Everyone would be following him, from the Romanos to the feds. Her sister's life hung in the balance of who got to him and the painting first.

Chapter Thirteen

Becker handed the keys over to the valet and escorted Olivia into the Ritz-Carlton.

Levi, Irish, Matt and Trace rose from the plush seating in the lobby and met them halfway to the elevators.

"We're going to catch a few hours of sleep," Trace said. "I wanted you to know we'll be up early to get to the jail before they release Nico. Levi and I will follow him wherever he goes for as long as it takes for him to get the painting."

Olivia nodded. "You might be wasting your time. He's not stupid. He'll know that he'll be followed."

"I'll be monitoring the internet for any sign of his coordinating a sale," Matt said. "Until he makes his move, we have nothing to go on."

"I know." Olivia's shoulders sagged. "I'm tired. I think I'll get a couple of hours' sleep too. Wake me if you hear anything?"

"I will," Trace said.

Becker's chest tightened. If he could, he'd take all her pain away. To do that, he'd have to free her sister. And that wasn't going to happen without that painting.

"I'm going up with her," Becker said. "I'll be down early for an update."

Trace nodded. "I'm sorry things didn't work out the way we'd hoped at the warehouse."

Olivia nodded. "Me too. Thanks for trying."

Becker walked with Olivia to the elevator. Once inside, he reached for her hand and held it all the way up to their floor and down the hallway to their room.

Once inside, he pulled her into his arms and held her.

She didn't move for the longest time, her cheek pressed to his chest, her arms wrapped around his waist.

He wanted to promise her they'd find and free her sister, but he wasn't sure they would. Not alive, anyway. Not after what had happened at the warehouse.

The Romanos were playing for keeps. Even with the death of one of their own, they would stop at nothing to get their hands on that painting. Including trying to kill Tacey Rogers. If Olivia's sister stopped being of value to them, they'd dispose of her as well rather than go to jail for kidnapping.

Becker stroked Olivia's hair back from her face and tipped her chin upward. "Are you going to be okay?"

She nodded. "It's not over yet. I have to be okay to see this through. As long as she's still alive, I have to fight to get my sister back."

His heart swelled at her loyalty and determination. "I'm with you on this. Whatever we have to do. Even breaking and entering."

Her lips quirked. "Yes, you did. And thank you for being there. I doubt very much I would have been able to crawl through that window so easily."

"Anything for a pretty lady," he said and bent to brush his lips across her forehead.

She tipped her head back and captured his lips with

her own. "I don't know what I would have done if you hadn't come into my shop to buy a vase for your mother."

"And I'm still wondering what it would be like to go out on a date with you."

She stared up into his eyes. "I think we're past the first-date awkwardness."

"Maybe," he said. "But we're not past the first date. I'm taking a rain check."

She chuckled. "You're on."

He brushed his thumb across her cheek. "You can have the shower first."

"Thanks." Olivia gathered her clothes and toiletries, entered the bathroom and closed the door.

Less than a second later, she opened the door and caught his gaze. "Wanna join me?"

He frowned. "Sweetheart, I don't ever want to take advantage of you when you're sad."

Her lips twisted. "Then can I take advantage of *you*?" She gave him a tentative smile.

He loved that she could tease when her world was upside down, how she made him feel when she was near.

Becker took a step toward her. "Are you sure this is what you want?"

She nodded and left the door open as she walked toward the shower, shedding her clothing as she went.

With a groan, Becker followed. He couldn't resist the beautiful artist, and he didn't want to. He went into the bathroom, closed the door and joined her in the shower.

They soaped each other's bodies, lingering beneath the warm spray until their skin pruned and the water chilled.

Drying her off was as captivating as washing her. Before he was halfway through, he'd gone well past his ability to control himself.

Becker scooped Olivia up in his arms and carried her into the bedroom, where he laid her on the bed and proceeded to make love to her, slow and gentle. She'd been through so much in the past couple of days. He wanted to relieve some of her stress, not create more.

He brought her to climax before he claimed his own. When they were both sated and sleepy, he pulled her into his arms and held her close for what was left of the night, loving the way she fit against him and how soft her skin was.

He could get used to holding her every night and waking with her in the morning. This was what he'd wanted when he was looking for love.

No.

She was who he'd wanted. Not just any woman to make a family with. He wanted someone who was loyal to the point she would sacrifice her own life to save her sister. Someone who was talented and humble yet independent and confident. Someone who inspired him to be a better man.

He held her closer, breathing in her scent, hoping what they were experiencing wasn't just a passing fling. It wasn't for him. He prayed she could see him as part of her future.

Not wanting to miss a moment with her, he lay awake until sleep claimed him.

MORNING CAME TOO SOON. The couple of hours of sleep he'd managed to get weren't enough but would have to do. Today could be the day they resolved everything outstanding in the case of the missing witness and one-of-a-kind painting.

Or it could be the day everything went to hell. Too

many variables were still up in the air for Becker to lie in bed, enjoying the company of a woman, no matter how beautiful she was.

They had to come up with a plan to save Olivia's sister and keep Nico Salvatore in jail.

Saving Jasmine seemed to boil down to finding that painting and trading it for her.

But only Nico knew where he'd stashed it. Letting him out of jail seemed to be the only way for them to locate it.

Becker lay for a long moment, taking in every detail of waking up with Olivia, from how warm and soft she was up against his body to the way she'd draped a leg over his in her sleep.

As much as he wanted to stay with her, he needed to see if Matt and Trace had come up with any other ideas on how to resolve the situation without anyone else dying.

Slowly, he eased out of the bed, careful not to wake her. He dressed in the bathroom and returned to the bedside.

Olivia remained asleep; Becker was glad. She'd barely gotten any sleep since her sister had been taken.

He jotted down a note telling her where he'd be and left it on his pillow.

Then he left the room and took the elevator down to the lobby lounge, where he found Trace and Matt with cups of coffee and pastries for breakfast.

"Morning," he grunted, not quite ready to converse until he'd had his own first sip of hot black coffee. He passed them and headed straight for the bar, where he ordered coffee. Once he had a cup in his hand, he joined the two men at a table, where Matt had his laptop open and humming.

He took a reviving sip and sighed. "Okay, what are we going to do to save Olivia's sister?"

"We need to find the painting," Trace said. "That's all there is to it. Without it, we can't negotiate her release."

"What about taking this to the police?" Becker asked.

"They'd go to Romano, he'd deny any wrongdoing and we'd be in the same place. Romano isn't going to keep her where the police will find her, and he won't admit he has her." Trace tapped his fingers on the surface of the table.

"I got a call from Deputy Jones just before I left my room," Matt said. "She was in contact with the jail where they're keeping Nico. When she inquired about his phone calls, they reported he'd made calls to his lawyer, his father and his wife."

Becker's cup was almost to his mouth when Matt mentioned Nico's wife. "He called his wife?"

Matt nodded. "At seven this morning."

"Probably making sure someone will pick him up when he's released," Trace said.

Becker shook his head. "We overheard Lana Etheridge talking about his relationship with his wife. She said his wife hated him and only stayed married so that she could continue to live at the Salvatore estate." He frowned at Matt. "Lana claimed Nico and his wife had not lived together for over a year."

"So?"

"Why would he call her after a year of living with his girlfriend?" Becker ran a hand through his hair. "It doesn't make sense."

"Unless he got her to stash the painting the night of the murder," Trace said.

"I thought the video cameras at the Salvatore estate

hadn't recorded any comings and goings that night and didn't have any gaps in footage," Becker said.

Matt's fingers flew over the keyboard. "I'm looking up Nico's phone records. He didn't make any calls around the time of the murder or even shortly afterward."

"Check Briana's—Nico's wife—phone records?" Becker asked.

"On it." Matt continued to work the keyboard, holding silent for a few minutes before he scowled. "She had a call come in after one in the morning from an unknown number and talked for several minutes. She called that number back thirty minutes later."

"That still doesn't account for the fact she didn't leave the Salvatore estate that night," Becker pointed out.

"Probably because she wasn't there that night. She has a charge on her credit card for three nights at the Hotel Zaza resort spa." Matt glanced up. "She could have met him somewhere for him to hand over the painting."

"Why would she do that?" Becker asked.

"Loyalty to the family that feeds her?" Matt suggested.

"But she hated him, according to Lana," Becker insisted. "She could have turned him in and he would have gone to jail, never to bother her again."

"He could divorce her from jail," Trace said. "And if he did, she wouldn't get to live with the family anymore."

"That's messed up," Matt said. "But then, she might not have a way of supporting herself. Especially if she's become accustomed to the lifestyle."

"True." Becker's eyes narrowed. "We need to watch her. Everyone will be watching Nico."

"When is Nico supposed to get out of jail?"

"I called earlier," Trace said. "They said they would

make a decision by nine o'clock this morning if the witness did not come forward."

Becker glanced at his watch. "That's only thirty minutes from now."

"The guy at the jail said they'd make the decision at eight, but they'd be sure to stretch out his release paperwork to make it last all day."

"That doesn't give us much time." Becker glanced across the table at Trace. "I'll stake out Mrs. Nico this morning."

"Who are we staking out?"

Becker turned to find Olivia standing behind his chair, wearing the black trousers from the day before and a cream-colored blouse. The contrast between the blouse and her black hair was stunning. Becker couldn't help staring at this woman, who'd been incredible in the shower and in bed just a few hours earlier.

"Briana Salvatore, Nico's wife," Trace said.

Her brow furrowed. "Why? I thought she hated Nico."

"Maybe, but he's been in contact with her since he's been in jail," Becker said. "And we just learned that she received a call in the middle of the night from a strange number the night of Eduardo's murder."

"You think she might have the painting?" Olivia pulled up a chair at the table and sat down.

"It's a possibility," Trace said.

"If she hated him so much," Olivia said with a frown, "why would she cover for him in a murder case?"

"Family loyalty?" Irish offered.

"Or maybe even more… A *test* of family loyalty," Matt said.

"Are we just going to follow her around and see if she leads us to the painting?" Olivia's glance shot from

Becker to Trace and back. "She may never do that. Or she could wait until days or weeks after Nico's release. Jasmine might not have that much time. The Romanos won't want to keep her that long."

Becker drew in a breath and let it out. "Then, if I can get her alone, I'll ask her point-blank if she has the painting."

Olivia met and held his gaze for a long moment. Then she nodded. "I'm ready when you are."

"Let's get a bite to eat before we spend the day sitting in a vehicle, waiting for Nico's wife to make a move."

"Okay, but I don't want to take any chances of missing her going to the painting." Olivia shifted in her seat. "I have the distinct feeling that we're running out of time."

Becker felt the same. With Nico getting out of jail, Olivia's sister was in even more danger than she would be if Romano got tired of dealing with her. Nico would also be after her to keep her quiet about witnessing him killing Eduardo.

If Briana knew where the painting was, they'd just have to get it from her.

OLIVIA AND BECKER opted to grab something to eat on the road at a fast-food restaurant rather than wait for a full-service meal that could take over an hour at the Ritz. Matt had given them the address of the Salvatore estate.

With no other clues as to the location of the painting or her sister, Olivia was ready to pull her hair out.

While she and Becker followed Briana Salvatore, Irish and Levi would watch Romano and follow him, hoping he would lead them to Jasmine.

Matt and Trace would follow Nico as his situation unfolded. So far, the authorities holding him were dragging their feet, processing "release" paperwork, which was both buying them time to find Jasmine and slowing them down on locating the painting.

What they had to keep in mind was that Nico may not need or want to dig up the painting anytime soon. He could sit on it for days, months or even years.

Olivia's heart sank to the pit of her belly at the thought of Jasmine languishing in whatever prison in which the Romanos had incarcerated her. She wouldn't give up on finding her sister. She just hoped the Romanos wouldn't give up on trying to make the trade for the painting.

Nico and his family would be searching for Jasmine as well, knowing Nico would go back to jail should she resurface. He would be less likely to bring the painting out of hiding to sell until he guaranteed her silence.

Killed her.

Olivia sat in the SUV beside Becker, her hands clasped in her lap to keep them from shaking.

Becker sat calm, cool and collected, as if he did this kind of thing on a daily basis.

Staking out thieves, fighting bad guys and searching for missing witnesses weren't on Olivia's résumé, nor did she want them to be. She'd led a pretty sheltered life with her artist parents, living in a small town, quietly throwing pottery that sold worldwide.

She'd gladly go back to that life as soon as she found her sister and brought her home safely. Maybe she'd convince Jasmine to stay in Whiskey Gulch and pursue her own artistic medium. She'd been quite good at painting with acrylics, oils and watercolors.

Perhaps she'd meet and fall in love with one of Trace Travis's Outriders, if he hired any more, as opposed to any of the men she'd grown up with. Life didn't have to be boring in Whiskey Gulch.

Heck, Olivia could *use* a little boredom after all that had happened in the past few days.

Becker had pulled off onto a rutted, overgrown farm road less than a tenth of a mile past the gated entrance leading into the Salvatore estate. He'd driven a mile past the gate before concluding it was the only logical entry and egress to the property situated north of Dallas in the ever-expanding suburbs.

Matt had tapped into Briana's most current cell phone records and determined she was still at the estate. She had also received another call from the jailhouse where Nico was being held.

With nothing else to do but wait and watch, Olivia glanced over at Becker. "I bet you didn't expect your first assignment as an Outrider to fall in your lap."

He chuckled. "I didn't expect the first woman I met in Whiskey Gulch to be so pretty, even when she was up to her elbows in mud."

A smile tugged at the corners of her lips. "All because you wanted to find a gift for your mother. I found that to be incredibly sweet. I hope she likes the vase."

"I loved it. The colors were what drew me to that particular piece." He glanced at her. "My mother had mentioned how beautiful your work was when she visited the Cavendish Gallery. She was right. You're very talented."

Her cheeks heated. As a lone artist working in a small town, she didn't often hear the words of praise that validated her creations. Sales helped, but words in person were even better. Coming from Becker…they were special. "Thank you."

"Where did you learn how to make pottery?" he asked.

"My parents," she answered. "Sort of. My mother painted in oils and acrylics. My father was a sculptor. I learned to love clay from him. He used a kiln for his work, and one day he bought a larger kiln that came with a pottery wheel. He gave me the older, smaller kiln." Olivia smiled at the memories. "When I asked about the wheel, my father got it out, dusted it off and taught himself how to throw pots so he could teach me."

"How old were you?"

"It was around my eighth birthday. He'd sit behind me and hold my hands around the clay, showing me how to work it while the wheel turned. The man had the patience of a saint. I would get frustrated when the pot was bottom-heavy or misshapen. He encouraged me to practice often. On my birthday, he gifted me with twenty-five pounds of clay, five different kinds of glazes, throwing tools and a monogrammed apron." She grinned. "The rest is history. I've even started sculpting. Since my father and mother died, I felt like I should carry on some of the family traditions."

"No painting?" Becker asked.

She shook her head. "Jasmine inherited that skill. She's really good too. Like Mom."

"Why did she work as a curator instead of an artist?"

Olivia shrugged. "She loves art of all kinds and loves discovering new artists and bringing their work to the attention of collectors." Her mouth twisted. "And they don't call them 'starving artists' for nothing. To survive as an artist, you practically have to sell your soul to make enough to pay rent. She works as a curator to pay the bills and paints in oils and watercolors in her spare time. It helps that she really loves her job and meeting people. She was always the more outgoing sister." Her smile faded. "I hope this doesn't change that about her."

Becker reached across the console for one of Olivia's hands. "You'll be there for her, as you have been all along."

She nodded. "I wish she'd move back to Whiskey Gulch, where I can keep an eye on her." Olivia looked over at him. "Is that being too overprotective? As the older sister, I feel like it's my responsibility to look out for Jasmine now that my folks are gone."

"It's natural to want to protect your family. And family can be more than just blood relations." He looked out the window at the gate to the Salvatore estate. "I'd do anything for my brothers in arms. They've been there for me and had my back on a number of occasions."

"As I'm sure you've had theirs," Olivia added quietly.

"When Trace left the Deltas to take over the family ranch, it felt as if we'd lost one of our own. Irish followed shortly afterward, ready to start a life outside the military. We grieved and were happy for him at the same time. It's hard to have a 'real' life when you're deployable 365 days a year."

"Is that why you left the military?" Olivia asked.

He nodded. "My last mission ended in a helicopter crash."

Olivia gasped and squeezed his hand. "Thank God you survived."

His mouth set in a grim line before he responded. "Yeah, well, that was the problem… I survived with some injuries—but I lived." His tone was harsh and emotionally ragged.

Olivia's heart pinched hard in her chest. "Others didn't," she said. Not as a question but a statement of fact. She could see it in his face and the way he stared into the distance, as if he was looking into the past.

"I pulled my best buddy out of the wreckage, but I couldn't get to the others before the craft burst into flames." His fingers tightened painfully around hers.

Olivia bore the pain silently, knowing what he felt was so much worse.

"Johnny had always dreamed of buying a house on a piece of land, settling his wife and newborn baby there and raising half a dozen more." Becker glanced down at her hand and loosened his grip. "He stayed with me until the medevac helicopter arrived. He wanted me to tell his wife and baby girl that he loved them. He wanted his wife to go on with life, be happy, marry again and have more babies. She was a wonderful mother who needed to have lots of kids to love. He made *me* promise to live life to the fullest and not wait for retirement to be happy."

Olivia nodded. "You never know when your number is up," she whispered. "I learned that from the death of my parents. They'd been saving for a long time to go on a trip to Peru. They'd wanted to see the ruins at Machu Picchu and visit the museums where they'd collected pottery from ancient civilizations. I was going to go with them."

"That was Johnny's point. Don't wait. Do the things you always wanted to. See Machu Picchu, have half a dozen children and a house on a couple of acres." He gave her a tight smile. "I was injured and my body recovered, but I couldn't unsee that helicopter on fire, my friends…my *family*…inside."

She looked at his pale face; the lines around his mouth and eyes were deeper than usual. "Is that why you held me back from the warehouse fire? Was that what you were seeing?"

He blinked as if coming back from his memories to where he was now, sitting beside her in the SUV, holding her hand. "I couldn't let you go into that building." His tone held so much pain, it made Olivia's heart ache.

"I'm glad you held me back. You were right. The firefighters were equipped for that kind of rescue. I would have added to their work." She glanced up as a movement caught her eye.

The gate to the Salvatore estate slid open, and a sleek white sports car drove through and out onto the highway headed into the city.

"Looks like a white BMW sports car," Olivia said.

"Matt said Briana has one just like that registered in her name." Becker shifted the SUV into Drive and pulled out onto the road, maintaining a reasonable distance.

Sitting on the edge of her seat, Olivia craned her neck, fully focused on following the woman to wherever she was going. She could be the key to getting Jasmine back.

Then, when the world returned to normal, Olivia might follow the advice Becker's friend Johnny had given him as he was dying.

Live life to the fullest.

She cast a quick glance toward the man effortlessly following the sports car.

Life could be full and satisfying if she let herself fall in love with a man like Becker. He was nothing like Mike.

Yeah, he sounded like he had PTSD and was in the process of starting over. He might have some baggage, having been stood up at the altar and losing his friends to war—but then, who *didn't* have baggage? Besides, her existence hadn't been all that rewarding. It had been what it was—just existing. Not living.

When she got her sister back and they returned to

Whiskey Gulch, she wasn't going to wait to start living her life to the fullest. She was going to cash in that rain check and go out on a date with this amazing man. She wondered if he'd be interested in traveling to Peru.

Chapter Fourteen

Becker had never opened up to anyone about what had happened that night when their Black Hawk had been shot down. Not even to the therapist he'd been ordered to see for the two months following his return to the States.

Why had he spilled his guts to Olivia? She had enough to worry about, with her sister missing and now having to follow a murdering thief's wife around.

Once they entered the metro area—and the heavy traffic always present on the highways—Becker struggled to keep up with the little white sports car. Built for speed and maneuverability, the car had no trouble weaving in and out of the clogged lanes.

The large SUV was a challenge. But, with Olivia's assistance, they managed to keep up with Briana all the way into the city. She continued deeper into the downtown area and finally pulled into the parking garage of a tall building not far from the Cavendish Art Gallery.

Becker closed the distance between the SUV and the sports car, afraid he'd miss her turning into a parking space before he could round the next corner.

It wasn't long before she parked and got out.

The woman wore a black dress that fit her slim body to perfection; a black hat with a broad brim; and a thin, shiny gold belt around her middle. She carried a matching shiny gold purse. She strode into the building in three-inch black stilettos like she was on a mission.

Even before Becker could park, Olivia unbuckled her seat belt and shoved open her door.

"Wait. What are you doing?" he demanded.

"I'm going to follow her in. You need to stay out here and watch her car in case I miss where she goes." Olivia didn't wait for his response. Instead, she jumped out and headed into the building, hot on the heels of Nico's wife.

"Damn," he muttered beneath his breath and backed into a parking space across from the white sports car. He got out of the SUV and hustled into the building after the elevator door closed with the two women inside.

He prayed Briana wasn't armed. She might be getting desperate and paranoid if she really did know where the painting was and had a date with the devil to return it. Nico wasn't above killing to get his hands on the artwork. Briana would be smart to be cautious. She'd have to be two steps ahead to stay alive in the Salvatore family.

Becker entered the glass-enclosed vestibule housing the elevator and watched the numbers from the elevator Briana and Olivia had gotten into climb. It stopped on the eleventh floor and then came down to the fifth.

Becker checked the list of businesses on the eleventh floor and frowned. "The Women's Health Group?"

He read the names of the gynecologists and obstetricians listed beneath.

Becker was glad he hadn't been the one to jump in the elevator with Briana; he would have struggled to come up with a reason for going to the exact same floor.

He went back to the SUV and climbed in. If Briana

was there for an appointment, it could take more than an hour before she and Olivia came back out.

With time on his hands, he called Trace to report in. "We followed Briana Salvatore to a building in downtown Dallas."

"Did you follow her in?" Trace asked.

Becker laughed. "No, and I'm glad I didn't. She's visiting a women's clinic. Olivia jumped in the elevator with her. I'm standing guard over her vehicle to make sure he doesn't slip past us."

"Good," Trace said. "Matt and I are outside the jailhouse, along with an army of reporters ready and waiting for Nico's release."

"No sign of that happening anytime soon?" Becker asked.

"No telling when it'll happen." Trace said something in the background to Matt that Becker couldn't make out. "Matt got a text from Irish and Levi. Romano is on the move. They're following."

"I'll probably be here at least an hour," Becker said. "Let me know if anything changes."

"Roger." Trace ended the call.

Becker sat across from the white BMW, tapping his fingers on the steering wheel, wishing he could be a fly on the wall of wherever Olivia was. He wasn't good at sitting still, preferring action to inaction. But he was smart enough to stay put.

If Briana gave Olivia the slip, he'd be there to follow. One way or the other, they needed to corner Briana and get her to hand over the painting. They'd do their best to keep her safe until Jasmine was freed and Nico was caught and sent back to jail.

With so much time on his hands and nothing to do

with it, his thoughts turned back in time to when he was engaged and what had gone wrong with that event in his life. He hoped he'd learned enough from that experience to not screw up his next foray into matters of the heart.

He'd never believed in love at first sight…until he'd met a certain artist with muddy hands and spots of clay on her face. She was strong and talented, and she cared about family.

Becker recognized he had a long way to go before he could face another fire without the flashbacks of the helicopter crash. His heart would always hurt when he remembered the friends he'd lost—but maybe, if he took it slowly with Olivia, they could build the kind of love he'd always dreamed of. One day, he might ask her to marry him. And as scary as it might be, he wanted kids.

As an only child, he'd always wanted brothers and sisters, and he'd dreamed of the day when he would have children of his own. He wouldn't stop at one. He wanted enough so that none of them would be lonely.

He wasn't sure how Olivia felt about children. Apparently, she was the oldest of the two sisters. She'd said Jasmine was the only family she had left. He wasn't sure when her parents had passed or how old Jasmine was when that had happened. Had Olivia shouldered the responsibility of raising her sister? Was she tired of being a parent?

She'd talked about the trip to Peru she'd planned with her parents. Was she more interested in travel than settling down to raise a family?

As much as he wanted a family, could he give up the idea if Olivia wasn't interested? He thought about the woman and how much he enjoyed being with her. Yes, he wanted kids. But kids grew up and moved away. If he married, it would be for life. His wife would be with him always. He could see himself growing old with Olivia. If she wanted to travel and see the world, he would travel with her and enjoy every second they were together.

He chuckled softly. "Dude, you're getting ahead of yourself. Relax. You don't want to scare her away by planning the wedding before you've gone out on your first date."

Pulling his thoughts away from dating and marrying Olivia, he went back through everything he knew about the murder, the stolen painting, Nico's wife and girlfriend, Giovanni Romano, and Tacey Rogers. Was he missing any clues?

He hoped and prayed Briana Salvatore could shed some light on the location of the Wyeth—before Nico left the jailhouse.

OLIVIA DIVED INTO the elevator as the doors closed, with no idea of what she might say or do.

"What floor?" Briana asked.

Olivia glanced at the number Briana had pushed and forced a smile. "We're going to the same place. How fortunate."

"I've been with Dr. Adams for the past four years. Which doctor do you see in the group?"

For a moment, Olivia went blank. *Doctor? Group?* She gave Briana a weak smile. "I'm new to the group, and I'm afraid to say—I've forgotten which doctor I have an appointment with."

Briana smiled back. "Don't worry. They'll have it in their system. Are you here for a regular visit or are you expecting?" She held up her hands. "Not that you look pregnant or anything. It's just that so many of the patients here are pregnant, I just assume they're either already pregnant, trying to get pregnant or have just had their babies and are back for a checkup."

Olivia laughed and avoided giving an answer by asking, "Which one are you?"

"For years, I was one of those trying to get pregnant… for all the wrong reasons."

Olivia frowned. "I don't understand."

Briana's lips pressed together. "I thought it would help save my marriage. It took a couple of miscarriages to realize nothing was going to save my marriage. He never loved me and never will."

"I'm sorry. That must be hard, losing a baby and knowing you're losing your marriage as well."

"Yeah, but you can lie around feeling sorry for yourself or you can get up and get on with living."

"That sounds like a healthy attitude." Olivia was beginning to like Nico's wife and was feeling really sorry for the woman married to such an uncaring man. And the fact that he was a murderer—well, that made for a lousy situation all around.

The elevator door opened into the lobby of the Women's Health Group.

"Good luck," Briana said. "I hope your appointment goes well."

"You too," Olivia said. She hung back, allowing Briana to check in for her appointment first. Once she had been escorted back to an examination room, Olivia found a corner to wait and watch for when Briana came back out.

While waiting, she studied the other patients. As Briana had said, many were young women in various stages of pregnancy—from smiling giddily and waving black-

and-white sonogram printouts to others who appeared to have swallowed a whole watermelon and could barely get out of the chair to waddle into the examination rooms.

Most were glowing with the expectation of a happy, healthy baby at the end of their pregnancy.

And every one of those women, even those with barely a baby bump, rested a hand on her belly as if reassuring or protecting the life within.

Without really thinking about it, Olivia's hand went to her flat stomach. What would it feel like to have a baby growing inside her? Would she be as ecstatic as most of the women in the room? She'd heard of morning sickness during the first three months of pregnancy—would she be one of the unlucky ones to experience it? And what about those who went into labor too early for the fetus to be viable? Or what if she was like Briana and miscarried, or what if she gave birth prematurely, before the baby had a chance to survive outside the womb?

All the things that could go wrong made the idea of procreating frightening.

But as she looked around the room at the loving smiles as the mothers-to-be looked down at their swollen bellies, all she saw was hope for the future. Of the baby, new beginnings and love.

Olivia's heart swelled. Even when she was dating Mike, she hadn't given much thought to children. She was just beginning to establish herself as an artist, starting to make a little money with her work and renovating the home she'd inherited from her parents.

Now that she was more financially secure, more settled and nearing her thirtieth birthday, she had begun to wonder if she'd ever have children.

Becker would make beautiful babies.

The thought popped into her head and shocked her with how easily it had come. And now that she'd thought it, she couldn't unthink the image of a little boy with shiny blond hair and blue eyes that would melt her soul. Or a little girl with long blond hair and blue eyes. She'd have her daddy wrapped around her little finger so fast…

The woman who married Becker would be very lucky. He was kind, funny, and loyal to family and friends. He'd take care of his own and be there when they needed him most.

What would it be like to have his baby growing in her belly? Her heart skipped several beats as she went over the past two nights with Becker. He'd used protection the first night.

Her stomach churned. Last night, they had been too caught up in each other to think about protection. What if…?

At that moment, Briana emerged from the door leading to the exam rooms. She slipped a pair of sunglasses over her red-rimmed eyes and dabbed her nose with a tissue; then she stuffed the tissue in the purse looped over her arm, squared her shoulders and headed for the elevator.

Olivia jumped to her feet and once again dived into the elevator as the doors slid shut.

Smiling brightly, she asked, "How did your visit go?"

Briana maintained her squared shoulders for exactly three seconds. Then she sagged and buried her face in her hands. "It's impossible. I don't know what I'm going to do." Her shoulders shook with her quiet sobs. "I'm so scared."

Olivia slipped an arm around the woman's shoulders. "You want to talk about it? I'm a good listener."

"It won't help. There's no way out of this mess. None." She pulled her sunglasses off and looked into Olivia's eyes. "And I'm pregnant," she wailed.

"Oh, sweetie. Where can we go to talk? I don't feel right leaving you alone."

"You can't help me. No one can." The door to the elevator opened up into the glass vestibule inside the parking garage.

"You can't drive," Olivia said. "Not in your state. Is there anyone you want me to call? Or would you rather I drive you somewhere?"

Briana dug in her purse and handed Olivia her keys. "Please, take me anywhere. Away from everyone. I need to get as far away from here as possible."

"What do you mean by 'here'? This building?" Olivia asked.

"This building, this city, Texas, this godforsaken country. I can't get far enough away to save this baby." She looked at Olivia and laughed, choking on a sob. "I don't even know your name and I feel safer with you than with my family."

"My name is Olivia Swann. I promise you I won't hurt you or your baby. Let's go find a place to talk. You can tell me what's wrong, and I'll see if I can help. If nothing else, you can bend my ear for a while." She gave Briana a little smile. "You can start by telling me your name."

"Briana," she said.

"Do you know of a coffee shop? Or, in your condition, maybe a smoothie shop would be better."

Briana dug her tissue out of her purse and dabbed at her nose, slipped her sunglasses over her eyes and stepped out of the glass vestibule. "There's one just around the corner. We can walk there and leave the car in the parking garage."

Olivia handed Briana her keys. "Then I won't need these for now. And hopefully, by the time we get back here, you'll feel well enough to drive." She held out her arm for Briana.

The young mother-to-be slipped her hand through the crook of Olivia's elbow and leaned on her as they walked past the dark SUV, where Becker sat behind the wheel, his gaze on Olivia.

She mouthed the words *I'll be back in one hour* and held up one finger, all out of Briana's view.

He nodded and waited until they passed and were stepping out of the garage and onto the sidewalk beyond before he got out of the SUV.

As Olivia and Briana turned to the right, Olivia glanced back to see Becker following them.

She didn't feel threatened by Briana, but being with the woman could be a threat in itself if Nico or any of the Salvatore clan decided to take her out. And they could have come to the same conclusion that she had the painting and were following her, hoping she would lead them to it.

Add in the fact the Romanos were probably looking for the painting, and Briana was definitely a target.

Fortunately, the smoothie shop was inside a mall, not on the street, where they would be vulnerable to a drive-by shooting.

All these thoughts raced through Olivia's head as she walked seemingly calmly alongside the ticking time bomb that was Nico Salvatore's wife, not knowing if or when she should run or duck for cover.

Chapter Fifteen

Olivia settled the distraught woman in a seat at the back of the smoothie shop after they'd ordered fruit smoothies and a plate of crackers and cheese.

"First of all, congratulations on your baby," Olivia said, starting off the conversation. She held up a hand when Briana opened her mouth to protest. "A baby is something to celebrate. Take it at face value." She held up her cup and tapped it against Briana's in salute to her pregnancy.

"I want to be happy. I've known for three months that I was pregnant, but I've miscarried two other babies in the first trimester."

"And you've made it past the first trimester." Olivia smiled. "Your baby has a better chance of making it through the entire pregnancy if it makes it past the first three months."

Briana nodded. "Yes. But it might have been better if I'd miscarried this one as well." She looked away while her hand rose to rest on her still-flat belly.

"Why do you say that? What could be so bad that you'd wish your baby away?"

"I don't want to bring him into the mess of my life."

"Who says you have to?" Olivia grimaced. "I don't

mean for you to get rid of your baby. Not at all. I can tell you care and want the best for him. But you don't necessarily have to bring the child into the life you live now. Can't you make changes to your world and make it better for your baby?"

Briana shook her head. "You don't understand. I'm Briana Salvatore. I made the mistake of marrying into the Salvatore family." Her voice became a choked whisper. "Once a member, you're a member for life."

"And by that, you mean the only way out is to end your life?" Olivia shook her head. "You can't think that way."

"I don't see any other way. I'm married to a man who has been accused of committing murder. You know him. His name is all over the news. Nico Salvatore."

"I know," Olivia said. "I understand they're releasing him today." She spoke the words in an even tone with no emotion. Inside, she was screaming and gnashing her teeth, wanting to get to her sister before Nico did. She had to keep cool. Briana was already at the end of her tether. She could drive her little sports car off a bridge, as distraught as she was. That couldn't happen until she handed over the painting.

She *had* to have the painting. She was Jasmine's last hope.

"They're going to release a murderer, and he's going to come after me." Briana closed her eyes and drew in a shaky breath. "I might not get to see this baby born. I might not live that long."

"Do you think your husband will hurt you?"

Briana nodded and then shook her head. "Yes and no." Her hand went to her belly again. "He's already threatened my baby. He'll kill it if I don't do what he says."

Her voice caught on another sob. "And when he finds out who's the baby's father, he'll probably kill me as well."

Olivia blinked. That was a twist she hadn't seen coming but should have. Though Nico's girlfriend had said Briana and Nico hadn't lived together for over a year, he still could have gone to his wife, had sex and left to stay at his girlfriend's house.

She bit down hard on her tongue to keep from asking who the father was. "He knows the baby isn't his?"

Briana nodded. "He told me I could keep the child if I did what he said and kept my mouth shut." She pressed her knuckles to her mouth and looked into Olivia's eyes. "And I'm telling you. He's going to kill my child."

Olivia took the woman's hand and squeezed it gently. "No, he's not. Not if we can keep him in jail."

"*We?* How will you be able to help? You don't know what he's capable of."

"I have a good idea," Olivia said. "You see, it's families like the Salvatores and the Romanos who terrorize people to get their way. I know because the Romanos are holding my sister hostage, and I can't find her to free her."

Briana's eyes widened. "The witness?"

Olivia nodded. "That witness has a name. Jasmine Swann. My little sister. She saw Nico murder Eduardo Romano and leave with the Wyeth painting."

Briana pushed to her feet so fast, her chair fell backward. "I can't…" She shook her head. "I have to go."

Olivia touched her arm without grabbing it and took a leap of faith that her gut was right. "Briana," she whispered, "I know you have the painting."

She shook her head, her eyes wide and wild. "No. This can't be happening. No one knows. No one would suspect a wife he hadn't seen or touched in over a year."

"It's only a matter of time before the authorities piece it together, as well as the Romanos and the rest of the Salvatore family."

"I'll deny it." She sank into the chair. "I never wanted to be involved. I should have taken it to the police… I was so afraid I'd lose this baby. I don't want to lose him. He's mine. He's the only good thing in my life." Her voice cracked, and tears slipped down her cheeks. "And he doesn't deserve this." She leaned across the table and gripped Olivia's hands. "Help me. Please. I don't know what to do."

Olivia scooted her chair around and pulled Briana into her arms. "I can help you put Nico in jail for good."

"How? He always has a way of getting out of trouble."

"My sister saw the murder. She will testify…if she can make it to the hearing." Olivia tipped Briana's face up and stared into her eyes. "That's where you can help me, her and your baby. We have to get to Jasmine before Nico does."

"How can I help you do that?"

"The Romanos want to make a trade." She held Briana's gaze. "My sister for the Wyeth painting."

Before Olivia finished speaking, Briana was already shaking her head. "I can't. He'll kill my baby. He'll kill me."

"Not if he's in jail," Olivia said. "The sooner we make the trade, the sooner my sister surfaces and the courts can't set Nico free. But we have to hurry. They're going to release Nico sometime today."

"I know. He wants me to get the painting to him somehow." Briana stared down at her hands held in Olivia's. "What if they let him out first?"

"Either way, we have to free my sister and protect her.

As soon as the authorities know she's alive and able to testify, they will arrest Nico again. We have people to protect her and you, if or when the time comes."

"It won't work. Nico never pays for his crimes. Never." She rubbed her arm. "He beat me so many times, and the police did nothing. I was glad when he moved in with Lana. Glad he left me alone." Her brows furrowed. "He murdered Eduardo."

"Did he tell you he killed Eduardo?" Olivia asked.

Briana nodded. "He told me he'd killed him and he'd kill me if I told anyone or if I told anyone he met with me that night."

"Briana. Will you help me free my sister? Will you help me put Nico away for good so that he can't hurt you or the baby?"

She chewed on her lip, her eyes wide, terrified. "It's the right thing to do," she whispered. "But I'm afraid." Again, she rubbed her arm as if remembering the times he'd hit her.

"If we put him away, he'll never hurt you again."

Briana nodded. "You know that if he's released, he'll come for the painting."

"Yes, he will," Olivia said.

"And he'll come for your sister." She snorted softly. "He won't be making a trade. He'll kill her like he killed Eduardo. And he'll kill the Romanos for trying to take the painting away from him. He says it's his. He wants to sell it, buy an island and move there with Lana."

Olivia's mouth twitched. "He'll be disappointed when she doesn't want to leave her boyfriend to go with him."

Briana's eyebrows rose. Then she laughed. "It would serve him right. He flaunted her in front of me. Nico never loved me. He only wanted me to have his babies and carry on the Salvatore name." Her mouth twisted into a crooked smile. "The joke's on him. It wasn't me who couldn't conceive. His sperm wasn't viable. And he'll be in a rage when he discovers the baby will carry on the Salvatore name. The baby's father is Vincenzo Salvatore." Her chin lifted, and she pushed back her shoulders. "Nico's father is the only member of the family who treated me with kindness when Nico beat me. The only man who doesn't treat me like dirt to be kicked in the corner."

Olivia shook her head, a grin spreading across her face. "You do have a complicated life."

Briana's shoulders sagged. "He doesn't know I'm pregnant."

"Why don't you tell him?"

"Because I don't know how loyal he is to his son. If I help put Nico in jail, will he hate me for betraying the family?" Briana shook her head. "I don't know."

"Briana, either way, you have to keep Nico in jail, or he'll hurt you and the baby. If the Salvatores take it badly, we can get you away from here to somewhere safe for you and the baby. You have to think of the baby now. He's your number one concern. As long as Nico sees you as a threat, he'll hold your baby's life over your head to get you to do what he wants."

"And there's no guarantee he won't hurt my baby anyway. He can't be trusted. He's not an honorable man." Briana chewed on her bottom lip. "You can keep me and my baby safe?"

Olivia nodded. "I know honorable former military men who will lay down their lives to protect you and your baby. But we have to hurry if we want to keep Nico in jail."

"I'm the only one who knows where the painting is. Even if Nico gets out, he won't know where to find it."

Olivia bit back her frustration. Already, another hour had passed while they'd been in the smoothie shop. One more hour closer to Nico going free, and the chance to trade for her sister's life was slipping away.

"Where is the painting, Briana?" Olivia asked.

"I can't tell you," she said. "I'll take you there." Her eyes narrowed. "But only you." She tipped her head toward the front window of the shop that looked out over the mall's courtyard, where Becker sat on a bench, pretending to read a newspaper. "He can't come."

Olivia nodded. "Deal."

BECKER PEERED OVER the top of the newspaper as Olivia exited the smoothie store and marched right up to him.

"She knows I followed you?" He folded the paper, his gaze on the smoothie store in case Briana tried to make a run for it.

"Yes. I'm going with her to get the painting. Just me."

His stomach knotted. "Not a good idea. She could be leading you into a trap."

"My gut tells me she won't."

"*My* gut tells me not to trust any of the Salvatores." He reached out and grasped her hand. "Let me go with you."

She shook her head. "I told Briana I would go alone. It will show her that I trust her."

"And why should you trust her?"

"Because she's pregnant and doesn't want to lose the baby." She leaned close and pressed a kiss to his lips. "Track my phone. I've shared my location with you. But don't follow close enough for her to see you. I'll be okay."

"I don't trust her. Hell, I don't trust anyone with your

life." He lurched to his feet and pulled her into his arms. "Olivia, I like you too much to let you out of my sight in this city. Heck, I might even be in love with you. So don't go and get yourself killed."

Her cheeks turned a pretty shade of pink at his words. "You love me?"

"I'm pretty sure. But if that scares you, I can say I like you and want to see where it goes." He winked. "I promised myself I'd take it slow and start with a date."

"I think we're past that stage in our relationship. I think we passed that the first night." She glanced across at the entrance to the smoothie shop.

Briana emerged, looked left, then right, and finally her gaze settled on Olivia and Becker.

"I have to go before she changes her mind. She's terrified of Nico. Can you work with Trace and come up with a plan for the trade? As soon as I have the painting, we need to make it happen. Hopefully before Nico is set free."

Becker nodded. "I'll be within a couple minutes of you. No matter what happens, hold on and I'll be there."

Olivia leaned up on her tiptoes and brushed a kiss across his lips. "It might be too soon—and it's crazy to even think it—but I think I love you too." She spun around and hurried to join Nico Salvatore's wife.

Given how dangerous the mafia family could be, Becker wasn't happy. The love of his life was walking away with a murderer's wife.

He was on his phone, calling Trace, as soon as the two women disappeared around a corner.

Trace answered. "What's happening?"

"Olivia is leaving with Briana."

"Did she agree to give her the painting?"

Becker talked while on the move. "So she said. Briana insisted Olivia go with her alone."

"You didn't let her, did you?"

Becker didn't answer.

"Right. She's a strong-willed woman with a mind of her own. I have one of those too. You have her phone on tracker?"

"Bringing it up now. Olivia wants us to set up the trade as soon as she gets the painting. She has the contact number, but we'll need to be there as backup."

"If I know the way these guys work, they will want her to bring the painting and come alone," Trace said.

"We can't let that happen."

"And we won't."

"That's right." Becker wouldn't send Olivia in to face the Romanos alone. They might renege on their promise to trade her sister. *And take the painting, kill the women and leave.* "We need to prime the engine," Becker said.

"'Prime the engine'?"

"Give the Romanos a sense of urgency."

"How?"

"Gunter Kraus needs to make an offer they can't refuse, with a time limit. That way, when they get word from Olivia that she has the painting, they're eager to make the trade in a hurry."

"What kind of time limit?"

"Before Nico is released."

"That might not happen," Trace said. "They're rumbling about running out of excuses, and Nico's attorney is putting the screws to them."

"All the more reason to make it happen in a hurry." Becker ended the call and emerged from the mall onto the street. Olivia and Briana were nowhere in sight. He jogged toward the parking garage. As he grew closer, the little white BMW sports car blew out of the building and sped away.

His heart pounding hard in his chest, Becker ran inside the parking garage, jumped into the SUV and raced to the exit. Using the tracker on Olivia's phone, he found her already three blocks away.

He pulled out into the traffic and was forced to stop behind several vehicles stopped at a red light. When the light turned green, the vehicles in front of him eased forward so slowly, Becker nearly ground his teeth into nubs. Two of them turned, giving him the break he needed to speed ahead.

To the next red light.

A glance at the location of Olivia's phone made Becker groan. They'd reached a six-lane high-speed highway and were quickly putting miles between them.

By the time he reached the same highway, they had turned off onto another road, zigzagging through smaller streets until they came to a stop.

He prayed Briana wasn't leading Olivia into a trap. No matter how hard Becker tried, he could not get there any faster. Every time he passed a car, another pulled in front of him, slowing him down. The SUV wasn't a sports car; it didn't maneuver through traffic as efficiently.

By the time he reached the exit off the main highway, Olivia's phone was moving again.

It was headed back the way it had come.

His phone rang. Olivia's number was displayed on the screen. He answered with "Tell me you're okay."

"I am. I have the painting. I'm ready to contact Romano to arrange the trade."

"We're close to the zoo. Meet in the parking lot in fifteen minutes," Becker said.

"We'll be there," she said.

Becker hung up with her and then placed a call to Trace. "Meet us in the parking lot of the Dallas Zoo. Be there in fifteen minutes or less. And give me Matt."

"On our way," Trace said. "Here's Matt."

"Can you patch me through to Romano and mask my phone number?"

"Yup," Matt said. "Give me a second."

Becker turned off at the exit for the Dallas Zoo. A minute later, he pulled to a stop in a parking space far away from other vehicles and shifted into Park.

"You still there, Beck?" Matt asked.

"Roger," he responded.

"Okay, you're on," Matt said. "Romano's phone is ringing. The caller ID will come up as 'Unknown.'"

The phone rang four times, then stopped. Romano didn't say "hello," "yeah" or anything, but Becker could hear sounds in the background. He knew he was there.

"Gunter here," he said. "I'm leaving town today and want to take the Wyeth with me. Four million dollars if it gets to me before I fly out of here in two hours."

After a long pause, Romano said, "How will I contact you?"

"Don't worry. I'll contact you. Four million transferred on the spot when you hand it over. Make it happen." Becker ended the call and prayed his bluff had lit a fire under Romano to do whatever it took to get that painting.

Chapter Sixteen

Olivia breathed a sigh of relief when she and Briana pulled into the parking lot of the Dallas Zoo.

Becker had given her his location, and he was there, as he said he'd be.

As soon as Briana pulled her sports car to a stop next to the SUV, Olivia was out of the vehicle with the painting wrapped in brown paper and tied with twine.

Becker pulled her into his arms and hugged her, painting and all. "I hate Dallas traffic," he said, and he bent to kiss her full on the lips.

Briana climbed out of the car and stood, twisting her hands. "I'm still not totally convinced I've done the right thing."

"You have. You're saving my sister's life. Between the two of your testimonies, you'll put Nico away for life."

"I hope so," she said. "Whether or not it works, I'm taking you up on that offer to relocate me to start over as far away from Dallas, Texas, as I can get."

Becker took the painting from Olivia's hands and untied the twine. "I want to see what all the fuss is about." He carried it to the back of the SUV, opened the hatch, laid the picture on the carpet and unwrapped the paper.

"I checked it over," Olivia said. "It's the real deal."

Wyeth had painted a naked woman walking away from the viewer through a field of ripe wheat. Her hair was the color of the wheat, and her naked body seemed to be a part of the field. The sky stretched over her head in a steely blue unbroken by clouds.

"It's beautiful," Olivia said.

"Yes, it is," Becker said.

"It belongs in a museum," Olivia said. "Not in someone's private collection."

"That's for the owners to decide," Becker said. "But I agree. It belongs in a museum for everyone to enjoy. The man had talent."

Matt and Trace arrived a few moments later, with Irish and Levi bringing up the rear.

They gathered around the tailgate of the SUV and stared at the painting that would buy Jasmine's freedom.

"Now that we're all here, I need to contact Romano," Olivia said. "We can't risk Nico being released. I promised Briana we'd keep her safe."

Nico's wife stood back from the others, rubbing her arms as if she were cold. "Go," she said. "Trade that painting for your sister. I don't want to be the only one testifying against Nico."

Olivia turned to the Outriders. "What's the plan?"

"When you talk to Romano," Becker said, "don't agree to meeting him alone. Insist on at least one of us going with you." He held up his hands. "It can't be me. Romano will remember me from the gallery. And you'll need some kind of disguise to keep him from recognizing you as Gunter's girlfriend, Monique."

"I have makeup in my purse," Briana offered. "We can change her appearance with it. I also have a light blue scarf she can cover her hair with."

"That should do it." Trace turned to Levi. "You'll go with Olivia to make the trade."

"Trace, Irish, Matt and I will get there ahead of you and be your backup," Becker said. "Whatever you do, don't give him the painting until you have Jasmine out of their reach."

Olivia nodded, pulled out her cell phone and brought up Tacey Rogers's phone number. She took a deep breath, met Becker's gaze and initiated the call to Romano.

"You still want to trade a painting for my sister?" she said into the cell phone.

Becker's heart swelled at how brave she was. Her voice was steady and her gaze met his, unwavering.

Now that they had the painting and a plan, she was ready to get her sister back. And nothing would stop her.

Becker would be there to make sure both women made it out alive. He wished he was going in Levi's place. But if Romano recognized him, he might spook and leave without the painting and with Olivia's sister. They couldn't risk it. Not when Nico would be released at any moment.

"I have the painting. Do you still have my sister?" Olivia paused. "I want proof of life," she said. "Let me talk to her."

A moment passed.

Olivia gripped the cell phone, her eyes filling with tears. "Jaz, baby. Are you all right? Hang in there. I'm coming to get you. Don't worry about me. We're going to come out of this and laugh about it later." Olivia frowned. "Don't hurt my sister, or the deal's off. Do you hear me? *Off.*"

She nodded. "I'll be there in twenty minutes. And just so we're clear… No sister…no painting."

She ended the call and looked up. "Twenty minutes

behind a warehouse near the rail yard. Not far from the one they torched the other night." She gave the address and started for Becker's SUV, where she rewrapped the painting and tied the twine. Then, with the painting in hand, she returned to the others. "Which vehicle are we taking?"

"You and Levi can take the SUV I was driving," Becker said.

Irish raised his hand. "Becker can ride with me."

"We'd better get moving," Trace said. "We want to get there before they do, if possible."

"What about me?" Briana asked. "What can I do to help?"

Olivia hugged her. "You've already done it. Without this painting, we wouldn't have anything to bargain with."

"We'll do our best to get it back," Trace said, "once we have the witness safely in hand."

Briana nodded. "I'd like to go along with you, even if I stay in the car when you guys go in." She glanced around. "I don't know where else to go. By giving you the painting, I've cut ties with the family. They will never trust me after this. I can't go back."

"You can come with us," Trace said. "You'll need to stay back, out of the line of fire, and lie low while the trade goes down."

Olivia nodded. "You won't want anyone to know you're around. If Romano's people find you there, it will place you and your baby in danger."

Briana snorted. "I get that. The Romanos wouldn't take kindly to having a Salvatore at their party. Even an ex-Salvatore." She nodded. "I'll stay out of sight. I have as much a stake in this trade as the rest of you."

"Then let's make sure we do this right the first time." Olivia lifted her chin. "There won't be any second chances."

BECKER RODE WITH IRISH, following the vehicle with Trace and Matt. They zipped through traffic on their way southeast to the rail yard where the warehouse had burned the night before, almost killing a woman inside.

They pulled into an alley a few blocks from the designated address, got out, and grabbed rifles and handguns.

Briana Salvatore parked behind their two vehicles and got out long enough to wish them luck. Then she climbed back into her car and locked the door. She slid low in her seat so that no one would see her sitting there.

Becker stopped beside her car and waited for her to lower her window a crack. "Be safe," he said. "If anyone shows up, be ready to drive off."

"I feel like I should do more to help," she said.

He shook his head. "Take care of yourself and your baby."

The men hurried through the streets to the meeting location Romano had specified, remaining vigilant, on the lookout for Romano's men.

With the noonday sun shining down overhead, they didn't have shadows to cling to. The men relied on moving silently and stepping between or behind buildings to avoid being seen by the traffic passing by on the road out front.

When they reached the address, they spread out, circled the block and took up covered positions behind whatever they could find.

Becker hunkered down behind a commercial trash

can and waited for Romano to show up with his people and Olivia's sister.

They had only been in position five minutes when a white van drove down the street between two warehouses and turned in behind the building where the Outriders lay waiting.

No one got out of the van. The engine remained running, and the windows in front were heavily tinted. Even in the sunlight, Becker couldn't see through.

Two minutes later, the black SUV arrived, with Levi driving and Olivia riding shotgun.

Becker held his breath, praying Romano didn't gun them down and leave with the painting and no witnesses left alive.

He raised his military-grade rifle to his shoulder and stared down the scope to the door of the van, ready to take down anyone who threatened Olivia or Levi.

As soon as Levi brought the vehicle to a halt, Olivia was out of the passenger seat, the painting in its brown paper wrapped in her hand, her jet-black hair wrapped neatly in the light blue scarf. Briana had worked magic with the makeup to contour Olivia's face, making her appear very different from how she'd looked the other night at the art gallery.

She held the painting in front of her like a shield, probably thinking Romano wouldn't shoot at her and risk damaging a four-million-dollar investment.

The side door of the white van opened, and Romano stepped down onto the pavement. He was followed by four men carrying semiautomatic rifles. They flanked Romano, providing royal protection for the mafia kingpin.

He reached inside the van and dragged a young woman

out by her arm. Her wrists were zip-tied behind her back, and her mouth was covered with duct tape.

Olivia stepped forward, her eyes narrowed, her mouth drawn into a tight line. "Release my sister, and I'll give you the painting."

"Show us the artwork," Romano demanded.

Olivia untied the twine and balanced the painting in one hand while pulling away the paper with the other. She turned the image to face Romano. "Send her over."

"We'll meet halfway," Romano said.

Becker didn't like that thought at all. He didn't want Romano within reach of Olivia.

"Show me your hands," Olivia called out.

Romano raised his hands, letting go of Jasmine for a second, to prove he held no weapons.

"Your man can do the same." Romano tipped his head toward Levi.

Levi held up his hands, then lowered them and cupped Olivia's elbow, holding her close.

"In the middle," Romano repeated. He started toward Olivia and Levi.

Olivia carried the painting, with Levi holding her arm, across the pavement.

When they were within two yards of each other, both parties stopped.

So far, so good, Becker thought. But his gut was telling him it wouldn't go down that easily. He didn't trust Romano. He sighted his weapon on the kingpin, ready to plug a hole in him if he tried to hurt Olivia, Jasmine or Levi.

He held his breath and waited for the next move.

"Hand me the painting," Romano demanded.

"Not until I have my sister," Olivia said.

"I'll send her over when I have my hand on the painting," Romano said.

Olivia stepped forward and held out the Wyeth.

Romano reached for it. When his hand was on the frame, Olivia held tight. "The painting is in your hand. Send over my sister."

Romano's eyes narrowed. With one hand gripping the frame and the other gripping Jasmine's arm, he had a choice to make.

Becker hoped the offer from Gunter was foremost in Romano's mind as he made his decision.

With a hefty shove, he pushed Jasmine toward Olivia.

Olivia stepped to the side, maintaining her hold on the frame. "Levi, take her to the vehicle."

"I'm not leaving you," he said.

Becker could have hugged him. His teammate didn't trust Romano any more than he did. He didn't want to leave Olivia alone with him for one second.

"Levi," Olivia said, her tone harsh, "take my sister to the vehicle."

"But—"

"Do it," she said.

Levi pushed Jasmine behind him and backed toward the vehicle.

Becker had his weapon trained on Romano.

Then, with a sudden jerk, Romano yanked the painting toward him, dragging Olivia with it.

She maintained her hold—to her detriment.

Romano let go of the painting and wrapped his arm around Olivia's throat.

Becker swore. He couldn't shoot the man without hitting Olivia. He could kick himself for letting Romano get his hands on her. Knowing how ruthless the man was, Becker should have seen it coming. He should have known Romano wouldn't just trade and be done.

"I know you have your people in position to take me and my men down," he called out. "But before you start shooting, I will snap this pretty lady's neck. Think about it. She is my ticket out of here with the painting. Let us go without any trouble, and I'll put her out on the side of the road, unharmed, once we're safely away."

"Don't do it," Olivia said. "Shoot him."

"If they do, they risk hitting you, my dear," Romano said.

"Shoot me," Olivia said. "That way you'll damage the painting, and it will be worthless."

"You wouldn't do that. It's worth millions," Romano said.

"I don't care what it's worth. It's not worth killing for. You never cared that your nephew died trying to steal a painting. You attempted to kill Tacey for daring to reveal my sister's location. You'd use me to buy your way out of here. Well, I'm not going for it."

Becker held his breath, cringing while his pulse raced through his veins. What was Olivia going to do? Whatever it was, he'd better be ready, because it was bound to make Romano mad enough to kill her.

Olivia, still holding on to the painting, went limp.

Romano adjusted to catch her and keep the painting from crashing to the ground. As he bent over, Olivia planted her feet hard against the pavement and came up sharply, her head hitting Romano in the nose.

He yelped, let go of her and staggered backward.

Olivia tucked the painting against her body and darted away.

When Romano lunged for her, Becker pulled the trigger.

The bullet hit the man in the chest. He fell where he stood and pitched forward onto his face.

His men raised their weapons and turned to take down the threat.

"You're surrounded," Trace called out in a booming voice. "Put down your guns, and you won't be hurt."

When they hesitated, Becker fired a shot at one of the men standing beside the van.

He hopped backward, threw down his gun and raised his hands.

The others followed suit.

With Becker covering for them, Levi, Trace, Irish and Matt zip-tied the wrists and ankles of Romano's men. Once all of them had been secured, Trace called an ambulance for Romano. Becker left his position by the trash can and hurried to join the others. He took the painting from Olivia's hands and laid it on the back seat of the SUV.

Then he turned and gathered Olivia in his arms. "When Romano grabbed you, I lost ten years off my life." He held her close, willing his racing heart to slow.

Engine noise echoed off the walls of the warehouses. A moment later, Briana's sports car raced down the road between the buildings and skidded sideways to a halt. She leaped out, her gaze going to Olivia. "It's Nico. He's free, and he wants me to bring the painting to him. Please tell me you still have it."

"We do. And we have the witness that can put him away for life," Olivia said.

Briana shook her head sadly. "You have to catch him first. He's not going to turn himself in. He has to be lured out with the promise of a big prize," she said.

"The painting." Olivia hurried over to her sister. "We

need to set up a trap to recapture him. Jasmine and Briana won't be safe until he's serving life behind bars."

Levi had cut the zip ties from Jasmine's wrists. She eased the duct tape from her mouth, careful not to rip her skin.

Once she was free of tape, Jasmine spoke. "If you're going to set a trap to capture Nico, let me deliver the painting."

Olivia shook her head. "I died a thousand deaths when Romano's men carried you out of the house. Please don't place yourself in danger again."

Jasmine captured Olivia's hands in hers. "I'm not a little girl anymore," she said. "I can make my own decisions, make mistakes and learn from them. Nico lied when he pleaded not guilty to murdering Eduardo. I saw him do it. He should pay for it and be taken off the streets before he kills again. So, please, let me do my part to bring the man to justice."

"No, let me," Olivia said. "We just got you back. You're safe now. I couldn't bear it if you got into trouble again."

Briana stepped forward. "I can't let you do this. He's my husband. *My* mistake. I should do this."

Jasmine frowned. "Who are you?"

Olivia nodded toward the blonde. "This is Briana Salvatore, Nico's wife. She gave us the painting we used to negotiate your freedom. She's also pregnant, so she can't meet with Nico."

Trace shook his head. "Nico is going to expect to see Briana with his stolen treasure. It will have to be Briana who delivers the painting and gives us enough time to surround and capture him. If not Briana, then someone with the same coloring. Briana is a blonde with long hair. Jasmine, from behind, looks a lot like her."

Jasmine smiled at Trace. "Thank you for the vote of confidence."

"Just don't get cocky," Trace said with a stern look. "You know how quickly things can go south."

She nodded, her smile fading. "I do." She turned to face Briana. "Where did you agree to meet?"

Briana sighed. "At a park playground in twenty minutes."

Jasmine shook her head. "He almost got away with murder. I want to see his face when he realizes he's not getting away with it. And all of this over a stupid painting."

Olivia laughed. "I never thought I'd hear my sister call a painting *stupid*. What is it you always preached? Every work of art deserves respect?"

Jasmine—dressed in the same clothes she'd been wearing for days, her blond hair a mess and her face dirty—planted her hands on her hips. "Yeah, yeah. Being held captive for three days can make even the most devout art enthusiast cranky." She turned back to Briana. "I'll need your clothes and a hairbrush. I'd also sell my soul for a toothbrush."

Becker's heart swelled at the happiness in Olivia's face that being with her sister inspired. He wanted to see her smile like that a lot more often.

But as Jasmine traded clothing with Briana, Olivia's smile faded, and the worry returned.

They had to see this through. Until Nico was behind bars for good, none of these women were safe.

Chapter Seventeen

Once again, the team took up positions in preparation for capturing Nico Salvatore. This time, instead of meeting in a deserted alley behind a warehouse, their quarry had chosen a playground crowded with small children and their mothers.

Becker and Olivia sat on one of the benches, holding hands like a young couple in love. On another bench nearby, Jasmine waited with the brown paper–wrapped painting that, although beautiful, seemed to be cursed. She'd cleaned her face, brushed her hair and dressed in Briana's black dress and stilettos. The broad-brimmed black hat shaded her face enough so that Nico would have to be right next to her to realize she wasn't his wife. She had Olivia's cell phone tucked beneath her dress, her hand on the button to record the conversation once Nico arrived.

Because they hadn't gotten the police involved, word would not have reached Nico that the witness had resurfaced.

Olivia's heart raced as she sat close to Becker, leaning her head on his shoulder while keeping her sister in her peripheral vision, praying she'd be all right. She hadn't lost her once just to lose her again.

A man dressed in gray trousers and a white polo shirt approached Jasmine.

Olivia stiffened, recognizing Nico Salvatore from the pictures plastered all over the news. “Here we go,” she whispered.

They were close enough to hear a little but not all. Olivia hoped it would be enough to know when to step in.

Trace said he’d wait until five minutes before the appointed time to call the detective in charge of the murder investigation. By now, he would have shared the news that the witness was alive and ready to talk. He’d have passed along the address of where they could find Nico to return him to jail. He asked them to come in with sirens off to keep from scaring the children.

Olivia worried about the children. If Nico got spooked, he might take one as a hostage.

Becker had assured her he wouldn’t let that happen, and he wouldn’t let Nico harm or abduct Jasmine. Olivia believed he’d do his best. But sometimes the best wasn’t good enough—bad things happened anyway.

Nico walked right up to the bench where Jasmine was sitting, her legs crossed at the ankle, her hat pulled low to hide her face.

With her heart in her throat, Olivia watched.

The murdering thief sat next to Jasmine and took her left hand in his.

“You’re not wearing my ring,” he said.

Olivia froze. They’d thought of the clothes, shoes, hat and hair, but they hadn’t thought of the wedding ring.

Jasmine only had to keep him long enough for the detective to arrive and arrest him again. If he happened to say something incriminating, all the better. Their main goal was to lure him out, have him take the painting and get caught with it.

Trace would work with the detective to get Briana a plea bargain: her testimony in exchange for the court overlooking her part in hiding the stolen painting.

"What happened to us?" he asked.

Olivia held her breath, praying Nico wouldn't recognize the difference in his wife's voice. Jasmine had practiced a few times to get the pitch and inflections right. Would it be enough?

"A marriage can't survive on lies," Jasmine said. "And it won't last if one partner abuses and threatens to kill the other."

Nico stiffened. "I only did what I had to. It was the only way I could get you to listen."

"No one deserves to be beaten the way you beat your wife."

"What's wrong with you? You never talked back to me."

"Maybe I've changed. Maybe I don't want to be married to a murderer," Jasmine said.

Becker's muscles tensed, ready to spring into action.

Across the playground, Olivia saw several dark sedans park along the curb.

Men in casual slacks and blazers got out and moved in.

The bench Jasmine had chosen was facing the playground equipment. Nico would have to turn to the side to see the men moving in on him.

He didn't. Instead, he laid his hand on the brown paper packaging. "Ed wasn't supposed to fight back. He wasn't a fighter. His family made him use his technical skills to disarm the gallery and steal that painting. They had questioned his loyalty. They told him it was his way of proving himself to the family. He didn't want to steal that painting. Or so I was told. I expected him to hand it over. When he didn't, I was forced to take it from him."

"No one forced you to take anything, Nico. You killed Eduardo in cold blood and took the painting."

"It doesn't matter. They have no evidence and no witnesses to prove anything." He stood up, taking the painting in his hands.

"I never should have helped you hide the painting."

He scoffed. "You're weak. When I asked you to marry me, you said you wanted children. And what have you given me? Nothing. Now you're pregnant, and it isn't even mine. All I had to do was threaten the bastard, and you crumbled. You're weak and unfaithful. I should kill you for carrying another man's child. You've tainted the Salvatore name."

"No—you, Nico," a voice said from behind the bench where Nico and Jasmine were. "*You* tainted the Salvatore name when you murdered Eduardo."

Nico spun around to face his wife, a frown creasing his brow. She wore Jasmine's dirty clothes, but there was no denying she was Briana Salvatore.

Becker and Olivia sprang to their feet, ready to come to Jasmine's defense.

"What's going on?" Nico demanded. "Who is this?" He whipped the hat from Jasmine's head and glared at her. "Who the hell are you?"

She rose to her feet and walked around the back of the bench, putting distance between her and Nico before answering. "I'm the witness."

His face burned a bright red, and he lunged for Jasmine.

The bench kept him from reaching her.

Becker grabbed him from behind before he tried to go over it. Nico struggled but was no match for Becker's strength.

Jasmine took the painting from him and handed it to the detective, who'd arrived in time to see Nico lunge for Jasmine. He snapped cuffs onto Nico's wrists and read him his Miranda rights. "But you already know them, don't you? And now that we have our witness and the missing painting, you won't be seeing the light of day for a long time."

"You've got nothing on me," Nico said. "It's my word against hers."

Jasmine held up the cell phone and replayed the recording of Nico confessing to the murder.

Nico cursed as the detective led him away. Another detective took the cell phone as evidence and thanked Jasmine for her part in helping to keep Nico Salvatore behind bars.

She tipped her head toward Olivia and the men of the Outriders. "Don't thank me—thank them. They didn't give up on me."

Olivia wrapped her arms around her sister and hugged her tight. "I would never give up on you. You're my family."

Jasmine shook her head. "How could the concept of family have such different meanings?"

Olivia shook her head too. "I don't know, but I'm glad *my* family is back." She hugged her sister again, her gaze going to the man standing nearby. The man who'd come to mean so much to her in such a short amount of time. A man who could easily become family, if she let him and if he was willing.

"Let's go home," she said, her words meant for Jasmine and Becker.

Jasmine climbed into the SUV.

Olivia waited beside the vehicle for Becker to finish talking to the detectives. When he finally joined her, she stood in front of him, a frown pulling her eyebrows low.

"What's wrong?"

"Does this mean your job is done?"

"This one is," he said. "I'm sure Trace has more work for me."

"So you'll be staying in Whiskey Gulch?"

He nodded and then frowned. "Do you want me to?"

Her face split open in a grin. "Yes. I do. We have yet to have our first date."

"I thought you said we'd moved way past a first date." He pulled her into his arms and stared down into her eyes. "I think what we're trying to say is, are we game for more? My answer is yes, yes and yes." He emphasized each *yes* with a kiss. "I told you not too long ago that I think I love you. I want to explore that thought until I know for sure."

"Good. I'm all in on this exploration. But I see no need to take it slow. I'm pretty sure I have all the data I need to make a decision sooner rather than later to take *I think I love you* all the way to *I* know *I love you*."

He brushed the hair away from her forehead and pressed a kiss there. "I concur. Now, let's go home."

Epilogue

"Did you get more nails at the hardware store?" Olivia called out as she emerged from the kitchen, carrying a tray of drinks for the men and women who'd converged on her house to help rebuild the walls.

"Got 'em," Becker answered.

She'd had to wait to rebuild until she could get the insurance adjuster out and then order the needed supplies to replace the windows and repair the siding.

"Where do you want me to put the sandwiches?" Jasmine asked, lugging a tray full of chicken-salad sandwiches out to the front of the house, where several picnic tables had been placed.

"On one of the tables," Olivia said. "Doesn't matter which."

Becker climbed the new wooden porch steps, took the tray of drinks from Olivia's hands and carried it out to the tables. "No alcohol until the work is done," he said to his teammates.

The Outriders groaned and laughed.

"I can't thank you all enough for coming to help. It will be nice to have the hole in my house closed up before the next rain."

Becker climbed the porch again and pulled her into

his arms. "They love any excuse to have a party. That, and I promised steaks and beer when the last nail is hammered in and the wall is complete."

"In other words, eat your snack and get to work," Irish said. "There's a steak with my name on it, just waiting to hit the grill." He grabbed Tessa around the middle and kissed her soundly. "We have the medical staff here in case someone steps on a nail or smashes a finger or toe."

She swatted his arm. "I'm pretty handy with a hammer too. I've been looking forward to this for weeks."

"Me too," Lily said. "Hammering is a great way to work out my frustrations."

Trace caught her from behind. "What could possibly frustrate you?"

She laughed. "You." She kissed him, grabbed half a chicken sandwich and danced away.

Levi helped Dallas buckle a tool belt around her slim waist.

"I heard they set the date for Nico's trial for three months from now," Dallas said.

"That's right," Becker said. "Olivia and I will be with Jasmine when we head back to testify."

"Did I tell you I heard from Briana?" Olivia picked up one of the sandwiches and carried it with her to sit beside Becker at one of the tables. "She decided to stay at the Salvatore estate."

"What?" Jasmine frowned. "Why would she do that?"

"So the baby could grow up with a father," Olivia said.

"Are you ever going to tell us who the father is?" Jasmine asked.

Olivia nodded, happy for her friend and the way things were working out. "The baby's father is Vincenzo Salvatore."

"Nico's father?" Aubrey exclaimed.

"I could have told you that," Matt said.

Aubrey lightly slapped his arm. "Then why didn't you?"

He shrugged. "Wasn't my business."

Aubrey huffed. "Men."

Rosalyn smiled across the table at Olivia. "You've been grinning nonstop since we got here. You look happier than I've ever seen you, and your face is practically glowing. What's up?"

Olivia's cheeks heated, and she cast a shy glance toward Becker.

He shook his head, a smile tugging at his lips. "You might as well tell them. You can't keep a secret to save your life." He held out his hand.

Olivia placed her hand in his. "We're going to have a baby."

Jasmine leaped up from the table. "How? When?" She spun around with a smile splitting her face. "I'm going to be an aunt?"

Olivia laughed. "*How?* The usual way. *When?* In eight months—and yes, you're going to be an aunt."

Becker leaned over and kissed Olivia and then raised her left hand so everyone could see the diamond solitaire on her ring finger. "And you're all invited to the wedding. She said yes."

"And when will *that* be?" Jasmine rolled her eyes. "I'm your sister. I should have known all this."

"We haven't picked a date yet, but the sooner, the better." Olivia laughed. "I want to fit in a wedding dress."

"We can have it out at the Whiskey Gulch Ranch," Rosalyn offered. "How's a month from now?"

Becker frowned. "That long?"

Olivia squeezed his hand. "That sounds perfect."

"I thought you didn't want to take it slowly." Becker brought her hand up to his lips and kissed the backs of her knuckles.

"Are you kidding?" Jasmine threw her hands in the air. "A month is barely enough time to find a wedding dress. Then there's the music, catering, florals, bachelorette party, showers… Good Lord. A month isn't enough."

"I don't care if we get married in jeans and a T-shirt in front of a justice of the peace, as long as she shows up and says 'I do.'" Becker grinned.

"I'll be there," Olivia said. "I've found the right one for me. Nothing could keep me away."

"That goes for me too."

"Then why wait?" Olivia turned to Rosalyn. "Could we move that date up to next weekend?"

Rosalyn laughed. "Of course."

Becker kissed Olivia and turned to his brothers. "You heard the lady. Wedding's next weekend."

A cheer went up around the tables.

"That doesn't mean you get to break out the beer yet," Becker warned. "We still have work to do. We have to have a place to live." He pulled Olivia into his arms. "I love you, Olivia Swann. I can't wait to make you my wife."

"And I love you, Becker Jackson. I can't wait to start the rest of our lives together."

* * * * *

LOOKS THAT KILL

AMANDA STEVENS

Chapter One

The house was old and creaky with the faint scent of mothballs and camphor wafting on the chilled air. Pulling the outside door closed behind her, Avery Bolt melted into the shadows to take stock of her surroundings. The situation warranted extreme caution. A misplaced step could prove deadly if the homeowner happened to be armed.

Motionless in the dark, she listened and waited. The house was silent except for the low hum of the central air conditioner and the rhythmic ticking of a pendulum clock somewhere nearby. No hurrying footfalls down the stairs. No telltale light streaming into the hallway. By all indications, the sole occupant of the home was fast asleep.

Following the thin beam of her penlight, Avery trailed her gaze over the spacious interior. The furnishings looked expensive and antique, at least what she could see of them. No security system. That was a lucky break, though surprising in such an exclusive neighborhood. Exclusive by small-town standards anyway.

Moonlight poured in through the French doors from which she had entered and glinted off the gilded frames that flanked the marble fireplace. She spent only a moment surveying the unknown ancestors before slipping across the polished wood floor of the parlor into the large entrance hall where double doors on the opposite wall opened into a smaller salon.

The drapes were closed against the night, throwing the room into pitch-blackness. As Avery stepped across the threshold, the beam of her penlight sparked off glittering eyes. Dozens of porcelain dolls in frilly gowns stared at her blindly from behind the leaded glass doors of a large curio cabinet.

Drawn by their fancy gowns and painted expressions, she moved silently across the room to stand in awe before them. The unblinking eyes were both magnetic and repellant. Something tugged at her subconscious, poking at a memory that remained just out of her reach. She'd experienced the same unnerving sensation numerous times over the past two weeks, ever since stumbling across a curious photograph online. Ever since she'd begun to investigate an old kidnapping.

Did she know this house? She wondered if she'd been here before, inside this very room, admiring these old dolls. She certainly felt something, but *familiarity* might be too strong a word.

Maybe the odd sensation of déjà vu was nothing more than a fantasy spawned by an unsolved disappearance and the feeling of displacement that had plagued her since childhood. Her devotion to her beloved father had only grown stronger after her mother's death a few years ago and yet the perception of not belonging had never gone away.

What would Luther say if he could see her now? Breaking into a stranger's house in the middle of the night out of morbid curiosity. Traveling to a town hundreds of miles from her home with no idea when she'd return. Handing over a thriving business to her partner, draining her savings account, packing up her car and driving through the night to arrive in Black Creek, Florida, just as the sun rose over the treetops.

She'd pulled to the side of the road and watched in fascination as the eastern sky had turned from gray to violet to blood red. The transformation had seemed like an omen, but Avery wasn't superstitious, nor did she have a tendency to second-guess even life-changing decisions. Once her mind was made up, she moved full speed ahead.

Exhausted from the long drive, she'd dozed off in her vehicle only to rouse an hour later to a cloudless sky as clear a blue as she'd ever seen. Maybe that, too, had been a sign.

Arriving in Black Creek, she'd driven through town several times to get the lay of the land before locating the lovely old Queen Anne–style house in the historic Crescent Hill neighborhood. She'd parked down the street for several hours to observe the comings and goings. No one had been in or out all day and there'd only been a single delivery. A tall, impeccably groomed woman had appeared in the doorway to retrieve the package and then quickly vanished back into the house. Avery hadn't seen her again, though she could have sworn she'd caught the twitch of a lace curtain at one of the front windows.

Had the woman somehow sensed she was under surveillance or was she paranoid by nature? Had someone called to warn her about a strange car parked down the street from her house?

Say her name. Say it.

Chapman. June Chapman.

A woman in her early seventies, who, by all accounts, had lived a tragic life. Her husband had died of a heart attack more than forty years ago, making her a young, rich widow, and then her only son had been killed in a horrific car accident before his twenty-first birthday. He'd fathered twin daughters before his death and one of the little girls had been abducted from her bedroom at the age of four, never to be seen or heard from again.

Say it. Say her name.

Maya Lamb.

The floor creaked beneath her black sneakers, and she stilled once more, her gaze trained on a blond, curly-haired doll with cornflower blue eyes and rose-red lips. Dressed in a dainty gown with a white lace collar, she was seated on a tiny rocking chair as if she'd been waiting forever for someone to free her from prison. Avery touched a gloved finger to the glass, tracing the doll's outline.

Can I hold her?

With those filthy hands? I should say not!

She snatched away her hand as if the glass had burned right through her glove. Heart hammering, she stumbled back from the cabinet, bumping her hip against a chair. The legs scraped against the wood floor, and she whipped her head around, listening intently for the slightest sound of someone stirring. When the house remained silent, she quickly left the room to make her way down the hallway, glancing in one door after another until she came to a solarium at the rear.

Moonlight glinted off the walls of windows and spilled down through a skylight, showering potted palms and lacy ferns with cool, silvery light. A Persian rug in vivid hues of cerulean, saffron and hints of emerald green cushioned the brick floor and silenced Avery's footsteps as she stepped into the lush space.

A large tabby rose from a cane chaise and stared at her balefully for a long moment, then shot past her into the hallway. Avery was so startled that she almost let out a yelp. Hand to her heart, she drew a deep breath to steady her nerves before she glanced around.

The sunroom was beautiful, but the exotic richness of the decor seemed out of place with the austerity of the rest of the house. The contradiction intrigued her. Despite her extensive research, she'd come across very little information about June Chapman and scant few images of the dour woman. She told herself it wasn't fair to pass judgment based on video footage of an interview from twenty-eight years ago. June Chapman's granddaughter had disappeared only days prior to the taping. No one would be at her best under such circumstances.

Still, her behavior throughout the interview had been chilling. No matter how hard Avery struggled to keep an open mind, she couldn't dismiss the icy glitter in the woman's eyes as she'd dissected the missing child's mother, stopping just short of accusing Reggie Lamb of murder.

So no, she couldn't imagine the June Chapman of that interview at home in such a sumptuous space. The rest of the house with the heavy drapery and dark wood paneling seemed more suited to her rigid comportment.

From the corner of her eye, Avery caught the subtle shift of a shadow out in the garden and wondered if she'd imagined the movement. Or perhaps the breeze had swayed a tree branch. Surely the human shape she detected in front of the boxwoods was a statue.

The statue moved and she caught her breath. Someone was out there watching the house.

Had she been made?

Her first inclination was to slip back into the darkness of the corridor, but her father had spent years training her to subdue her impulses in compromised situations. He had taught her to think and evaluate before acting. *Use your head, Avery. Don't get complacent or reckless and never, ever make assumptions.*

She quickly assessed her current predicament. She'd broken into the home of an elderly woman, not to steal, but to explore and gather data. She doubted the police would believe her story or care about her motive. They would only be interested in her actions. Not that it mattered at the moment because the person outside in the garden wasn't the police. The interloper's black attire and stealthy movements led Avery to deduce his intentions were nefarious.

She didn't dare change her position for fear of giving herself away. She waited until the sound of a passing car out on the street caught his attention before she slipped back through the doorway. Then she tracked the dark figure from the safety of the hallway. He came right up to the solarium and pressed his masked face against the glass before vanishing into the shadows.

Avery whirled and headed for the end of the hallway, hurrying as fast as she dared while mindful of the sleeping occupant upstairs. If the woman awakened to find someone in her house, she might shoot first and ask questions later. She certainly wouldn't give Avery the benefit of a doubt about a second intruder.

What were the chances that tonight of all nights, someone else had decided to break into June Chapman's home? It had to be a coincidence because Avery hadn't told anyone of her plans. No one even knew she was in Black Creek. The masked invader could kill her, dump her body in a lake and no one would ever be the wiser. She'd simply disappear without a trace the way Maya Lamb had done twenty-eight years ago.

Disappearing actually sounded like a very good idea at the moment, but she couldn't leave without taking precautions. Removing a prepaid phone from her back pocket, she called 911 and, in a rushed whisper, reported the suspicious activity at the Chapman home without identifying herself. Sliding the disposable back in her pocket, she entered the front parlor and stole across the wood floor to the French doors through which she had entered earlier. She reached for the brass lever and then dropped her hand to her side.

The door stood ajar. She'd closed it earlier. She remembered distinctly the sound of the clicking latch in the silent room. The wind could have blown the door open, but there was only a mild breeze tonight. Had the person in the garden already rounded the house? Or worse, did he have an accomplice, someone who had been inside the whole time she'd been there?

Avery vacillated for a moment before she once again crossed the parlor to the foyer, peering up the staircase where the landing was dimly lit by moonlight and crystal sconces. Beyond the island of pale illumination was only darkness and presumably June Chapman's bedroom.

She climbed the stairs slowly, her senses on full alert as she listened for any sign of another intruder. Halfway to the top, she paused to stare back down into the foyer. Nothing stirred. No sound came to her at all. Even the air conditioner had clicked off.

Thwack.

She whirled, her attention darting to the top of the stairs. The sound had come from just beyond the landing, like a book being slammed against a table.

Avery again checked her impulses, assuming a cautious approach rather than flinging herself headlong into the action. A second *thwack* froze her on the landing as a muzzle flash lit up an open doorway. Now she recognized the noise. Someone had fired off two rounds from a suppressed weapon. Almost instantly she heard the thud of running footfalls coming straight toward her.

She lunged for the shadows, pressing her back against the wall. The assailant rushed past her and bolted down the stairs, skidding to a halt as he reached the foyer to glance back up at the landing. Through the eye slits in the mask, gleaming orbs met hers in the dark. Before she could melt deeper into the shadows, he lifted his weapon and fired up the stairs. *Thwack. Thwack. Thwack.*

Avery dropped to the floor as the bullets buried in the wall above and beside her. She waited a beat, then crawled to the railing and glanced through the spindles down into the foyer. The front door had been flung wide.

Her first instinct was to pursue the shooter, but she was unarmed and in unfamiliar territory. And somewhere in the house, an elderly woman might be at that moment clinging to life.

Scrambling to her feet, Avery hurried down the hallway. Only one door stood open to the corridor. She hugged the wall, pausing once more to check her surroundings. Then easing up to the threshold, she swept the space with a single glance.

Moonlight flooded through French doors into an ornate bedroom of satin and lace. A woman lay sprawled on the floor beside the bed, blood blooming on the chest of her white silk pajamas. Her eyes were closed. She didn't appear to be breathing. A silver-plated hammerless pistol with pearl handgrips lay on the floor beside her.

Avery stared down at June Chapman, taking in the sharp cheekbones, the slope of the aristocratic nose, the thin, rigid lips. Mostly she noticed the pallor of her skin and thought the woman must surely be dead, in which case there was nothing to be done but flee the scene. The call to 911 had already alerted the authorities. *There's nothing more you can do here. Get out before the police come!*

Instead, she knelt and gingerly checked for a pulse. A hand clamped around her wrist and clung for dear life. Avery was so startled that for a moment she could do nothing but gape.

"Who are you?" June Chapman whispered, her grip tightening with surprising—perhaps even superhuman—strength. "Who sent you here?"

In full-blown panic, Avery flung off the woman's hand and scrambled away. She wanted nothing so much as to sprint for the stairs and disappear into the night as the shooter had done moments earlier. But she couldn't leave a gunshot victim to bleed out on the floor. She had to do something.

"Tell me!" the woman rasped. *"Who sent you to kill me?"*

A chill slid down Avery's backbone. Her response came out in a shocked croak. "No one sent me! I didn't do this!"

But June Chapman never heard the denial. Her eyelids fluttered closed, and her head lolled to one side as she lost consciousness.

Avery berated herself as she inched back to the victim. She'd never been a hand wringer in emergency situations, but she found herself in a daze and at a loss. Why oh why had she come here tonight? Stupid, stupid, stupid to think she could break into someone's home without consequences. Not that she hadn't done it before whenever necessary, but never on impulse. Never without thorough reconnaissance and a sound backup plan. But how could she have predicted that someone would break into an old woman's house to murder her in her sleep—

Do something!

Now was not the time to obsess over her stupidity. June Chapman might die if she didn't act quickly.

Leaping to her feet, she grabbed a towel from the adjoining bathroom and then dropped once more to the woman's side. She used her right hand to apply pressure to the wound while retrieving her phone with the left. For the second time in the space of five minutes, she placed an emergency call. Speaking in the same hoarse whisper, she explained the circumstances, gave the address and disconnected the call yet again without supplying her name.

Luckily, she'd had the foresight to pick up a stash of disposable phones in convenience stores along the route from Texas to Florida. Though not entirely untraceable, burners always came in handy in her line of work. One could mitigate the risk of tracking by activating in a crowded location and forgoing personal phone calls and text messages. Even if the number could be traced to point of sale, she always used cash.

But none of that was luck, she reminded herself. Training and preparation had become second nature to her by now, or so she'd thought. But Luther Bolt's daughter from a month ago would never have ended up in her current predicament. The avid pupil who'd soaked up her father's life lessons would be back in Houston right now, safe and sound in her apartment. Or on surveillance, bored out of her mind while she waited for the money shot.

No time to fret about any of that now. Already she could hear sirens. By the sound of it, at least one squad car had already turned down June Chapman's street. Avery waited until she heard a car door slam before she eased pressure on the wound. The compression seemed to have done the trick.

She checked the woman's pulse a second time before slipping through the French doors out onto the balcony. The garden below lay in deep shadows. Behind her, she could hear footsteps pounding up the stairs. In another few minutes, the grounds would be swarming with police.

Pulling the French doors closed behind her, she swung her legs over the balustrade and climbed down a two-story trellis. A few feet from the ground, she heard something snap, and the lattice sagged beneath her weight. She pushed away from the wall and jumped, twisting her ankle as she landed in a crouch. Pain shot up her leg, but she ignored the fiery needles as she made her way through the dense foliage to scramble over a brick wall into the adjoining backyard.

She half expected to be confronted by a snarling guard dog, but when no attack was forthcoming, she took a moment to grind her heel into the burner and bury it beneath a crape myrtle bush. Rising, she inched along the wall, in-

Chapter Two

Max Winter stood at the third-story window of his cramped office and rubbed the back of his neck as he surveyed the nightscape. Not a lot to see from his vantage. The low-rise office buildings across the street had gone dark hours ago. It was after midnight and even the bail bond businesses near the county jail had turned off their garish signs and closed up shop for the evening. The streets around the courthouse appeared deserted, but the calm was deceiving. Lurking shadows in a maze of alleyways hinted at an underground nightlife that thrived in the dark, even in a backwoods place like Black Creek, Florida.

Max knew all about that nightlife. There'd been a time in his teenage years when he'd been drawn to an after-hours lifestyle. Crawl out his bedroom window, shimmy down a drainpipe and step through the veil of night that had allowed him to shed his real-life skin and assume an anonymous persona. In those alleyways, no one asked his name. No one recognized his face. No one knew or cared that his father had been *the* Judge Winter, a renowned jurist who'd been gunned down on the courthouse steps in broad daylight by the wife of a convicted murderer, thus posthumously cementing his status as a local legend.

Max sometimes found it surreal that he now occupied an office in the very building where the Honorable Clayton tent on finding a gate. Just when she thought she was home free, a light came on in the house and she once again dived for the shadows.

Winter had once presided with an iron fist over his courtroom on the first floor. Growing up in his father's shadow, Max had never aspired to follow in the old man's footsteps, yet here he was. No regrets. He liked his job as an assistant district attorney well enough. He enjoyed punching holes in a carefully crafted defense almost as much as he relished sparring with opposing counsel. Mostly he liked winning. But sometimes on a moonlit night, the old restiveness would creep in, making him wonder what his life might have been like if he'd chosen the road less traveled.

Stuffing his hands in his pockets, he rocked back on his heels and watched the street for another long moment before returning to his work. The courthouse was eerily quiet this time of night. Sometimes when everyone else had gone home, he liked to walk the halls, perusing the portraits and framed documents as he pondered witness testimonies or formulated a closing argument.

On rare occasions, he would sometimes go outside and sit on the courthouse steps to watch the night. Most people would consider it a ghoulish pastime considering what had happened out there, but Max had never been too concerned with what others thought of him.

Settling back in at his desk with a lukewarm cup of coffee, he opened the case file that had consumed his every waking moment for the past two weeks, ever since the regional DA had dropped the thick folder on his desk. The twenty-eight-year-old cold case had the potential to either make or break Max's career. Considering the lack of concrete evidence, he very much feared the latter.

"Take a look and see what you think, but use discretion," his boss had cautioned. "Nothing leaves this office until we determine the most prudent way to proceed."

"Aren't you jumping the gun?" Max had countered. "There hasn't even been an arrest."

"The local police seem to have hit a dead end with their

investigation, but the decision to bring charges against Denton Crosby ultimately rests with this office. Stay on them. Without sufficient evidence, we can't move forward, but if word gets out we've declined to prosecute one of Maya Lamb's kidnappers, we'll be crucified in the court of public opinion. I'm counting on you to make sure that doesn't happen."

"I'll do my best."

"Let's hope that's enough."

Stuart Masterson was an ambitious politician who knew how to cover his ass. If the prosecution managed to win a conviction, he'd claim the glory. If the case fell apart midtrial, he'd make a show of axing one of his most successful assistant DAs.

Max was neither motivated nor intimidated by the politics of his job, but he accepted the reality. In this particular instance, he happened to agree with the need for discretion. Maya Lamb's family had been living a nightmare ever since she'd been taken from her bedroom nearly three decades ago. He didn't want to give her mother and sister false hope after everything they'd been through. Without physical evidence or eyewitness testimony, he feared justice for little Maya might still be a long time coming.

What he did have was the deathbed confession of one Nadine Crosby, an ex-con house cleaner who, before her passing, had opened up to a Black Creek police detective. Nadine had claimed that she, her brother, Denton, and a man named Gabriel Jareau, the detective's father, had been responsible for the child's disappearance.

According to Nadine, an unknown party had paid the trio to abduct Maya and her twin sister from their home. Before the plan could be carried out, however, Jareau had been murdered. Acting alone, Denton Crosby had managed to nab one of the little girls and flee. He and Nadine had transported the child to a prearranged drop point and watched her get into a car with strangers. Nadine swore they'd never seen Maya Lamb after that night. Her brother, Denton, insisted the story was a complete fabrication.

With two of the three kidnappers dead and nothing but his sister's unsubstantiated confession tying Denton Crosby to the abduction, the police were reluctant to make an arrest. Even Crosby's alleged complicity in the more recent death of an elderly man was far from a slam dunk. Denton Crosby was clever. He knew how to cover his tracks, which was how he'd remained free all these years.

Max's ringtone jarred him from a deep contemplation. He glanced at the screen and then picked up the phone. The call was from Cal Slade, an old friend in the Criminal Investigations Unit. This time of night, communication from any homicide detective wouldn't be good news.

"There's been a shooting in Crescent Hill," Cal informed him. "Looks like a home invasion. It just happened so I don't have any of the details. I'm giving you a heads-up because it's possible the incident could be connected to the Maya Lamb case."

Max straightened, his previous restiveness forgotten. "Connected how?"

"The victim is June Chapman, the missing kid's grandmother."

Normally, the nearly thirty-year span between a disappearance and a home invasion would diminish the chances of a link. However, the recent kidnapping of another child in Black Creek had put the Maya Lamb case back in the news and had prompted Nadine Crosby's confession. Once the floodgates opened, people sometimes came crawling out of the woodwork.

"Is she alive?" Max asked.

"The responding officer found her unconscious on her bedroom floor with two bullet wounds to the chest. The EMTs are on the way."

"What about the gunman?"

"Still at large. I'm less than five minutes away," Cal said. "If and when she regains consciousness, I want to be the first to talk to her."

Max pushed back from his desk. "I'll meet you there. This could be the break we've been waiting for."

He pocketed his phone, grabbed his briefcase and jacket and locked his office door on the way out. It wasn't until he was outside in the parking lot that he allowed himself a moment to explore the memory that had been flickering at the edge of his subconscious for days. He lifted his face to the night breeze and willed the vision to take shape. Yes, there it was. Two little girls clutching hands on June Chapman's front porch steps.

Max had been only five at the time, but he remembered the day vividly because he'd just come from his mother's funeral. His house had been filled with his father's friends and colleagues, all of whom had observed him with the same pitying glances as they whispered to each other about his fate.

He hadn't understood much of what he'd heard that day. All he knew was that his mother wasn't coming home from the hospital this time and his father had locked himself in his study, leaving Max to cope with the well-meaning strangers. Suffocated by too many embraces, he'd slipped outside to sit on the porch by himself. That was when he'd noticed the little girls across the street. He'd gone over to stand on the sidewalk to stare up at them. One wore a frilly yellow dress, the other a pink one. He'd never seen anyone or anything so beautiful in his young life as that delicate pair.

"What's your name?" the one in yellow asked him.

"Max."

"I'm Thea. This is my sissy. We're twins."

Max cocked his head as he squinted up at them. "How come you don't look alike?"

"We do so look alike! We're exactly the same. Our mama says we're like two peas in a pod."

"Well, you don't look the same to me," Max insisted.

"That's because you're dumb!"

"Shush, Sissy!" The one in the pink dress glanced over her shoulder toward the front door. "You don't want her to come out here, do you?"

The one called Thea folded her arms in defiance. "I'm not afraid of her."

"But she'll be mean to Mama if we're not good." She turned back to Max with a shy smile. "Sissy was just playing with you. You're not dumb."

"That's okay." He kicked at a rock as he eyed the girl in pink. "What's your name?"

"Maya."

A month later she was gone, abducted from her bedroom in the dead of night while her twin sister lay sleeping beside her. A box had been dug up in the woods containing a doll and the child's DNA, but no other trace of Maya Lamb had ever been found.

For nearly three decades the trail had remained cold. Until now.

AVERY HUNKERED IN the bushes trying to ignore her throbbing ankle as she pulled cobwebs from her hair. She shuddered to think of the spider that might even now be creeping across her scalp or down her collar. Running fingers through her hair, she shifted her position to accommodate her ankle, and then ducked lower when someone came out on the covered porch and splayed a flashlight beam across the garden. The illumination just missed her hiding place.

The elderly man wielding the light seemed too captivated by the commotion playing out behind the brick wall to give more than a cursory search of his own backyard. He hurried down the steps and strode across the grass with purpose. A wrought iron gate, which had been hidden by darkness and a thick curtain of ivy, squeaked open and he poked his head through.

Light glinted in his silver hair as a powerful beam raked over him. He threw up a hand to shield his eyes as someone yelled, "Hey! You there! Stay where you are!"

The older man called back, "It's all right, Officer! I live here. I heard all the sirens and came outside to investigate."

"You live where?" a disembodied voice demanded.

"1304 Alice Lane." The man stepped away from the gate to allow the officer to peer through the wrought iron rods. "My name is Tom Fuqua."

"The state senator?"

"Retired. I haven't been in politics for over a decade. I'm surprised anyone remembers my name."

"My uncle used to be the local police chief. He always said you were a good friend to the boys in blue going back to when you were a prosecutor."

"Your uncle is…?"

"Will Kent."

There was a brief pause. "Ah, yes. I remember Chief Kent. One of the best we've ever had in Black Creek. What's he up to these days?"

"Retired, like you. Bought a place on the river near Myrtle Cove. Fishes all day and plays poker all night. What a life, right?" The light beam shone through the gate and arced over the yard. "So this is your house. Niiice."

"I've lived here for nearly forty years," Tom Fuqua said with a hint of pride. "My late wife and I raised our family here."

"You must know all your neighbors pretty well by now."

"Yes, but the only one I'm concerned about at the moment is June Chapman. The commotion seems to be coming from her place. Is she all right?"

The officer ignored the man's worried query. He stepped through the gate and targeted his light toward the bushes. The small talk had made Avery antsy, but she didn't dare move a muscle even though she could feel the scurry of tiny feet down her backbone. She resisted the urge to sprint from the bushes, tearing at her hair and clothing. Arachnophobia was a very real thing for her. She'd been terrified of spiders ever since a brown recluse had crawled up her pants leg and bitten her behind the knee. She'd only been ten or so at the time, but she still remembered the awful stomach cramps and violent tremors that had accompanied the puncture, not to mention the necrosis that had left a sizable scar. Armed assassins she could handle; eight-legged creepy-crawlies, not so much.

Suppressing a shiver, she drew as deep a breath as she dared and tried to regain her focus.

"Have you been home all night, Mr. Fuqua?" the officer wanted to know.

"I was out earlier. I played bridge at Evelyn Carmichael's place until around ten and then I walked home and went straight up to bed."

"Do you normally keep this gate locked?" The officer examined the latch and then squatted to search the ground on both sides of the wall.

"There's never been a need to. June and I respect each other's privacy."

"You're friends, I take it?"

"Not really. She isn't much of a socializer. She minds her own business and expects everyone else to do the same."

The officer stood. "Okay with you if I take a look around your property?"

"Yes, certainly, but I wish you would tell me what or who you're looking for. Maybe I can help."

"I've got it covered, thanks."

Avery tried to sink deeper into the shadows as the policeman moved into the garden. Her snap judgment was of an average-sized man with an oversized ego, but nerves may have colored her assessment. He sauntered around the yard, probing the bushes with the beam of his flashlight. Like the shooter, Avery was dressed from head to toe in black. She was well hidden for now but if he came any closer—

"You say you walked home earlier?" He traced the beam along the back wall as if gauging how difficult it would be to scale the brick facade.

"That's what I said, yes."

"Did you see or hear anything unusual during that walk?" The officer crouched once more, putting himself at eye level with Avery as he examined the edge of the flower bed and all along the ground. Could he see her footprints in the grass? Or the disturbed dirt where she'd buried her phone?

She was usually so careful about covering her trail, but the night's events had knocked her off her game. She was still shaken by the shooting. Still rattled by June Chapman's assumption that she had been sent to kill her.

"What do you mean by *unusual*?" Tom Fuqua asked.

"Did you notice any vehicles on the street that didn't belong in the neighborhood? A delivery truck or repair van, anything like that? Or an unfamiliar car parked at the curb?" The officer moved the beam slowly over the lawn, searching and searching. *Almost as if he knows I'm here.* He picked up something from the grass and examined it in the light. What had he found? Not the smashed burner, surely.

Avery tried to tamp down her panic as she took stock of her gear. She hadn't inadvertently dropped anything, had she? Her tools and car fob were stored safely in her backpack—she'd made certain of that—and her personal smartphone was back at the hotel, along with the other possessions she'd brought with her from Houston. Nothing could be traced to her. *Nothing.*

A thought occurred to her as she tried to shift her weight ever so slightly off her throbbing ankle. What if the shooter had come this way, too? What if he was also hiding in the bushes? Seemed unlikely, but after tonight, Avery discounted nothing.

Tom Fuqua echoed her curiosity. "What did you find there?"

"Cigarette butt. You a smoker?"

"Never touch the filthy things. Maybe someone from the yard crew dropped it earlier. I'll have a word with the owner."

The officer bagged the cigarette butt and stuffed it in his pocket. Then he picked up a pebble from the flower bed and flung it into the bushes, frightening a cat that had been hiding in the azaleas. Startled, the officer jumped to his feet, his hand flying to his weapon as the feline leaped to the top of the wall with a disgruntled yowl.

"I knew something was back there! Damn thing's lucky I didn't shoot it."

"There's no cause for alarm," Tom soothed. "It's just Dexter, June's old tabby. Poor thing probably got scared off by all the ruckus."

"God, I hate cats." The officer muttered an oath with an exaggerated shudder. "They ought not to be allowed to run loose."

"He's harmless. Wouldn't hurt a fly, would you, Dexter?"

The cat crouched directly above Avery on the wall, his gaze riveted on her motionless form. She willed him to move on before his intense focus drew the officer's interest to her hiding spot.

"Did you see anyone else out walking on your way back home tonight?" he asked the neighbor.

"No, but Evelyn only lives a few houses down the street. It only took me a couple of minutes to get home and then as I said, I went straight to bed. There was nothing out of the ordinary about the night until the sirens awakened me a few minutes ago."

"What about earlier in the day?"

"Not that I recall." Tom paused. "I don't mind answering your questions. I'm happy to help in any way I can, but I'm worried sick about June. I'd probably be a lot more helpful if I knew what happened."

"There was a break-in," the officer grudgingly informed him.

"At June's house? Why didn't you say so?" The older man sounded genuinely apprehensive and not a little perturbed by the officer's reticence. "Was she home when it happened? Is she all right?"

"I'm not at liberty to say anything more at the moment. If you really want to help, then go back inside and lock your doors. If you have an alarm system, make sure you turn it on."

"Are you saying—"

"The suspect is still at large. He's armed, dangerous and possibly hiding out somewhere nearby." The flashlight beam swung over the yard once more. "I suggest everyone in the neighborhood take precautions until the perp is apprehended."

"Yes, of course," the older man agreed. "Thank you for the warning, Officer."

As the policeman moved back through the gate, Tom Fuqua took out his phone and placed a call, speaking softly to the person on the other end. "Your sister's boy was just here. Yes, the cop," he clarified impatiently. "Seems there was a break-in at June Chapman's house tonight."

He listened for a moment, then said, "I don't know any of the details. I couldn't get anything out of him. If we're lucky, they'll assume it was a random burglary. There's no reason to believe it's connected to that other business, but for now we should both lay low. And be careful what you say to your nephew. I got the impression he's sharper than he looks." He slipped the phone in his pocket and walked quickly back to the house. A few minutes later, the lights went out.

Chapter Three

Avery waited in the bushes until she felt reasonably certain Tom Fuqua had retired for the night and then she eased out into the moonlight. She stood for a moment staring up at the facade of his two-story Colonial. Like all the houses on the street, the place looked immaculate in the moonlight, the lawn and gardens meticulously tended. On first glance, Crescent Hill seemed pleasantly somnolent, an affluent neighborhood of shady streets and wide verandas, but in Avery's experience, it was the kind of place where secrets could fester for years.

She'd come to Black Creek trying to pick up the trail of an old kidnapping. Now the victim's grandmother had been shot in cold blood and a neighbor with a political past seemed to know more than he'd let on to the police officer. What was the "other business" he'd referred to and what did it have to do with a retired state senator and a retired chief of police?

Zigzagging her way from Tom Fuqua's backyard to the front, she kept to the shadows as she moved out onto the sidewalk. The homes on this block were dark, the residents still fast asleep and blissfully unaware of the shooting.

A dog barked somewhere behind her and she paused yet again, listening to the night. From her current location, she could easily make her way back to the alleyway where she'd left her vehicle. The patrols would be out soon, canvassing the neighborhood on foot and in squad cars with powerful spotlights. She had a few minutes' head start, but no time to waste. Once in her car, she could drive back to the hotel—or better yet, to Texas—with no one ever being the wiser.

Instead, she recklessly cut back over to June Chapman's street and found another hiding spot near a construction project that gave her a clear view of the house. She watched and waited as more squad cars arrived on the scene. The perimeter had already been roped off and no one except authorized personnel was allowed up the walkway, much less onto the porch or inside the house.

The EMTs had arrived next, and a few moments later, a black SUV with tinted windows pulled to the curb very close to where Avery crouched in the bushes. She thought at first the unmarked vehicle might belong to the county coroner or the medical examiner's office, but the man who got out seemed in no hurry to join the other officials. He stood outside his vehicle for the longest moment, allowing Avery a pretty good look at him in the streetlamp. She guessed him to be in his early to mid thirties, tallish and lean with dark wavy hair that brushed the back of his collar. Though she could only see his profile, she knew that he was good-looking. He carried himself with the kind of poise and unaffected grace that came with supreme self-confidence. Not arrogance or conceit, but an assurance of success in every aspect of his life.

After a moment, a middle-aged woman in a robe came out of the house directly across the street from June Chapman's and called his name. *Max.*

Who was he? A detective? Despite the heat and late hour, he was dressed in a suit, but his coat was open, and his tie loosened. There was something about his demeanor that Avery found inexplicably compelling.

Intrigued or not, she was foolish to linger so close to the

crime scene, yet she couldn't seem to tear herself away. Not until she knew if June Chapman was still alive. Not until she could determine the newcomer's business. *If you're not a cop or the coroner, who are you?*

He turned suddenly to search up and down the street, almost as if he'd sensed her eyes on him. The lush vegetation hid her from his view, and she was too much of a professional to give herself away by an inadvertent movement. Despite the pain in her ankle, she could remain frozen for as long as she needed to. *You won't catch me unless I want you to.*

Still, when he finally turned away, she couldn't help expelling a breath of relief.

He gave the woman on the porch a slight nod before striding up the sidewalk to the large Georgian-style home adorned with gleaming columns and arched windows. She met him at the top of the veranda steps. The man, Max, placed his hands on her shoulders, seemingly to offer comfort or to calm her. By their ages and body language, Avery assumed a familial connection. Mother and son, most likely.

They were too far away for her to pick up their conversation and she didn't dare ease any closer. She was already putting herself at risk just by being there. Once the police started canvassing the area, they'd eventually spot her car in the alley and the out-of-state plates would immediately trigger an alarm. Best she hightail it back to her hotel and scour the internet for updates.

She stayed put, her attention captured by the curious pair. Something about the woman's frantic gestures and the man's patient demeanor sparked a feeling that seemed almost like a memory. Had Avery known either of them in another life? She wished she could get a closer look, but right now she needed to concentrate on making a clean getaway. She needed to head back to her room and record everything she could remember about the night's events, and then figure out her next move.

The shooting hadn't been random. Why else would the wounded woman have assumed that Avery had been sent to kill her? No, this wasn't the act of a panicked burglar but someone who had deliberately targeted June Chapman. Which raised the question of who stood to benefit from the woman's demise.

The trick for Avery was to somehow impart this knowledge to the police without admitting to being in the victim's house at the time of the shooting. She was a stranger in town with no one to vouch for her integrity. She had to be very careful how she handled herself.

Reluctantly, she shifted her focus from the pair on the porch to June Chapman's front door. They were bringing her out now. Avery welcomed the sight of the IV bag and tubing attached to the gurney, which meant the woman was still alive. But that presented a whole new dilemma. June Chapman had seen her face. She'd certainly had a good enough look to identify Avery in a lineup.

Again, she contemplated the wisdom of leaving town. That would be the sensible thing to do. She could drive all night and be back in Houston by midday tomorrow. She could even arrange for an alibi if the need were to arise.

But she'd come to Black Creek looking for answers and she wasn't about to leave without them. The attempt on June Chapman's life was merely the starting point on a trail that could eventually lead her all the way back to the night when a little girl named Maya Lamb had gone missing from her bedroom.

MAX STOOD WITH his stepmother, Gail Mosier, on the veranda of his childhood home as they watched the activity across the street. By the time he'd arrived on the scene, squad cars and emergency vehicles had already lined the curb in front of June Chapman's house. He'd called Gail on the way over because he knew she'd be worried when she heard all the commotion. She was a therapist and usually had a firm handle on her emotions, but waking up to sirens and revolving blue lights outside one's window was enough to frighten anyone.

There'd been a time, Max was ashamed to say, when he wouldn't have been overly concerned about his stepmother's welfare, much less her peace of mind. He hadn't approved of his father's second marriage to a younger woman even though his mother had already been dead for nearly ten years. He'd resented someone new coming into the family home and he'd acted out his disapproval by ramping up his rebellious nature.

When his father had been gunned down on the courthouse steps, no one would have blamed the young widow for shipping a recalcitrant stepson back to the boarding school where he'd aleady spent two years or to the nearest blood relative. Instead, Gail had sat him down after the funeral and told him that the house in Crescent Hill would always be his home. They were family and needed to stick together. Eventually, Max had come around and they'd managed to form a close bond, but it had taken a long time. He'd never be able to repay her steadfast loyalty and patience. No telling where or how he would have ended up if she'd turned him out after his father's death.

She wrapped her arms around her middle and shivered as the EMTs loaded the stretcher into the back of the ambulance and closed the doors. She'd thrown a cotton robe over her pajamas, not having bothered to dress before coming outside to monitor the situation. Her hair was tangled, her face devoid of makeup. She looked pale and tense in the reflected blue light from the nearest squad car, and every one of her fifty years. Max was a little jolted seeing her so unkempt even though it was the dead of night and she'd been hustled from bed by the sirens. She was usually so meticulous about her appearance.

"That poor woman," she said in a hushed voice. "To have this happen after everything she's been through. Makes you wonder what this world is coming to, doesn't it? That someone would break into an elderly widow's house and murder her in her sleep."

"She's not dead yet," Max said. "And from everything I remember about June Chapman, she's as stubborn as they come. I wouldn't bet against her chances."

His reassurance fell on deaf ears. Gail took a step toward the edge of the veranda as she stared intently at the house across the street. He saw her gaze travel up to the second story where lights blazed from all the windows. "Her bedroom is at the back of the house. No one would have seen anything," she murmured.

"You didn't hear the gunshots?"

"What? No." She seemed to rouse herself. "I didn't hear anything until the sirens woke me up." She rubbed a hand up and down her arm. "Max, how could something like this happen here? Crescent Hill has always been such a quiet neighborhood."

"Violence can happen anywhere to anyone. You and I know that better than most," he reminded her. "It's dangerous to become lulled into a false sense of security no matter where you live. Why do you think I dogged you for so long about installing an alarm system? It only makes sense in your line of work to take precautions. You never know when a disgruntled client might show up on your doorstep some night."

She gave him a quick smile. "In all my years as a therapist, I've never once felt afraid for my safety. But it's nice to have a son who cares."

Stepson. Though Max rarely made the clarification aloud these days.

"It's a shame June doesn't have anyone looking after her," Gail said. "She rattles around over there by herself in a house full of antiques and valuables. Even her old doll collection must be worth a fortune. I tried to talk to her about a security system when you had mine installed, but she wouldn't hear of it. She's always been set in her ways and not a little arrogant. She told me if anyone was stupid enough to break into her home, she was perfectly capable of taking matters into her own hands."

"She said that?" Max sighed. "Arrogant and naive."

"That's June Chapman in a nutshell. Impervious to anyone or anything outside her little bubble. She probably thought no one would dare to violate her sanctum, but you're right, Max. This just proves that no place is completely safe, and no one is invincible, even June Chapman."

They watched in silence as the ambulance pulled away from the curb and sped down the street, rushing the injured woman to the nearest ER. Depending on the severity of her wounds, she would either be stabilized at the local hospital or immediately life-flighted to a trauma center in Jacksonville. In either case, the next few hours would be telling.

The night seemed strangely silent as the siren died away, even though cops came and went from June Chapman's house and a few neighbors had gathered on the street. Through the wrought iron side gate, Max could see flashlights arcing through the backyard. He swept his gaze up and down the street, searching manicured lawns and the shadowy flagstone paths between houses. The shooter had undoubtedly fled the scene, yet an inexplicable chill crawled along Max's backbone as he peered into the night. *Are you out there watching us? Are you enjoying the chaos you've created?*

Down the street, something moved in the bushes. For a moment, he could have sworn disembodied eyes stared back at him through the leaves. Then he shook himself and turned back to his stepmother.

"When was the last time you saw June?"

Still visibly distressed, Gail leaned a shoulder against a column as she closed her eyes and thought back. "It must have been last weekend. Sunday, I think. I went out for an early morning walk, and she was already working in her garden."

"How did she seem?"

Gail shrugged. "She seemed like June. She's never been one for small talk. We said good morning, I complimented her garden and then she went back to her watering."

Max took off his suit coat and tossed it onto a wicker rocker. It was still hot despite the late hour. "Have you noticed any unusual activity in the neighborhood? Unfamiliar vehicles driving slowly past June's house or parked at the curb?"

Gail straightened in alarm. "You think someone cased her house in advance?"

He shrugged as he rolled up his sleeves. "It's possible, especially if we're dealing with professionals."

"Professionals?" She seemed shocked.

"I mean like a burglary ring," he said. "They target houses in neighborhoods like this."

"You don't think they'll come back, do you?"

He nodded toward the police cars. "They won't risk it with this kind of heat. But make sure you keep your doors locked and the security system engaged, even during the day. And keep an eye out for any suspicious activity in the area."

"Now you're really scaring me, Max."

"I don't mean to frighten you. Just be aware of your surroundings and circumstances, okay?"

She nodded. "I'm usually so tired by the time I get home from work that I probably wouldn't have noticed anything out of the ordinary. But I promise to be more observant from now on."

"Good."

They both turned back to the street. The front door of June's house was open. Max could see a police officer stationed inside the foyer. If Cal Slade took lead, he'd try to limit personnel inside the home until the forensics team completed their search. Max itched to cross the street and find out what they'd turned up so far, but an assistant DA at a crime scene could create an unnecessary and unwelcome distraction. He'd hang back for a bit and then contact Cal for a walk-through.

"What is it, Max?" Gail prompted.

"Nothing. Just lost in thought." He turned, searching her drawn features in the light spilling out from the front windows. "Does June have any enemies that you know of? Anyone holding a grudge or hard feelings against her?"

She stared at him in silence. Then, "Why would you ask that if you think she was the victim of professional thieves?"

"It's too early to rule out anything," he explained. "The police have barely begun an investigation."

"Speaking of the police, shouldn't they be over here asking these questions instead of the assistant district attorney?"

"They'll come." He motioned up and down the street. "They'll want to talk to the immediate neighbors, but right now securing the crime scene is priority. Besides, we're all on the same team last time I checked."

"Yes, of course. I didn't mean to suggest that you're overstepping your bounds. It's just..." Her hand crept to her throat. "This is all so upsetting."

"Yes, but you've handled worse."

"I know. I'm usually a rock in most situations. I don't know why this is hitting me so hard."

"Because it happened too close to home," Max said. "I would be worried if you weren't upset."

"It's more than fear. I think the shooting has triggered a lot of painful memories." She closed her eyes on a deep sigh. "Sometimes I remember the day Clayton was murdered like it was yesterday. Other times, it seems like a half-forgotten dream."

"For me, too."

She brushed the back of her hand across her cheek and straightened her shoulders. "But to answer your question, I don't know of any enemies that June might have, but she's never been the easiest person to deal with. She can be dictatorial, egotistical and sometimes unforgivably cruel. It wouldn't surprise me if she'd rubbed someone the wrong way. Look at the way she treated Reggie."

"Reggie Lamb?" His attention was caught by the name. She was the mother of the little girl who'd gone missing all those years ago. He saw her from time to time when he had lunch at the diner where she waited tables. He conjured an image of a wiry, haggard woman who wasn't afraid of hard work.

"You were just a baby when June's son died so you won't remember how bitter June became," Gail said. "She blamed Reggie for the car crash."

"Why? Was Reggie driving the vehicle?"

"No, but she and Johnny had been out drinking all night. He'd just dropped her off when he wrapped his sports car around a light pole. I guess you could argue that Reggie should have taken his keys, but if anyone was to blame for that crash besides Johnny, it was June. She never should have bought an immature man-child such a dangerous toy, but she catered to his every whim. When he started seeing Reggie, June was absolutely devastated. No one would have been good enough in her eyes, but Reggie Lamb was from the wrong side of the tracks and a rough-around-the-edges party girl to boot. When I think of some of the awful things June used to say to her…" She trailed off as her mouth thinned. "It's not hard to imagine someone holding a grudge against that woman all these years."

"Someone like Reggie?"

"She was always far more forgiving than I would have been in her shoes." Gail slid her hands into the pockets of her robe as she stared out into the night. "After Johnny's memorial service, Reggie asked me to come with her to June's house so that she could pay her respects in private. June met us on the veranda. She told Reggie in no uncertain terms that she would never be welcome in her home and that she and her brats would never see a dime of her money. She said Reggie had taken the only thing that meant anything to her in this world and if there was any justice to be had, Reggie would someday know the same kind of pain and loss that she'd inflicted upon June."

"How did Reggie react to that?" Max asked.

"She just turned and walked away. I think she must have been as stunned as I was by June's viciousness. That a woman could talk so callously about her grandchildren when her son wasn't even cold in his grave. Can you imagine cutting those innocent babies out of your life just to spite their mother? Or wishing something bad would happen to one of them so that Reggie would suffer?"

"People sometimes say and do extreme things when they're grieving." Max had certainly had his moments.

"Knowing June, she meant every word of it." Gail sounded angry as she sat down on the top step and smoothed her robe over her knees. Her earlier sympathy for June Chapman seemed to have vanished. "I've never seen anyone look at another person with the kind of hatred I saw in her eyes that day. I felt so bad for Reggie. She's certainly had her share of troubles over the years, more than any one person should have to bear. I don't know how she's coped. Not knowing what happened to your child must be the worst kind of hell."

"The two of you used to be close, didn't you?" Max leaned a hip against the railing as he studied his stepmother's profile in the dark.

"We grew up together. We were like sisters all through school." She hugged her knees. "We've talked about this before so you're already aware that I was at her house the night of the kidnapping."

Max sat down beside her. "I'd like to hear your account again if you feel like talking about it."

She turned. "I know that tone. Your wheels are turning. What's going on, Max? You don't think what happened to June has anything to do with Maya's kidnapping, do you? Not after all these years."

"A connection seems unlikely," he admitted. "But as I said, it's too early to rule out any possibility."

He felt a little guilty for not telling her about Nadine Crosby's confession, but there were reasons the police department and the DA's office had agreed to keep that information under close wraps. Certainly to protect the victim's family and the district attorney's political aspirations, but also because emotions still ran high in Black Creek when it came to Maya Lamb's abduction. It wasn't hard to imagine a vigilante justice situation if Denton Crosby walked.

"You're keeping something from me," Gail said. "I can always tell."

He opened his mouth, to deny or deflect, he wasn't quite certain, but a shout from down the street brought both their heads around. Two of the uniformed officers across the street took off running. A third came out of the house to join them. Max rose and hurried down the steps to track their bobbing flashlights.

Gail came up beside him. "Max, what's going on?"

"They've spotted something." He turned with a frown. "Go back inside and lock the doors."

"What about you?"

"I'll see what I can find out." He went back up the stairs and grabbed the flashlight his stepmother had brought out on the porch earlier. "Wait for me inside. I'll be right back."

Instead of following the armed officers, he took off down the sidewalk toward the spot where he'd noticed movement earlier. He couldn't say why he chose that route except that he couldn't shake the hunch someone had been watching him. The farther he got from the action, the darker the street became. He knew it was his imagination, but the streetlamps seemed dimmer, the shadows thicker.

A new building was going up in an overgrown lot where an old house had been torn down. The foundation had been poured and the walls and roof erected. Max stood on the sidewalk and shined his light around the property. Nothing. No movement, no errant sound. Yet the feeling persisted that someone was there.

He moved up the sidewalk and stepped through the doorway. He could see straight through the wall joists to the back entrance. He trailed the flashlight slowly around the area and then moved the beam up the stairs to the second story, where a shadow darted into the deeper recesses of the skeletal house.

Chapter Four

Max bolted up the stairs without stopping to consider that he was alone, unarmed and possibly in the presence of the person who had just shot an elderly woman in cold blood. Such a person wouldn't think twice about defending himself, especially if he felt cornered. Why June's attacker wouldn't already be miles away from the scene of the crime was anyone's guess. Perhaps he was wounded or had unfinished business in the neighborhood. Maybe he was overconfident and reckless.

Pausing at the top of the stairs, Max shined his light through the wall studs. The beam caught the eyes of the intruder, startling them both. The cat bounded past him, nearly knocking him backward as he tried to scramble out of the way. The tabby dashed across the subfloor and shot out the front door, leaving Max relieved but feeling foolish.

He raked the beam through the open walls once more before turning to leave. Below, a shadow moved in one of the framed rooms off the foyer as a board creaked somewhere else in the house. He thought at first the tabby had come back, but then he saw someone in black lurking in a corner. Before he had time to seek cover or to even to call out, a bullet from a suppressed weapon splintered a two-by-four just inches away. A second slug grazed the flesh of his left arm.

Stunned by the piercing sting of the bullet, he grabbed a support as he teetered at the top of the stairs. His knees buckled and down he went, hitting the stairs hard and cracking his head on the edge of a wooden step. He must have blacked out for a second because the next thing he knew, he lay sprawled on his back at the bottom of the stairs. Someone in a ski mask stood over him pointing a weapon at his chest. Dazed and half-blinded from pain, Max threw a hand up as if he could somehow shield himself from another bullet.

He thought he was a goner for certain. He wouldn't survive a bullet through the heart at such close range. Then something unexpected happened. He heard a loud thud and the gunman went down on one knee. His weapon was kicked aside as another figure in black drew back a board. Max's rescuer tried to hit the shooter again, but he was too quick this time. He lunged, dodging the blow, and then he was on his feet, shoving the newcomer to the floor with brute force as he grabbed his weapon and scrammed from the building.

The scuffle was over so quickly Max would later wonder if he'd imagined the whole thing. He tried to lift his head, but even so slight a movement made him dizzy and the pain in his arm had become excruciating. He was only half-aware of someone kneeling beside him and ripping his shirtsleeve.

"This just isn't my night," a female voice muttered. "Yours, either, apparently."

A woman. With dark hair and luminous eyes.

"Don't worry. It's just a flesh wound," she assured him. "I'm no doctor, but there's very little blood. Well, it's not gushing at least. That's a good sign. But you hit the stairs pretty hard and then rolled all the way down. You need to take it easy. You may have broken something."

Ignoring her advice, he struggled once more to sit up.

His head spun. He put a hand to the bump at the back of his head and drew back bloody fingers. “Who are you? What were you doing in here?”

“Saving your butt. Let’s not make a habit of that, okay?” She rose. “I think you’re good, but call for help once I’m gone.”

“Wait…” He tried to catch her hand, except she moved quickly out of his reach. “Do I know you?”

“I don’t see how.”

“Who are you? Tell me your name.”

She gave a funny little laugh. “I would, but you’d never believe me.”

SURELY HE HAD more sense than to try to follow her. Avery watched from across the street as the wounded man stumbled out of the doorway, pausing to cling to a post while he struggled for balance. He was on the phone. Any minute now the police would have the whole area surrounded.

So go! What are you waiting for?

She may have lingered too long. Making a clean getaway wouldn’t be so easy now. Even in his unsteady state, he was already looking for her. He left the porch and moved down the walkway, gaining strength with each step. By the time he got to the street, his shoulders were back, his posture erect. *Who are you, Max? Why did you come alone and unarmed to an empty house? How did you know the bad guy would be hiding inside? How did you know I’d be watching?*

If she hadn’t been keeping an eye from the bushes…if she hadn’t decided to follow him inside that house, his evening might have ended very differently.

She wasn’t a hero nor did she have a savior complex, far from it. Normally, she was more interested in looking out for number one, but twice in a single night she’d been forced from her comfort zone to offer assistance to strangers. Unlike June Chapman, the Max guy would probably be fine by morning. He'd have a sore arm and a tender place on his head, but he was damn lucky she hadn't gone back to her hotel room five minutes earlier. Maybe things really did happen for a reason.

Do I know you?

"No, Max, you do not know me. No one in town knows me and I'd like to keep it that way," she whispered.

A low profile was imperative in her line of work. Luther always said that whenever possible it was best to operate from the shadows. After tonight, that might no longer be an option. By coming to a stranger's rescue, she'd placed herself in an even more precarious position. Both victims and the shooter could identify her. Not only was her investigation compromised, but also her safety. Her only hope was that the dark house and the assailant's mask had sufficiently obscured his vision.

Avery searched up and down the street. Was he still out there or had he finally fled the neighborhood? And why had he remained in the area for so long after the shooting?

She thought about earlier when she'd first noticed the French door ajar in the parlor and had wondered if the intruder in the garden had an accomplice who was already inside the premises. Maybe that explained why one of them had been hiding out in a construction zone. The pair had split up, possibly to search for the only witness to their crime besides June Chapman. It was unnerving to think that even now she was being hunted.

Across the street, Max finished his call and slipped the phone in his pocket. She assumed he would either head back up the street to seek medical attention or hunker in place until backup arrived. Instead, he crossed the street and peered into the bushes dangerously close to where she was hidden.

"I know you're still here," he said. "I know you're watching me."

She remained motionless, hardly daring to breathe as she tracked him through the leafy branches. She could see him clearly from where she crouched. His presence had an almost visceral effect on her though she had no idea why. She didn't know him. Not in this life. He was a stranger and yet there was something so disconcertingly familiar about him.

"Why did you run away? You saved my life. I'd like the chance to thank you properly."

Just go, Avery silently pleaded. *Leave me alone.*

"No worries. I'll find you," he promised as he turned and walked away without a backward glance.

WHEN AVERY FINALLY got back to her hotel, she climbed the fire escape up to her room on the second floor rather than chance being seen in the lobby by the night clerk or, worse, getting caught on a security camera. She crawled through the window she'd left open earlier and plopped down on the bed to peel off her shoes and socks so she could examine her ankle. The joint was still painful, but she didn't think it was fractured or sprained. Ice and elevation was all she needed.

Stripping, she took a long, hot shower, vigorously scrubbing her flesh and scalp in case any cobwebs remained. Then she threw on a robe over her pajamas and fetched a bucket of ice from the machine at the end of the hallway. Finally tucked in bed with her laptop and a makeshift ice pack on her ankle, she closed her eyes for a moment and let the tension from the past hour drain out of her.

I really stepped in it this time, Luther.

Then figure out a way to step back out of it, kid.

Her father's phantom voice drifted away as she opened her laptop and searched the local sites for news of the shooting. It had been less than an hour since she'd heard the suppressed gunshots in June Chapman's home, so it wasn't surprising that word had yet to get out. She opened a blank document and typed out everything she could remember of the night's events. Then grabbing her notebook and a pen from the nightstand, she jotted down the names that she'd overheard in the neighbor's backyard:

Tom Fuqua (June Chapman's neighbor and a retired state senator)

Will Kent (Retired Black Creek police chief)

Max...?

The woman on the porch?

The shooter?

A possible accomplice?

So many questions. She doodled for a moment as something teased at the back of her mind. She opened her file on the Maya Lamb kidnapping and scanned through the Word documents. Yes, there it was. Will Kent had been the police chief at the time of the child's disappearance. He'd remained in the position for another fifteen years before retiring a decade ago.

Avery went back and adjusted her notes:

Will Kent (Black Creek police chief at the time of the kidnapping. Now retired)

She did a Google search using both men's names. The only hit was an archived article from a local paper with the headline "Senator Tom Fuqua Eulogizes a Local Legend."

A photograph taken at a graveside service accompanied the headline, followed by a lengthy article highlighting Judge Clayton Winter's illustrious career on the bench. Senator Tom Fuqua and Police Chief Will Kent had served as honorary pallbearers. According to the article, the trio had fought together in Vietnam and had then returned to their hometown, each to serve the community in his own way.

Avery scanned the article and then added Judge Winter to her list:

Clayton Winter (Circuit court judge, murdered. Friends with Tom Fuqua and Will Kent)

She scrolled back to the top of the article and enlarged the photograph, scrutinizing the grim faces until she recognized Tom Fuqua. She hadn't gotten a good look at him in the dark earlier and he would be considerably older now, but she was reasonably certain he was the same man. Then she was jolted to see another face she recognized. A teenage boy stood just to Tom Fuqua's right and slightly behind him, half-hidden by the shadow cast by the state senator.

Her heart thudded as she studied his features. *Max, is that you?*

On Tom Fuqua's left was a slender woman in a veil. The camera had caught the boy shooting daggers at her.

Intrigued, Avery scrolled down to the bottom of the article where the obituary had been linked. She quickly read through the surviving family members: A wife, Dr. Gail Mosier, and a son, Max Winter.

She paged back up to the photograph before opening a new window to search *Max Winter, Black Creek, Florida*. Dozens of links popped up along with a more current photograph.

"There you are," she murmured in triumph. "I found you first."

Maximus Clayton Winter, an assistant district attorney. *That's some name, Max.*

So the man had resources he could employ to track her down if she wasn't careful. But no need to panic just yet. Maybe she could turn things around and use those same resources to her benefit. After all, she was Luther Bolt's daughter, wasn't she?

A plan was already starting to form as she read back through her notes. For the next hour, she clicked links and scanned articles until the words on the screen started to blur. Before putting away her laptop for the night, she took one last look at the photograph that had started her on this mission.

Enlarging the image, she scrutinized the woman's features as she'd done a hundred times before, taking note once again of the wavy blond hair blowing back from a solemn face dominated by vivid blue eyes and a generous mouth. Special Agent Thea Lamb. A woman who'd made it her life's work to search for missing and exploited children. The heavy toll of her profession haunted her eyes and hardened her mouth. In many ways, she looked to be a formidable person and yet there was something achingly vulnerable about her expression when she'd been caught off guard by the photographer.

Closing the laptop lid on the image, Avery turned off the light and slid down under the covers. She lay on her back for the longest time, unable to sleep. Finally she got up and padded over to the window, crawling out onto the fire escape for a breath of fresh air.

The night had finally cooled. She tilted her face to the breeze, drinking in the intoxicating fragrance of jasmine that drifted up from the courtyard. The night was very still except for the sound of a bamboo wind chime somewhere nearby. The melodic clacking of the hollow pipes stirred a powerful memory.

Or was it a dream?

She closed her eyes, letting the odd music seep into her consciousness. Another sound came back to her, mingling with the chimes. The distant baying of a coonhound. Then a child's tremulous voice whispering from the farthest corner of her memory.

I'm scared, Sissy.

Chapter Five

The sun had already risen over the treetops when Max arrived the next day at his stepmother's house. He was surprised to find her still in her nightclothes. She was usually dressed and out the door by eight, but from the looks of her unkempt hair and the dark circles under her eyes, she'd spent the early morning hours tossing and turning.

He handed her a disposable cup as she opened the screen door. "I brought coffee."

"You're a lifesaver. I didn't think to set the timer before I went to bed. Not that I couldn't have pushed a few buttons this morning, but when it comes to caffeine, I'm all about instant gratification." She took a quick sip and sighed. "Just what I needed. Thanks."

"Least I could do for showing up on your doorstep before breakfast."

"Why *are* you here so early?" She took in his suit and tie as she came out on the veranda. "Looks like you're headed to the office. I was hoping you'd take a few days off to recuperate."

"No recuperation necessary. My arm is fine. Just a scratch."

Her mouth tightened with worry. "Don't try to downplay what happened. You were shot, for God's sake."

"I was grazed. The bullet barely touched me. The ER

doctor said I'll be good as new in a day or two." His arm was sore as hell and he had a goose egg at the back of his skull, but he felt strangely exhilarated now that the case was starting to heat up. Where the events of last evening would lead, he had no idea, but it was time to start looking for the mysterious woman who had come to his rescue.

Gail's free hand crept to her throat. "When I think about what could have happened to you… Don't ever do that to me again."

"I'll try not to make it a habit."

"I'm serious, Max. You're not a cop. It's not your job to track down dangerous criminals. You're just supposed to put them away."

"Who says I can't do both? I'm kidding," he quickly added when she scowled her disapproval. "There's no need to worry about me. Most of my time is spent in the office or a courtroom." Not that that would be of much comfort to a woman whose husband had been gunned down on the courthouse steps.

"Did you at least get a look at the gunman?" She sat down in one of the wicker rocking chairs and smoothed her robe.

"No, as I explained last night, he wore a ski mask. And I only caught a glimpse of him anyway."

"What about the person who came to your rescue? A woman, you said."

"Yes." He glanced out over the garden and tried to conjure her image. Nothing came back to him. He could hear her voice. He could even imagine the scent of her hair, but he couldn't seem to recall her features. It had been too dark, and he'd only been semiconscious while she'd tended his arm.

Do I know you?

I don't see how.

"I have no idea who she is," he said. "I'm certain I've never seen her before. But she probably saved my life."

Gail seemed less than impressed. "Odd that she happened to be in that construction project at just the right moment."

The same thought had crossed Max's mind. "Lucky for me that she was."

"Why would the man who attacked June stay in the neighborhood after he shot her? Why didn't he flee immediately afterward? It makes no sense to me."

"Maybe he was waiting for a getaway car. Or maybe he wanted to make sure she was dead."

His stepmother grew pensive as she traced a finger around the lid of her cup. "Do you know how she's doing this morning? I called the hospital earlier, but they wouldn't tell me anything. Is she still at Memorial or did they transfer her to a trauma center?"

"The police have instructed the hospital not to give out any information. She's alive. That's about all I can tell you at the moment."

"Of course. Her safety is paramount. I don't suppose you can talk about the investigation, either."

"There isn't much to discuss. I'm meeting the lead detective at her house in a few minutes. You remember Cal Slade."

"*Calvin* Slade?" She grimaced. "How could I forget him? The pair of you must have taken ten years off my life after you came back from boarding school. Who would have ever thought that kid would end up on the right side of the law?"

Max grinned. "No one who knew either of us back then, but he's turned out to be a fine detective. I've asked him to walk me through the crime scene and bring me up to speed on any evidence that's been recovered."

She gave a vague nod. "I still can't believe it happened. I talked to one of my neighbors just before you arrived. Tom said a cop searched his backyard last night. He was pretty upset. We all are. We don't expect this kind of crime in a close-knit neighborhood like Crescent Hill."

Max sat down in the second rocker and placed his cup on the glass-topped side table between them. "I don't mean to pick at an old wound, but I was hoping we could continue our conversation from last night."

She frowned. "What conversation is that?"

"You were telling me about the night Maya Lamb went missing."

"Yes, and I asked if you thought there could be a connection to June's shooting." She gave him a narrowed stare. "Do you?"

"I still think it's a long shot, but the police aren't ruling anything out at this point. Do you mind talking about the kidnapping?"

Gail sighed. "Not if you think it will help."

"You never know."

"It's funny, but even after all this time, I still remember the hours after she went missing as if it happened yesterday." She turned to stare out into the garden as she rocked gently to and fro. "I must have gone back over that night hundreds of times in my mind. Every now and then someone still wants to do a story. People never seem to lose interest. We'd all like to believe she's somehow alive and well, but the reality is, that child was probably dead within twenty-four hours after she was taken."

"The statistics in stranger abductions are grim," Max agreed. "Why were you at Reggie's house that night?"

"She threw a big party almost every weekend. That night things got wild even by her standards. I stayed over because she'd had too much to drink, and I wanted to be there in case the twins needed anything. They were such sweet girls, especially Maya. She had a smile that could melt your heart."

"I remember seeing them at June's house once." Max's gaze moved across the street. "They were sitting side by side on her veranda steps."

"Oh, I think you must be mistaken, Max. I can't imagine June ever having those girls at her home."

"No, they were there," he insisted. "It was the day of my mother's funeral, so I remember the incident vividly. They both had on frilly dresses. Maya's was pink and Thea's yellow."

Gail turned in surprise. "With little bows at the waist?"

"That I couldn't tell you. I just remember thinking they were dressed fancy for a weekday."

His stepmother shook her head in wonder. "My goodness. I'd forgotten all about those dresses. Reggie had them made for their fourth birthday. She must have scrimped and saved for months. They turned out so sweet with pearl buttons down the back and those tiny bows at the waist. The girls adored them. They wanted to wear them everywhere." She paused on another sigh. "So you really did see the twins at June's house. Reggie never said a word to me about a visit."

"Maya disappeared a few days later," Max said. "It probably didn't seem important."

"No, of course it wouldn't." Gail paused, thinking back. "Nothing seemed important after that night. Maya's disappearance changed everything. When I close my eyes, I can still see myself walking into their room and finding that empty bed. I wasn't even certain at first which girl was missing. They looked so much alike in their sleep. Later I learned they'd swapped places sometime during the night. Thea usually slept in the bed nearest the window. She was always such a brave little soul. I can only imagine how often she must have thought of that arrangement over the years. If they hadn't switched beds, she would have been taken instead of Maya. It wasn't her fault, of course, but try reasoning with a child who's lost her twin sister."

According to Nadine Crosby's confession, both twins were to have been taken, but Gail had no way of knowing that. "I imagine it's been a living hell for Thea," Max said. "I would also guess that's why she joined the FBI and why she works almost exclusively on cases involving missing and exploited children."

"I can still see her little face that morning," Gail said dreamily. "She was only four years old, and we tried to protect her as best we could, but she knew something terrible had happened to her sister. She knew far more than anyone wanted to believe."

Max had read the official file at least a dozen times in the past two weeks. He knew what was coming, but he still listened intently to his stepmother's personal account of those first few hours after Maya Lamb had gone missing.

"It seems surreal even now," she murmured.

"Did you know right away that she'd been taken?"

She shook her head slowly. "The window was open, but I didn't think much of it at first. The old air conditioner in Reggie's house never cooled the bedrooms. I assumed she'd left the window open so the girls could catch a breeze. I checked the bathroom and kitchen and then I woke up Reggie. The two of us tore the house apart and then we searched all around the yard. The back gate was open. I remember wondering if Maya might have been sleepwalking. Maybe she'd somehow climbed out the window in her sleep, opened the gate and wandered into the woods. It was scary enough thinking of her out there alone, lost and frightened and not able to find her way back home. I kept worrying about the cave, but I didn't want to say anything to Reggie. We were both out of our minds by that time."

"As anybody would be," Max said.

She folded her arms around her middle. "The police arrived, and search parties were organized. The hours ticked away without any trace of Maya. It was as if she'd vanished into thin air. Some of the neighbors came over and made sandwiches and iced tea for the volunteers. Night fell. The search was called off until morning so that everyone could get a hot meal and some sleep. One of the neighbors stayed to watch Thea while Reggie and I kept looking. We went all the way to the cave calling Maya's name. Reggie wanted to go down into the passageways, but I talked her out of it. It was too dangerous, just the two of us out there alone. We went home so hoarse and exhausted we could barely speak, but neither of us could sleep. We stayed up all night clutching hands. The police came back the next morning and brought dogs. One day blended into another until hope began to dwindle and we were left with nothing but an awful, waiting dread."

Max felt inexplicably shaken by his stepmother's recollection. It had been nearly three decades since Maya Lamb had been abducted from her bedroom, but the slight tremor in Gail's voice brought home the deep and lasting pain from her disappearance.

"Did you ever wonder if someone at the party had taken her?" he asked.

Gail nodded. "Yes. I mean, it was only human nature to wonder. Reggie hung out with a rough crowd back then. The worst of the bunch was the creep she dated."

"Derrick Sway?"

"He never had much use for the girls even when he was sober. When he was drunk..." Gail trailed off on a shudder. "I never saw him lay a hand on them, but it's not hard to imagine his temper getting the better of him. He was a mean drunk. Why Reggie put up with him for as long as she did, I'll never know."

"What about Reggie?" Max asked. "Did you ever wonder about her?"

Gail answered without hesitation. "Not once. She had her faults, but she loved her little girls. She would never have done anything to harm them."

"Some people would disagree with you," he said. "Some still think to this day that Reggie Lamb murdered her daughter and buried her body in the woods."

Gail's expression darkened. "That was June's doing. She went on that local crime stoppers television show and planted the seed, all but accusing Reggie of murdering the child. After that interview, people started looking at Reggie differently, whispering about her behind her back. Calling her nasty names to her face. June made her a pariah in her own hometown."

"Did you ever talk to Reggie about it?"

"About the interview? Not really. By that time, she and I had already started to drift apart. She put up walls after Maya disappeared. I didn't blame her. She needed to protect herself. I only meant to give her some space, but you know how it is. You get busy with your own life and before you know it, you've both moved on. I went back to school and Reggie found religion."

"Do you think she carried a grudge against June for that interview?"

"Max, for goodness' sakes!" Her eyes blazed with sudden indignation. "You can't possibly think Reggie Lamb broke into June's house and shot her last night."

"No. Not really. But I wanted to hear what you thought. Do you know of anyone who would benefit financially from June's death?"

Gail settled back down. "Certainly not Reggie. I think June would sooner take a lit match to her fortune than to see Reggie inherit a dime. It's possible she made provisions for Thea in her will, but I doubt it. The only other living relative that I know of is a nephew by marriage. His name is

Paul Bozeman. He owns an antique shop on Main Street. I believe he has a daughter that runs the business with him."

"Have you ever met either of them?"

"Not that I recall, but I know there was bad blood between the two families. I don't know the details, but I gather June's late husband came from old money. His sister was disowned for some reason, so he inherited the bulk of the family fortune, which went to June upon his passing. You can imagine the resentment that created. Years ago, when June and I used to have coffee from time to time, she once mentioned that Paul Bozeman would steal her blind if he thought he could get away with it. She said things had a way of turning up missing when he came around. Silver candlesticks, a piece of jewelry. Even one of her prized dolls. She could never catch him in the act, but she was certain he and his *delinquent daughter*—her words, not mine—were coming into her home and taking things while she was out."

"Yet she refused to install a security system."

Gail nodded. "Her arrogance again. Though I do wonder if the alleged thefts were anything other than her imagination. June has a tendency to think the worst of people. Throw in a healthy dose of paranoia and who knows if there was any real basis for her accusations. Still, you should probably check them out."

"I'll let Cal know."

"Is that his car?"

An unmarked vehicle pulled up across the street in front of June Chapman's house. A tall, lanky man in his midthirties climbed out with a cell phone pressed to his ear. He strode up the walkway and removed the police tape across the front porch and then the door and let himself inside.

Gail seemed fixated on the house across the street.

"You okay?" Max asked.

"What?" She gave herself a little shake as she brought her

attention back to him. "Yes, of course. Just a little tired this morning. Not enough sleep and too many old memories."

"I'm sorry if talking about Maya upset you."

"No, don't be silly. I still think about her often." She made an effort to lighten the mood. "You must be chomping at the bit to see what the police have uncovered. Go on over there and talk to Calvin. I need to get ready for work anyway."

"Are you sure you're all right?" Max asked. "You've had a shock. Maybe you're the one who should take the day off."

"I've got appointments all morning, but maybe I can come home early this afternoon. We'll see. Please don't worry about me. I'm fine. Just keep me posted, okay?"

"Yes, as much as I'm able to." They both rose. "Remember what I said last night. Keep your doors locked and your security system engaged when you're here alone."

"I'm not likely to forget to do that anytime soon." She patted his arm. "I'll call you later. Maybe we can have an early dinner together."

He waited until she'd gone inside before jogging down the steps. Gail was right. He was eager to find out what the forensics team had recovered from the crime scene. A connection to the kidnapping might well be a long shot, but it could also be the break he and the police had been waiting for.

In the meantime, he had a couple of leads to pass along to Cal Slade. Paul Bozeman and his daughter would need to be checked out. So would Reggie Lamb despite his stepmother's objection.

Something else swirled at the back of Max's mind, a vague supposition that seemed too dark to even consider. Had June Chapman somehow been involved in her granddaughter's kidnapping?

He tried to recall what little he knew about the woman.

His family had lived across the street from her for years, but he'd never paid much attention to her. Couldn't remember ever carrying on a conversation with her. To him, she was just the cranky old lady who lived in the house with all the flowers. Suddenly, though, a particular encounter came back to him, and he paused on the walkway, his gaze going to the lush garden across the street.

He'd been ten or eleven at the time and bored out of his mind. All his friends were either on vacation with their families or had gone off to baseball camp for a month. He'd had to stay in town to attend summer school because of one measly D on his report card. His old man had been adamant. No son of his would be a slacker.

After the morning session was over, he'd been kicking a soccer ball down the sidewalk when he happened to notice a bunch of white flowers in June Chapman's garden. The sweet scent carried all the way out to the street. He only meant to pick the bloom closest to the sidewalk—mostly out of spite—but before he knew it, he'd waded into the garden and snapped every last stalk. Then he stuffed the fragrant blossoms in a grocery bag and rode his bike all the way out to the cemetery to place them on his mother's grave.

Unbeknownst to Max, June Chapman had witnessed his thievery from one of her front windows. She must have nursed her outrage all day because she'd marched across the street the instant his father's car had pulled into the driveway. Max, hiding in the bushes at the side of the porch, had eavesdropped on their entire conversation without the slightest qualm. After a testy back-and-forth, his father had assured June that suitable punishment would be meted out to his son and that she would be compensated for the damage to her garden.

She'd grudgingly accepted the apology and had turned

to go back home when she suddenly stopped in her tracks and whirled.

"That boy needs a firm hand or else he's headed for trouble."

"Like your boy, you mean?"

Her mouth tightened. "That was low even for you, Clayton Winter. Johnny was a good kid until he took up with that awful girl. It only takes one bad apple. Max spends too much time alone. No supervision. No role models. He's restless and spoiling for trouble. If you're not careful, stolen flowers will be the least of your worries."

His father sighed. "I told you he'd be punished. What more do you want?"

"I want you to take an interest in your son. Teach him some boundaries. He needs to know he can't go around taking things that don't belong to him."

His father paused for the longest time, then said quietly, "That's rich coming from you, June. You know all about taking something that doesn't belong to you."

MAX OPENED JUNE CHAPMAN'S front door and glanced inside. In all the years his family had lived across the street from her, he couldn't remember ever having been in her home. Even on the hottest day of that summer when he'd had to weed her garden as punishment for his misdeed, she'd never invited him inside for so much as a glass of water. Instead, she'd tracked his every move from the cool comfort of her solarium, taking perverse satisfaction in his misery. Or so it had seemed to Max.

Considering what he did remember of her, the gloomy interior was hardly a surprise. She'd always been a somber woman. Paneling darkened the foyer, creating a feeling of oppression despite sunlight spilling in through the sidelights. Portraits in heavy frames lined the hallway and an impressive mahogany staircase curved up to a wide landing with an ornate rail and spindles.

Cal Slade was just coming down the stairs when he spotted Max in the doorway. He held up a finger as he answered his phone. A veteran detective who'd spent the early part of his career with the Jacksonville Police Department, Cal had returned home to Black Creek three years ago with a new wife and baby. He and Max went all the way back to middle school. There'd been a time, as his stepmother well remembered, when the two of them had thumbed their noses at rules and convention, but that was all in the past. Cal was a devoted family man now and Max had sorted out his priorities a long time ago.

The detective spoke with some urgency to the person on the other end of the call. For so early in the morning, he looked a bit harried. His tie was loosened, and his sleeves rolled up to accommodate the summer heat. He was tall and fit with a hairline that was just starting to recede. Max still had a full head of hair, but there were days when he cut his five-mile run in half. Thirty-three was far from old, but there were times when he didn't feel so young, either.

"Sorry about that. Lot of fires to put out with the chief gone for a few days." Cal put away his phone and motioned for Max to enter the foyer. "Don't worry about contamination. Forensics has been over the house with a fine-tooth comb."

"Did they find anything?" Max stepped across the threshold.

"The usual assortment of prints and fibers. Hopefully, the lab can sift through the haystack and find us the proverbial needle. In the meantime, I'll show you what we've got so far." He turned and went back up the stairs and Max followed a few steps behind him.

Cal pointed to a trio of bullet holes in the wall above the landing. "Angle of entry suggests the gun was fired from the foyer. We dug three 9 mm slugs out of the plaster. You'd be surprised how thick the walls are in these old houses. Three shots here and the two in the bedroom that wounded the victim. Five rounds total, yet not a single neighbor we've talked to heard gunfire."

"My stepmother didn't hear anything, and she lives just across the street," Max confirmed.

Cal angled his head in the general vicinity of the yard. "I'm surprised she's stayed in the same house all these years. Place brings back a lot of memories. I can only imagine what it must be like for her. And for you."

"It's a good house. I don't see her getting rid of it anytime soon." Max shrugged off a sudden tug of nostalgia. "Anyway, back to the shots. Since the gunfire didn't awaken her, I'm assuming the intruder used a silencer."

"That strikes me as a little unusual for a run-of-the-mill break-in," Cal said. "Not unusual that he had a weapon, but that he had the forethought to bring a noise suppressor."

Max went over to the carved banister and glanced down into the foyer. Then he turned back to the hallway. "I'll take a stab at what happened. The victim heard a noise that roused her from sleep, and she came out here to investigate. The intruder saw her on the landing, panicked and fired up at her. She fled back to her bedroom, and he pursued her. Which means there's a good chance June Chapman saw his face."

"Not a bad deduction, but you haven't yet seen what we found in the bedroom." Once again Cal took the lead as they headed down the hallway. Then he stepped aside so that Max had a view into June Chapman's bedroom.

The room was spacious and luxuriously decorated with satin drapes and tufted upholstery, but the opulence seemed heavy-handed to Max. The bed was unmade, the nightstand drawer open. Nothing else seemed amiss except for two Xs marked on the floor with blue painter's tape.

"She was found lying next to the bed." Cal moved across the room and pointed to the first X. "A pearl-handle, hammerless revolver was found beside her."

"Hers?"

"We're checking the registration, but it's a pretty safe bet. You don't come across a vintage piece that well-preserved every day."

"I'm surprised the gunman didn't take it. Must be worth a lot to the right collector." Max imagined the elderly woman awaking suddenly to a noise in the house. Instead of reaching for her cell phone to call the police, she'd grabbed for her weapon thinking she could protect herself.

"Maybe he thought a piece like that could too easily be traced," Cal said.

Max nodded. "What about the second X?"

"That's where things start to get interesting. The EMTs found a folded towel covering the victim's wounds, presumably to stop the bleeding. It's possible she made it to the bathroom, grabbed the first thing she could find and stumbled back out to the bedroom before she collapsed, but it doesn't seem likely. There's no blood trail to the bathroom."

Max gave him a skeptical look. "You're not suggesting the shooter administered first aid before he fled the scene, are you?"

"No." Cal's eyes gleamed. "I'm *telling* you there was a third person in the house at the time of the shooting."

Chapter Six

Cal's certainty of a witness intrigued Max. June Chapman lived alone as far as he knew. Who else would have been in her house at the time of the shooting? An accomplice? He thought about the woman who'd come to his rescue last night. Like his stepmother earlier, he wondered about the timing of her appearance. But if she'd gone into the vacant house to meet her partner, why come to the aid of a stranger? On the other hand, why flee the scene of a crime if she wasn't afraid of facing the police?

"Do you have any idea who this third person might be?" he asked. "Or why he or she was in June Chapman's house last night?"

"There's no sign that anyone else is staying here. Whoever she is, we think she used a burner phone to call 911 a few minutes after midnight to report suspicious activity at this residence."

"She?"

Cal nodded. "Approximately four and a half minutes later, another anonymous call was placed from this location reporting shots fired and requesting an ambulance. The phone went dead after those two calls. No way to trace it except through the old-fashioned method of triangulation, but my guess is it's already been ditched. We can obtain the call log from the carrier, but I doubt it will tell us anything. We seem to be dealing with a savvy individual. The operator said she spoke in a hoarse whisper as if she was trying to disguise her voice."

"Or maybe she didn't want to be overheard. The operator is certain the caller was female?"

"Not a hundred percent, but reasonably certain. I've asked the lab to run a voice analysis on the recording. Hopefully, they may be able to pick up something in the background that'll give us a clue to her identity."

Max's rescuer had spoken in a hushed but normal tone in the empty house. Funny how he could recall her voice but not her face. Everything had happened too fast and the fall down the stairs had dulled his senses. Not to mention the white-hot sting of the bullet grazing his flesh. He flexed his arm now, as if the sudden pain might sharpen his memory.

Was she their anonymous caller? If so, why had she been in June Chapman's house in the middle of the night?

"I don't think we can rule out the caller as an accomplice just because she called 911," he said. "Maybe she and her partner broke into the house together, but when June woke up and caught them in the act, the partner panicked, pulled a gun and shot her. Maybe the accomplice also panicked and called 911, then tried to render aid to the victim before the police arrived. That could explain why she fled the scene."

"Yes, but it doesn't explain why she brought a burner phone to a robbery. Or why the shooter equipped his weapon with a silencer. I agree it makes sense to assume they were working together, but I can't shake the feeling that we're dealing with two separate suspects with two separate agendas. Call it gut instinct or intuition or just plain guesswork. Something doesn't feel right to me."

Max glanced around again. "Do we know how they got in?"

"At least one of them came through the French doors in

the parlor. We found scuff marks on the strike plate and doorjamb. It's the most logical point of entry. Trees block the streetlight on that side of the house and the heavy vegetation would have hidden an intruder from the neighbors. The front door was wide open when the officers arrived. We think that's how the shooter exited the premises." He nodded across the room. "The French doors in here were also unlocked."

"June may have thought it unnecessary to secure second-floor entrances," Max said.

"True, but it's also possible one of the suspects exited by way of the balcony. There's a trellis fastened to the wall within reach. Some of the slats near the bottom are loose."

They both went over to check out the balcony doors. Max stepped outside and glanced down. "Long way to the ground," he said. "If the trellis had snapped at the top, someone could have ended up with a broken neck." Which would further suggest the caller was desperate to get away before the police arrived.

Max studied the garden for a moment longer and then went back inside. "Gail told me earlier there's a nephew by marriage in the picture. His name is Paul Bozeman. He and his daughter own an antique store on Main Street. Evidently, there's bad blood between the two families. Resentment over an inheritance or something. June once told Gail that Bozeman would steal her blind if he thought he could get away with it. She was convinced that he and his daughter were coming into her house while she was out and stealing her silver."

"Did she file a police report?" Cal opened the closet door and glimpsed inside.

"I doubt it. She's always been the type to handle things privately. May not be anything to it, but I thought I'd mention his name just in case."

"Lots of antique shops and thrift stores along Main

Street, but I'm pretty sure I've heard that name before. Bozeman Antiques." He closed the closet door and turned back to Max. "My mother used to shop there so they must be a reputable outfit. She was like a bloodhound when it came to cheats. I guarantee she checked them out from one end to the other before she spent a dime. Most of their stuff was too pricey for her anyway, but she liked to browse. I'm trying to remember what she said about the owner. She always had an opinion."

"I liked that about her," Max said. "You never had to guess where you stood with Mrs. Slade."

"She always liked you, too. She thought I was a bad influence on you."

"You were."

Cal grinned. "Funny, I remember it the other way around." He glanced inside the open nightstand drawer. "My honest opinion about the Bozeman dude? He sounds like a long shot, but I'll do some poking around and see what I can find out about him."

Max nodded. "Let me know if anything turns up. Speaking of long shots, you said last night you thought the shooting could be connected to the Maya Lamb case."

Cal shrugged and replied candidly, "I figured that was the quickest way to get you involved. Nothing like a little heat from the DA's office to loosen the purse strings. You know what it's like at the station right now. Everything has to be budgeted right down to the Post-it Notes. I'd like to assign another investigator to the case, but without any evidence to support a connection, I'm not likely to get it. Unless you can convince your boss to do a little arm-twisting. Even then…" He trailed off. "I will say this. At the very least, the timing is curious. Just when Maya's case is once again splashed all over the news and internet, her grandmother is shot in her own home. Could be nothing more than coincidence, but I've never been a big believer of coincidences."

"Yeah, me either," Max agreed. "Gail mentioned something else that got me to thinking. Nadine Crosby claimed she, her brother, Denton, and a man named Gabriel Jareau were hired to abduct Maya and Thea Lamb. We've been operating under the assumption that someone who wanted the girls for their own agenda paid to have them kidnapped. Child trafficking was a fast-growing criminal enterprise even back then. Not to mention illegal adoptions. But what if someone just wanted the girls gone? Someone with a lot of money whose only intention was to punish the children's mother?"

Cal frowned. "Someone like June Chapman, you mean?"

"According to Gail, she blamed Reggie Lamb for her son's death. After his funeral, June told her that if there was any justice in the world, Reggie would someday know the same pain and loss that June had suffered."

Cal rubbed the back of his neck. "I'll admit that's an interesting angle, but how would someone like June Chapman come into contact with the likes of Nadine and Denton Crosby? They don't exactly move in the same circles."

The better question was, how had Max's father known about June's complicity in the kidnapping? Was Clayton Winter the missing link? As a circuit court judge, he'd seen all manner of criminals come in and out of his courtroom. He could have easily put June in touch with the Crosby siblings.

A chill skirted along Max's spine, agitating his nerves and making him jittery until he reminded himself that his recollection of the conversation between his father and June Chapman could be faulty. Even if the dialogue unfolded the way he remembered, his father's parting taunt could have been referring to something completely unrelated to Maya's kidnapping. Max was jumping to all sorts of conclusions based on nothing more than an old memory.

He shook himself and forced his attention back to Cal's question. "People with June's kind of money can make almost anything happen. Think about it. Why would Denton Crosby hang around in the area when he knows the police are trying to tie him to the kidnapping? Not to mention to the suspicious death of an elderly man whose car Crosby allegedly stole. He could have blown town the moment you had to release him. Instead, it almost seems as if he's daring you to pick him up again."

Cal swore under his breath.

Max nodded his agreement with the sentiment. "But maybe that's just what he wants you to think. Maybe the real reason he's still in Black Creek is to tie up loose ends. His sister is dead. Gabriel Jareau is dead. The only person who can connect him to Maya's abduction is the person who hired him."

Cal played devil's advocate. "Why would he turn on her now when they've kept each other's secret for nearly thirty years?"

"Because of his sister's confession. If his own flesh and blood would rat him out, how can he trust June Chapman to keep her mouth shut?"

"But she can't finger him without incriminating herself," Cal pointed out.

"No, but maybe Crosby decided he couldn't take that chance. She's getting on in years. Maybe he was worried she'd want to clear her conscience before she died. I know this sounds like a lot of grasping at straws," Max said. "But if we're on the right track, June Chapman's shooting could be a major break in a case that's been ice-cold for almost three decades."

"I'll carve out some time to go back through the old case file," Cal said. "Fresh eyes and all that. Will Kent was the chief of police back then. Might be a good idea to get his input on your theory."

"I know him. He and my old man were big buddies back in the day. I can give him a shout, tell him to expect your call."

"Or better yet, you could go talk to him yourself," Cal suggested. "He might be a little more cooperative with someone he knows. I hear he can get pretty defensive when it comes to the Maya Lamb case."

"Sure, I can do that," Max said. "I'll try to make a run out to his place in the next day or two."

"In the meantime, I'll station an officer at the hospital for a couple of nights just in case Denton Crosby or anyone else decides to try and finish the job. That's about the best I can do and even that's pushing it. June's condition is still critical so it could be days before we can talk to her. If ever."

"You could always bring Crosby back in and see if he's rattled enough to let something slip," Max said.

"It'll take more than forty-eight hours in a holding cell to loosen that guy's tongue. He's had nearly thirty years to perfect his story. But we'll keep tabs on him as much as our limited manpower will allow." Cal turned and retraced his steps down the hallway to the landing, pausing once again to study the three bullet holes in the wall. "Let's assume for a minute that the caller and the gunman did have separate agendas. Let's also assume the caller was already in the house when June Chapman was shot. If she had started up the stairs to investigate, she would have heard the shooter coming down the hallway toward her. There wouldn't have been time to hide. All she could do was press herself against the wall and hope for the best." He positioned his body against the wall so that the bullet holes surrounded him.

"The shooter would have been in flight mode," he continued. "He ran down the stairs, maybe glimpsing something out of the corner of his eye. When he got to the bottom, he looked back, saw her up here hiding in the shadows and fired off three rounds before bolting out the front door."

"Like this." Max hurried down the steps to the foyer, lifting his gaze and a pointed finger toward the landing.

Cal stepped to the banister. "She would have had a good view from up here. It was dark and if the gunman was the same guy that attacked you, he was probably wearing a mask. But it's possible she noticed a tick, a tattoo, a piece of jewelry, *something* that could help us identify him."

"Then we'd better find her before he does," Max said.

AFTER CAL LEFT for the station, Max lingered in the house to walk the crime scene alone, going back over in his head the information that his stepmother had shared earlier that morning. If anyone had known Reggie Lamb's state of mind twenty-eight years ago, it was Gail Mosier. The two women had been the best of friends all through high school and beyond, but the kidnapping had driven them apart. Understandable. Gail was the one who had discovered Maya missing. She would have been a constant reminder to Reggie of what had happened to her little girl. Not to mention Reggie's guilt. According to Gail, her friend had been too drunk to look after her own children that night. What would the weight of that kind of remorse and self-loathing do to a person over the course of twenty-eight years? Might she eventually go looking for someone else to blame?

Max didn't know Reggie well. He'd mostly interacted with her when she waited his table at the diner. Even so, he was hard-pressed to imagine her breaking into June Chapman's house and shooting her in cold blood. But if he'd learned anything from his time in the DA's office, it was that people could sometimes fool you. Ever since Denton Crosby's case file had landed on Max's desk, he'd spent a lot of time researching Maya's disappearance. After devouring countless articles and interviews, he'd deduced early on that Reggie Lamb was a far more complicated individual than her appearance and lifestyle would suggest.

So was June Chapman, a near shut-in who had been either the victim of a random break-in or the target of a calculating killer. Like Cal, Max didn't put a lot of stock in coincidences, particularly considering June's connection to Maya. He'd seen enough in his career to know that people were capable of doing unspeakable things to one another, but a woman having her own grandchildren kidnapped just to torment their mother was almost a bridge too far even for him to accept.

Yet if you dug down past the instinctual revulsion of such an act, June Chapman's involvement in the kidnapping made a perverse kind of sense. It could explain why Denton Crosby had refused to leave town when he had the chance. He needed to take out the one person who could tie him to Maya's abduction. The one person who had had the means and motive to hire the likes of Crosby and his sister, Nadine.

Max had been so lost in thought that he hadn't realized how much time had gone by since Cal's departure. He glanced at his phone and swore. He needed to get moving. He had less than an hour to get to the office and glance over his case files before heading into court. Nothing on the schedule that morning was particularly complicated or noteworthy but the docket was packed. He'd spend most of his day filing motions and haggling back and forth with various defense attorneys and then, of course, there'd be the inevitable postponements and rescheduling to deal with.

He'd much rather devote his time to going back through his notes on the kidnapping case, or even better, heading over to Main Street to interview Paul Bozeman and his daughter. But, as his stepmother had been quick to point out earlier, he wasn't a cop. He needed to back off and let the Black Creek Police Department do their job.

When he came out of the house a few minutes later, he was surprised to find a woman sitting on the veranda. The street in front of the house was empty. No cars parked in the drive or at the curb. He wondered where she'd come from. Brazen of her to cross a police barricade in broad daylight.

Reclined in one of June Chapman's elegant wrought iron chairs, hands clasped behind her head, she stared out over the garden, apparently so engrossed in the scenery or lost in thought that she wasn't aware of Max's presence. He locked the door, then took a quick assessment before he spoke. She wore jeans, sneakers and a baseball cap over a dark brown ponytail. Slender. No more than thirty, the best he could tell from her profile. He didn't have a clue who she was until she turned and trained her vivid blue gaze upon him.

For a moment, he felt unaccountably tongue-tied, like an awkward teenager bumping into his first crush. Then he said in shock, "You!"

"And *you*," she countered. "It's gratifying to see that you remember me. I wasn't sure you would."

"You're not that easy to forget," Max replied with a candor that surprised even him. He leaned a shoulder against the doorframe and folded his arms as he regarded her with open suspicion. "Who are you and what are you doing here?"

"No beating about the bush, then." She shrugged. "I saw the other guy leave. He looked like a cop. I knew you were alone so I thought I'd come over and find out how you fared after our little adventure last night."

A warning bell sounded as he frowned. "How could you know I was alone unless you were watching the house?"

"I was watching the house."

At least she didn't try to deny it. "Why? What were you hoping to discover?"

She returned his scrutiny with equal intensity. "First things first. You're okay, I take it?" Her gaze danced over him. "You look okay."

"I'll live, thanks to you."

Her tone sobered. "I wasn't too concerned about the bullet. Even in the dark, I could tell the wound was superficial, but you took a hard spill down those stairs. I was worried you'd suffered a concussion or worse. You're lucky you didn't break your neck."

"I'm tougher than I look, I guess." He searched her upturned face, noting those blue eyes again and the enticing curve of her lips. In the morning light filtering down through the oak trees, he could detect a faint sprinkle of freckles across her nose and a tiny scar at her jawline. Once again, she held her poise under his frank inspection, not giving anything away of what she might be feeling. Her unwavering regard stirred something akin to a memory for Max, a strange sense of déjà vu that simultaneously fascinated and unsettled him.

He straightened and moved across the veranda toward her. "Don't get me wrong. I'm glad to have the opportunity to thank you in person, but you're about the last person I expected to bump into this morning. I was prepared to spend a lot of time and resources tracking you down. And here you are."

"Here I am." She glanced away as if discomfited by his gratitude. "Let's not make a big deal of it, okay? I did what anyone would do under the circumstances."

"I doubt that. Attacking an armed suspect with a piece of lumber took guts. What I don't get is why you ran away. And why you were watching this house." He waited a beat. "I'll ask you again… Who are you? What's your name?"

She smiled, almost stopping him dead in his tracks. "You sure ask a lot of questions, Max."

That did stop him. "How do you know my name?"

"We'll get to that, but for now, let's jump back to your first question. I didn't run away last night. I left in pursuit of a suspect."

He gave her a skeptical look. "You're a cop?"

"Private detective." She handed him a card.

He scanned the information and glanced up. "You're a long way from Houston, Avery Bolt."

"I go where my clients need me," she said with unnerving nonchalance.

"If you're a licensed PI, then you must be aware that fleeing the scene of a crime *is* a crime."

"There were extenuating circumstances and time was of the essence. As you well know," she added.

He sat down at the wrought iron table across from her. Instead of returning her card, he slipped it in his jacket pocket for future research. "Why were you in that empty house last night?"

She folded her arms on the table and entwined her fingers. The freckles and ball cap made her seem young, but Max had a feeling she was older and wiser than he would have initially guessed. She was certainly composed. She didn't seem the slightest bit rattled by their second encounter. Unlike Max, who still felt a twinge of unease in the pit of his stomach.

"Two days ago, I received a call from June Chapman at my Houston office." Her voice was still smoothly matter-of-fact. If she had a tick or a tell, Max couldn't detect it. "She indicated our agency had come highly recommended by someone she trusted."

"Why not contact someone a little closer to home if she needed a PI?"

"I asked her that. She said she didn't want to use a local agency because the matter was delicate and discretion was of the utmost importance. For those same reasons, she would only speak to either my partner or myself in person. She asked that one of us come to her home here in Black Creek to discuss her security needs."

"You didn't think that request unusual?"

"Unusual but acceptable considering she offered to triple our daily rate plus expenses."

"She didn't give you any idea as to why she wanted to hire a private detective?" Max asked.

"Yes, she certainly did." Her gaze met his. "She thought someone was trying to kill her. And considering what happened here last night, I'd say she was right."

Max stared back at her as he absorbed the shock of her revelation. "Did she name names?"

"She wouldn't discuss it over the phone. She was adamant about that. When I pressed, she dug in her heels. I got the impression she's a very headstrong woman, someone who is used to having her own way. People like that tend to make enemies."

Max tried not to reveal how thoroughly off guard she'd caught him. He didn't know what to make of her story. It sounded plausible, but he couldn't help wondering why someone with June Chapman's resources would go all the way to Houston, Texas, to hire a private detective. Something about Avery Bolt's explanation didn't sit well with him, but at the moment, he was willing to give her the benefit of a doubt. After all, she had saved his life.

"Why didn't she call the police?" he asked.

"Apparently bringing the authorities into the matter wasn't an option."

"Why?"

She lifted a shoulder. "You would have to ask her. As I said, she was very guarded as to how much she would tell me over the phone. That's not so unusual. Trusting strangers isn't easy even when they come highly recommended."

"What else did she say?"

"That's about it really. We came to a financial agreement and I rearranged my schedule so that I could leave for Black Creek immediately. We were to meet this morning here at her home. I arrived a day early so that I could get a feel for the town and my surroundings."

"Did you contact her when you arrived?"

"No. She was very specific as to the time and place of our meeting. I checked into a hotel and spent the remainder of the day familiarizing myself with the neighborhood and staking out her house."

"None of the neighbors reported seeing a strange vehicle in the area," he said.

"I wouldn't be very good at my job if they did. Blending in is key to the services I offer."

She may have blended in with the neighbors, but she certainly stuck out in Max's mind. Her heroic efforts on his behalf aside, he was drawn to her in a way he couldn't explain. Her sudden arrival in his life both captivated and unnerved him, yet there was also something oddly...comforting about her presence. Like running into an old friend who had been gone for a long time, but had remained the same person that one remembered. "You were here when June Chapman was shot last night, weren't you? In this house, I mean. You were the one who called 911."

"Yes. I saw someone sneaking through the garden just after midnight. I made the call and then decided to check out the house. I found one of the parlor doors open." She nodded toward the left side of the house. "I didn't know if the intruder I'd spotted in the garden had already gained entry or if he might have a partner already inside the house."

"So you unlawfully entered the premises."

"I did and without hesitation. From the moment I accepted Mrs. Chapman's retainer, it became my job to protect her. Unlawfully entering her house was the least of my concerns. I knew there was a very good chance the intruder had come to kill her. What was I supposed to do? Wait for the police to arrive?"

"Take me through it," Max said. "Don't leave out even the smallest detail."

She nodded. "Everything played out quickly, but I'll do my best. After I entered the premises, I took a moment in the parlor to get my bearings and then I went out into the entrance hall. I assumed Mrs. Chapman's bedroom was on the second floor so I started up the stairs. I was halfway to the top when I heard two shots fired from a silenced weapon. Then I heard footsteps running down the hallway toward me. I barely had time to rush up to the landing and step into the shadows before the masked shooter darted past me. When he got to the bottom of the stairs, he glanced up. I guess he must have spotted me because he fired off three rounds in my direction before he ran out the front door."

More or less the scenario Cal Slade had described earlier.

"What did you do then?"

"I wanted to go after him but I didn't know how badly Mrs. Chapman might be hurt. Her safety was my first priority. I found her lying on the floor of her bedroom with a pistol beside her. I assume she heard the intruder and reached for her weapon, but she never got off a shot. I checked her pulse and then applied pressure to the wounds until I heard the sirens on the street outside her house. When I was certain help had arrived, I went out the balcony doors and climbed down the trellis."

"Fleeing yet another crime scene," he said. "Two for two."

Her gaze narrowed slightly as if his accurate observation annoyed her. "Yes, and both times for the same reason. I assumed the gunman could still be in the neighborhood and on foot since I didn't hear a car engine. Again, time was of the essence," she stressed. "Even if the police had bothered to check my credentials, they could have detained me for hours if not days and I didn't want to sidetrack their efforts or waste precious time answering endless questions. I climbed down the trellis and went over the back wall, then made my way back around to the street. That's when I saw you approach the empty house."

He still wasn't sure if he believed her or not, but she was very good at making him want to buy whatever she was selling. Her particular blend of mystery and sincerity was exceptionally potent. "Did you know the suspect was inside?"

"I wasn't certain, but it seemed like a pretty good place to hide if he wanted to keep track of police movements. Or to find out if his mission had been successful."

Max sat back in his chair seemingly relaxed but more wired than he'd felt in years. Whatever else happened, this was exciting. *She* was exciting and he had no desire to end their meeting despite his tight schedule. "You never thought to warn me when you saw me go inside?"

"Why would I? For all I knew you could have been the bad guy. Or *a* bad guy. I had no way of knowing we were on the same side until you were shot."

"Getting shot doesn't prove anything," he said.

Her eyes glinted. "I know you're one of the good guys, Max. I checked you out."

He didn't know whether to be flattered or irritated. "Checked me out how?"

"I heard someone say your name so I looked you up. Have you googled yourself lately? You're all over the internet. A young, dynamic prosecutor who has never lost a case. That's impressive."

He wasn't sure he appreciated the way she summed up his career. Maybe it was his imagination, but he thought he detected a faint undercurrent of derision, and he hardened his voice accordingly. "Maybe I just know how to pursue winnable cases."

"I don't think you're that jaded."

"You don't know anything about me," he was quick to point out. "Looking me up on the internet doesn't give you any special insight into my ethics or ambition. As for you…" He shrugged. "Maybe you're telling the truth and maybe you're not. I haven't yet decided if I believe you. I know one thing…" He allowed himself a tight smile. "You're not telling me everything."

"What more do you want to know?"

"Save it for the police. You'll need to give them a statement as soon as possible, and I would advise you not to hold anything back."

"Pouring my heart out to the assistant DA isn't good enough?"

"I'm not in charge of the investigation," Max said. "Cal Slade is the lead detective and he happens to be a friend of mine. I can arrange a meeting this morning. The sooner he has your official account of last night's events, the less time and fewer resources he'll need to expend looking for you. In fact, I'm on my way to the courthouse now. I can drop you off at the police station."

"That won't be necessary. My car is nearby."

Max searched the empty street. "Then I'll follow and make sure you don't take a wrong turn."

She smiled but her eyes had cooled. "You don't trust me to go in alone?"

"No, I don't."

"I guess that's fair." She rose from the table and adjusted her cap. "Let's get this over with, then. I've places to go and people to see. But if they throw me in jail, I'm counting on you to pull some strings to get me out. I'm really not kidding about that." She paused. "Speaking of pulling strings, I don't suppose you could get me in to see Mrs. Chapman?"

"No one's allowed to see her at this time."

"She's still alive, then. That's a relief. Can you at least tell me where she's being treated?"

"No."

She lifted a brow at his blunt answer. "Any pointers on dealing with Detective Slade?"

"Don't be coy or evasive and don't assume you can pull the wool over his eyes because he's a small-town detective. Cal Slade is as sharp and intuitive as they come."

"Duly noted. Oh, wait a second." They had both started for the steps but she turned, searching the table as she patted her jeans. "My phone."

He nodded toward the railing. "Over there."

"Thanks."

"Is that your personal phone or another burner? You know, like the one you used to call 911 last night."

Something flared in her eyes, but she merely shrugged. "No law against using a prepaid, is there? I find them useful in my line of work."

He said nothing to that, but instead turned and descended the steps while she retrieved her phone. He waited at the bottom for her to catch up. Halfway down, she paused again to glance over her shoulder. This time her gaze went to the front door as if she could somehow peer into June Chapman's private domain. Maybe it was her bemused expression or her suddenly tense body language, but Max felt a prickle of anxiety at the base of his spine.

What aren't you telling me, Avery Bolt? Why are you really here?

And why did he feel as if they'd met before? Whether in the past or in a dream, Max wasn't quite certain.

Chapter Seven

Judge Wilcox seemed determined to make a large dint in the overcrowded docket before he left on his yearly fishing excursion. Max didn't get out of the courtroom until midafternoon. Instead of grabbing a snack from the vending machines on the way up to his office, he decided to walk over to the diner and have a decent meal before he settled in at his desk.

The temperature had climbed into the midnineties while he'd been cooped up inside the courthouse. He took off his jacket and loosened his tie as he crossed over to the shady side of the street. A car horn honked and he glanced around to check traffic before scanning the sidewalk behind him. A few pedestrians were out and about, cell phones plastered to their ears as they walked briskly to and from the courthouse. He acknowledged the people he recognized and nodded to the others, but he didn't linger to chat with anyone. He wasn't in the mood for casual conversation or any conversation for that matter. After hours of arguing back and forth, he wanted to enjoy the solitude of his walk.

His phone rang as he neared the diner. He didn't recognize the number and started to ignore the insistent ringtone, then accepted the call and brought the phone to his ear. "Hello?"

He thought no one was there at first, then the timid voice of an elderly female said, “Who is this?”

“Max Winter. Who is this?”

“Max Winter.” She repeated his name in confusion. “Would you happen to be Judge Winter’s son?”

“I am. Did you mean to call me?”

“I think so. I must have heard your name somewhere. Or maybe I read about you in the paper. I can’t seem to recall.”

“How did you get my number?” Max asked.

“It was in my book. You’re somebody important, right? Like your father?”

“That depends on who you ask,” he said with a note of irony. “How can I help you?”

“I don’t mean to bother you. It’s just… Someone needs to know.”

“Know what?” When she didn’t respond, Max coaxed, “Are you all right? Do I need to call someone for you?”

“No, please don’t tell anyone about this conversation.”

“Why not?”

“People will think I’m a senile old woman. Maybe you already do.”

“I don’t think anything at the moment,” Max said. “I’m still very much in the dark as to why you called me. Can you at least tell me your name?”

“I’d rather not.”

“Then how can I help you?”

A long pause. “I saw her.”

Max stopped and stepped into deeper shade. “You saw who?”

“Maya Lamb.”

The name was a shock even though he reminded himself that people had reported sightings of Maya ever since she’d disappeared. Some were sincere but most were either crank calls or people looking for attention. Now that the kidnapping was on everyone’s radar again, the calls were bound to start back up. Why the woman had contacted him instead of the police, Max had no idea. He decided to humor her for a moment before he ended the call. "When and where did you see her?"

"Oh, she looked just like an angel with light falling all around her," she said. "And as sweet and lovely as I remembered her. I thought I might have been dreaming, but I wasn't. I even wrote it down so I wouldn't forget."

"Where did you see her?"

"I don't want to say. She could still be in danger."

"From who?"

"From the people who took her."

Max frowned. Maybe she wasn't as muddled as she sounded. "Do you know their names?"

"I might have once, but my memory isn't what it used to be. My granddaughter tells me to write things down, but sometimes I forget to. Not this time, though. The note is right here on my desk. It says, *Today I saw Maya*." Another long pause. "Do you believe me?"

Max gentled his voice. "Is it possible you saw her picture in the paper recently? Or on the news perhaps?"

"On the news?"

"Yes, her photograph has been on TV a lot recently. That could explain why she looked the way you remembered her."

"Like an angel," she said on a sigh.

"Are you sure you won't tell me your name?" Max asked. "You sound distressed. Maybe we should contact your granddaughter to come and look after you."

"No, please don't do that. She worries enough as it is. This was a very bad idea. I can see now that I should never have bothered you."

"You haven't bothered me," Max said. "I'd like to help if I can." But his assurance came too late. She'd already severed the call.

He didn't spend much time dwelling on her claim. She was obviously an elderly person easily confused and probably lonely. Undoubtedly, she'd viewed Maya's photograph on TV or online and had convinced herself that she'd seen the missing child in person. The bigger mystery was why she'd called him. She seemed to know who he was. He thought about trying to call her back, then shrugged and pocketed his phone. Probably best to leave well enough alone.

By the time he got to the diner, most of the lunch crowd had dispersed. Only a handful of patrons remained scattered about the room so he had his pick of tables. His gaze went immediately to one of the back booths where Avery Bolt sat hunched over her phone, apparently deep in concentration.

No way she could have known he'd be at the diner in the middle of the afternoon so their third encounter had to be a coincidence—unless she'd called his office to find out his whereabouts. However, his assistant was discreet to a fault so maybe he was being paranoid. He still didn't trust her opportune appearance in the empty house last night or the way she'd turned up on June Chapman's veranda that morning. Why confide in him instead of going straight to the police? No doubt she had an agenda, but what role he played in that plan, he had no idea.

She didn't glance up until he stood beside her table and then she gave him a sly smile to let him know that she'd been tracking him. She feigned surprise anyway and mimicked his previous greeting. "You!"

"And you." His tone was colder than he'd meant it. Suspicion had a way of chilling even a lighthearted greeting. He mustered up a slight smile and angled his head toward the empty bench across from her. "May I?"

"Be my guest," she said with a little wave. She wore the same baseball cap she'd had on earlier. The bill shaded her features, but somehow the freckles across her nose and cheeks stood out more prominently than he remembered. Or maybe he was becoming a little too aware of her nuances. He didn't know if that was a good thing or not. One thing he did know. She still intrigued him.

He slid in opposite her and said in a more cordial tone, "Sorry to interrupt your lunch. I'll try not to take too much of your time."

"You aren't interrupting anything. I haven't even ordered yet. As long as you're here, you may as well join me. I've never minded eating alone, but it's nice to have company for a change."

Her affable, chatty tone took him aback. "If you're sure you don't mind."

"Not at all."

"I was wondering how it went at the police station," he said as he settled in.

"I'm not in jail so I'd say the interview went as well as could be expected. You can save your bail money." She flashed another smile and Max felt a surge of unexpected attraction that he quickly tried to stifle. Not a good idea until he knew more about her.

Sharing a meal was an unexpected turn of events, but he couldn't say he dreaded the prospect of spending a little more time with her. He didn't trust her, of course, and he'd be a fool to let down his guard, but he also might learn something interesting about her.

He dropped his suit coat on the bench seat and slid off his tie.

"How do you wear those things?" she wanted to know. "I would feel like I'm being perpetually choked."

"You get used to it. Actually, that's a lie. You don't get used to it. You just learn to ignore the suffocation."

"I admire your candor." She placed her phone on the table and sat back against the padded booth, seemingly relaxed. They were both a little too comfortable considering they were complete strangers, but Max decided not to overanalyze. There'd been a time in the not too distant past when he hadn't been so conventional or uptight. When he would have considered spending time with an attractive woman a good thing regardless of her motive. Somewhere along the way, he'd turned into a bureaucratic automaton, weighing every angle and perception before making a move.

"What did you tell the police?" he asked.

"I gave a full and detailed account of my activities since arriving in town. But I'm guessing you already know that."

"I haven't spoken to anyone about the interview," Max said. "I've been in court all day."

"Then feel free to call Detective Slade if you need verification."

"That won't be necessary." *At this moment.* He idly lined up his flatware. "How did you two get on?"

"As you said, he's a very savvy and intuitive investigator. And a lot more open-minded than I expected. He agreed that I could be of more use to the investigation on the outside rather than locked up in a holding cell."

Max glanced up. "He actually said that?"

"Not in so many words," she admitted with a shrug. "But I choose to believe that's what he meant."

"I wouldn't put words in his mouth if I were you. The last thing you want is to get on his bad side. The Cal Slade I know doesn't have much use for private investigators or anyone else muddying up his investigations. My advice is to tread lightly while you're in town."

"Thanks for that, but I'm not just any investigator." She leaned in, blue eyes glinting like gemstones in the light shining in through the plate glass window. "I can help you, too, if you'll let me."

He gave her a dubious look. "Help me how exactly?"

"DA's are often assigned their own investigators, aren't they? Someone who doesn't have to divide her time and attention among dozens of other cases like an overworked police detective does. If I'm on your team, my focus is single-minded. I'm not just blowing smoke here. I'm very good at what I do."

"Oh, I'm sure you have a very particular skill set."

She ignored his sardonic tone. "As a matter of fact, I do. I'm an excellent tracker and an even better researcher. I can find people that are trying very hard not to be found. I can dig up information that's been buried for decades."

Curiosity stirred even as Max warned himself that he, too, should tread lightly. Despite her assurances to the contrary, he'd bet good money she'd withheld information from the police. He had a well-honed BS detector, but he may have met his match in Avery Bolt.

So why was he still sitting here allowing her to spin a web around him? Was he that bored with his day-to-day routine?

"Number one, the investigators we use are assigned to us by the police department," he explained. "And two, give me an example of what you've been able to dig up."

She took a moment to enjoy his cynicism before springing her first surprise. "I know about the confession."

He tried not to give away his shock. "What confession would that be?"

She glanced around the diner, then leaned in even closer. "Before she died, a woman named Nadine Crosby told a local police detective that she, her brother and the detective's father were paid to kidnap Maya and Thea Lamb."

He held her gaze. "Where did you hear that?"

She sat back. "I never disclose my methods and sources. Unless we come to a working arrangement, that is."

Now it was Max who leaned in, his voice sharp with apprehension. "Only a handful of people know about that confession. For many reasons, it's not for public consumption. I need to know where you came across that piece of information."

"If you're worried about leaks in your office or the police department, don't be. No one told me. I found out by accident. I take it from your tone and expression that it's true."

"We don't know if it's true. We have only a dead woman's story."

"You have less than that," Avery said. "You have a potentially biased police detective's account of the dead woman's story. Which is why, I'm guessing, Denton Crosby is still a free man. None of what his sister told the detective is admissible in court."

"Correct."

"And the police haven't been able to dig up anything else that ties him to the kidnapping. I'm not the police. I can find that evidence. I can get you everything you need to put Maya Lamb's kidnapper away for life."

Her bold self-assurance was refreshing, especially since it came without a hint of bluster. "You're not lacking in confidence. I'll give you that."

"Why waste your time with false modesty? I was trained by the best. That's just a fact."

"Be that as it may, I still need to know how you came by the information." When she remained silent, he took a stab in the dark. "Someone must have made the mistake of leaving you alone in Cal Slade's office. You snooped through his confidential files."

"You won't find my fingerprints on anything in that office."

"That's not a denial."

She took off her ball cap and tucked back her dark hair. "You're focusing on the wrong thing, Max. It doesn't matter how I found out. All you need to know is that I have no intention of broadcasting that confession. My only interest is whether or not there's a connection between Denton Crosby and June Chapman's shooting."

"What did Detective Slade tell you?"

"He doesn't know I know about the confession."

"So you didn't give him a *full* account of your activities after all."

She sighed. "You really are determined to paint me as a bad guy, aren't you?"

"Why shouldn't I? You've given me no reason to trust you."

"Except for saving your life."

He conceded her point with a shrug.

She picked up her phone. "Call my office. Ask for Sam Cusack. He's my partner. He'll back me up."

"I've no doubt," Max said. "But that just means the two of you have your stories straight."

"It's not a story. It's the truth," she insisted.

"And if June Chapman survives the shooting? Will she back you up?"

She looked momentarily discomfited by the notion. "What if I told you—" She broke off abruptly and glanced out the window with a frown.

"Go on. Tell me what?"

She closed her eyes and released a long breath. "Nothing. I need a minute, okay?" She slid out of the booth.

"Are you coming back?" he asked.

She stared down at him. "Of course I'm coming back. I'm not that easy to get rid of."

AVERY GLANCED UNDERNEATH the stall doors in the restroom before calling Sam Cusack. She'd talked to him the night before from her hotel room, but for her own peace of mind, she needed to make sure he knew exactly what to say should anyone decide to question him.

"It's a little late to be worrying about that now," he told

her. "I took a call this morning from a Detective Slade in Black Creek, Florida. Never heard of the place until you mentioned it last night. I had to look it up. He sure had a lot of questions about you."

Avery gripped the phone anxiously. "What did you tell him?"

"Exactly what you told me to say if anyone called. You're the one who took the call from June Chapman—whoever she is—and you're the one who agreed to take her on as a client. You made all the arrangements yourself, including a trip out of state to speak with her in person."

She closed her eyes in relief. "Good. That should put you in the clear."

"Put me in the clear from what?" he demanded. "What are you doing in Florida? Why is a police detective from some burg I can barely find on a map calling about a client who doesn't exist?"

"You're exaggerating the size of the town. It happens to be a county seat. And for your information, June Chapman does exist. I just massaged the truth a bit about our arrangement. But you don't need to worry. I've got everything handled."

"Sure you do. That's why you asked me to lie to the police."

"It wasn't precisely a lie."

"Did June Chapman call you?"

"…No…"

"Did you agree to take her on as a client?"

"I would have, had she called."

He sighed. "Exactly which part of the story I fed to the police *isn't* a lie?"

"I am in Black Creek, Florida, working a case."

"Which case?"

"The less you know, the better," Avery said.

She could imagine him rearing back in his chair with a big scowl on his face. "I don't like the sound of that one bit."

"I know you don't. But there's no reason to worry. I'll tell you everything as soon as I'm able. In the meantime, I need to make certain Detective Slade believed you."

He sounded offended. "Who do you think you're talking to? Of course he believed me."

She nodded, even though he couldn't see her. "You may get another call from an assistant DA named Max Winter. Make sure you tell him the same thing you told Detective Slade. No improvising details, okay? They're apt to compare notes."

"As if you need to give me pointers on running a cover. I've been doing this for a lot more years than you have, kiddo."

"I know and I'm sorry, Sam. I didn't mean that the way it sounded. It's just… This is really important to me."

"So why won't you tell me what's really going on?" he said gruffly. "Let me help you."

"This is something I have to do on my own."

He was silent for a moment. "I know Luther's death hit you hard. It was a body blow to all of us. I also know you've been dealing with some pretty deep issues since he passed. But you're not alone. Marie and I are still your family," he said, referring to his wife, who was also the agency receptionist. The pair had known Avery from the time she was a little girl, when her mother used to dress her up in ruffles and lace and take her into the office for Marie to ooh and aah over. The Cusacks had never had a child of their own. In many ways, Avery had been their surrogate daughter.

Her eyes stung with unexpected tears. "That means everything to me. I don't know what I'd do without you two."

"Then level with us. Marie is worried sick. You come into the office and announce you're taking some time off—maybe a week, maybe a month. You don't know when you'll be back. Then you pack your bags and leave town without letting anyone know where you're going. It's not like you to be so secretive. I can't help wondering…" He paused and his voice lowered. "Does this have something to do with what happened to you as a kid?"

"Please, just let it go for now. I'm working through some things. Trust that I know what I'm doing and I'll explain everything when the time is right."

"What do I tell Marie in the meantime?"

"Tell her I love her. I love you both."

His voice roughened. "I guess that'll have to do for now, but if you need anything, I'm only a phone call away. You know that, right? I can fly into Tallahassee and rent a car at a moment's notice. And watch your back over there. I have a feeling you're digging up something that might be best left buried in the past."

She slid the phone back in her jeans pocket and then rinsed her hands at the sink. Grabbing a paper towel, she frowned at her reflection in the mirror. She still wasn't used to the straight dark hair, though in some ways the style and color suited her more than her naturally blond waves. Leaning in, she stared herself straight in the eyes. *Who are you anyway? What's your story?*

That's for you to find out.

And find out she would, no matter the cost. She couldn't let it rest now. She couldn't leave those secrets buried in the past no matter how much Sam and Marie might wish her to. Funny how one little photograph—happened upon purely by chance—had the potential to change the course of her life. She could be risking everything—her career, her savings, her peace of mind. Even her life. Fine. That was a gamble she was more than willing to take, but it wasn't fair to involve Sam. Putting his reputation on the line to corroborate her cover story was asking a lot, even of a man who'd gladly take a bullet for her.

She'd have to make it up to him somehow, but she couldn't worry about that now. She still had a job to do, an old mystery to unravel, and she needed to stay focused in order to keep her own lies straight.

Tossing the paper towel in the bin, she exited the bathroom, still so deep in thought that she bumped into a man coming down the narrow hallway that led from the dining room back to the restrooms and a rear exit. He grabbed her arm to steady her and she recoiled, the hair at the back of her neck lifting inexplicably.

He looked to be in his midfifties, not tall, not short, stout but not heavy. There was nothing about his appearance that would stand out on first glance, but as Avery stared up at him in the dim light, she saw something in his eyes that sent a chill skidding down her backbone. She wasn't a particularly spiritual person, and yet in that moment she had the paralyzing notion that she was staring into the face of evil.

She'd never seen the man before. Not that she could remember, at least. She was seven hundred miles from home so the likelihood of their having crossed paths was slim unless…

Could he be the man she'd seen in June Chapman's house last night? She searched his eyes, but his return stare was so darkly intense she had to glance away.

His voice was low with a hint of gravel. "Better watch where you're going, little lady."

The smell of cigarette smoke on his clothing permeated the close confines of the corridor. She took another step back from him. "I'm sorry. My fault entirely. I'll be more careful from now on."

"Say, do I know you?" He narrowed his eyes as if trying to remember where he'd seen her.

"There's no way," she blurted.

He cocked his head. "You sound pretty certain of that."

"I'm not from around here. I've only been in town a couple of days," she explained.

"I'm not from around here, either. At least not anymore. Where you from?"

"If you'll excuse me, I really need to get back to my table." Avery started around him, but he stepped in front of her.

"Now hold on. No need to take that tone. I'm just trying to be friendly. A pretty little gal like you stands out in a place like this. You can't blame me for taking notice."

She glanced over his shoulder, hoping to see someone advancing toward them down the hallway. "Sir, please step aside."

He propped a hand against the wall, still with a canted head and slitted eyes. "You plowed into me. The least you can do is tell me your name."

Avery had no idea what had come over her. She'd never had the slightest reservation about defending herself, but she couldn't seem to muster the courage to break eye contact with this stranger, much less push him out of the way. She felt light-headed all of a sudden as perspiration dampened her forehead. *Get a grip! He's just a creep in a hallway.*

She lifted her chin as she started past him. "I said step aside."

He put his hand on her arm and before he had time to wipe the smirk from his face, she'd flung off his hold, grabbed his collar with both hands and shoved him up against the wall. He looked momentarily stupefied. "What the hell do you think you're doing?"

Avery rammed her forearm against his windpipe. "Don't touch me. Don't you ever try to touch me again."

He threw his hands up in acquiescence. "Okay, I get it." He muttered an expletive as he massaged his throat. "What is wrong with you?"

"Come near me again and find out."

He swore again as she turned away.

When she got to the end of the hallway, she glanced back. He was still standing in the same spot staring after her. A slow smile spread across his face, as if he'd just figured something out. Those same icy fingers clawed down Avery's backbone as the phantom smell of cigarette smoke clogged her nostrils.

Their gazes held for the longest moment and then he lifted a finger to his lips as if to warn her to silence.

Chapter Eight

"You okay?" Max asked.

Avery slid into the booth and grabbed her napkin. "Of course. Why wouldn't I be?"

"I don't know. You look a little pale."

"I bumped into someone in the hallway outside the restroom. I wasn't watching where I was going and he took issue."

Max frowned. "What did he say to you?"

"It doesn't matter. People can be jerks for no reason."

"It matters if he upset you." He glanced back through the diner toward the restroom area. "Where is he? Point him out to me."

She rolled her eyes on a sigh. "I'm not going to point him out to you. For one thing, I don't even see him, and for another, I don't need you or anyone else coming to my defense."

He turned back with a lifted brow. "Where did that come from?"

"Sorry," she muttered. "I guess he got under my skin more than I realized."

"No apology necessary and for what it's worth, I know you don't need my help. I've seen you in action, remember? This guy sounds like a real piece of work. Maybe I just want to know who he is so I can avoid him."

She gave him a skeptical look. "Sure you do." With an effort, she shrugged off a lingering chill. "Let's just forget about that creep. If we're lucky, he went out the back way and neither of us will ever have to deal with him again." She raised an arm to signal a server. "I don't know about you, but I'm starving."

Surprisingly, her short fuse didn't drive him off. Instead, he leaned back against the seat, completely relaxed, as a waitress hurried over to refill their water glasses.

He glanced up at the woman and smiled. "Thanks, Reggie."

Reggie? Reggie Lamb, the missing child's mother?

"You bet," she said. "You folks ready to order or do you still need a minute? Lunch special is available until four or would you rather look at a menu?"

For a moment, Avery couldn't answer. She felt the same quiver of nerves she'd experienced in the hallway with the unpleasant stranger, though her reaction wasn't as visceral. She tried not to stare, but she couldn't seem to tear her gaze away. This was the woman June Chapman had accused of murdering her little girl and burying her body in the woods. And here she was twenty-eight years later waiting tables in the same small town.

She didn't look at all as Avery would have imagined and yet she couldn't picture Reggie Lamb any other way. Life hadn't been kind to the woman. That was obvious in her haggard appearance and in the wary way she carried herself. Her once-blond hair had gone a sort of dirty gray and deep crevices carved into her leathered skin seemed like a road map to all the dark places she'd been. She was tiny—scrawny, one might even say—but there was toughness in her posture and demeanor and despite everything she'd endured, there was kindness in her eyes.

"Avery?"

Max's voice startled her back to the immediate present.

She glanced away awkwardly when she realized she'd been staring for too long. "I'm sorry. What?"

He observed her curiously from across the table. "Do you want to look at a menu?"

"Uh, yeah. I'll take a peek. You go ahead and order."

"I'll have a burger medium well and might as well add an order of fries to go with it."

Avery stared down blindly at the laminated menu, unable to focus on the choices. First the stranger outside the bathroom had thrown her for a loop and now an unexpected encounter with Reggie Lamb had knocked her off her game. Not to mention Max Winter turning up in the diner just minutes after she'd been seated. No way he could have known she'd be there, but had she subconsciously staked out an eatery close to the courthouse in the hopes of running into him again?

The man was insanely handsome with that gorgeous wavy hair and those dark brown eyes. Not to mention his sensuous mouth and razor-sharp cheekbones. Avery had purposely steered clear of men like Max Winter all her adult life. His looks were intimidating and she didn't like feeling inferior, but it was his insight that worried her the most. She had a feeling every time he looked into her eyes he could see past the lies and half-truths and had quickly come to the conclusion that she wasn't to be trusted. Which was a fair assessment under the circumstances and shouldn't bother her in the least, but for some reason, his opinion seemed to matter.

"You need another minute, hon?" Reggie prodded in her heavy country accent. The rasp in her voice only enhanced her careworn appearance, but her blue uniform was crisp and her white sneakers spotless. She might not be vain but she was certainly conscientious.

"A burger sounds good." Avery returned the menu to the holder and glanced up. "I'll have exactly what he's having."

"Two burgers, two fries." Reggie dropped her pen on the floor as she turned toward the kitchen. Avery bent to retrieve it, then used the opportunity to give the woman a closer appraisal as she returned it.

"Thanks." Reggie held up her right hand tightly wrapped with a pressure bandage. "Can't seem to get used to this blasted thing."

"What happened?" Avery asked. "That is, if you don't mind my asking."

"Banged up my wrist in a car accident a couple weeks back."

"It was a bad wreck, from what I hear," Max said. "I'm surprised to see you back at work so soon."

"Bills won't pay themselves." Her matter-of-fact tone didn't invite sympathy. "Won't be able to lift food trays for a while, but I can take orders and help out in the kitchen." She tucked the pen behind her ear, old-school. "Anything else I can get for you folks?"

"I'm fine," Max said.

"Me, too." Once she was gone, Avery said, "You called her Reggie."

"Yes. Reggie Lamb."

She watched in fascination as the woman rounded the counter and turned in their ticket. "So that's her. The notorious Reggie Lamb."

"I doubt she'd appreciate the description," he said. "How do you know about her anyway?"

"Her name came up in my research. There isn't much to be found on the internet about June Chapman except for an interview she gave a few days after her granddaughter disappeared. She didn't come right out and say it, but she left little doubt that she believed Reggie had murdered the child."

"I've seen that video," Max said. "It's pretty brutal."

Avery winced. "I'd call it an evisceration. Refined and

subtle but an evisceration nonetheless. Was there any basis for her accusation?"

"A box was dug up in the woods behind Reggie's house containing a doll and Maya's DNA. Reggie had a wild reputation back then so people were inclined to think the worst."

"What kind of reputation?"

"She was a party girl from what I've heard. Hung out with a bad crowd." He glanced out the window, frowning into a shaft of sunlight that shone down through a hole in the awning. "You have to understand how it was in this town after Maya went missing. People didn't want to believe it could happen to their child so they were quick to look for a bad guy that could give them back their peace of mind. Reggie made an easy target. She became a scapegoat for their fears."

"But that's so unfair." Avery was surprised at how quickly she'd come to a stranger's defense.

"It's human nature," Max said. "The abduction of a child is gut-wrenching no matter the location, but in a place like this where everyone knows everyone, you don't want to believe your next-door neighbor or someone you grew up with could be a child predator. Far easier to accept that a high-strung young mother was negligent and tried to cover up her crime." He idly drummed his thumb against the table as he gazed out the window, apparently lost in thought for a moment. "Maya's disappearance changed this town in ways an outsider can't begin to understand. Nothing has ever been the same since her abduction."

"Did you know her family?"

He turned back, his gaze meeting hers, and she felt a little quiver of anticipation in the pit of her stomach. "Not really. I grew up in the house across the street from June Chapman, but I only ever remember seeing Maya there once. I gather that was a rare occurrence since June never wanted anything to do with her grandchildren."

"Why?"

"It's a long story. Goes back to the death of her son."

"What was she like?"

"June? She's always been a bit eccentric."

"No, I mean Maya."

He gave her a wry smile. "I was five years old at the time of the kidnapping. I'm not sure what kind of insight you expect from me here."

Avery leaned forward, inexplicably eager for whatever crumb he could give her. "After all this time, you still remember seeing her so she must have made an impression."

If he thought the comment or her behavior odd, he didn't let on. "I'd just come from my mother's funeral. That's why I remember the day so vividly."

"I'm sorry," she said with genuine sympathy. "Losing a parent is hard at any age, but for a five-year-old… I can only imagine how devastated you must have been. How lost and lonely you must have felt."

His dark eyes regarded her thoughtfully. "I'm getting the impression you speak from experience."

She nodded. "My mother died when I was in high school and my dad passed away just last year. It was sudden. He went to sleep one night and never woke up. Sometimes I still can't believe he's gone. Then I walk by his empty desk and it's all too real."

"I'm sorry."

"Yeah, me, too." She waited a moment until she trusted herself to speak. "We were close. He always had my back no matter what and I had his."

"You worked together?"

"Since I was in high school. He taught me everything I know about our business. Not a day goes by that I don't miss him."

"As you said, losing a parent is tough at any age, but especially when it's sudden and you've had no time to brace or prepare."

She swallowed past the lump in her throat. "Now I think you're the one speaking from experience."

He glanced away with a shrug. "It was a long time ago, but my father's death was also unexpected."

Avery thought about the photograph from Judge Winter's funeral and how the photographer had inadvertently caught Max glaring at the widow. "Were the two of you close?"

"No. We didn't understand each other at all. Which is why I spent the better part of two years away at boarding school," he said with a humorless smile. "It took a long time and a lot of patience on her part, but my stepmother and I finally have a good relationship. I think the old man would be happy about that. I wasn't exactly magnanimous when he and Gail got together."

"Gail?" Avery repeated the name absently.

"Dr. Gail Mosier. Don't tell me you've met already."

"Not that I'm aware of." *Gail Mosier. Gail Mosier.* Something fluttered at the back of her mind. June Chapman had mentioned someone named Gail in her interview, but Avery couldn't remember now what had been said. "I've only spoken with two people at any length since I've been in town. You and Detective Slade."

And, of course, June Chapman. They'd conversed just long enough for the wounded woman to jump to the conclusion that Avery had been sent to kill her.

She ran a finger down the side of her glass, tracing a drop of condensation as she wondered how she'd allowed the conversation to become so intimate. She rarely let down her guard for a reason. People couldn't be trusted. She had no reason to assume Max Winter was any different. Still, despite his daunting good looks, he was easy to talk to, low-key and empathetic. But that just meant she needed to watch her step—and her back—with him.

"I don't know how we got so sidetracked," she said. "You were telling me about the day you saw Maya Lamb at her grandmother's house."

"There isn't much to tell. It was a brief encounter. She and her sister were all dressed up in matching outfits. That stands out because it was the middle of the week and I wondered where they were going." His brow furrowed as he thought back. "There is one thing I remember about Maya. I got the impression she was afraid of her grandmother."

"Afraid, afraid?"

"*Intimidated* might be a better word. Not that I blamed her. June Chapman has always been a formidable woman."

"What was Thea like?"

Max smiled. "She was outspoken as a four-year-old. She became more guarded as she grew older, but on that particular day I made the mistake of saying she and Maya didn't look like twins and she lit into me."

"What did you do?"

"Nothing. I think I was awestruck by the pair and maybe a little smitten. I do remember that Maya took up for me. She said I wasn't dumb."

"That was a bold assumption on her part."

His grin flashed again. "Yes, I appreciated her leap of faith."

Avery grew serious. "I've seen a recent photograph of Thea. She's an FBI agent, right? She came back to Black Creek when another child went missing from Reggie's house. How strange was that incident? According to the news accounts I read, the similarities between the two kidnappings were uncanny."

"Not uncanny. Calculating and clever." Max waited a beat, then said, "The case is pending so I won't comment further except to say Agent Lamb very likely saved that child's life. Her efforts during the rescue were nothing short of heroic."

Avery couldn't help wondering if he was still a little smitten with the valiant Agent Lamb. "Do you think she joined the FBI because of her sister's disappearance?"

"I'm sure of it. Maya's kidnapping changed her and Reggie's lives forever." He gave her a reflective look. "I'm surprised you know so much about them considering June only contacted you two days ago."

"I told you, I'm good at what I do and research happens to be a specialty."

She was saved from further comment as a server brought over their food. Reggie was busy at the far end of the diner wiping down tables with her left hand. Once they were alone, Avery used her knife and fork to skillfully cut her burger into four manageable pieces. Not Max. He attacked his meal hungrily, all the while watching her fastidious dissection in amusement.

They ate in silence for a moment and then Avery picked back up on their previous conversation. "You mentioned Reggie was an easy target because of her reputation. Did *you* ever wonder if she had anything to do with Maya's disappearance? You personally, I mean. Did you ever think her capable of murdering her own child?"

He took a break from the burger and wiped his hands on a paper napkin. "I assume you're asking about my opinion as an adult."

"Yes, and as a prosecutor."

He seemed to consider his answer carefully as he took a drink of water. "I'd be lying if I said the thought never crossed my mind. Everyone in town must have wondered at one time or another if Reggie was responsible for her daughter's disappearance. The way the child vanished without a trace was odd."

"What was odd about it? Children disappear all the time, unfortunately."

"Yes, but Maya was taken in the middle of a party. Dozens of people were in and out of Reggie's house that night. Granted, most of them were probably hammered, but even so, the kidnapper took a big risk nabbing the child with that many people around."

"Doesn't seem strange to me," Avery said. "All the noise and confusion of the party made for good cover."

"Maybe so, but anyone at any time could have walked into the girls' bedroom or around the house as the kidnapper carried her across the yard and through the back gate. The guy's timing or his luck was impeccable that night."

Avery sat forward, the half-eaten burger forgotten. "You think it's possible someone at the party gave him the all-clear signal? Or created a diversion while he slipped away with the child?"

"The police have always considered the possibility of an inside man. Reggie's boyfriend at the time was a creep named Derrick Sway. Both the locals and the FBI questioned him any number of times after Maya went missing. He made for a good suspect. A petty thief and drug dealer with a violent temper."

"But why wouldn't Nadine Crosby have mentioned him in her confession if he was involved?"

"I can't answer that. She also claimed not to know the identity of the person who bankrolled the operation. It's possible her brother kept her in the dark about certain details of the arrangement to protect her."

"Or because he didn't trust her. Do you know of any connection between the Crosbys and Derrick Sway?"

"No. But I'd never heard of Denton and Nadine Crosby until a few weeks ago." He frowned pensively. "My father was good friends with the then chief of police. Until the day he retired, Will Kent swore Derrick Sway was somehow involved, but he could never prove it."

"Will Kent," Avery repeated. "Why do I know that name?"

"You would have run across it in your research. Big guy,

strong personality. He remained the face of the investigation in the media even after the FBI took over the case."

No, the name struck a chord because of the overheard conversation in Tom Fuqua's backyard the previous night. Will Kent was the man the ex-state senator had called to warn about the break-in. *If we're lucky, they'll assume it was a random burglary. There's no reason to believe it's connected to that other business, but for now we should both lay low.*

According to the article, Tom Fuqua, Will Kent and Clayton Winter had been friends going back to their Vietnam War days. How they were all linked to June Chapman and "that other business," Avery had no idea. It seemed unlikely such an illustrious trio would have been involved in Maya Lamb's kidnapping, but why else would Tom Fuqua be worried about a break-in at June Chapman's house?

She decided not to mention the conversation to Max just yet. If his father had somehow been involved, it could at best create a conflict of interest and, at worst, the need for a cover-up. She wanted to believe Max Winter was a straight arrow, but small-town politics could be treacherous and deeply incestuous.

"Whether or not anyone at the party was involved, the reality is that Denton Crosby is still a free man," Avery said. "And the person who hired him remains hidden."

"For now," Max agreed.

She nibbled on a french fry as she watched Reggie Lamb fill salt and pepper shakers at the end of the counter. "She deserves to know about that confession."

Max glanced over his shoulder. "She will, but we don't want to play our cards too soon. We'll only have one shot at a conviction so I hope you meant what you said about discretion."

"Don't worry, Max. I'll keep your secret. But I'd like something from you in return."

He glanced up from his plate. "What?"

"We agree to share information. I'll come to you with anything I dig up and you keep me in the loop regarding the investigation into June Chapman's shooting. It doesn't have to be an official arrangement. No one else has to know."

"I'll think about it."

She was stunned that he hadn't turned her down flat. "Is that the best you can offer after all we've been through?" she goaded good-naturedly.

"I'm afraid so."

"I won't press my luck, then. While you consider my proposition, I'll share a name to prove I'm operating in good faith. Paul Bozeman. He owns an antique shop in town and is apparently related to June Chapman by marriage. Might be a good idea to find out if he was at Reggie's party the night Maya went missing."

Max stared at her in astonishment. Then he very deliberately pushed aside his plate. "Where did you hear that name?"

"People talk, I listen."

"Sounds a lot like eavesdropping to me." She didn't deny it and he didn't bother to hide his irritation. "How long were you left alone at the police station anyway?"

"Long enough for certain people to forget I was there," she admitted. "After I gave my statement to Detective Slade, I drove back over to Crescent Hill. One of June's neighbors offered to speak with me if I helped her weed a flower bed. She had no qualms about putting a stranger to work." She held up a blistered thumb. "Afterward she served me homemade lemonade on the veranda and we had a nice, long chat. She and June Chapman have been neighbors for decades. She said June's late husband came from a wealthy family."

"Not just wealthy," Max clarified. "Old money with all the baggage and expectations that come with it."

"Then I'm probably not telling you anything you don't already know. You can stop me if I'm being repetitive." She paused, but he motioned for her to continue. "Her husband's name was Robert Chapman and apparently his younger sister was something of a wild child. Their father kicked her out of the house when she got pregnant by someone he didn't approve of and he later wrote her out of his will when they eloped. The old man left everything to Robert, who in turn left everything to his widow, June. The daughter, Sarah, tried on two separate occasions to contest the will but her lawsuit was thrown out each time. June wasn't very sympathetic to her sister-in-law's plight and the two women became bitter enemies. When Sarah died, her son, Paul Bozeman, and *his* daughter, Sidney, continued the feud with June. According to the neighbor, the Bozeman family has been trying for over forty years to get back the fortune they believe is rightfully theirs."

"Which probably explains why June is convinced they've been stealing from her," Max said.

Avery said in surprise, "You know about that? Mrs. Carmichael—the neighbor—told me about an experience she had in their shop sometime back. She noticed a pair of silver candlesticks that she was certain had come from June's house."

"Did she tell June?"

"Yes, but she said June refused to call the police. Said she'd handle the situation in her own way." Avery glanced around to see if anyone had taken a seat within earshot. She leaned in and lowered her voice. "In her confession, Nadine Crosby claimed that someone paid her, her brother and a third man to kidnap both Thea and Maya Lamb. I was sitting here wondering about motive when you walked in."

"What did you come up with?"

"The twins were June's only living relatives. With those children out of the way, Sarah and her son, Paul, may have thought they had a shot at an inheritance should June die suddenly. Or at least, a better chance of winning a settlement against her in court."

"It's an interesting theory," Max said. "I like that you're thinking outside the box, but here's the problem. Nadine claimed she and her coconspirators were each paid a large sum of money for their services. Bozeman Antiques may be reasonably lucrative for a small-town business, but it's doubtful the family would have had large amounts of cash lying around to pay kidnappers."

"Maybe they took out a loan using their business as collateral. Granted, it would have been a risky endeavor, but you're talking an investment of thousands with the possibility of a return in the millions. When the third kidnapper was murdered and Denton Crosby could only take one of the twins, June was still left with a flesh-and-blood heir in Thea. Maybe that's why Paul and his daughter have resorted to stealing from June. They feel the antiques in her home are their due. Question is, why does June put up with it? Guilt?"

"She's never struck me as the type to be bothered by a conscience," Max said.

Avery tapped her palms lightly on the tabletop as an idea struck her. "You know what we should do? We should go talk to Paul Bozeman and find out his whereabouts on the night of the kidnapping."

Max gave her a look. "You think he'll volunteer that information, do you?"

"You're a prosecutor. It's your job to get the truth out of him."

"You seem to think my job is interchangeable with that of a police detective."

"Funny, you seemed to think the same thing last night."

He conceded her point. "Fair enough, but last night's lapse in judgment aside, I don't make a habit of showing up at a place of business to prematurely interrogate a potential witness. If you're smart, you'll refrain from interfering in a police investigation."

"And if they never get around to questioning him? This is a small town with a limited police force. How much time and attention can they afford to devote to each case? Cal Slade may be a great detective, but he's only one man."

"He said almost exactly the same this morning," Max admitted.

"See there? We'd be doing him a favor."

"Gotta love your justification."

She gave him a knowing look. "You want to do it. I can see it in your eyes. You're dying to get in on the action."

He remained unflappable. "Maybe you see what you want to see."

"Or maybe I see more than you want me to see. I know one thing." She nodded to the crumpled tie on the seat beside him. "You couldn't wait to get out of that straitjacket." When he didn't respond, she pressed on. "Aren't you just the tiniest bit excited by the prospect of something new and different?"

"Some*thing* or some*one*?" he challenged.

"Either or both. Are you in?"

He sat back in his seat with an enigmatic gleam in his eyes. "I haven't decided yet."

Chapter Nine

As Max cruised down the center of town searching for Bozeman Antiques, he told himself he was merely satisfying a niggling curiosity. His impulse had nothing to do with Avery Bolt's suggestion that they talk to Paul Bozeman together. In fact, she wasn't even aware of his intention. He'd left her at the diner with the promise that he would consider her proposition, but on further reflection, teaming up with a woman he barely knew and didn't trust seemed like a very bad idea. He could only imagine the kind of trouble she could make for him.

But… He had to admit her theory about Paul Bozeman and his mother bankrolling Maya Lamb's kidnapping intrigued him. It echoed Gail's earlier revelations about the lawsuits filed against June Chapman by her late husband's estranged family. Interesting how quickly an outsider had drilled down on that premise after having heard Paul Bozeman's name at the police station only that morning. Or so she said. For all Max knew, Avery Bolt could have begun her investigation long before arriving in Black Creek. For all he knew, she could have an agenda that had nothing to do with protecting June Chapman.

Taking out the card she'd given him that morning, he called the number of her Houston office as he inched along in congested traffic. The call went straight to voice mail. Max left a brief message for Sam Cusack, then disconnected.

All the while, he kept an eye out for the store. He must have driven past Bozeman Antiques dozens of times over the years, but he couldn't remember the exact location of the building. That only mattered because now that both father and daughter were on his radar, he wanted to get a better handle on their situation. A failing business might generate the kind of desperation that could lead to a home invasion—or worse—particularly if the homeowner was regarded as the enemy.

Of course, the last thing he wanted was to steamroll over the police's investigation, but Cal Slade hadn't seemed all that interested in the Bozeman connection earlier. He'd considered their involvement a long shot while simultaneously lamenting the limited resources of his department. He'd even asked Max to speak with Will Kent rather than trekking out to the lake himself to consult with the former police chief. Cal would do his best to cover the bases, but now that he'd been appointed acting chief in Nash Bowden's absence, he was spread even thinner than usual. Last night's shooting was only one of dozens of active cases on his plate. Maybe Avery was right. Maybe Max would be doing his friend a favor by looking into the Bozeman angle on his own time.

Gotta love your justification.

Avery might be right about something else, too. He was itching for some action regardless of the risk. Or maybe because of the risk. Being cooped up in his musty office reading through briefs couldn't have sounded less appealing at that moment.

He circled the block, glancing from time to time in the rearview mirror. He'd spotted a silver SUV that had stayed two cars behind him ever since he'd made the turn onto Main Street. The only person he could think of who would be tailing him was Avery. Had she followed him back to the courthouse and then waited for him to leave just as she'd waited for Cal to exit June Chapman's house that morning?

Max berated himself for not being more situationally aware. By the time he and Avery had parted ways outside the diner, his thoughts had already turned to the mountain of case files waiting for him back at the office. Preoccupied as he was, he could have easily missed a tail.

He'd had every intention of working all afternoon and well into the evening as was his usual practice, but he'd only made it to the second floor of the courthouse before abruptly reversing course and heading out the rear door to the parking lot. Then he'd called his assistant to cancel an afternoon appointment, offering the flimsiest of excuses, which she seemed to buy without question. And why wouldn't she? He never canceled appointments without good reason, never skipped meetings, never, in all the years he'd worked at the DA's office, called in sick or left work early. At the ripe old age of thirty-three, he'd become the thing that had once repelled him the most—a single-minded workaholic.

He found a tight space between two cars and parallel parked. The silver SUV turned down a one-way street and kept going. The realization that he was under surveillance unsettled him more than he cared to admit. He'd always considered himself a good judge of character, but he couldn't get a read on Avery Bolt. Was *she* one of the good guys?

Again, Max questioned the wisdom and motivation behind his actions, but in the end, he merely dismissed his qualms and climbed out of the vehicle. Crossing the street, he pretended to window-shop as he made his way along the sidewalk until he stood outside Bozeman Antiques. Flanked on one side by a vintage-clothing boutique and on the other by an art gallery, the shop was centrally located in the trendy section of downtown where dozens of thrift stores and resale businesses had intermittently thrived and withered for decades.

He couldn't remember the last time he'd been to this part of town. In recent years, the area had become something of a tourist attraction, creating a traffic nightmare on weekends. Max avoided the chaos whenever possible, which was probably why Bozeman Antiques had escaped his attention. He took a moment now to observe the discreet sign with gilded lettering that hung from a wrought iron rod over the door and the artful display of antique oil lamps in the plate glass window.

A bell chimed as he entered the shop and he stood for a moment taking in the crowded space as the door closed softly behind him. He appeared to be alone in the store. Wednesday afternoon was evidently a slow time in the antique business.

At the back of the main showroom, a long glass counter displayed small collectibles—everything from turquoise jewelry to silver pillboxes to gilded hand mirrors. Larger pieces like candlesticks and heavy crystal vases were displayed on long rows of shelving behind the counter. A jumble of furniture and rolled rugs could be glimpsed through a wide archway, and at the very back of the building, double doors likely led to the warehouse.

Max glanced out the front window as he pretended to browse the wares. Avery stood on the opposite side of the street near his vehicle. She had on sunglasses and the ubiquitous ball cap to disguise her appearance, but he had quickly come to recognize the confident way she carried herself—shoulders back, posture perfect. He'd never met anyone like her. Assertive to the point of arrogant at times and yet she'd allowed a pushy jerk in a dimly lit hallway to get under her skin.

And why the hell was she following him?

As he stood watching, she crossed the street and walked

past the shop without glancing in. He leaned into the window to track her, then turned at the sound of a cleared throat behind him.

A man had materialized behind the counter. He looked as if he'd been hard at work in a hot space. His cotton shirt clung to his skin and beads of sweat glistened on a high forehead. He kept the barrier between them as he took out a white handkerchief and vigorously mopped his brow.

"Hello," he said. "I didn't know anyone was out here. The buzzer in the warehouse must be broken."

"That's all right," Max said. "I haven't been here long." His gaze was drawn momentarily to the maze of tattooed vines and roses on the man's forearms. His own tattoos were more discreet and less intricate—and less professional, if he were honest. The kind of skin art that came from a rebellious impulse and a tattoo parlor at the end of a dark alley. Afterward, Max had taken great care that his old man didn't catch sight of them, but he'd ended up in boarding school anyway so, in hindsight, he might as well have flaunted his ink. There was a reason why he hadn't. He could take his father's anger and disappointment, but the old man's contempt was a whole different matter.

"You'll have to excuse me for looking like something the cat dragged in," the shopkeeper said in an amiable drawl as he unrolled his shirtsleeves and fastened the cuffs. Max wondered if the man had misinterpreted his appreciation of the detailed inkwork as disapproval or even derision.

"No problem," he said.

"We just got in a large delivery from an estate sale and our warehouse help was a no-show today," the man explained. "Can't say I blame him. Place is like an oven back there."

"I can only imagine," Max said. "It's nearly a hundred outside."

"Yes, well, I'm the owner so I don't have the luxury of calling in sick no matter the weather."

"I get it," Max said. "Things being what they are, you do what you have to do to keep a business going."

The man nodded appreciatively and plucked a card from a holder on the counter. "Paul Bozeman." He slid the card across the glass top while simultaneously giving his forehead a final swipe. "How can I help you?"

"I'm not sure yet. I came in on a whim," Max admitted, allowing a hint of uncertainty to creep into his voice. "I hope that's okay. I understand some shops in the area are appointment only except on weekends."

"Not us. We still have regular operating hours, Tuesday through Saturday, ten to four. Drop-ins during business hours are always welcome. Feel free to take your time and look around." A smile flashed, followed by a note of regret. "Of course, we do have some limitations. No unsupervised children allowed in the store. No food or drinks. Most of our inventory is one of a kind and can never be replaced if stained or damaged."

"I'll remember that." Max pretended to examine an amber ring through the glass countertop as he covertly took Bozeman's measure. He looked to be in his early fifties, tall and wiry with a sprinkle of silver at his temples that might have lent an air of sophistication to his appearance on normal days. At the moment, however, he merely looked hot, tired and slightly seedy.

He returned the scrutiny as he wordlessly took out the ring and placed it on a felt square in front of Max. Then he removed a cloth from underneath the counter and pretended to wipe away fingerprints from the glass.

Was he the intruder who had shot June Chapman twice in the chest last night only to later take aim at Max as he lay at the bottom of the stairs? Max tried to conjure an image of the masked intruder, but he couldn't honestly say that the body types matched. He'd only had a glimpse of gleaming eyes through the mask before Avery had brought the man to his knees.

He felt a surge of admiration at the memory, but he quickly shuttered the image as he picked up the ring. "Beautiful stone. I've never seen anything quite like it."

"Baltic amber set in 18K gold. You'll never see another like it."

Max returned the ring to the felt pad. "I'm not actually looking for jewelry. Maybe something a little less personal." He glanced around. "You certainly have a lot to choose from. I've lived in Black Creek for most of my life, but I don't believe I've ever been inside your shop before."

"That doesn't surprise me. You don't exactly strike me as a collector," Bozeman observed.

"You can tell that about me in the few minutes we've been talking?"

"That and more." The man's smile turned enigmatic. "When you've been in the business as long as I have, you learn early on to differentiate the passionate collector from the casual buyer and the casual buyer from the curious browser. It saves everyone a lot of time."

"Well, you're right," Max said. "I don't know the first thing about antiques. I came in looking for a gift for my stepmother. She has an appreciation for old stuff like this. She says every piece tells a story."

"Smart woman. Is she one of our regulars?"

"I have no idea."

"I only ask because it might make it easier to point you in the right direction." Bozeman tucked the dust cloth underneath the counter and stood back, giving Max some space while still observing him with a keen eye. "Of course, if you'd rather look around and choose something on your own, that's fine, too. Feel free to ask questions if you see something you like."

"No, I'd welcome your input. Gail's pretty picky about

what comes into her home." Max nodded to the shelves behind the counter. "She likes silver candlesticks and I notice you have a lot of them."

"Are you looking for a certain period or maker?"

Max shrugged in confusion, then pointed to one of the more elaborate pieces. "I think she'd like something like that."

Bozeman turned and carefully extracted the candlestick from the shelf, then placed it on another felt square in front of Max. The piece was much too ornate to suit Gail's classic style but Max thought it would have been right at home in June Chapman's house. And maybe it once had been.

"A Victorian rococo from the late nineteenth century," Bozeman told him. "It makes for a nice presentation, but it's not all that rare. If your stepmother is particular about her pieces, maybe she'd favor something a little more… exclusive."

Which translated to more expensive, no doubt. "I see your point."

"What's the occasion, if you don't mind my asking?"

"No occasion. I just felt like doing something nice for her. She lives in the same neighborhood as the woman who was shot last night. I'm sure you must have heard about it." Max waited for a response. "It's been all over the news," he prompted.

Something flickered in Bozeman's eyes, a look of curiosity quickly replaced by one of distrust. "You're talking about the incident in Crescent Hill? I heard something about it on the local radio station this morning on my way downtown. They seemed to think it was a burglary or home invasion gone wrong."

"My stepmother lives on the same street as the victim. She's pretty shaken up, as you can imagine," Max said. "The whole neighborhood is in an uproar. Nothing like that has ever happened in Crescent Hill."

"I haven't heard the latest," Bozeman said. "Have the police caught the guy who did it?"

"Not that I'm aware, but I'm sure they must have one or more individuals under surveillance. Hopefully, it's only a matter of time before they make an arrest."

"Hopefully," Bozeman muttered.

Max observed the man's reaction before continuing in the same conversational tone. "Of course, there are some crimes that never get solved. Take the little girl that was kidnapped from her bedroom. How long has it been since she went missing? Nearly thirty years? And the police have only now caught a break in the case."

Bozeman's gaze shot to Max. "Are you talking about Maya Lamb? What break?"

"Could be just a rumor," Max hedged. "But her case has generated a lot of media hype lately because of the other kidnapping. It's possible someone has come forward with new information."

"New information? After all these years? If someone knows what happened to that little girl, why would they wait until now to come forward?" Bozeman's tone also remained casual, but there was an undercurrent of anxiety that sharpened his pitch. Max searched for other tells—the twitch of a muscle or the jump of his pulse.

"Did they mention on the radio that the shooting victim is the missing child's grandmother?" Max asked. "That alone is enough to make you wonder about a connection."

"What kind of connection?"

"Maybe you could tell me." Max picked up the candlestick and pretended to examine the maker's mark on the bottom.

"What's that supposed to mean?" Bozeman's tone had noticeably cooled.

"You're related to both victims, aren't you?"

A long silence, then, "I don't know what you're talking about. There's no relation."

Max glanced up. "Oh, come on. You may not be related by blood to June Chapman, but her late husband and your mother were siblings. That makes you her nephew by marriage and a second cousin to Maya Lamb and her sister, Thea."

Bozeman snatched up the amber ring and shoved it underneath the counter. Then he grabbed the silver candlestick from Max's hand and moved it out of reach. "Who are you? A reporter?" He made a production of locking the glass case. "It's obvious you didn't come here to shop for your stepmother or anyone else. What is it you want?"

"I'm with the DA's office." Max took out a card and handed it to him. "My name is Max Winter. I'd like to ask you a few questions regarding one of my cases."

Bozeman picked up the card, scanned the information and then flicked it back across the counter. "You've got the wrong guy. I can't help you."

"How do you know? I haven't told you which case I'm working on."

"Doesn't matter. I don't know anything about anything. I run a legitimate establishment here. Been at the same location for over twenty years. You can ask any of my associates or clients. I work hard, pay my taxes, keep my nose clean and out of anyone else's business."

Max took note of his defensiveness. "I'm sure you're an upstanding citizen and businessman. A real asset to the community," he said without a trace of irony. "Nevertheless, I still have a few questions."

"I *said* I can't help you."

"I would reconsider if I were you. A little cooperation can go a long way, Mr. Bozeman."

He drew a breath and released it slowly as if counting to ten in his head. "I would be happy to cooperate if I had anything helpful to offer. Unfortunately, I don't. But ask your questions anyway," he added grudgingly. "Make it quick. I have a business to run."

"When was the last time you spoke to June Chapman?"

He shrugged. "We don't speak. I barely know the woman."

"Have you had any communication with her since you and your mother contested her husband's will?"

If the question caught the man by surprise, he didn't let on. "That's ancient history. We lost in court, took our lumps and moved on."

"You don't feel any animosity toward June Chapman for inheriting a fortune that some would consider rightfully yours?"

"I don't like the woman, but I don't wish her any ill will. Now, if that's all you've got—"

"Where were you on the night Maya Lamb went missing?"

That question did take him by surprise. His jaw slacked, his eyes hardened and, for a moment, he appeared speechless with shock or anger or a combination of the two. Then he collected himself and sputtered, "What the hell kind of question is that?"

"The simple, straightforward kind."

Bozeman's hands balled into fists at his sides. He shoved them in his pockets and then rocked back on his heels as if trying to present a composed demeanor. But there was something in his eyes Max couldn't define. Something bobbing behind the anger and fake outrage that might have been fear.

"Mr. Bozeman, are you going to answer my question?" he pressed.

"How do you expect me to remember where I was thirty years ago?"

"Twenty-eight years to be precise. Most anyone in Black Creek can tell you where they were the night Maya Lamb went missing. Her disappearance shook this town to its core. You're related to the victim so the time frame in which she vanished must stick out in your mind."

"Why? I didn't know the kid." Bozeman clamped his mouth shut as if realizing how heartless he sounded. He returned the candlestick to the shelf, fiddling with the placement. When he turned back to the counter, his demeanor and tone had noticeably softened, but not without effort, Max thought. "I'm sorry she got taken, but it had nothing to do with me."

"Did you know her mother?"

"It's a small town so I saw her around from time to time, but I wouldn't say I knew her. I heard the rumors about how June treated her after Johnny was killed. Didn't surprise me, of course, but I felt for the poor woman just the same."

"Were you at her party the night Maya was taken?"

A myriad of emotions flashed across the man's features. He looked torn between keeping his cool and the baser urge to punch Max in the face. "I just told you I didn't know the woman. Why would I attend her party?"

"That's a no, then?"

"Look, Mr. Whatever-you-said-your-name-was—"

"Max Winter."

"I don't know what you're trying to pull here, but I'm about thirty seconds away from calling my attorney. He's a pit bull and I'm not afraid to use him."

"That's your prerogative," Max told him. "I'm merely trying to ascertain who was at Reggie Lamb's house the night her daughter disappeared. There's a partial list in the case file. I'm hoping to fill in the gaps."

"After all this time?"

"You never know. The passage of time can sometimes intensify the need to clear one's conscience." Max paused to let that sink in. "Just so I'm straight on the facts, you're saying you weren't at Reggie Lamb's party the night her daughter went missing."

Max could see the wheels turning in the man's head. What if someone had come forward and placed him at the party? Was it better to out and out lie or continue to equivocate in case he later needed to change his story? Bozeman chose the latter.

"I'll say it again. I don't remember where I was that night, but I know I wasn't kidnapping a little girl."

Max let it go for the moment. "How about last night? Do you remember where you were between the hours of midnight and two a.m.?"

"Where most folks were—home in bed."

"Alone?"

"Yes, alone, although I don't see how that's any of your business."

"Is there anyone who can vouch for your whereabouts?"

"Why would I need someone to vouch for me when I haven't done anything wrong?"

Max gave him a pointed stare before glancing through the arched doorway. "Is your daughter around? I'd like to have a word with her as well."

"She's not here."

"Would you mind telling me how I can get in touch with her?"

"She's gone for the day." Bozeman's gaze narrowed. "Why do you want to talk to Sidney?"

"I have a few questions for her." He peered through the archway as if searching for the elusive Sidney Bozeman. "Did you know June Chapman told some of her neighbors that she believes you and your daughter go into her house while she's out and help yourselves to her valuables?"

His accommodating facade slipped. "I have no control over what that old bitty says."

So…not quite as indifferent to the woman as he'd earlier let on.

Max let his gaze scan the shelves of silver candlesticks before he vectored back in on Bozeman. He slid his card across the counter once more. "Keep my number. You never know when something may come back to you."

As he turned to walk out, Bozeman said from behind the counter, "I meant what I said about calling my attorney."

"You do what you have to do, Mr. Bozeman. I'll be in touch."

Chapter Ten

Avery waited until Max was inside the store before crossing the street and hurrying down the narrow alleyway that led to the back of Bozeman Antiques. Mindful of the earlier run-in at the restaurant, she kept glancing over her shoulder to make sure she wasn't being followed. Ironic, she supposed, since surveillance was a big part of her business as a private investigator. Case in point, just minutes ago, she'd tailed Max from the courthouse, and earlier that morning, she'd staked out June Chapman's house so that she could approach him as soon as he was alone.

She wasn't motivated by mere curiosity, though she freely admitted to a certain level of fascination and even attraction when it came to Max Winter. No, an assistant DA could be a valuable ally in a place like Black Creek, but she needed to make sure she wasn't being blinded by his good looks and charm.

But…back to the man at the restaurant. Avery had no idea who he was or why she'd been repelled by his mere presence, but she certainly didn't relish another encounter, especially in a dead-end alley. The very thought of his hand on her flesh gave her the creeps and made her feel cornered. Made her want to run back to her hotel room, pack her bags and flee homeward as fast as she could. That wasn't a typical reaction for her. She never backed down from a bully or succumbed to irrational fears. She hadn't cowered behind a locked door since she was a little girl plagued by bad dreams.

Taking one last glimpse behind her, she rounded the corner where the alley intersected with a small parking area at the rear of Bozeman Antiques and the adjacent shops. A cinder block wall separated the row of buildings from the backs of the businesses on the next street over. Some of the establishments had loading docks where vans and moving trucks could empty cargo straight into the warehouses.

The overhead door was open at the rear of Bozeman Antiques, but Avery couldn't detect any activity inside. She waited another few minutes before hitching herself up on the platform and slipping through the door.

The space inside was packed with antique and vintage furniture that had been organized in rows for easier access and inventory, but the back of the warehouse looked chaotic with boxes and plastic bins stacked to the ceiling and a mishmash of shelving units for storing lamps, vessels and other items in need of cleaning or repair.

"Hello? Anyone here?" Avery's voice echoed back to her in the cavernous space. For some reason, she thought again of the man at the restaurant and the sly way he'd lifted his finger to silence her. She glanced back through the open bay, consumed once more by the urge to run until she took a deep breath and berated herself for overreacting. Luther had taught her better than that.

He had also taught her to heed her instincts. She didn't seem to be in any danger at that very moment, but her nerve endings prickled a warning just the same.

"Hello?" She went slowly up one aisle and down another, not really knowing what she hoped to find. Experience had taught her that she would recognize it when she saw it.

As she emerged from one of the aisles, the sound of a slammed door followed by a female voice sent her scurrying for cover. She planted herself behind the mirrored door of a mahogany chifforobe where she could peek around the edge.

A young woman dressed in denim shorts and a faded T-shirt appeared at the top of a wooden staircase that led up to a loft area. She looked to be around thirty with a deep suntan and the trim, hard calves of a runner. Tucking a clip-board underneath her arm, she continued to argue with the person on the other end of the call. The conversation grew more and more heated until the door to the shop opened and a man called out, "Sidney, you back here?"

"Up here, Dad. What is it?"

"Can you come down here for a minute? We need to talk."

The woman mumbled something into the phone and then slipped it into the back pocket of her shorts before she quickly descended the steps. Avery lost sight of her until she eased away from her hiding spot and inched to the end of the aisle, stopping short when the man came into her view. He was tall and thin with a receding hairline on a high fore-head. Leaning a hip against a nearby desk, he took out a white handkerchief and mopped his brow. Avery wished she could do the same. It was sweltering inside the ware-house despite the industrial fans rotating overhead. Sweat stung her eyes and dampened her shirt, but she remained motionless, her gaze riveted on the man she assumed was Paul Bozeman.

"I'm just finishing the inventory checklist," the woman said as she hurried across the warehouse toward him. "What's up?" Then she added in concern, "Are you okay? You look like you just saw a ghost."

"Someone from the DA's office stopped by. A man named Max Winter."

"Max Winter?" She sounded shocked. "I've been seeing his name all over the news lately. He's hard-core and kind of a big shot. What did he want?"

"He was asking a lot of questions about that missing kid, if you can believe it." He coughed into his handkerchief before stuffing it back in his pocket.

"Are you sure you're okay?" the woman pressed. "I'm worried about your color."

"I got a little overheated earlier. Nothing a good night's sleep won't take care of. I'll be fine."

"I could tell you weren't feeling well. You should have let me unload the truck by myself," she admonished.

"I said I'll be fine," he snapped.

"Okay, okay. No need to take my head off. Why was Max Winter asking questions about the missing kid?" She spoke in a conciliatory tone as she went over to an old refrigerator and took out a bottle of water, which she brought back to her dad. "Here, drink this. Didn't they catch the person who took her? And why would someone from the DA's office come to see you about a missing kid anyway?"

He took a long swig of chilled water and then replaced the cap. "I'm not talking about the one that disappeared a couple of weeks ago. That little Kylie girl. He had questions about Maya."

"Maya? Maya *Lamb*? But she disappeared years ago."

"Twenty-eight years to be precise."

A long silence followed. Then, in a softer voice, she said, "What's going on, Dad?"

"I wish I knew."

"What did he say, exactly?"

"He *implied* that someone has come forward with new information."

"About you?"

"About the kidnapping, I guess. He was vague about that part. He wanted to know where I was the night Maya got taken. He asked straight up if I'd gone to Reggie Lamb's party."

The woman's ringtone sounded. She glanced at the screen, frowned, then turned off her phone and tossed it onto the desk. "Dad, this sounds serious. What did you tell him?"

"I told him I don't remember."

She pulled up a chair and sat down at the desk, swiveling around so that she could stare up at him. "Don't take this the wrong way, but do you really think that was the best way to answer him?"

"Why not? It's the truth."

"Dad." Her tone turned slightly admonishing. "You honestly can't remember where you were the night Maya Lamb disappeared? Her kidnapping was a huge deal in this town. People still talk about it."

"So?"

"So, people who were around back then remember where they were when it happened."

Bozeman jumped up from the desk. "Are you calling your own father a liar?"

She didn't seem at all fazed by his outburst. Instead, she merely shrugged. "Don't take this out on me. I'm just trying to figure out what's going on. Regardless of what happened that night, I'm on your side. I'm always on your side. You know that."

He took no comfort in her assurances. "What do you mean, regardless of what happened?"

She leaned forward, her voice hushed. "It's just you and me in here now. Max Winter is long gone so you can be straight with me. Were you at that party?"

"I said I don't remember." He remained sullen and defensive, which made Avery wonder about his veracity. He was obviously hiding something. What if he had been at Reggie's party? What if he'd been the lookout for Denton

Crosby, making sure the coast was clear for the kidnapper as he climbed through the bedroom window and took little Maya back out the same way?

Avery could picture the scenario in her head. She could almost hear the music and boisterous laughter from the party and the nearer sound of soft breathing from the sleeping children. Bozeman would have planted himself in a spot where he could keep an eye on their bedroom window. When the time was right, he would have given the signal—the flick of a cigarette lighter maybe or the wink of a flashlight. Then he would have waited for the dart of a shadow across the yard, a silhouette at the window, and when it was over, he would have slipped away from the party as quietly as he'd entered.

Shaken by the image, Avery drew a deep breath and then another to slow her suddenly racing pulse. After decades of dead-end trails, was the Maya Lamb kidnapping case about to be cracked?

Sidney Bozeman's voice dropped Avery back into the blistering warehouse. "Dad? Did you hear what I said?"

"Okay," he said with reluctance. "I may have stopped by the party at some point during the night, but I didn't stay long and no one saw me. No one who would have remembered the next day."

His daughter's tone remained even, but Avery detected a note of worry at the fringes. "Why did you go?"

He sat back down on the desk, grasping the edge with both hands as his voice turned hard and resentful. "Not to kidnap Maya Lamb, if that's where you're going with this."

"You know that's not what I mean. You weren't friends with Reggie, were you? Why would you go to her party?"

"I don't know. I was a young man back then and I guess I was curious. Her parties were legendary. I wanted to see for myself what went on out there."

"Did you go alone?"

"Yes."

Another long silence.

So no one to corroborate when he had arrived and when he left.

"What are you thinking?" Bozeman prompted.

"I'm just trying to work out why you didn't tell Max Winter the truth. Why did you feel it necessary to keep that information from him?"

"Use your head, Sid. How would it look if I admitted to being at that party after keeping silent all these years?"

"Why did you keep silent?" Apprehension crept back into her voice along with the slightest hint of accusation.

"No one ever asked and I saw no reason to volunteer the information. Why would I? I was only there for a few minutes. I figured out pretty quick it wasn't my kind of scene. I didn't see or hear anything that could help the police. Your grandmother was still alive back then, but she was already sick. Those lawsuits took a lot out of her emotionally and physically. After everything that went down with June, I didn't want the cops coming around asking a bunch of questions that would upset her."

"Now, see? That makes sense," Sidney said. "Totally understandable that you'd want to protect her. Okay, let's just think about this for a minute." She got up and started to pace. In the interim, Avery tried to shift her position so that she could see both father and daughter. She lifted her face momentarily to the breeze created by the overhead fans. Being from Houston, she was used to the heat, but she was starting to feel a little claustrophobic. She had a sudden vision of all that stacked furniture tumbling down upon her where she crouched. Shaking off the image, she forced her attention back to the pair at the front of the warehouse.

"According to Max Winter, someone has come forward with new information about the kidnapping," Sidney mused as she walked over to the bay door and glanced out both ways.

Bozeman waited until she came back to the desk to respond. “He didn’t outright say it, but that was the strong implication. He was vague on details.”

She seemed to contemplate his response for a moment. “Sounds like he was fishing. I seriously doubt anyone has come forward with new evidence, much less an eyewitness. After twenty-eight years? Come on. He’s got nothing.”

“You don’t know that for certain,” Bozeman fretted. “This is a cutthroat business. I’ve made my share of enemies over the years. For all either of us knows, someone could be out to ruin me by spreading rumors. And anyway, fishing or not, this Winter guy came across to me as a man on a mission. I don’t trust him. A person like that will do whatever it takes to make a name for himself.”

“Unfortunately, you could be right about that.” She walked back over to the open doorway as if she couldn’t quite settle in one spot. Or as if she was expecting someone.

“Can you please stop that pacing?” Bozeman finally said in exasperation. “You’re making me nervous.”

“Sorry.” She remained in the doorway surveying the parking area. “I was just thinking that for anyone with political aspirations, closing the Maya Lamb case would be a huge feather in his cap. If Max Winter is bluffing about new information, then something else must have put him on your trail. Any idea what that could be?”

“Isn’t it obvious?”

“June Chapman.”

At the mention of her name, a strange pall seemed to descend over the warehouse. Paul Bozeman grew jittery and wary, glancing over his shoulder as if he were afraid his old nemesis had somehow materialized behind his back.

“It was all over the news this morning.” Sidney turned away from the door, watching her father intently for a moment before once more closing the distance between them. "Apparently, it's a big deal when someone like her gets shot. Not so much for the rest of us. But why would the police think you had anything to do with it?"

"It's not rocket science," Bozeman said. "There's been bad blood between our families going back decades."

"But that's been over since Grandma died."

His voice lowered. "Come on, Sid. You and I both know that's not true."

The ensuing pause seemed somehow loaded. "Do you think June might have said something to the police?" Now Sidney was the one who sounded anxious and jittery. "Assuming she's still alive, of course. The news accounts have been pretty sketchy about her condition."

"God, I hate talking about that woman," Bozeman grumbled. "I don't even like hearing her name."

"You make it sound as if she has some strange power over you. She doesn't. She's just a moneygrubbing old hag who took something that doesn't belong to her and now someone has finally made her pay. She's lucky one of us didn't put a bullet in her years ago."

He seemed momentarily speechless by her outburst. Then, "For God's sake, don't let anyone else hear you say that."

"Relax. No one is going to hear me." But her tone sounded strained. "If June Chapman really is the reason the authorities are suddenly all up in our business, then why did Max Winter question you about Maya's kidnapping? Why not grill you about the shooting?"

"He seems to think there could be a connection."

"How could there be a connection? Maya went missing nearly thirty years ago. How could her disappearance have anything to do with someone popping an old woman in her sleep?"

Bozeman's tone subtly altered. "I never said she was shot in her sleep."

"I heard it on the radio."

"The report I heard was vague. You said yourself, they're being careful about giving out details."

"Well, as *you* said, it's not rocket science. They broke into her house in the middle of the night. There's a strong likelihood she was asleep. Focus, Dad." She snapped her fingers, either to get his attention or to distract him from his current train of thought. "Where's the connection to the kidnapping? And more important, where's the connection to you? It must be something pretty compelling for an assistant DA to show up here in person."

He ran a hand through his thinning hair. "June has been telling her neighbors that you and I have been coming into her house when she's gone and stealing her antiques."

Sidney swore loudly. "She said that? She implicated both of us?"

"You haven't been back to her house, have you, Sid? You didn't—" He broke off abruptly and turned to scour the warehouse.

"What is it?" she asked.

"I thought I heard something."

Avery closed her eyes and steeled herself. She was certain she hadn't inadvertently moved or made a sound, but she'd heard the screech, too. Glancing over her shoulder, she tried to pinpoint the sound. She caught sight of someone behind her and started. Then she realized she'd glimpsed her own reflection. The mirrored door on the chifforobe had swung open on squeaky hinges. She must have left it open earlier or else the breeze from the powerful fans had loosened the ancient latch. Neither father nor daughter could see her from their vantage, but if they came down the aisle to investigate—

"I didn't hear anything," Sidney said.

"Shush, just listen for a minute."

Avery glanced around for a new place to hide as her heart thudded. She reminded herself that she'd been in tighter spots than this. What would Luther tell her if he was at her side? *Panic is your worst enemy. Keep your cool and ride it out.*

"You're starting to sound paranoid," Sidney said. "That guy really rattled your cage, didn't he?"

"It's not every day I get interrogated about Maya Lamb's kidnapping, so yeah, he rattled my cage." Bozeman paused. "Are you sure we're alone?"

"Yes, I'm sure. The truck left an hour ago. I've been working back here by myself ever since. I would have known if anyone else was around."

That seemed to temporarily tamp down his paranoia. "Where were we?"

"June Chapman told her neighbors we've been stealing from her."

"You haven't, have you, Sid?"

"What? No!" She sounded more defensive than offended. "I haven't been inside her house in years. Though by rights, that place should be ours." Her voice rose. "Don't look at me that way. I'm telling you the truth."

"It's just you and me," he said, echoing her earlier comment. "You can tell me anything."

She waited a beat before she said in a quieter tone, "What are you accusing me of?"

Funny how the tables had suddenly turned, Avery thought. Their bond seemed a little frayed around the edges by mutual distrust.

"Nothing," Bozeman said. "I just want you to tell me the truth. Where were you last night? I tried to reach you several times. My calls went straight to voice mail and you never called me back."

"I was out with some friends. I didn't get home until late. I figured you were in bed by then."

"Is there someone who can vouch for your whereabouts?"

"Why do I need someone to vouch for my whereabouts?"

"Max Winter asked about you," Bozeman told her. "He wanted to know how he could reach you."

"What did you tell him?"

"I said you were gone for the rest of the day and wouldn't be in until tomorrow."

"Do you think he'll be back?"

"I think we have to assume that he will and prepare for the worst," Bozeman said. "It's possible the police can get a warrant on whatever information Winter thinks he has on me. You need to make sure your alibi for last night is airtight and you need to make damn sure they don't find anything in here that can be traced back to June Chapman."

"You don't need to worry about that. Everything's clean including my alibi. I really was out with friends last night."

"Good." He sounded relieved.

"Really, Dad. Don't get yourself all worked up over this," she said. "I'll admit it's a bit nerve-racking, but we just have to keep our cool until it all blows over. Remember what the doctor said. If you want to avoid another heart attack, you need to avoid stress. Business is slow today. No law says we can't close early. Go home and get some rest. If Max Winter comes back, I'll handle him."

Handle him how? Avery wondered.

The pair spoke for another few minutes and then Bozeman went back through the door to the shop. Sidney took out her phone and called someone as she unlocked one of the desk drawers. She rummaged inside for a moment, then turned her attention to the call.

"Hey, it's me," she said. "We've got a problem. Somebody from the DA's office came snooping around the store a few minutes ago. Dad's all upset." She listened for a moment, then said, "Yeah, yeah, I know you warned me. I should have left well enough alone, blah, blah, blah, but it's too late now for second-guessing. I need you to get over here and move those boxes out of the loft and take them to my personal storage unit. Bring the van. I've got some other stuff for you to do while you're here." Another pause. "Yes, right now. I don't give a damn what you're in the middle of. Drop everything and get your ass over here or I'll call your girlfriend and let her know how you've been spending your Sunday afternoons."

She severed the call and slid the phone back in her pocket. Then she took a gun from the desk drawer, inserted a magazine and tucked the weapon in the back waistband of her jeans before following her father into the store.

Chapter Eleven

Avery waited until she was sure the coast was clear and then eased from her hiding place and headed for the wooden staircase. She intended to get a look at whatever was packed inside those boxes before they were moved off site. A fair bet the contents were stolen or at least incriminating based on Sidney Bozeman's intent to extract them from the property before the police arrived with a warrant.

Whether or not the items had come from June Chapman's house remained to be seen. Whether the pieces had been taken before or after the shooting also remained to be determined. At the moment, Avery was certain of only one thing. Father and daughter were hiding something—from the police and, by all indications, from each other.

She had to move fast. At any moment one or both Bozemans could return to the warehouse and she had no good reason for being there. On more than a few occasions, she'd been able to talk her way out of a dicey situation, but the 9 mm tucked into Sidney Bozeman's jeans made her worry about the acceptance of a glib explanation. Better to avoid a confrontation altogether.

The treads creaked beneath her sneakers as she climbed the stairs. They were steep and didn't have a guardrail. One false step and she could end up at the bottom with a broken leg or neck. She had a sudden image of Max tumbling down a similar set of steps the night before. Despite the shock of a bullet grazing his arm, he'd had the presence of mind to tuck, roll and protect his head. And then as he'd lain on his back at the bottom of the stairs, the gunman had advanced. Why? Why not flee since Max had been in no shape to follow him? At least not immediately. Why the attack? Had the gunman recognized Max? Did he have an agenda that included taking out an assistant DA?

Those were questions to ponder at a later time, Avery decided. Right now, she needed to stay focused.

At the top of the stairs, she turned to sweep her gaze over the warehouse. The door to the showroom was still closed and no one had approached the open bay on foot or in a vehicle. So far so good.

The massive loft area contained open storage, but Avery's interest was riveted on a closed door right off the landing. She doubted stolen antiques would be kept out in the open, at least any that could be traced back to the scene of a shooting. She took another quick glance over her shoulder before putting her ear to the door. She listened for a moment and then, satisfied that no one was inside, tried the knob. The door swung inward and she stepped quickly across the threshold, her gaze darting about the space as she kept her senses attuned to any noise from below.

The first thing she noticed was the chilled air on her face and arms. After the oppressive heat of the warehouse, the air-conditioning was a welcome respite. She'd expected to find a storage room behind the door, but instead she'd stepped into a loft apartment decked out in what looked to be a mix of high-end furniture and priceless antiques. Stylish accommodations for whoever occupied the space. Avery assumed Sidney Bozeman lived in the apartment since she'd been coming down the stairs earlier when her dad had called out to her.

Sunlight streamed in through a tall window that looked

out on the roof of a neighboring business. Avery went over and glanced out to get her bearings. The alleyway from which she'd approached the back of the building was directly below her. To her right, she could glimpse traffic on the cross street and to her left, nothing but a dumpster in front of a cinder block wall where the alley dead-ended. Not exactly a picturesque view, but the apartment itself was impressive.

Turning, she surveyed the space in one sweep. A couch and two armchairs were grouped around a low coffee table facing a freestanding electric fireplace that separated the living area from the sleeping area. Straight across from the window was a small kitchen with marble countertops and stainless-steel appliances. Bold artwork hung from white walls, and the tabletops and mantel were adorned with unique bowls, boxes and statues, most of them probably antique and therefore expensive. At any other time, Avery might have enjoyed examining the individual pieces, but she'd caught sight of several cardboard boxes stacked on the other side of the fireplace.

She went back to the door and cracked it open to peer down the stairs. The coast was still clear. Closing the door softly, she hurried into the bedroom. There were at least half a dozen medium-sized moving boxes sealed tight with packing tape. A handheld tape dispenser and a utility knife lay on top of the bed.

Avery used the knife to slice open the tape on one of the boxes. The contents were protected by several layers of Bubble Wrap, which had also been sealed with packing tape. It took some effort to unravel a gold pocket watch with an intricate engraving on the case. The second piece was a silver hand mirror inlaid with ivory and jade. Both pieces looked very old, very delicate and extremely valuable, the kind of priceless heirlooms one might find tucked away in a jewelry box or displayed on a dressing table in

June Chapman's opulent bedroom. Avery snapped a few shots with her camera phone, then carefully rewrapped the antiques and resealed the box.

Rising, she returned to the living area and headed straight for a small desk that had been placed against a wall near the window. The drawers were secured and she didn't take the time to jimmy the locks. Instead, she scanned the paperwork strewn across the top, vectoring in on a stack of unfinished sales tickets. The items listed on one of the tickets included the pocket watch and the hand mirror. Small objects that could easily be ferreted away in a bag while a burglar made good his or her escape.

She assumed the contents of the other boxes were similarly itemized on individual tickets, each containing the names and addresses of various businesses and dealers. They were unsigned and undated, leading Avery to speculate that Sidney Bozeman may have been in the process of fabricating the sale and provenance of stolen collectibles.

Spreading the receipts across the desk, Avery snapped shots with her camera phone and then returned everything to the way she'd found it. There were other areas in the apartment she wanted to explore, but she'd been upstairs for too long as it was. Time to make good her escape. She'd just taken a step toward the door when she stilled and turned her head to listen. Someone was coming up the stairs.

Adrenaline pumping, she looked around for a place to hide. No time to crawl under the bed, much less to locate a closet or a second exit. Instead, she dived behind the couch and pressed herself against the soft upholstery. She barely had time to draw herself into a ball when the door opened and Sidney Bozeman came into the room. At least Avery assumed it was Sidney. She couldn't see the front door from her current position.

She listened intently, following the sound of footsteps across the room. When she wasn't immediately spotted, she eased to the end of the couch so that she could peer around the arm. Sidney stood at the desk with her back to Avery. She seemed deep in contemplation for a moment before she grabbed the itemized receipts and fed them into a shredder. Then dumping the remnants into a trash bag, she tied up the handles before heading into the bedroom.

Avery backed herself on hands and knees to the opposite end of the couch nearest the entrance. She had no choice but to make a run for it. The longer she lingered, the greater her chances of being caught, and then what? Sidney Bozeman was locked and loaded and within her rights in the state of Florida to shoot an intruder first and ask questions later.

Crouching, Avery braced herself to make a dash for the door, then dropped to the floor once more when Sidney came out of the bedroom carrying one of the boxes. She went back and forth, stacking the cartons just outside the door on the landing. If she'd noticed the tampered seal, she gave no indication. She didn't appear anxious or hurried, but she was methodical. Returning to the desk, she grabbed the trash bag with the shredded receipts and exited the apartment, locking the door behind her.

Avery let out a relieved breath and rose. She waited until she was certain the woman wasn't coming back into the apartment before she went to the door. As physically fit as Sidney Bozeman appeared to be, she wouldn't have had time to carry all of the boxes downstairs, so for all Avery knew, she might be waiting just outside on the landing for her helper to show up.

Putting her ear to the wood, Avery listened for several beats, then carefully tried the knob before realizing the dead bolt was the kind that could only be unlocked with a key on either side.

So maybe the woman had noticed the fresh tape on the box. Maybe she'd locked Avery inside the apartment until her backup arrived so that they could dispose of her body along with the contents of the boxes.

And maybe you need to stifle your imagination and find a way out of here.

Right. There had to be a spare key somewhere.

The desk seemed the most logical place to search, but she came up empty-handed. She rummaged through the nightstands in the bedroom as well as the kitchen drawers, the end tables and the mantel, all the while keeping an ear attuned for footsteps on the stairs.

After five minutes of frantic digging, she decided to go to plan B. She pushed up the window and leaned out. Not much of a plan after all. Jumping from a two-story window onto pavement was hardly a viable escape route.

Then she spotted an old metal ladder fastened to the brick wall beneath the window. Probably once used as a fire escape, the rusty apparatus looked as if it hadn't been touched in decades. The top few rungs were missing, rendering the ladder virtually inaccessible from the window except to the desperate. Avery wasn't afraid of heights and not adverse to a certain amount of risk. Besides, what were her options? Remain locked inside the apartment until Sidney Bozeman returned with her 9 mm Glock or take her chances on the ladder?

Lowering herself over the windowsill, she dangled her legs for a moment until she felt the uppermost rung with her toes. Then she eased the rest of the way over the sill, clinging to the edge with her fingertips while testing her weight on the ladder. She stepped down onto another rung and then another, releasing her grasp on the window ledge while simultaneously reaching for the handrail. The ladder creaked and groaned, but the ancient bolts held and she quickly descended.

Several feet from the pavement, she ran out of rungs and stepped down into nothing but air. Her fingers slipped on the handrails and she very nearly lost her balance, just managing to pull herself back up to the bottom step as a panel van turned down the alleyway and headed straight for her.

Under the cover of darkness, she could have flattened herself against the wall and possibly gone unnoticed, but in broad daylight with the van barreling down the narrow side street toward her, she might as well have waved her hands for the driver's attention.

He bore down on her with surprising speed considering the constriction of the alley. Avery now had two choices. Go back up to the apartment and take her chances with Sidney Bozeman or jump and pray the driver had enough room to swerve away from her. The bottom rung gave way, making the decision for her. She dropped to the pavement, landing hard on her butt and then her back. Her breath swooshed from her lungs and momentary panic set in before she scrambled to her feet.

The van was nearly upon her. Instead of braking, the driver veered toward her. Deliberately. No question of his intention. He would run her down in the alley or crush her against the wall. She had only a glimpse of his bearded face before she turned and sprinted toward the dead end.

The vehicle was so close she could feel the heat of the engine against her back. Ignoring the fiery pain in her ankle, she searched for a door, a window, any means of escape. The brick buildings formed a solid wall on both sides and the alley was barely wide enough to accommodate the van. No way to get around it and head back toward the street. She was trapped. Without a weapon, nothing she could do but run.

Glancing over her shoulder, she saw how close the vehicle truly was and redoubled her efforts. The dumpster she'd spotted from the window was situated against the cinder block wall at the end of the alley. Avery sprinted toward it, jumping up to clutch the edge and then hitching herself to the top a split second before the van screeched to a halt just inches away. She hunkered on the metal top, peering through the windshield for a better look at the driver before determining her next move. The driver stared back at her, gunning the engine and rocking the van as if taunting her to make the first move. Then he eased forward until the bumper connected with the dumpster, jolting the bin just enough to throw her off balance.

He backed up and came at her again, ramming the trash bin so hard she was forced to her knees. Farther down the alley, she saw someone hanging out the window of Sidney Bozeman's apartment. The woman screamed something down at the driver, but Avery couldn't hear what she said over the noise of the engine. Whether they were intent on harming her or merely scaring her, she had no idea. She could only assume the worst, but at least no one was shooting at her yet.

The driver reversed yet again and in the split second before the bumper collided with the bin, Avery jumped for the top of the cinder block wall that divided the rows of buildings. She fought for purchase, digging her fingertips into the hard surface until she could boost herself up.

Safe for the moment, she glanced back for one final look at the driver before she jumped down on the other side.

A FEW MINUTES LATER, Avery emerged from a second alley onto a busy street. Glancing behind her to make sure she wasn't being pursued, she took a moment to gather her bearings and then headed for the nearest intersection. As she came around the corner, she spotted Max's vehicle up ahead. She limped up to his car and rapped on the side window. He looked momentarily startled, then quickly unlocked the door. She jumped in and slunk down in the seat. "Drive!"

He checked the rearview mirror before careening away from the curb, tires screaming in protest.

"No need for dramatics," she muttered.

"It seemed like you were in a hurry," he said. "I'm driving but where am I going?"

"Doesn't matter. Circle the block a few times." She checked the mirror. The van driver sprinted from the alleyway onto the street, pausing to glance both ways. She slid down farther in the seat.

Max had spied him in the rearview. "Friend of yours?"

"Never saw him until a few minutes ago when he caught me climbing down the fire escape outside Sidney Bozeman's apartment and then he tried to run me down with his van. I think he must work for the family. It's possible he was trying to scare me away, but he took it a little too far for comfort."

Max shot her a glance. "What happened? Be specific. I'd appreciate it if you wouldn't leave out important—i.e., incriminating—details. If I'm an accessory after the fact, I need to know what I'm getting myself into."

She gave him a quick rundown of her exploits.

He frowned out the windshield as he took it all in. "So how did you end up in Sidney Bozeman's apartment in the first place?"

"I told you, she has a loft on the second floor of the warehouse. I stumbled upon it by accident." Now that the adrenaline rush was subsiding, her ankle had started to throb. She leaned down to rub the tender joint and winced.

"What happened there?" Max asked.

"I aggravated a previous injury. Nothing a little ice won't take care of."

"You should get it looked at. Could be a hairline fracture."

"No, I just twisted it the wrong way. Turn here," she

said, trying to divert his attention from her injury. They had far more pressing issues to discuss. "Where were we?"

"You stumbled upon Sidney Bozeman's apartment by accident. Or, as some might say, by snooping or more accurately breaking and entering."

Now she was the one who gave him a look. "What do you think a private investigator does anyway? Snooping is our lifeblood."

"I would expect you to operate within the confines of the law, particularly when you find yourself in a state for which your license doesn't extend."

"How do you know I'm not licensed in the state of Florida?"

"Are you?"

"No," she conceded. "But technically a license isn't required."

"*Technically*, you still have to abide by the law."

"The door was open in both the warehouse and the apartment and I even called out to see if anyone was there before I entered a place of business. So *technically* there's no case for breaking and entering. Trespassing, maybe, but let's not get all tangled up in semantics. Aren't you more interested in what I found out?" She watched the mirror as she gestured with her hand for him to turn again at the next intersection. "I don't think he's following us."

She settled back against the seat to catch her breath. Just a few blocks over from one of the busiest areas in town, they'd entered a quiet residential neighborhood of quaint bungalows and tree-lined streets. Avery lowered her window and the jungle scent of palm trees drifted in, mingling with the sticky sweetness of the jasmine that grew profusely up lampposts and arbors. The area reminded her of the neighborhood in Houston where she'd grown up. A powerful nostalgia tugged at her senses and for a moment sadness and grief pressed down like an anvil upon her shoulders. Funny how a scent could stir memories and evoke such a powerful reaction.

"You okay?" There was something in his voice now—a sudden softness—that caused her heart to flutter.

"What? Yes. Just needed a bit of fresh air." She raised the window as she steered the conversation back to a less personal topic. "I think it's safe to say Bozeman Antiques isn't entirely on the up and up. Apart from my suspicion that one or both are dealing in stolen antiques, it seems more plausible than ever that Paul Bozeman has some sort of connection to Maya Lamb's kidnapping. Why else would he lie about attending Reggie's party that night? Why keep his whereabouts secret for all these years if he has nothing to hide?"

"Tell me again what you overheard."

She recounted in as much detail as she could remember of the conversation between father and daughter and the subtle way that they'd turned on one another. Then she walked him slowly through her exploration of Sidney Bozeman's apartment, including the discovery of the unsigned and undated receipts and the contents of the box she'd opened.

"Okay, let's back up for a minute," he said. "You heard Paul Bozeman admit outright that he was at Reggie's party the night of the kidnapping. You didn't just infer it."

"Absolutely not. He couldn't have been clearer, although he denied knowing anything about the kidnapping. He said he was only there for a few minutes. He never mentioned it to the police because his mother was sick and he didn't want her upset by a lot of questions. I guess that's plausible enough considering their history, but it doesn't explain why he never said anything after his mother died."

"Maybe by then he thought coming forward would look suspicious. And maybe by then he had other things to hide."

"Yes, that's my feeling, too." Avery turned and studied

Max's profile. He appeared deep in thought. She let her gaze linger on the contours of his jawline and shivered. No one should be that good-looking. No scars, no freckles, no flaws of any kind that she could discern, but no one was perfect. She just needed to look harder to find them. "I'm willing to make a statement to everything I saw and heard, but I realize my entering the premises without an invitation could be problematic."

"It also boils down to your word against theirs," he said.

"Right. I'm an outsider and Paul Bozeman is a respected local businessman."

"It matters in a small town."

"Who you know matters everywhere," she said. "Okay, so a statement may be premature, but at least we now have a solid lead. An hour ago, we had nothing but a theory. There must be someone who saw Paul Bozeman at Reggie's party that night. We just have to find that person and jog his or her memory."

"Easier said than done after all this time. People forget, move away, don't want to get involved. Besides, Bozeman's presence at that party doesn't prove anything." He checked the rearview mirror, causing Avery to turn and glance out the back window.

"It may not prove his complicity, but it certainly gives him opportunity. We already know he had motive."

Max shrugged. "Still innocent until proven guilty. Let's just slow it down and try not to get ahead of ourselves," he advised. "Justice is a marathon, not a sprint."

She laughed outright. "You did not just say that."

He gave her a sheepish look.

She rolled her eyes. "Sounds like a very bad campaign slogan. I hope it's not yours."

He half smiled. "God forbid. I'm no politician."

"Maybe not yet."

"Not ever, but that's a discussion for another time. Right now, let's talk about the contents of those boxes."

"I only had time to open one. I'm no expert, but both the watch and the mirror looked extremely old and valuable. The mirror especially. The inlay was so beautiful and delicate. I've never seen anything quite like it. Seems more like a piece you'd find in a museum or private collection rather than a small-town antique shop. I could also see it on June Chapman's dressing table." She got out her phone and skimmed through the images. "Given the conversation I just overheard, it's not exactly a leap to think the items in those boxes were taken from her home, maybe over months or even years. Sidney Bozeman in particular seems to think June's house and the contents therein rightfully belong to her and her father. But without June's corroboration, I don't know how we prove it since she never filed a police report."

"Text me the images," Max said. "Especially the ones of the mirror. I'll show them to my stepmother. If the piece is as unique as you seem to think, she might remember seeing it."

"Wouldn't that be lucky?"

They exchanged phone numbers and Avery texted the photos, then leaned back against the seat and tried to relax. "At the risk of getting ahead of myself..." She waited for him to respond.

"Go on."

Excitement crept into her voice. "I really think we're on to something. Why else would Paul Bozeman warn his daughter about having items in her possession that could be traced back to June? Why else would she be so anxious to move those boxes out of the warehouse after he warned her about a search warrant? By the way, is that a possibility?"

"With what we have now? No."

"That's what I thought." She stared out the window for

a moment, lost in thought as she absently tapped a knuckle against the glass.

"What are you thinking?" Max asked.

"Whether Sidney was involved in the shooting or not, she's hiding something. They both are. From the authorities and from each other. That gives us a golden opportunity to turn them against each other."

"How do you propose we do that?"

She shrugged. "I don't know, but I'll think of something."

"Considering your track record since I've known you, that worries me."

He was rightfully skeptical considering her recent antics, but there was an unmistakable edge in his voice that Avery interpreted as anticipation. Or was that wishful thinking? Maybe he'd been right earlier when he accused her of seeing what she wanted to see, hearing what she wanted to hear. She'd been at loose ends ever since Luther's death. Maybe her melancholy had caused her to seek out an unlikely partner in crime because she desperately needed a challenge.

But was Max Winter really so improbable a partner? Even when deep in concentration, he had a restive quality that Avery knew she hadn't imagined. The way he moved, the way he spoke, the sometimes faraway look in his eyes revealed a discontent that he tried to keep masked behind a by-the-book persona. But he'd gone to the antique store to question Paul Bozeman himself rather than leaving the interview to the police, and his objections to her unconventional methods seemed token at best. She couldn't help feeling that for whatever reason, he needed to shake things up, too.

He pulled to the curb and shut off the engine.

She glanced around. "Why are we stopping?"

"We need to get a few things straight." He turned, draping an arm over the steering wheel as he gave her a long scrutiny. His eyes were dark and extremely intense. Unnerving really. She'd never in her life been so captivated by a person's stare.

She swallowed and nodded. "Okay."

"I admire your enthusiasm and your ability to think outside the box, but from what I've seen so far, you also have a tendency to push or even cross certain boundaries. That makes working with you a problem for someone in my position. I could get fired or even disbarred for prosecutorial misconduct if I knowingly use tainted evidence."

It was as if he'd read her mind. It was as if he needed to convince himself as to why their partnership wouldn't work.

"Don't you ever push boundaries?" she asked.

"Not anymore and never as an assistant DA."

Not anymore? His equivocation intrigued her. "When was the last time you crossed a line? I'd love to know the circumstances."

He wasn't about to give up anything. Not yet anyway. "Let's stick to the matter at hand. The information you uncovered back at that warehouse could prove valuable, but how you came by it calls into question admissibility. It would be one thing to turn a blind eye if the only thing at stake was my reputation. It's another matter entirely when a twenty-eight-year-old kidnapping case is involved."

"Yes, I'm well aware of the ramifications," Avery said. "But when I entered that warehouse, I was following up on a lead the police have no interest in pursuing. You said so yourself. Isn't that the reason you decided to interrogate Bozeman in person? You didn't trust your detective friend to act on the information you gave him."

He looked as if he wanted to argue the facts, but instead he took another tack. "Be that as it may, there are lines that should never be crossed. There are real-life consequences to crossing said lines. Cases get thrown out every single day on the smallest technicalities. Could you live with yourself if your actions allowed Maya Lamb's kidnapper to go free?" He paused as he searched her face. "I understand your priorities are to your client. Mine are to Maya's family. They've lived in limbo for nearly three decades. For most of Thea's life. I can't imagine the hell she and her mother have been through. They deserve justice and whatever closure a conviction can bring them. I won't allow you or anyone else to compromise that objective."

The raw passion in his voice took her breath away. His dogged pursuit of justice for a child who had disappeared when he was five years old was extraordinary. "I understand," she said. "I'll be careful from now on. You have my word."

"That's not to say…"

"What?"

"If you find something you think I need to know, don't hold back. You can still come to me so long as you haven't broken any laws. And if it's something I need to know about regardless, well, just try to find a way to make it legal."

"That could prove a tall order," she murmured. "Can I ask you something? Would you have gone to see Paul Bozeman today if I hadn't pressed the issue? Would you have considered him a suspect in Maya's kidnapping if I hadn't told you about my theory?"

"Maybe. He'd already caught my attention, so who knows? I'm going to be completely honest here so that you know where I'm coming from. You worry me. Not only because of the way you conduct your investigations, but also because you're tapping into something that I've had to work very hard to control."

Now she was even more intrigued. "What do you mean?"

"You're a risk-taker. You're impulsive and sometimes

reckless and that hits a little too close to home. There's a part of me that's always been attracted to danger and adrenaline."

She said in surprise, "You think I'm dangerous?"

"I think you could be."

"Then why are you still here?"

He met her gaze head-on. "Because I like you. Because, against my better judgment, I enjoy spending time with you. You're smart and funny and I haven't been able to talk to anyone this candidly in a very long time. Also, you're easy on the eyes," he added in the same serious tone.

"Not compared to you," she blurted.

He flashed an appreciative grin and suddenly she was the one in imminent danger. Her heart pounded so hard she could barely think straight, but at that moment, she didn't want to think. She wanted to act on the impulse that had been tugging at her since the moment she'd first clapped eyes on Max Winter.

Chapter Twelve

She didn't know who made the first move. Probably she did, but it hardly mattered because the second Max's lips touched hers, she was a goner, lost in the heat of pure lust. She couldn't remember a kiss ever catching her so completely off guard, but she didn't feel trapped or vulnerable, far from it. She felt powerful.

She slid an arm around his neck and pulled him closer.

After several long moments, he drew away, but his hands still cupped her nape. He caressed her jawline with his thumb. "That was probably a mistake."

"Funny, it didn't feel at all like a mistake to me."

Heat flared in his eyes and for a moment, she thought he would kiss her again, but he held back, possibly reviewing in his head all the reasons why another kiss would be an even bigger mistake. "Would it sound like a cliché if I said I've never met anyone like you?"

"Yes," she replied bluntly. "But I've never met anyone like you, either. I should probably confess, however, that a social life hasn't always been a priority for me so my experience is somewhat limited. Normally, I avoid guys like you."

He lifted a brow. "Guys like me?"

"Look in the mirror if you don't know what I mean."

He cocked his head as he studied her features. "You really have no clue, do you?"

"About what?"

"Your effect on men. On me. Confidence can be a powerful turn-on."

"Is that so?" she murmured.

He trailed his hand down her arm and entwined his fingers with hers. "As much as I would like to see where this leads, we'll have to put it on hold for now. I have to get back to the office for a meeting with my boss."

For now. She latched on to those two simple words. "And later?" she asked boldly.

He lifted her hand and brushed his lips against her fingers. "I'd like to ask you to dinner, but I really think it's best if we keep things professional for now."

For now. Those two words again. "That might have been possible until a few minutes ago."

"Let's at least try."

She sighed. "Fine. I've got plenty to do this afternoon to keep myself occupied. I probably won't have a spare moment to think about you anyway. Out of sight, out of mind."

"You don't have to make it seem *that* easy." He still held her hand even when his mood sobered. "Whatever you've got planned for the afternoon… It's probably best I don't know the details. But you should stay away from that warehouse. Let things cool down for a bit."

She shrugged noncommittally.

"I'll take that as your agreement," he said.

"Take it however you like, but it might ease your mind to know that first and foremost on my agenda this afternoon is finding a place to stay. You wouldn't happen to know of any short-term rentals or sublets in the area, would you?"

The change of subject seemed to throw him. She saw something flash across his features that might have been concern. Was he that worried about having her around? Did he really view her as that much of a temptation? The notion secretly thrilled her.

"I thought you were staying at the Magnolia," he said.

She wrinkled her nose. "It's a little too vintage-y for my taste. Besides, I don't care for hotels in general. I prefer having space to spread out. I like being able to fix breakfast in the morning and dinner at night. Cooking relaxes me."

He was silent for a moment. "Does this mean you're planning on staying in town for a while?"

"For as long as it takes. Could be a day, a week, a month..." She trailed off. "Is that a problem for you?"

"It might be for reasons we just discussed. And for reasons we haven't discussed." He finally released her hand but his gaze was still on her. "Those same reasons could also be a problem for you."

"Meaning?"

"Whoever shot at you in June Chapman's house likely saw your face. If not there, then later at the construction site when you came to my rescue. My point is, the gunman knows there's a witness."

"He wore a mask. I never got a look at this face. Besides, you're a witness as well as a victim," she reminded him. "What's to prevent him from coming after you? Even if he caught a glimpse of me in the shadows, he doesn't know who I am. You're well-known in this town. It's very possible he recognized you. Maybe that's why he shot at you."

"Food for thought," he said. "But don't make the mistake of thinking anonymity can protect you. Not in this day and age. And not ever in a small town. You've already talked to the police. Word will spread faster than you can imagine. Once the gunman has your name, all he has to do is call around and find out where you're staying."

"Yet another reason why I should move out of the hotel," she said. "Look, I appreciate your concern. I do. But I can take care of myself."

"So you keep telling me, but there may be a tendency for

someone accustomed to operating in a big city to become lulled into a false sense of security in a place like this."

She glanced out the window, taking in the green lawns and shaded porches, the splashes of lush color in the flower beds and the songbirds flitting through the trees. The setting was peaceful on the surface, but she couldn't help wondering about the secrets contained behind all those walled gardens. Maybe it was her imagination, but the past seemed to hang heavy over Black Creek.

"If anything, the opposite is true," she said. "I'm in unfamiliar territory here. There's something about this town..." She trailed off on an inexplicable shiver. "I can't explain it, but I sensed it from the moment I first arrived. Even in broad daylight, it feels like that moment when twilight deepens to darkness and you suddenly sense the nearness of a night creature on the hunt."

"Wow," he murmured.

She gave herself a little shake, then turned back to him. "I don't know where that came from. I'm not usually so melodramatic. I apologize for disparaging your hometown."

"No apology necessary. I've never heard anyone sum up my feelings about this place quite so succinctly."

"You feel it, too?"

He glanced away. "Sometimes."

"And yet you stay on."

"I'm often surprised by that fact," he admitted. He got out his phone. "Back to your current living situation. I have a good friend who's a real estate agent. If there are any sublets or short-term rentals to be had in the area, she'll know about them. I'm texting her information to you."

"Thanks. I appreciate that," Avery said as her phone dinged, but in the back of her mind she couldn't help wondering just how good a friend this Realtor person might be. And why was his personal life any of her business anyway? One kiss did not a relationship make. And that was absolutely fine by her because she hadn't come to Black Creek looking for romance. She came here looking for answers and maybe that kiss was the jolt she needed to remind herself of her own objectives. "I'll let you know how it goes. In the meantime, if you could just drop me off at my car..."

He leaned forward and pressed the ignition button, but before he pulled away from the curb, he turned with that enigmatic smile she was coming to know so well. "I'll say this. For good or bad, life hasn't been boring since you hit town."

For good or bad. She could live with that.

WHEN MAX GOT back to the courthouse, he went around to the front entrance to avoid the pair of attorneys deep in conversation at the rear door of the building. The last thing he needed was an ambush. He wanted to spend the short trek to his office thinking about Avery Bolt and contemplating when he might see her again. Despite his lofty suggestion that they keep things professional, he was already pondering how much trouble he could be in if he let things go too far. A part of him didn't really care. There was something to be said for living in the moment, a lifestyle he'd once embraced wholeheartedly.

That was before he'd chosen a profession requiring the kind of dedication and resolve that could wear you down over time and the kind of compromises that could leave you jaded. Sometimes he fantasized about walking out of the courthouse never to return. Just get in his car and drive until he got to the Gulf and then find a little place to live on the beach until his money ran out. *Someday*, he thought as he headed up the wide walkway to the courthouse. Someday he might do exactly that, but not today.

It was late afternoon by this time, but the sun still blazed overhead and the humidity was killer. He stopped in the shade to re-knot his tie. His straitjacket, he thought. Avery was nothing if not perceptive.

Halfway up the steps, he paused as he almost always did to reflect on his father's murder. The bloodstains had long since faded and his memories of that day had waned over time, but he still remembered the mind-numbing shock and disbelief upon hearing the news. It had taken a long time to process his emotions. He and his father had never been close, and even now some of the old resentments still surfaced from time to time. He'd once promised himself he would be his own man, yet he'd somehow ended up following in his father's footsteps and he still didn't know why.

The hair at his nape prickled as he stood with his back to the street. He lifted his gaze to the *Lady Justice* statue near the entrance, focusing on her blindfolded eyes as he tried to will away the eerie sensation of being watched.

Slowly, he turned to the street, his gaze skimming over the pedestrians and passing cars and then lifting to the roof of the building across the busy thoroughfare where a sniper would have a clear shot of the courthouse steps.

It was crazy to think that someone would be brazen enough to try and take him out in broad daylight, but then his father had been shot at two in the afternoon. The woman had walked right up to him, raised her gun and opened fire. He'd never seen it coming.

Like his father, Max had made enemies over the years. Everyone involved in the criminal justice system dealt with death threats. But he sensed a different kind of danger. He remembered Avery's warning that he was not only a victim, but also a witness and could be considered more of a threat to the shooter than she was. If June Chapman's attack really was connected to Maya Lamb's kidnapping, then the masked gunman they'd both encountered would likely be as ruthless in eliminating eyewitnesses as he was in tying up old loose ends.

DUSK HAD FALLEN by the time Avery got back to the hotel. She found a place to park on the street and then went in through the front lobby, nodding to the clerk behind the desk before climbing the stairs to her third-story room rather than taking the elevator. The public areas were well lit but deserted. She felt anxious from everything that had happened since her arrival in Black Creek and found herself glancing over her shoulder in the stairwell and again in the hallway as she headed for her room.

The afternoon had been fairly productive in spite of the fact that the white panel van had disappeared by the time she'd circled back around to the warehouse after Max dropped her off. She'd staked out the alley for over an hour until Max's real estate agent friend had returned her call and arranged a meeting. The woman had been extremely helpful. She'd shown Avery a fully furnished duplex in a quiet, but convenient part of town. The owner offered a month-to-month lease for the summer and Avery had put down a deposit and first month's rent on the spot. If her references checked out—and they would—she could possibly move in as soon as the following day.

She considered calling Max to thank him for his help, but she knew that was just an excuse to talk to him again. He was probably right about keeping things professional. As much as she would have liked getting to know him better over dinner and a bottle of wine, she decided to settle instead for a hot shower and room service. Plus, she wanted to enter her notes in her Black Creek file while everything that had happened at the warehouse was still fresh on her mind.

Inserting her key card in the slot, she waited for the lock to disengage and then stepped inside. And froze. Her gaze darted about the shadowy interior as a breeze from the open window drifted across the king-size bed and down the narrow entrance hall where she lingered. The window had been closed when she'd left early that morning to stake out June Chapman's house. She was always careful about securing her accommodations, especially when traveling. Possibly, someone from housekeeping had opened it to air out the room while they cleaned and then forgotten to close it when they left. Or, a darker explanation, someone had climbed up the fire escape and jimmied the lock.

Avery's mind went first to the man outside the diner restroom and then to the driver of the white panel van. The latter had tried to run her down in the alley, seemingly intent on crushing her against the brick wall. As gruesome an image as that conjured, she was more unnerved by the notion of the creepy stranger from the diner slinking through her room and touching her private things. She still had no idea who he was or why she'd been so instinctively repelled by his presence. Or why she couldn't seem to get him out of her head. She'd been accosted by creeps before. She knew how to handle herself during a contentious encounter. Yet everything Luther had taught her about self-defense had fled, rendering her momentarily paralyzed in that hallway.

She felt gripped by the same icy inertia as she vacillated on the threshold, torn between fleeing back into the hallway and advancing into the room to face an unreasonable fear.

Letting the door close softly behind her, she crept along the tiny corridor, peering into the bathroom and then hovering once more at the foot of the bed while she checked the room. The gauzy curtains rippled ghostlike in the breeze, tripping her pulse and making her wish for the weapon she'd left locked in the glove compartment of her vehicle. The state of Florida shared a reciprocity agreement with the state of Texas, meaning she was lawfully allowed to conceal-carry while she was in town. Being a stranger in Black Creek, she hadn't wanted to be caught with a firearm on her person. But as she stood in her hotel room, heart pounding in her ears, she decided it was time to seriously reconsider that decision.

She backtracked and checked the closet. When she was a little girl, she'd had recurring nightmares about someone hiding in her closet or underneath her bed. Luther would come in and check her room thoroughly while her mother cradled her in her arms and sang to her. Her loving protectors were both gone and Avery was on her own now.

Grabbing a flashlight from her bag, she dropped to the floor and angled the beam underneath the bed. No one was there, of course. Whoever had been in her room was long gone.

Or was he?

The base of her spine tingled a warning as she peered over the edge of the bed. A man stood on the fire escape just outside the window. She could see him silhouetted through the white curtains. He hadn't been there a moment ago. He'd crept onto the landing while she checked underneath the bed.

Springing to her feet, she caught him in her flashlight beam and for a moment, she had the terrifying notion that he would dive through the window and snatch her.

"Who are you?" she called. "What do you want?"

He remained so still that for a moment, Avery thought her imagination had raised him from the shadows. Then he whirled and a split second later, she heard his footsteps clattering down the metal rungs of the fire escape.

Without stopping to consider the possible outcome of her chase, she flung herself across the room and climbed out the window. Pausing on the landing, she peered through the metal grate until she spotted him on the steps one story below her.

"Stop!" Ignoring her injured ankle, she propelled herself down the metal stairs at a breakneck speed.

When he got to the bottom, he spun to stare up at her. Avery couldn't make out his features, shielded as he was by a hoodie and the deepening twilight. But a familiar chill crept over her, slowing her steps and repressing her resolve. She faltered, grabbing the iron handrail for balance as their gazes clashed for the longest moment.

When he made no move to flee or to come up after her, she called out again, "Who are you?"

His husky reply seemed to drift up to her on the wind, along with the faintest hint of cigarette smoke. "Who are *you*?"

An iron fist clamped around her heart. She knew who he was now. They'd met face-to-face only hours earlier in the dim hallway outside the diner restroom. She remembered the gravel in his voice and the taunt in his eyes. The eerie way he'd lifted a finger to his lips to silence her.

The encounter hadn't been happenstance after all. He must have followed her back to the restroom and waited for her to come out, planting himself in the hallway so that she would have to brush against him. But why?

Across the street, the unseen wind chimes clanked in the breeze, the sound of the hollow reeds eerie in the fading light. Avery resisted the urge to close her eyes and let the mysterious melody carry her back into the farthest recesses of her memory.

"Your hair is different," he said.

How did he know she'd changed her appearance before coming to Black Creek? Had he been following her since before she left Houston?

"Tell me who you are," she demanded. "How do you know me?"

"That's a long story."

The icy needles at the base of her spine intensified. Her knees trembled so violently she had to tighten her grip on the handrail. Over the pounding of her heart, she could hear Luther's voice in her ear. *Don't let him see your fear. Never, ever show weakness to an enemy.*

She steeled her spine as she gazed down at the stranger.

"Why were you in my room just now? What were you looking for?"

"The same thing you are. The truth."

He put his hand on the rail as if he meant to come up and confront her face-to-face. Avery stood her ground even though she wanted nothing so much as to run. He was danger. She felt his evil with every fiber of her being and yet she wouldn't run away. She wouldn't give him the satisfaction of knowing her fear.

As if testing her mettle, he started up the steps and then stopped as the sound of laughter drifted in from the street. A moment later, the courtyard gates burst open and a small group of rowdy partiers stormed through, heading for the pool in a cacophony of whoops and chortles.

In all the confusion, the stranger backed down the stairs and fled through the open gate, vanishing so quickly into the night that he might have been nothing more substantial than a figment from one of her old nightmares.

Chapter Thirteen

Max was surprised to find Avery waiting in the small reception area outside his office when he returned from court the next day. She'd been concentrating intently on her phone but put it aside and rose when he came in. She wore her usual uniform of jeans, T-shirt and sneakers minus the baseball cap. Sunlight glinted in her dark hair as she tucked the loose strands behind her ears and gave him a tentative smile.

Mindful of his assistant's avid interest, he merely nodded and then motioned for her to follow him into his office. She closed the door and glanced around curiously at the shabby furnishings.

"Interesting place you've got here. Did you decorate it yourself?" she teased.

"Yes, right down to the water-stained ceiling."

She cocked her head as she glanced upward. "Looks kind of like a horse."

"It's abstract," he said.

"That explains the three eyes." Her smile disappeared as she moved into the room, the old wood floor creaking beneath her sneakers. Max was sorry to see her humor vanish. He enjoyed their banter more than he should. It was actually the only bright spot to an otherwise frustrating day.

"I was surprised to find that your office is located in the courthouse," she said. "Is that usual for a district attorney?"

"It is when the courthouse has spare office space and the regional DA's office has other budgetary priorities. No frills for a lowly ADA." He glanced around, seeing the stains and scars through her eyes. "It's convenient. That's about all I can say for the place."

"I think it suits you."

"I'm not sure how to take that." He placed his briefcase and phone on the desk and folded his arms on the back of his chair as he watched her.

"Take it as a compliment. These old courthouses have character and history, unlike so many of the sterile new-builds I so despise." She nodded toward the window behind his desk. "May I?"

"Not much to see, but be my guest." He tracked her as she walked up to the window and glanced out. His gaze dropped, then quickly lifted. She wore her jeans extremely well.

"I see you have a nice view of a bail bond office across the street."

"Adds to the character," he assured her. "You should see it at night when the neon sign is lit. Nothing like flashing greenbacks to instill unshakable faith in our judicial system."

She leaned into the window, staring down three stories onto *Lady Justice*. "Working here must be hard for you," she murmured.

"Why do you say that?"

Her expression remained somber. "Your father was murdered on the courthouse steps by the wife of a man he'd sent to prison. I would imagine that image comes back to you every time you look out this window."

He frowned. "How do you know about that?"

"I told you yesterday morning, I heard your name and

I looked you up. I wasn't exaggerating when I said you're all over the internet."

"Still, you must have done a deep dive into my history to uncover that chapter." He pulled out his chair and sat down, swiveling to face her. He wanted to be annoyed by her prying, but he wasn't. Everything on the internet was fair game. Besides, it was flattering to think he'd sparked her interest. "I don't dwell on the past nor do I consider myself damaged by it. Bad things happen every day and life goes on."

Too late, he remembered she'd only recently lost her father. A look of sadness descended before she quickly turned back to the window. He wanted to say something comforting or murmur an apology for being so flip, but he instinctively knew to let the moment pass.

He fiddled with his favorite ballpoint pen as he studied her profile. "Why don't you take a seat and tell me why you're here."

She remained at the window gazing out. "I was just thinking. How long have we known each other, Max?"

The casual use of his name took him by surprise, as did the question. What an odd thing to ask. "Two days if you count Tuesday night."

"Doesn't it seem longer than that to you?" She turned to meet his curious gaze. "It seems longer to me."

"In some ways it does," he agreed. "You saved my life. That certainly helped to break the ice." When she didn't respond, he gave her a prompt. "Where are you going with this?"

She left the window and took a seat across from his desk, leaning forward earnestly as her gaze intensified. "I feel like we have a connection. I don't mean attraction, although…" An understanding passed between them, quick and electric. "I'm talking about a real connection. It's not just me, is it?"

"No," he replied candidly. "It's not just you."

"You're the only person in this town I feel I can trust."

Her mood was starting to concern him. "What's going on?"

"I'm here to ask a favor. It could put you in an awkward position with someone you've probably known your whole life."

He sat back, intrigued. "Go on."

"I understand the former chief of police, Will Kent, was a good friend of your father's."

She never ceased to amaze him at the things she'd uncovered in such a short amount of time. "What about it?"

"The archived article I read about your father's murder also mentioned that Chief Kent was an honorary pallbearer at his funeral, along with a state senator named Tom Fuqua. Their friendship went all the way back to their time together in Vietnam."

Max scowled across the desk at her. "I know all this. What's the favor?"

"I'd like to talk to Mr. Kent, but I doubt he'll agree to see me unless someone he knows and trusts vouches for me."

Since he'd already planned a visit with the former police chief, it would have been an easy favor to grant, but Max took a moment to contemplate her request. Did he want to talk to Will Kent alone or would it be helpful to have Avery at his side? And, more important, what was she up to?

He decided to do a little fishing. "Why do you want to see Will Kent? He retired years ago. I doubt he can tell you anything about your client that you don't already know."

"I'm not sure that's true," Avery said. "I'm willing to bet he still has contacts in the police department, including a nephew who was one of the first to respond to the 911 call from June Chapman's house."

"Your 911 call," he reminded her.

"Yes."

"How do you know about his nephew?" He tried to keep his tone and demeanor casually inquisitive, but she was sharp enough to see right through him.

"Why all the questions? We're working toward the same end, remember? I trust you, but you still don't trust me, is that it?"

He decided to be completely open with her. "Not yet, but I'm getting there."

"Maybe this will help." She slid forward until she was sitting on the edge of her seat. She looked nervous and for the first time since he'd met her, unsure of herself. *Oh, boy,* Max thought. *This is going to be good.* "There's something I haven't told you about the night of the shooting."

"Oh?"

"I wasn't sure of the significance, but the more I've thought about it…" She paused. "Remember how I explained about climbing down the trellis to avoid the police?"

"You didn't want to waste time answering questions or risk being taken to the station while the suspect fled."

She nodded. "That's right. What I didn't tell you was that I hid out in the garden next door until the coast was clear."

"So… You weren't in hot pursuit as you claimed?"

"Not immediately. The cops were already swarming the area so I had no choice but to take cover."

"Which neighbor's garden?"

"Tom Fuqua's. Of course, I didn't know it was his house at the time or even who he was. He came outside and talked to Will Kent's nephew. After the officer left, Fuqua called Kent to tell him about June Chapman. I'm paraphrasing but he said they had no reason to believe the break-in or the shooting had anything to do with that other business, but the two of them should keep a low profile until things blew over."

"What other business?" Max asked.

"That's what we need to find out." She got up and returned to the window, leaning back against the ledge and resting her hands on the sill as she faced him. "Will Kent was the chief of police when Maya Lamb went missing. You said yourself he was the face of the investigation even after the FBI took over the case. What if he knew something he never put in the official report? What if the *other business* Tom Fuqua mentioned was Maya's kidnapping? Maybe he and Will Kent were somehow involved in a cover-up."

She certainly had his attention, but he remained skeptical. "That's a pretty big leap."

"Is it?" She shrugged. "I'm not so sure."

"You should be careful throwing around an accusation like that," he warned. "Those two men have a lot of admirers in this town, including me. I can't see either of them covering up something so monstrous as the abduction of a child. What would be the motive?"

"Child trafficking was already big business back then."

He stared at her for a moment. "Again, you're talking about two of the most respected members of this community."

"I realize that, but people get caught up in all kinds of bad things. Maybe it wasn't even about money. Maybe they found out about June Chapman's involvement and covered up evidence to protect her."

"Why would they do that?"

"I don't have all the answers. Or any answers," she said in frustration. "I have nothing but a gut feeling that the other business is somehow connected to Maya's disappearance."

He glanced past her out the window where the sky was blue and cloudless. A typical day in the Sunshine State, yet something dark gripped Max's soul. At the time of Maya's disappearance, Will Kent and Tom Fuqua had been best friends with his father. A police chief, a state senator and a circuit court judge wielded a lot of power in a place like Black Creek. They could have covered up a crime without anyone being the wiser, but the question of motive remained. Why would they risk their reputations to protect June Chapman? Or anyone else for that matter.

"If you feel that strongly, why did you wait until now to mention this conversation?" he asked.

"I had to know that I could trust you. I had to make sure you're the type of prosecutor who is only interested in the truth, no matter where that truth leads you."

"You've known me for little more than twenty-four hours," he reminded her.

"Not true. It's going on forty-eight hours." She paused and a smile flickered. "But it seems longer."

Yes, it did seem longer. Max wanted to trust her, too, but he couldn't help worrying about a secret agenda. What else wasn't she telling him?

Despite his lingering doubts, he was on the verge of recounting what his father had said to June Chapman all those years ago while they were discussing an appropriate punishment for the theft of her prized flowers. *You know all about taking something that doesn't belong to you.*

Max had managed to convince himself the overheard conversation was innocuous. No telling what his father had been referring to. Or maybe Max's memory was at fault. He'd had his problems with his father and had never tried to sugarcoat their strained relationship. But he'd always considered Clayton Winter a man of honor and integrity and there was no way he would have been involved in the cover-up of a kidnapping. Giving voice to that memory might somehow give credence to Max's secret fear.

"Will you go with me to see Will Kent?" Avery pressed.

He forced his attention back to the present conversation. "Yes, I'll go with you. But you need to let me do the talking. He's old-school law enforcement. He won't have much use for a private detective."

She accepted his terms with a nod. "But if I feel the need to jump in, I will," she warned.

"That's hardly a shocker."

She went back over to her seat and plopped down. She still seemed nervous and fidgety and in no hurry to bring their meeting to an end.

"Something else on your mind?" he prompted.

"I wasn't sure I should mention it. I don't want to worry you."

"Now I am worried."

"Someone broke into my hotel room last evening. They didn't take anything. At least I don't think so, but I'm certain my belongings were searched."

He said in alarm, "Are you okay?"

"Yes, I'm fine. There was no physical altercation, but I just thought you should know. Apparently, you were right yesterday when you said anonymity wouldn't protect me. I don't know how he found out where I was staying, but he got into my room by climbing up the fire escape."

"How do you know it was a he?"

"I saw him."

"Okay, back up a minute," Max said. "Tell me exactly what happened."

"I went back to the hotel after a meeting with your Realtor friend. I put down a deposit on a duplex, by the way, but we can talk about that later. When I opened the door to my room, I noticed the window was open. I knew it had been closed when I left that morning. I'm careful about security."

Max didn't like the sound of this at all, especially coming as it did after two harrowing events—the shooting and the chase in the alleyway. Someone had obviously made her. "Was this person still in your room?"

"No, he was on the fire escape looking into my room. When I went after him—"

"Wait… You went after him? After everything that's happened?"

She gave him a puzzled look. "What else was I supposed to do?"

"Just a suggestion, but you could have called the police. Or me."

"He would have been long gone by the time you got there." She gave him a pointed look. "You do remember that I'm a licensed investigator, right? I'm trained in self-defense among other things."

"Point taken. Continue."

"He had a good lead on me, but he stopped at the bottom of the fire escape and turned to stare up at me. I asked who he was and what he wanted. He said he wanted what I wanted. The truth." She ran her hands up and down her arms as if trying to rub away goose bumps.

"What do you think he meant by that?"

"I don't know, but Max…" She leaned forward. "I've seen him before. He was the man I bumped into at the diner yesterday as I was coming out of the restroom. I recognized his gravelly voice and he had the same stale cigarette smell clinging to his clothes."

"Did you get a good look at him?"

"It was dark and he wore a hoodie, but I know it was him. He must have followed me from the police station to the diner yesterday. He saw me go into the restroom and waited in the hallway for me to come out just so he could…" She tightened her arms around her middle. "I don't know why. I just know that I've never felt such fear and revulsion for another human being in my life. I'm talking irrational, paralyzing fear."

"And you have no idea who he is? You've never crossed paths with him before? Maybe he followed you here from Houston."

"That occurred to me, too, but I don't think so. I could be totally off base but… Can you describe Denton Crosby?"

"I can do better than that." Max opened his laptop, then turned the screen around to face her. "This shot was taken a few years ago according to his sister, Nadine. She provided the photograph to the police. Since he was never arrested or processed through the system, we don't have a mug shot."

"He was questioned, though, right?"

"Questioned and released," Max said. "Not enough evidence to hold him."

She scooted her chair closer to the desk as she studied the image on the screen. Then she glanced at Max. "That's him. That's the guy at the diner. I'm certain he's the man I saw outside my room last night. He knows I can place him in June Chapman's home at the time of the shooting. Why else would he be following me?" Her eyes gleamed with excitement. "You know what this means, don't you?"

"That you're in danger?"

"It means we were right about a connection between the shooting and Maya's abduction. With his sister dead, the only witness who can tie Denton Crosby to the kidnapping is the person who hired him. June Chapman. He broke into her house night before last to make sure she never talks."

"It doesn't prove any of that," Max said. "But it does strongly suggest the possibility of a connection. Let's assume you're right for a moment. Denton Crosby shot June Chapman because she's the only person still alive who can link him to the kidnapping. And now you're the only person who can tie him to the shooting. See the problem?"

She merely shrugged. "I never got a good look at him that night. If he'd left well enough alone, he'd be home free."

"He couldn't take that chance, though, could he? He's remained a free man all these years because he's cautious."

"Or because someone covered for him," she said, bringing the conversation back around to the original point of her visit. "I still don't understand why he fired at you, though. Why not flee the area while he had the chance and then take care of me later? Winging an ADA is the opposite of cautious."

"Maybe he was waiting for someone," Max said. "Maybe the shot wasn't meant to take me out, but to warn away whoever he'd gone there to meet."

"A fourth kidnapper," she said.

AVERY STARED OUT the window as they followed the river to a place called Myrtle Cove, a fisherman's paradise of stilted houses, boat docks and long, shady decks overlooking the water. The farther from town they drove, the more primal the scenery. The thick canopy across the road triggered an uncomfortable feeling of claustrophobia, as pervasive as the kudzu that crept over tumbledown barns and snaked up blackened tree trunks. The air smelled of mud and rain and old nightmares. Avery's hand slipped to her throat as she turned to study Max's profile, wondering if he, too, felt the smothering gloom of the landscape, or if her shivery aversion was merely a manifestation of everything that had happened.

They'd barely spoken since leaving his office. Avery wasn't sure why. She'd wanted to discuss strategy on the way to Will Kent's house, but instead she found herself succumbing to the kind of soul-crushing dread she hadn't experienced in years. Not for the first time, she wished Luther was here to quell her fears the way he had when she was little.

"You okay?" Max's voice cut into her reverie. She hadn't realized she was still staring at him until their gazes met and he lifted a brow. "You seemed a million miles away just now."

"I'm a little apprehensive about the meeting." She glanced back out the window. "Do you think we should have called ahead? He may not react favorably to an ambush."

"No, it's better if we catch him by surprise," Max said. "Otherwise, he'd just find an excuse to avoid us if he doesn't feel like talking."

"How long has it been since you've seen him?"

His brow furrowed in thought. "Probably since my father's funeral. He's become something of a recluse since his retirement."

"What if he doesn't remember you?"

"He'll remember."

And that was the end of their conversation until Max turned down a long gravel driveway shaded by willows and pecan trees.

"This is the place." He parked at the side of the house and they got out. A light breeze rippled through the trees, carrying the scent of something lush and spicy layered over the fecund fragrance of the river. They each paused to survey their surroundings before wordlessly climbing the porch steps side by side.

A gray-haired woman of indeterminate age answered their knock. She wiped her hands on a floral-print apron as she gazed at them curiously through the screen door. "May I help you?"

"I'm ADA Max Winter." He held up his ID for her to scrutinize through the screen. "This is my colleague Avery Bolt. We'd like to have a word with Chief Kent about one of his old cases if he can spare us a minute."

"Max Winter." A delighted smile replaced her initial wariness. "Clayton's boy?"

"Yes, ma'am."

She beamed and unlatched the screen. "Well, my goodness. Haven't you grown into a fine-looking young man?" When Max responded with a courteous smile, she said, "You don't remember me, do you? I'm Martha, the chief's housekeeper. It's been a long time and I'm a lot grayer than I used to be." She patted her hair with a good-natured chuckle.

"Yes, of course I remember you," Max said. "You made the best brownies I ever ate."

"Sour cream is the secret." She winked at Avery and then her smile vanished as she turned melancholy. "You look so much like your father. The judge was always so handsome and elegant. Always a perfect gentleman. Such a tragedy what happened and he had just married that lovely young woman after so many years of being alone. What was her name? I can't seem to recall..."

"Gail Mosier," Max supplied.

"Yes, Gail. I know some thought she was too young and maybe a little too ambitious, but I admired her for the way she turned her life around. Coming from the background she did, it's a wonder... But never mind all that now. You came here to talk to the chief, not to listen to my babbling nonsense."

Max gave her a gentle prompt. "Is he home?"

"He took the boat out a few hours ago. You're welcome to come in and wait if you like."

"We don't want to trouble you," Max said.

"Any idea when he'll be back?" Avery interjected.

Martha cocked her head slightly as she gazed through the screen at Avery. "I'm sorry. What did you say your name was?"

"Avery Bolt. I'm a—"

"She's a colleague of mine," Max said.

Martha gave her a puzzled frown. "I have this feeling we've met before, but I don't know of any Bolts in this area."

Her perusal was a bit unnerving. "I'm not from around here," Avery said. "I guess I just have one of those faces."

"About the chief," Max said. "When do you expect him?"

She reluctantly tore her gaze from Avery. "He missed lunch so he should be back anytime now. Why don't I bring you out some iced tea. You can wait here on the porch where it's nice and breezy."

"That's very kind of you," Max said. "But please don't go to the trouble. We'll just walk down to the water and see if we can spot his boat coming in."

"If he didn't catch anything, he'll be in a mood," she warned.

"We'll keep that in mind."

Avery heard her latch the door as they turned and exited the porch. At the bottom of the steps, she glanced over her shoulder. The housekeeper was still standing behind the screen watching them. Watching her.

"What an odd woman," she murmured as they moved down the sloped yard toward the riverbank.

"What makes you say that?"

"You didn't find it strange the way she kept staring at me?"

Max shrugged. "She thought she knew you. It happens. People in small towns think they know everyone and most of the time they do. The familiarity can get annoying."

"She certainly remembers you."

"My father cast a tall shadow. Hard to get away from it sometimes."

"You seem to be doing okay," Avery remarked. "One of the hottest young prosecutors in the state, according to the article I read." She gave him a sidelong glance. "You're good at your job, too, or so they say."

She thought at first the wordplay had gone over his head,

but he turned with a look in his eyes that caused her heart to thud. "If we decide to charge Denton Crosby, I guess we'll see how good I am."

"I have faith."

He lifted a hand to tuck back a strand of windswept hair from her face. His knuckles brushed against her cheek and she closed her eyes on a shiver. "Must be blind faith since you don't know anything about my career except what you've read online."

"You might be surprised," she said. "I bet I know a lot more than you think I do."

"That's probably alarmingly true."

She started to respond in the same lighthearted manner, then turned toward the water. "I hear a boat."

They watched as a small fishing boat putt-putted up to the dock and a man dressed in jeans and a fishing vest cut the engine and climbed out to tie off. He looked to be in his late sixties or early seventies, tall, lean and tanned with a smooth helmet of white hair swept back from a high forehead. He seemed oblivious to their presence, taking his time unloading a cooler and his fishing tackle. All this was a secondary observation as Avery's gaze was initially drawn to the weapon strapped to his hip.

"Need any help?" Max called as he started toward the dock. Avery hung back for a minute.

The man whirled in surprise and lifted a hand to shade his eyes. "Oh, now you ask after I've already hauled everything out of the boat."

"Sorry," Max said. "Didn't think it a good idea to startle you." He nodded to the holstered weapon.

"Good call." Will Kent propped a foot on the cooler and folded his arms across his thigh. His gaze went to Avery and then back to Max. "What can I do for you folks?"

"I don't know if you remember me. I'm Max Winter. Clayton's son."

"I remember you all right. I seem to recall running you in a few times for curfew violations. And a couple of other times on more serious charges but I don't want to think hard enough to recall what they were right now."

No wonder Max had been so certain the man would remember him. He'd once been trouble. She thought he might still be deep down.

Will Kent straightened. "What brings you all the way out here, son?"

"I'd like to talk to you about one of your old cases." He turned as Avery walked up beside them. "This is Avery Bolt. She's an investigator I'm working with."

Avery extended her hand. "Pleasure to meet you, sir."

Will Kent's eyes narrowed as they briefly shook. "Private investigator?"

"Yes," she said. "I'm with a security firm out of Houston."

"Houston? You're a long way from home, young lady."

She suspected his use of the moniker was to put her in her place, but she let it go without comment. "I have a client in Black Creek. June Chapman."

He folded his arms and rocked back on his heels as he gave her a tense inspection. Then he said in a highly dubious tone, "June Chapman is your client? *The* June Chapman?"

"Yes, sir, she is."

He eyed her for another long moment, then shook his head. "You'll have to do better than that. I've known June for more than forty years. There's no way in hell she'd hire a private investigator, especially one from another state. That woman doesn't trust anybody."

"She might if she thought her life was in danger," Max said.

The former chief's suspicious gaze remained on Avery. "Why would she think her life was in danger?"

"That's what she hired me to find out," Avery said. "And considering the fact that she was shot in her bedroom the night before last, she was right to be afraid."

"She was shot during a burglary gone bad," he said. "I talked to her that very morning. If she was afraid for her life, she would have told me or I would have picked up on something in her voice. She was fine. Same old June. Never said a word about hiring a private detective."

"What did you talk about?" Avery pressed, despite Max giving her the side-eye.

"That's between her and me."

"Are the two of you close?" Avery asked.

"Depends on what you mean by *close*." He bent down and grabbed a beer from the cooler. "You don't mind if I indulge while we talk, do you?" This to Max. "Worked up a sweat out on the water."

"Go right ahead," Max said. "Do you talk to June often?"

"Once a week ever since her husband died. Fifty-two weeks times forty years is a lot of conversation. Robert was a good friend of mine and I made it a point to check in on his widow whether she appreciated it or not." He took a long swig and then set the bottle on top of the cooler. "You said you wanted to talk about one of my old cases. What's June Chapman got to do with it?"

"Some new information has surfaced about Maya Lamb's disappearance," Max explained. "We think it may be connected to the shooting."

He gave them a sage look. "I figured someone would come out here sooner or later. You're talking about the gal's claim that she and her brother and another fellow were hired to kidnap Maya and Thea Lamb."

"You know about that?" Max sounded exasperated. "We've been trying to keep a lid on Nadine Crosby's confession until we find evidence or another witness that can corroborate her story."

Will Kent scoffed at the notion. “You won’t find any corroboration. She made the whole thing up.”

“Why would she do that?” Avery asked. “She was a dying woman.”

“Maybe that’s why. Maybe the cancer affected her brain. Who’s to say? People confess to crimes they didn’t commit for all sorts of reasons. Most of the time it’s because they crave attention. Sometimes it’s for revenge. If she had it in for her brother and wanted to get back at him, that would be a pretty damn good way of going about it. She dies, leaving him holding the bag.”

“You don’t put any credence in her confession at all?” Avery asked.

He shrugged.

“Did you know Nadine and Denton Crosby at the time of the kidnapping?” Max asked.

“I knew of them,” he said. “Mostly because of what happened to their folks. They got hit head-on by an eighteen-wheeler when the girl was still little. I helped the highway patrol work that scene. It was bad. One of the worst I ever saw.” He suppressed a shudder. “I lost track of the kids after that. I think they ended up in foster care.”

“What about Sarah Bozeman and her son, Paul. Were they on your radar?” Avery asked.

He frowned. “I knew about the lawsuits if that’s what you mean. June complained about them often enough, but that was a civil matter. No reason for me to get involved.”

“Did you know Paul Bozeman was at Reggie Lamb’s house the night of the kidnapping?”

“So?”

“So?” She tried and failed to conceal her exasperation. “Did it ever occur to you that he and his mother might have had motive for getting rid of June Chapman’s only living blood relatives?”

He folded his arms again and spread his feet apart in

a stance orchestrated to intimidate. Or was he merely defensive? "I'm going to say my piece about this matter and then I'm going up to the house and have some lunch. I don't know what you two are trying to imply, but here's the truth about that case. I never worked a case harder than I did Maya Lamb's kidnapping. I can't even begin to tell you the number of interviews I conducted or the endless man-hours my department racked up before all was said and done. We were on the case before the FBI arrived and long after they left. We never stopped looking. The conclusion I finally came to is what I still believe today."

Max and Avery waited in silence.

"Something happened to that little girl at that party. Maybe it was an accident, maybe it wasn't. My gut told me she was dead before she ever left the house. Finding that box in the woods with her DNA pretty much cinched it for me. I figured Reggie's boyfriend lost his temper, struck the child and things got out of hand. He and Reggie panicked, got rid of the body as quick as they could and then went back later and moved it. They wouldn't admit it and I couldn't prove it, but you'll never convince me otherwise no matter how many crazies come out of the woodwork to confess."

"What if you're wrong?" Avery asked.

He shook his head. "I'm not wrong. Even after all these years, it hurts like hell to say it, but Maya Lamb is dead. She has been for twenty-eight years."

Chapter Fourteen

After their meeting with Will Kent, Avery went back to the hotel, packed up her belongings and moved everything into the duplex. She made a grocery store run for immediate supplies, and then afterward set up a workspace at the kitchen table. She entered everything she could remember of their conversation with the former chief of police in her Black Creek file, closed the laptop and stretched.

What she really needed to do at that moment was go out for a run. Familiarize herself with her new neighborhood while she worked out the kinks. Instead, she curled up on the porch swing with a glass of tea and an ice pack for her ankle until the sun went down and then she got in her vehicle and drove to the aging neighborhood on the outskirts of town where Reggie Lamb lived.

Finding the address had been dead easy. What she intended to do once she got to the house was a matter still to be determined. Knock on the door and ask Reggie to recount what had happened to her daughter twenty-eight years ago? Demand to know what she knew of June Chapman's shooting?

In the end, Avery parked at the end of the street and circled through the woods on foot to come up behind Reggie's house the way the kidnapper must have done on that fateful night. The sun was just setting as she took to the trees and the landscape soon grew shadowy. Mindful of her weak ankle and the rugged terrain, she kept to an old trail that dead-ended at Reggie's back gate.

She didn't immediately step through, although trespassing had never been that much of an impediment. No, something else held her captive behind the chain-link gate, a strange premonition that her investigation might reveal far more than she had ever bargained for.

The house looked familiar, but that was to be expected. She'd seen pictures of Reggie's modest ranch online, along with a close-up of the very bedroom window through which Maya had been taken. She couldn't see the window from behind the fence, so after a bit, she opened the gate and slipped through the fragrant backyard until she stood at the corner of a latticework shed connected to the garage. Clumps of oleanders hid her from the street, but from her crouched position she had an unobstructed view of the side of the house, including the infamous bedroom window. Had the kidnapper stopped here, too, waiting for a signal that the coast was clear?

Dusk had fallen by this time and the shadows behind her deepened. The breeze picked up and she could smell rain in the air. She told herself to head back while she could still find her way through the woods. She didn't move.

The air was hot and sticky despite the breeze, but she grew more chilled the longer she fixated on that window. The hair at the back of her neck lifted and she tore her gaze away to scour the woods behind the fence. She wondered if someone was back in the trees watching her, but how could anyone know she was there unless she'd been followed? Unless she'd been too preoccupied to pick up a tail? That wasn't like her, but nothing about her trip to Black Creek was normal behavior for her.

She listened to the nocturnal sounds emanating from the woods for the longest moment before turning back to the house. A light came on in the bedroom, startling her. She pressed back against the outbuildings, her heart tripping as a silhouette appeared in the window. For a moment, she had the wildest notion that the kidnapper had returned to the scene of the crime. Then the window opened and Reggie Lamb propped her hands on the sill as she leaned out into the night. The wind blew back her gray curls and stirred the ornamental windmill in the backyard. The woman seemed mesmerized by the rhythmic click-click-click until a sharper breeze blew open her back gate.

The sound of the metal gate clanking against the chain-link fence jolted Avery. Had she failed to drop the latch back into place or had someone come through behind her?

At the window, Reggie's head whipped around as she peered into the darkness. "Maya?"

The name drifted across the yard on the wind. Avery thought at first her imagination had conjured the sound, but then Reggie's voice grew louder, more heartbreakingly plaintive. "Oh, my sweet, sweet girl."

Avery closed her eyes and wished herself miles away. She had no right being here. When was it ever appropriate to invade a tortured mother's privacy? But she couldn't steal away now without being seen. Nothing she could do at the moment but hunker in the bushes and blink away the sting of sudden tears.

"I know you're still alive. I can feel you." Reggie put a hand to her heart. "I'm here, Maya. I'm right here."

WHEN AVERY PULLED into the driveway on her side of the duplex, she was still so lost in thought that she was out of the vehicle and halfway up the sidewalk before she realized someone was sitting on the porch swing. Her first thought was that Denton Crosby had somehow found out about her new place, but in the next instant, she realized it was Max.

Relief washed over her. The last thing she wanted at that moment was to be alone.

She murmured his name. He couldn't have heard her, but he rose and came down the porch steps just the same, pausing at the bottom as he faced her in the moonlight.

There was something about the way he stood there watching her…a look on his face she couldn't comprehend. "What is it?" she breathed. "What's wrong?"

"I think I've finally figured it out," he said in a strange voice.

"What? The shooting?" When he didn't respond, her heart started to thud in trepidation. "What did you figure out, Max?"

"You're her. You're Maya Lamb."

Chapter Fifteen

"Answer me," he demanded. "Are you Maya?"

Avery walked past him and sat down on the porch steps, pulling her knees up and wrapping her arms tightly around her legs. "I don't know. I might be."

He sat down beside her. She could feel his gaze on her in the dark. The intensity made her shiver.

"That's why you came to Black Creek. You never talked to June Chapman, did you? She never called your office in Houston. She never hired you. All that was just a front for the truth."

"I needed a reason for being in her house the night of the shooting, one that would hopefully keep me out of jail. I counted on my PI license to help sell the story and I knew my partner would back me up if anyone called him."

"That was clever." Miraculously, he didn't sound angered by her deception, but perplexed and curious. He rested his forearms on his thighs as he gazed out across the yard. His voice sounded warm and familiar in the dark. A comforting sound to Avery despite the circumstances.

She glanced at him. "I'm sorry I lied to you."

He shrugged. "I knew there was something about you. I couldn't put my finger on it. I convinced myself you really did have one of those faces, but you don't, actually. You're beautiful enough to be memorable."

Her heart skipped a beat at the intimacy in his tone.

He turned to study her again. "Maya had curly blond hair as a child."

She swallowed. "I colored and straightened mine before I came here. I was afraid my looks would make me a target if I'm really Maya. I didn't want to take the chance someone would notice a resemblance. But apparently Denton Crosby has his suspicions."

"Even with the dark hair, I can see Thea in your features and sometimes Reggie," Max said.

"You didn't, though, until you started to consider the possibility that I could be Maya. Now you see what you want to see."

"That may be true. There is such a thing as the power of suggestion," he conceded. "I'm curious, though. When did you consider it a possibility? Did you have a flashback… a memory? What was the catalyst after all these years?"

She hugged her knees tighter. "It wasn't a sudden thing. At least, not entirely. There's always been an element of mystery to my background and adoption. I was told that I'd been left at a fire station in Houston when I was four with no trace of who I was or where I'd come from. The social worker assigned to my case concluded I'd suffered severe psychological trauma because I didn't speak for over a year. Not a single word."

"So you couldn't tell anyone your name or what had happened to you."

She nodded. "My parents—Luther and Charity Bolt—had been trying to adopt for years. They'd applied at every private and public agency in the state, but my dad's job was a problem. He worked for an international security firm back then and traveled a lot. He was sometimes out of the country for months at a time. He'd just accepted a long-term assignment overseas when they got the call about me. I don't know how they managed it, but they were granted permission to take me out of the country. We lived in Germany for three years before moving back to Houston."

"That does seem an unusual arrangement. By the time you returned, Maya's disappearance would have faded from the news," he mused. "You don't have any memories before your adoption?"

She didn't know how to explain the odd feelings that came over her from time to time when she heard a certain sound or experienced a particular scent. Or the dreams she used to have about people she didn't know, accompanied by a sense of loss that would linger for days. "Sometimes bits and pieces come back to me, but they're not real memories, more like feelings of déjà vu. I remember the sound of a bamboo wind chime, for instance. I have no idea why that sound is important, only that it is." She added almost furiously, "I need to say something now before we go on. I know you must be wondering about my parents. I saw the way you looked when I told you about Germany. Luther and Charity were wonderful people. I loved them very much. I'm grateful every day of my life for everything they gave me, for everything they instilled in me. Whoever or whatever brought me to them… They didn't do anything wrong. I'll never believe otherwise."

He looked on the verge of challenging her assertion, but wisely held his tongue.

She drew a long breath. "Having said all that, I still need to know the truth. That's why I'm here. You asked about a catalyst. I mentioned before that I'd seen a photograph of Thea online right after the little Buchanan girl's rescue. There was something in her face, the way she held her head…" Avery trailed off and regrouped. "It wasn't anything concrete. We don't even look that much alike. I can't explain it, but I knew she was someone important to me. A part of me." She closed her eyes on a shiver. "I googled her name. An FBI agent makes the news so I started with Kylie Buchanan's kidnapping and that led me to Maya."

"Did you find pictures of Maya?"

"Yes, but I didn't have the same reaction as I did to the photo of Thea. Which makes no sense if I'm Maya. The video file of June Chapman's interview impacted me the most. Her absolute certainty that Reggie Lamb had killed her little girl struck some kind of chord, I guess. I decided to come here and find out for myself what had happened."

"So you broke into June's house. Why not Reggie's?"

"I'm not sure, really. Maybe deep down I was afraid of what I'd find, although I've fantasized about driving to her house and knocking on her door. I finally worked up the courage to go over there earlier. It was almost a compulsion. Even at the diner yesterday, a part of me just wanted to blurt it all out to her."

"You didn't recognize her?"

"Not really, but I did have an emotional reaction. But that could also have been the power of suggestion."

"What about when you went to June's house?" Max asked. "Anything there spark a memory?"

"Something came back to me about a doll. I wasn't allowed to touch it because I had grubby hands. I think it was June who told me that."

"That sounds like her."

They were silent for a moment, each lost in thought. The night was very still except for the occasional passing of a car and the distant barking of a dog. Avery touched Max's thigh and his hand closed over hers. She was grateful for his presence. For the first time since Luther died, she didn't feel so alone.

"Now that you know I gave a false statement to the police, what are you going to do?" she asked. "You have obligations. I understand that."

"For the moment, this stays between us," he said. "You've

seen how quickly word spread about Nadine Crosby's confession. Denton Crosby has been following you, but he hasn't yet made his move. I'm guessing that's because he wants to be certain. We have to make our move first."

"What move?"

He squeezed her hand. "I've got a plan."

AVERY PULLED TO the curb behind Max's car and shut off her engine. Across the street, June Chapman's house lay in darkness except for a lone porch light that illuminated the yellow police tape crisscrossing the front door. There was no sign of life inside or out.

Max got out of his car and waited on the walkway for her to join him. From the safety of her vehicle, she studied the stately lines of his childhood home, raking her gaze over the wide veranda and up the graceful columns. Unlike the house across the street, nearly every downstairs window was lit. Avery could see his stepmother on the veranda, waiting for them at the top of the steps.

Max opened her door and offered her a hand. They walked up the steps together. His stepmother glanced from one to the other and smiled, but Avery saw something in her eyes that didn't seem quite so welcoming. She was dressed in jeans and a white blazer accessorized with a gold chain around her throat and tiny pearl studs in her lobes. Her hair was pulled back and fastened at her nape. She was every inch the polished therapist, both her attire and demeanor carefully nonthreatening.

"This is Avery Bolt," Max said as they reached the top of the steps. "Avery, this is my stepmother, Dr. Gail Mosier."

The woman's smile never faltered as she extended her hand. Neither did the hard glint in her blue eyes. "Pleased to meet you, Avery," she said in a pleasant drawl. "Would you like to come inside?"

"That's very kind, but I feel this is a terrible imposition," Avery said.

"Not at all. I have some time before my Thursday night group session."

She stepped aside so they could enter the foyer. Max put his hand on the small of Avery's back and ushered her through. Her trepidation waned as her curiosity took over. So this was the house where Max had grown up.

It was a far different residence from the bungalow in southwest Houston where she'd been raised. Her childhood home had been cozy and inviting with comfortable furniture in the den for lounging around a big-screen TV. Avery doubted there was a television in the whole of the downstairs in Gail Mosier's home. The interior looked like something from a design magazine. Everything from the area rugs to the upholstered furniture to the abstract art on the walls was in varying shades of cream, beige and white.

Gail led them down a wide hallway into a room that looked only fractionally less formal. They sat side by side on a white sofa, just close enough that their thighs occasionally brushed. When their gazes met, Max gave her an encouraging nod.

"Would either of you like a drink before we get started?" Gail asked.

"No, thank you," Avery said.

Max declined as well. "I explained what I could over the phone, but I'm sure you have questions."

"Yes, quite a lot of them, in fact." Gail sat down in a chair opposite the sofa and crossed her legs. Despite the flattering lamplight, her features looked drawn as if she'd put in a very hard day at work and the lines around her mouth and eyes were far more defined than Avery had initially noticed. "You have gaps in your memory, I understand."

"More like one big gap," Avery clarified. "I don't remember anything before the age of four or five."

"That's not unusual, although recent studies suggest that on average a person's earliest recall can go back as far as age two."

"That early?" Max said in surprise. "I don't remember anything that far back."

"You only think you don't. People have a tendency to misdate their early childhood memories. In other words, something you recall happening when you were four may actually have occurred when you were three or even two. Researchers have concluded there is a vast pool of early childhood memories that one can tap into."

"Even if the person experienced a severe psychological trauma?" he asked.

"Trauma-related amnesia is a different matter entirely," she said. "You asked on the phone about hypnotic regression. I'll tell Avery what I told you. Recovering lost memories through hypnosis is unreliable at best and can be extremely detrimental to the patient. I don't recommend it except in extreme cases. False memories can too easily be implanted in a susceptible subject."

"What do you suggest?" Avery asked.

"We can try tapping into your memory pool. There are certain relaxation techniques I can teach you. The earliest memory you can recall often causes another to surface, then another and another and another."

"It's that easy?" Max asked.

"With some coaching. As I said, I can walk you through the exercises. If you still feel the need for regression therapy, then I would be happy to refer you to someone qualified in that field."

Max's phone rang just then. He fished it out of his pocket and glanced at the screen.

"Max," Gail admonished. "No phones."

"Sorry." He stood. "I have to take this. You two continue. I'll be right back."

He quickly left the room and a moment later, Avery heard the front door close. She rubbed her hands against her thighs as she gave Gail a tense smile. "I don't know how I feel about all this. It was Max's idea to come here."

"Why don't you tell me a little bit about yourself while we wait. Max said you were adopted. I take it the repressed memories date back to before the adoption?"

Avery nodded, wondering how much Max had told her. He wouldn't have mentioned Maya. He'd been adamant that their suspicion remain secret for the time being.

"You were born and raised in Houston?"

"I was raised there except for the three years my family spent in Germany. I don't know where I was born."

"What's your earliest memory?" When she saw Avery's reaction, she said in a soothing voice, "Just relax. No pressure. No hurry. Take your time and think back."

"Will you excuse me?" Avery stood abruptly. "Sorry. I just need to speak to Max for a moment." She hurried out of the room before Gail had time to protest. Max was just putting away his phone when she opened the front door and stepped out. "Everything okay?"

He looked grim. "That was Cal Slade. June Chapman suffered a massive coronary earlier this evening. They don't expect her to make it through the night."

Avery closed the door. "Should we go to the hospital?"

"I'm headed there now, but I don't think you should come. You won't be allowed to see her."

"I know. It just seems like the right thing to do."

"Regardless of who you are, you don't owe her anything." His voice softened. "It's better if you stay here and work with Gail. She's good at what she does. She can help if you'll allow yourself to trust her."

Avery remained skeptical. "If it was that easy to tap into my memories, why haven't I done so already?"

He put his hands on her shoulders. "Just talk to her. What have you got to lose? I'll call as soon as I know anything. In the meantime, don't say anything about June's condition. Cal will release a statement when the time is right."

She watched as he ran down the steps and hurried out to his vehicle. He pulled away from the curb and in the next instant he was gone.

The door opened behind her. "Everything okay?" Gail glanced around the porch. "Where's Max?"

"He was called away on an emergency."

"What kind of emergency?"

Avery shrugged. "The legal kind, I guess." She turned back to the door where Gail still hovered. "I should probably go, too. I still don't feel right about barging in on you like this. Maybe we could resume at a later date in your office."

"Nonsense. You're already here. Let's talk for a bit. Besides," she added with a deprecating smile, "I'm sure Max has already sung my praises so I feel I have something to prove."

"Not to me you don't." Avery reluctantly followed her back into the house. Gail had poured them each a glass of wine while she'd been on the veranda with Max.

"I thought you had a group session later," Avery said in surprise.

"One glass of wine won't hurt. Besides, it seems we can do with a bit of an icebreaker. It's a very good cabernet if I do say so myself."

Avery reached for her wineglass, glad to have something to do with her hands. She sipped slowly as she glanced around the room. She noticed a framed photo of Max on a walnut credenza. She fixated on his image as she sipped.

"You were telling me about your earliest memory," Gail prompted.

"It was my first Christmas Eve in Germany," she said. "My mother had a Saint Nicholas doll on the mantel that terrified me. I would see his face peering in my window every night when the lights were turned out."

"Did you tell her the doll frightened you?"

"I didn't speak that year."

"At all?"

Avery shook her head, her gaze still on Max's photo. She could see the whirl of the ceiling fan reflected in the glass. The movement was mesmerizing. Or maybe that was just the wine. She'd emptied her glass without even realizing it and now she felt a bit boneless. She let her head fall back against the seat and closed her eyes for a moment.

"Sorry," she murmured. "That hit me harder than I expected."

"It's all about relaxation. Let yourself go, let yourself float back in time." Gail's voice sounded strangely distant and eerily hypnotic. "Do you remember the plane ride to Germany?"

"Yes. My mother brought a book and read to me until I fell asleep. Funny I hadn't remembered that until now. She had the sweetest voice, my mother. And the softest hands."

"Try to go deeper into your memory pool," Gail coaxed. "Deeper and deeper until you remember a time before Germany. You're floating. You're drifting. The memories are coming back to you now."

She *was* floating, drifting far, far away from Germany, from Houston, until her mother's voice faded, replaced by a tremulous whisper she somehow knew was her own. *I'm scared, Sissy.*

"What is it, Avery? What do you remember?"

"Mama's wind chimes," she murmured. "And our neighbor's coonhound baying in the woods."

"Are you in Germany?"

"No."

"Are you Houston?"

She shook her head.

"Where are you?"

"In my bedroom with Sissy."

She could have sworn she heard Gail's breath catch. "What else do you remember?"

"Whispering."

"Someone is whispering to you?"

"To each other. It's dark in the room, but I can see them at the end of my bed."

"Can you hear what they're saying?"

She said in a loud whisper, "Take one and come back for the other. Hurry up. We don't have much time."

The wineglass slipped from Avery's hand and shattered against the wood floor. The sound jolted her back to the present and she offered a stuttered apology. She wanted to clean up the shards, but her limbs had grown heavy and unresponsive while she'd been floating and her vision blurred. Somehow, though, she was cognizant of the fact that a third person had entered the room.

Had Max come back?

"Now do you believe me?" Gail demanded. "I told you it was her."

A shadow moved in front of Avery. She could smell stale cigarette smoke on the newcomer.

"What did you give her?"

"A sedative. It's strong, but you never know how someone will react."

He hunkered in front of Avery. "Her eyelids are fluttering. Can she hear us?"

"Not for long. Another few minutes and she'll be out."

"Good. I've been doing some snooping out at McNally's Cave. They've demolished the hell out of that place, but there's still enough room at the main entrance to shove a body through. Once they seal the hole, she's gone for good."

"I thought we were going to put her in her car and drive it into the river?"

"Too many houses along the river," he said. "Too many prying eyes. Besides, you don't want to take the chance her body will eventually float to the surface. Better that it's blown into a million pieces. No corpse, no case. Relax, okay? I know what I'm doing."

"Then why is June Chapman still alive?"

"The old broad's tougher than I gave her credit for, but she'll be dead soon enough. Two bullets to the chest at her age? No way she comes back from that."

"You better hope not."

"*You* better hope not. You've got a lot more to lose than I do. But one problem at a time." He reached over and gave Avery a push. She toppled sideways without resistance. "I'll load her up in the back seat of my truck. Follow me out there in her car. But first..." He tugged at Avery's T-shirt. She tried to slap his hand away, but her wrist was too limp. "Still got a little fight left, huh?"

"What do you think you're doing?" Gail demanded.

"Swap shirts and find a cap to go over your hair. From a distance, nosy neighbors will think she's leaving of her own accord. Afterward, we'll get rid of the vehicle and I'll bring you back here. It'll be like nothing ever happened."

She knelt in front of Avery and lifted her eyelid to check her pupil dilation. "You need to pass out now. Stop fighting it. Just close your eyes and let it happen."

"You want me to help her along?" Crosby asked.

"No, leave her alone." She brushed back Avery's hair. "I'm sorry, Maya. I really am. It would have been so much easier on all of us if you had just stayed dead."

Chapter Sixteen

Max texted Cal Slade when he arrived at the hospital and the police detective met him at the elevator on the ICU floor. Underlying his grim demeanor was an edge of nervous excitement.

"How is she?" Max asked.

"Not good. She's slipped into a deep coma. The doctors say it's just a matter of time. We've notified Agent Lamb. She's the next of kin as best we can determine. She's on her way."

"That's good, I guess." He thought about Avery back at Gail's house. "What about Reggie?"

"Given their history? I figured I'd let Thea make that call."

"You're probably right," Max said. "Just seems like she should know." Reggie Lamb had a right to know about a lot of things, but Max couldn't worry about that now.

"Something odd happened earlier," Cal said. "Although one of the doctors says a rally right before death isn't unusual."

"What do you mean *a rally*?"

"Two hours before she suffered the heart attack, June regained consciousness. She asked to speak to the detective in charge of her case. When I got here, she seemed completely lucid. Amazingly so after what she'd been through.

She asked to make a statement." He motioned for Max to follow him out of earshot of the nurse's station. "Your instincts were right. She owned up to everything."

"Everything as in…?"

"She admitted to paying those people to take Thea and Maya from their bedroom, though she claimed she had no personal interaction with the kidnappers. Someone else put the plan together for her. That person brought Nadine and Denton Crosby on board, and they recruited Gabriel Jareau."

"Who put the plan together?"

Cal shifted his gaze to the nurse's station. "I'm getting to that. June said a couple of months before the kidnapping, she was put in touch with an underground organization that I would have sworn was nothing but an urban legend. This group was comprised of former cops, FBI agents, judges, social workers—various professionals who had vast first-hand experience dealing with the inequities and failures of our criminal and social justice systems, especially when it came to abused and at-risk kids. According to June, this group would step in as a last and desperate resort once the courts, law enforcement and child protective services failed to remove a child from imminent danger."

"Stepped in how?"

"The children would just disappear. Once in this group's custody, they were moved through an underground network of safe houses until they could be given new identities and backstories and placed with new families."

Urban legend sounded about right, Max thought. He remained skeptical. The story struck him as a way to divert blame. But then, he'd heard stranger tales. "How did she manage to find this group, let alone convince them that Maya and Thea Lamb were in imminent danger?"

"She was vague about the connections. My guess is, even on her deathbed, she's still protecting someone."

Max thought about the phone conversation Avery had overhead between Will Kent and Tom Fuqua, men who had worked inside the system for most of their lives and had made a host of powerful contacts. He thought about his father's comeback to June Chapman: *You know all about taking something that doesn't belong to you.*

He glanced past Cal toward the ICU room where June Chapman still fought for her life. Or had she already given up? Now that she'd finally come clean about the terrible thing she'd done, had she decided to take the easy way out?

"You said she claimed someone else put the plan together. Did she give you a name?"

"She did." Cal put a hand on Max's shoulder. "It was Gail. June paid her a million dollars to kidnap her best friend's children."

It was Gail. It was Gail. It was Gail.

The three words pounded inside Max's head as he careened to the curb in front of his childhood home and jumped out, barely taking the time to kill the engine. He rushed up the veranda steps, rang the bell and then rapped loudly on the door with his fist. Avery's car was gone and the house was dark. Maybe she'd gone straight home after Max left and Gail had returned to her office for the group session. No use assuming the worst. Gail didn't yet know of June's confession. He hauled out his phone and called Avery again as he headed back down the steps. Still no answer. Still no use in assuming the worst. Maybe she just wanted to be alone.

An elderly neighbor strolled down the sidewalk with her dog. She paused underneath a streetlamp and gave Max a curious stare. "You looking for Gail?"

He hurried toward her. "Yes. Have you seen her?"

"She was on the veranda earlier with the young lady who

weeded my flower bed yesterday. Beautiful girl. Looked just like an angel when the light hit her a certain way."

The description struck a chord. "Wait," Max said. "Are you Mrs. Carmichael?"

"Call me Evelyn."

"I think we spoke on the phone yesterday. I'm Max Winter. Clayton's son?"

"Max Winter." Her head canted slightly. "I'm sure you're right but I can't for the life of me remember why you called me."

"You called me," Max said.

"Did I? I'm sorry." She shook her head. "My memory isn't what it used to be. What did I say? Nothing rude, I hope."

"No, ma'am. You said you thought someone should know that you'd seen Maya Lamb."

She broke into a smile. "Oh, yes! Now I remember. I did see her. Plain as day, only..." Her brow furrowed. "That can't be right, can it?"

"I don't know," Max said. "Was she the same young woman who weeded your flower bed?"

"No, that can't be, either. She said her name was Avery."

"You saw Avery on the veranda earlier. Did you see her leave?"

She nodded. "Oh, yes. She left a little while ago. I was sitting out on my porch like I do every evening around this time. There's always a cool breeze and I like to smell the flowers. She got in a silver vehicle and drove off."

"Did you notice anyone else leave the house?"

She thought back. "I don't think so."

"But you're sure it was Avery? What was she wearing? Did you notice?"

"Blue jeans, I think, and a white shirt. Maybe a T-shirt. And the same red baseball cap she had on when she came to see me yesterday."

"Did she seem okay?" Max asked. "She wasn't visibly upset or frightened?"

"Frightened? Oh, dear. She's not in some kind of trouble, is she?"

"That's what I'm trying to find out."

"Come to think of it, she did seem in a bit of a hurry. She made a U-turn in the street instead of going down to the intersection."

"Which way did she go?"

She turned and pointed.

If Avery had left Gail's house under her own steam, then she was okay, Max reasoned. But she still wasn't answering her phone and when he drove by her duplex, her vehicle was gone. So where could she be that she didn't want to answer her phone?

There was only one place he could think of. Maybe a memory had surfaced that had finally driven her to Reggie's front door.

THE TRUCK BUMPED to a stop and the dome light came on when Denton Crosby opened the door. Avery sensed his gaze on her, but she didn't open her eyes. Instead, she remained motionless even though she'd been semiconscious for several minutes. She couldn't yet mount an attack because her limbs were still rubber. If Luther had taught her anything, it was patience. Wait to strike until the likelihood of success was greatest.

He opened the rear passenger door and gave her shoulder a shake. "You awake yet? Hey!" He slapped her cheeks a few times. She didn't so much as flinch.

A car pulled up behind them. She thought she recognized the sound of her vehicle's engine. A car door slammed and Gail's voice cut through the dark. "Let's get this over with. I need to get to the office in case Max comes by."

"This time of night? You work too hard," Crosby said

with a grunt as he grabbed Avery underneath her arms and hauled her out of the vehicle, dumping her unceremoniously on the ground.

Gail trained her flashlight directly in Avery's face. "She's still out?"

"Didn't hear so much as a peep the whole way out here. You gave her some of the good stuff."

"I told you, the reaction to certain pharmaceuticals can be unpredictable."

A drizzle had begun to fall. The cool mist on Avery's face was bracing.

Gail said, "Let's get going."

He tugged Avery up by the arms and hoisted her over his shoulder. "I'm getting too damn old for this."

"If your sister had kept her mouth shut, we wouldn't be in this predicament."

"She always did have a tender heart and a soft conscience."

"Unlike you," Gail said.

"Or you, I reckon."

"Let's just get on with it."

"Open the gate," he said. "I broke the lock when I was out here earlier."

Avery heard the gate squeak and then they walked up a slight incline before Crosby once again dumped her on the ground. She tried not to wince as she hit the rocky surface.

"Anything you want to say before I do the honors?"

"Just shut up," Gail snapped. "I never wanted this."

"We all make our beds," he said.

"Yes, we do."

Avery physically started at the sound of a gunshot not three feet from where she lay sprawled on the ground. Reacting instinctively, she drew herself into a ball to protect her vital organs. She expected another shot to ring out at any minute, but when she recovered from the initial shock, she lifted her head to reconnoiter. Gail had her back turned as she struggled to drag Denton Crosby's prone body toward the cave opening.

Rolling onto her stomach, Avery pushed herself up on hands and knees and then rose to a crouch. Gail was still preoccupied with the body. Grunting and gasping from the strain, she hadn't yet noticed Avery. Now she was squatting, putting all her strength and focus into rolling the body down into the cavern. If Avery hadn't still been under the influence, she would have tackled and disarmed the woman. Instead, she moved as quietly as she could down the slope. She was almost to the fence when the first shot rang out.

She wasn't hit. She didn't fall. Instead, she stumbled through the gate and plunged into the woods. Gail wasn't far behind. Avery could hear the crunch of twigs and leaves as the hunter closed in on her prey.

Avery kept going, half stumbling, half running until after a bit, she realized that she wasn't so much running away from someone as running to someone. Reggie's house was somewhere up ahead.

Don't stop. Keep Going. You're almost home.

MAX WHEELED INTO Reggie's driveway and jumped out. To his surprise, she hurried around the corner of the house as if she'd been expecting him. "You got here fast." Then she stopped cold, her gaze going to his vehicle in the drive.

"Reggie, it's me. Max Winter. From the diner?"

She said in confusion, "What are you doing here? I was expecting the cops."

He approached cautiously so as not to alarm her. "Why did you call the police? What's happened?"

"I was sitting out on my back porch and I heard gunshots in the woods. One shot, then three more in rapid fire. *Bang, bang, bang.* People used to target practice out there but not at night and no one's been coon hunting in ages. It may be nothing, but it got my hackles up."

"Reggie." He tried to keep the low-grade panic from his voice. "I need to ask you something. It won't make much sense at first but—do you remember the woman I had lunch with yesterday at the diner? Brunette, slender build. She asked about your wrist."

"Wore a ball cap," Reggie said. "I remember thinking how pretty she was. What about her?"

"Have you seen her in the last hour or so?"

"My shift ended at three so if she came to the diner after that—"

"No, I mean here. Did she come by your house this evening?"

She took a step toward him as if she sensed what was coming. "Why would she come here?" She stopped mere inches from him so that she could peer up into his face. "Who is she?"

"We don't know for sure. That's important to remember. We don't yet have conclusive proof. We think… I think she could be Maya."

Reggie said nothing, just stared straight into his eyes.

"Are you okay?" Max asked.

Still no reaction.

Then without warning, her knees collapsed. Max grabbed her and held her.

"Maya…" The way she whispered her daughter's name was like nothing Max had ever heard before. She kept saying it over and over, almost like a prayer chant.

His grasp tightened on her arms as he held her away from him. "Listen to me carefully, Reggie. I know you're in shock, but I need you to do something. This woman—whoever she is—could be in danger—"

A gunshot sounded in the woods, echoing back to them through the trees.

"That one was closer," Reggie said.

"Go into the house," Max said. "Lock the doors and call the police station. Ask for Detective Cal Slade. Tell him I said it's a matter of life and death."

AVERY'S BAD ANKLE turned and she went down hard just as a bullet exploded in a nearby tree trunk. If she hadn't tripped, she might have been hit. She tried to scramble to her feet, but Gail was already on her. "Stop right where you are."

Avery lifted her arms and slowly turned to face her.

Gail motioned toward the trees with the gun. "We're going back to the cave. Nice and slow. I wouldn't try running again if I were you."

"Why does it matter? You're going to kill me anyway."

"I'll tell you why it matters. Reggie Lamb still walks these woods looking for Maya. She's been spotted out here at all hours of the day and night. If I shoot you here, she's likely the one who will find your body. You don't want to put that on her. Not after everything she's been through."

Avery gave a nervous laugh. "You're worried about Reggie Lamb? After what you've done to her?"

There was enough moonlight filtering down through the trees that Avery could see the woman's face. She looked genuinely distressed. "You have to understand, I never wanted to hurt her. She was my best friend, but I had to do right by you girls. Reggie was a horrible mother back then. June was right. You and Thea deserved so much better."

Avery remained unmoved and cut right to the chase. "How much did my grandmother pay you?"

"I won't lie, the money was important," Gail said. "You have no idea how much a million dollars meant to someone like me. A girl who came from *nothing*. It was enough to turn my life around. I've been able to help so many people because of the education that money provided. And you were never to be harmed. That was made clear from the onset. You and Thea would be given far better lives than anything Reggie could ever provide."

"But that was a lie," Avery said. "All you have to do is look at Thea. Look how her life has turned out."

"She's who she is because of your disappearance. Reggie's a different person, too, but who's to say what kind of life any of you would have had if she'd continued on the same destructive path."

"You've had years to work out your justification," Avery said. "But sooner or later the truth will come out."

"Maybe," Gail said on a tremulous breath. "But not tonight." She gestured again with the gun.

A twig snapped nearby, freezing them both in their tracks. Gail whirled, turning her ear to the sound while simultaneously lifting a finger to her lips to silence Avery. She started to call out for help, but what if Reggie was out there?

Instead, she held her tongue and waited for the right moment.

Another twig snapped. Someone was closing in on them. Avery braced herself.

Then a male voice called from the woods, "It's Max. I'm coming toward you. Don't shoot."

The sound of his voice seemed to stun Gail. Then she said, "Stay where you are, Max. Don't come any closer. Please. Just go away."

"I can't do that, Gail. I know what you're planning to do. I know what you've already done." He stepped out of the woods then, hands raised in the air as his gaze went from Gail to Avery, then back to Gail. "If you kill her, you'll have to kill me."

"Don't," Gail pleaded. "You're my son. Please just go away and let me end this."

"It's over," he said. "June Chapman regained consciousness a little while ago. She gave a full statement to the police."

"I don't believe you."

"She told us how you set everything up including the recruitment of the kidnappers. You kept Reggie out of the way that night, didn't you? Did you drug her drink?"

"I didn't have to," she said. "She made it easy for me."

An agonized cry sounded from the woods, followed by a single gunshot. Gail's hand flew to her chest where she had been hit. The gun fell from her limp fingers as she dropped to her knees.

It all happened in the blink of an eye. Suddenly, Reggie was there, pistol balanced in both hands as she advanced toward Gail with purpose. How she had fired so accurately with her damaged wrist, Avery would never know.

"You were my best friend. My *sister*. You walked these woods with me, calling my little girl's name and all the time you *knew*. You sat holding me in your arms night after night while I cried my heart out and you *knew*." She was standing over Gail now. "You knew. You *knew*."

Max said, "Reggie, don't do this. She'll be punished for what she did. She'll spend the rest of her life in prison, I promise."

The gun never wavered. Reggie was stone-cold resolved.

He tried a different tactic. "She took Maya from you once. Don't let her do it again."

Avery had remained silent, caught up in a frenzy of emotion and shock that had rendered her speechless. But she had the power to stop this now with a single word "Mama?"

The gun fell from Reggie's fingers as she gave a keening cry. She rushed to Avery and wrapped her in a tight embrace. They collapsed to the ground, rocking back and forth. "Mama's here, sweet girl. Mama's right here."

Chapter Seventeen

Hardly anyone showed up for June Chapman's funeral. Even without the slow drip of news about the kidnapping, who would have wanted to pay respects to a woman who had basically alienated anyone with whom she'd come into contact?

After her son's death, she'd lived most of her life as a recluse. It was to be hoped that she'd spent at least a portion of her alone time wallowing in guilt, but the June Chapman Max had known was more likely to have closed herself off so that she could bask in the dim glow of her self-righteousness. For whatever reason, she'd felt the need to come clean before she died so maybe she had a conscience after all. Or maybe she'd wanted to stick another knife in Reggie Lamb's back.

He stood away from the handful of people who had gathered at the gravesite. He wasn't sure why he'd felt compelled to attend and he'd been even more shocked to see Avery at the service, flanked on either side by Reggie and Thea Lamb. He felt reasonably certain they hadn't come to mourn, but to somehow find closure.

Paul Bozeman was undoubtedly there to try and squelch the talk that he and his daughter had been stealing from June for years. Rumors were bad for business. And maybe he and his daughter were still hoping to find themselves in June's will.

Max's gaze traveled over the group, resting for a moment on Will Kent and Tom Fuqua. He still had his suspicions about their involvement, but their secret had gone with June to her grave. And his father? Max would have to somehow make peace with his doubts.

He left before the service was over. He didn't want to intrude on Avery's time with her family. Besides, he had work to do. Loose ends of his own to tie up.

Two days later, he finally pulled back into Reggie Lamb's driveway and cut the engine. Avery and Thea were sitting side by side on the front porch and it took him back to that day twenty-eight years ago when he'd been captivated by a pair of four-year-old twins on June Chapman's veranda.

Thea got up when he approached. She touched his arm briefly and smiled. "Good to see you again." Then she turned and went inside the house.

Max sat down beside Avery. "Hello."

"Hello." She gave him a long scrutiny. "I was beginning to wonder when I'd see you again. If I'd see you again."

"You knew you would eventually."

"I hoped."

"You knew." He put his hand on her knee and she clasped it. "I don't even know what to call you now."

She shrugged, her gaze bold and bright. "It doesn't matter. I'm still the same person you met a few days ago."

"I doubt that's true. I'm not even the same person I was a few days ago."

"A lot has happened," she agreed.

"Which is why I haven't been by before now. I wanted to give you some space." He glanced over his shoulder. "How's it going?"

She took a moment to answer. "It's awkward and scary

and surreal. Reggie and Thea have been wonderful, but we all need some time. It's just hard…you know?"

He squeezed her hand.

"Have you been to see Gail?" she finally asked.

He was definitive about that. "No, and I don't plan to."

"It's okay if you want to see her," Avery said. "She's family. Feelings don't change overnight."

"Maybe in time." He shrugged. "It's best I keep my distance while the preliminary legal proceedings are being arranged. Another ADA will be assigned to her case, of course. I'm done with it all."

She turned. "What do you mean *all*?"

"I turned in my resignation."

Her eyes widened in surprise. "When did this happen?"

"Yesterday. It wasn't sudden. I've been considering a change for a while now."

"Wow." She digested his news for a moment. "What will you do now?"

"I don't know. I've got some options. I could open a small private practice in Tallahassee. I might enjoy that. Or maybe I'll try something completely different. I don't have to decide right away."

"Something different," she mused. "It's funny you should mention a change. Just today I started thinking about opening a branch office in Tallahassee or Jacksonville so I can be near Reggie and Thea. I could use a good detective on my team, one who will keep me on the straight and narrow."

"And you think I'm the man for the job?"

"We've made a good team so far," she said. "Might as well see where it goes."

"When you put it that way." He fell silent as he glanced out over the yard. "When I drove up just now and saw you and Thea on the porch, it took me back to the first time I ever laid eyes on you. You had on a pink dress."

She shook her head in wonder. "I can't believe you remembered that after all this time."

He lifted her hand to his lips. "No one in this town ever forgot you, Maya."

Her eyes glistened. "Everyone remembers what happened to me. You remembered me."

"Coming from my mother's funeral that day, it seemed like the end. How could I have known when I saw you on June Chapman's veranda that it was really just the beginning?"

* * * * *

MILLS & BOON

THE HEART OF ROMANCE

A ROMANCE FOR EVERY READER

MODERN

Prepare to be swept off your feet by sophisticated, sexy and seductive heroes, in some of the world's most glamourous and roman locations, where power and passion collide.

HISTORICAL

Escape with historical heroes from time gone by. Whether your passio for wicked Regency Rakes, muscled Vikings or rugged Highlanders, a the romance of the past.

MEDICAL

Set your pulse racing with dedicated, delectable doctors in the high-p sure world of medicine, where emotions run high and passion, comfo love are the best medicine.

True Love

Celebrate true love with tender stories of heartfelt romance, from the rush of falling in love to the joy a new baby can bring, and a focus o emotional heart of a relationship.

Desire

Indulge in secrets and scandal, intense drama and plenty of sizzling action with powerful and passionate heroes who have it all: wealth, st good looks...everything but the right woman.

Experience all the excitement of a gripping thriller, with an intense mance at its heart. Resourceful, true-to-life women and strong, fearle face danger and desire - a killer combination!

To see which titles are coming soon, please visit

millsandboon.co.uk/nextmonth